The NOTCH

Tom Holleuw

This special
signed edition of

THE
NOTCH

is limited to
1,000
numbered
copies.

The NOTCH

by Tom Holland

CEMETERY DANCE PUBLICATIONS

Baltimore

2020

Cemetery Dance Publications
132B Industry Lane, Unit #7
Forest Hill, MD 21050
www.cemeterydance.com

First Cemetery Dance Printing

ISBN: 978-1-58767-721-2

Cover Artwork and Design © 2020 by Elderlemon Design
Cover and Interior Design © 2020 by Desert Isle Design, LLC

For Kathi.

Book 1:
THE FIRST DAY

CHAPTER 1

Joe "Bear Claws" Arachro drove the ATV at a good clip along the wash. The desert was flat here, the sand crunchy beneath the fat tires. The sun was just rising with the breaking dawn, the scrub brush beginning to cast shadows, the wildflowers just opening their petals to the sun.

He went up the bank into the flat stretch of sand that stretched out and up against the low mountains, the bigger peaks rising out of the earth behind them, far in the distance. Joe slowed, just tooling along on the four-wheeler. He loved the desert at dawn.

It was clean, scrubbed by the wind and blowing sand, watered by the sudden storms and washed by the flash floods. It was quiet, too, only the sounds of nature. Joe was mostly Indian, Tonto Apache, but the rest was white and mestizo, whoever happened by over the centuries. He didn't care, but it was the red man in him that the desert spoke to.

He could hear it, the prairie dogs sticking their heads out of their holes, the rattler sliding sideways under the scrub brush with a soft whoosh as he rode by. He slowed to a crawl. The coyotes silently stalking their prey, the mule deer munching at whatever vegetation could be found, the scrape of the beetles in the sand and spiders in the shade. Joe heard them all, saw them, too, when he became quiet and still like them. Sometimes it could take hours, but if he just sat in the shade of some elephant tree he could see the desert life waking around him.

His love of it had made him quit drinking and dope taking and open his four-wheeler shop with Terry Lathrop. They'd become best buds during recovery. Nothing like being in 12 Step to make you love—or hate—someone. Joe and Terry's Dune Buggies and Dirt Bikes, they called it. It was right on the main highway, due south. He'd be back by noon and then Terry would take a few hours off, go back to the little house they had close to it.

It worked perfectly for them both. It was off-season now, the heart of the summer, and too hot for anyone but people like him and Terry. Lovers of the sand.

With that thought, he slowed to a crawl, trying to take it all in. There were saguaros around and some dead trees along with the scrub, but that was about it. Otherwise it was all flat grainy sand with a brownish cast. Until the first spring rain came, if they were lucky enough to have any, and then it would explode with the color of wild flowers.

He pulled to a halt on a small hillock, looking across the flatness as it rose up into a sudden flat top mesa, higher than it was longer at the top. Joe frowned. He'd never seen that mesa before and he'd grown up on the res, which was part of the Tonto National Forest. He narrowed his eyes, lifting his sunglasses for a better look.

There was another jagged butte tilting at an angle next to the mesa, not as wide or long, more like God giving the world the finger. It made a notch between the two. They were both cast up from the desert like an afterthought in a battle between giants eons ago.

Joe gazed around. The desert was familiar, but not those buttes. It was like they just appeared from nowhere, dropped down here, in the middle of the desert. But when he peered at them harder they looked like they had been there forever. Rubble was piled up at the bottom of both, the sides cut and smoothed by a millennium of wear.

Joe Bear Claws was pushing past fifty, had spent his life here, but he had somehow missed the tabletop and the jagged spire next

Book 1: THE FIRST DAY

to it. Only explanation. But, Christ, he hadn't been that stoned and drunk for so many years that he'd miss them. Had he?

He pulled out the makings and some paper and began to roll himself a smoke. They said it was bad for you, but living out here was bad for you, if you didn't know the ways, and living in the city was pure death. If your fellow addicts and hustlers didn't kill you, the drugs and booze would. Joe frowned, the makings forgotten as he spotted something in the shimmering glare in the notch between the two buttes. He squinted, trying to see better.

Someone was walking out of the sun, surrounded by the blazing rays. Joe wore an old floppy canvas fishing hat with a strap underneath to keep it on and polarized sunglasses, but now he took both off, squinting harder, trying to figure out what was appearing out of the sun between the notch in the buttes.

It was a boy, thin and straight, his face cast in black by the blazing sun behind him.

Joe blinked, swiping at his eyes with his forearm, and when he looked again, the boy was closer. Much *too* close, given where he had just been. Like he'd jumped ahead of himself. His features were still hidden by the blinding rays behind him, his face shadowed in the golden glow that framed him. He wore a pair of ragged khaki pants and a loose, short-sleeved shirt that billowed in the early morning breeze. What looked to be old-fashioned, canvas topped Keds sheathed his sockless feet. They weren't tied tight and should have scraped his skin raw, but the kid seemed oblivious.

Joe Bear Claws didn't know what he was seeing, but he knew it was special. He blinked again, this time consciously, and sure enough the boy was closer yet again. A lot closer. Maybe thirty feet or so away, walking steadily toward him, his skinny arms swinging loosely at his side.

Now Joe could see his face. It was well made, longish, pale, the skin clear with a light sprinkling of freckles. He looked like a Cub

11

Scout with a touch of Tom Sawyer. But it was the hair that stopped Joe. It was pale, like him, but beyond pale. It was almost without any color at all. White? No, that wasn't it. When the sun hit, it reflected a light gold. It was like all the color had been washed out of him, with just a hint left, but it came and went with every step he took. Yet the face was perfect. A raggedy kid who could've gone missing from down the street, a neighbor's kid a few doors over, but here he was, striding across the desolate desert with an easy but determined stride.

The boy was almost upon him now. He had a thin nose and couldn't be more than ten years old or so, but far enough along that he had control of his body.

He moved with a natural grace, almost flowing across the desert with his relaxed movement. There was something beautiful about it, as though he were one with the sea of sand around him.

Now Joe could see his eyes. They were startling, almost colorless, not golden white like the hair, but with a hint of sky blue, as though they were there and weren't. Then the boy was walking past. His gaze met Joe's once and then slid away, hardly noticing him. It was as if the boy had a place to be at an appointed time and mustn't tarry.

Joe reached out for him, not wanting to let him get away. He was so extraordinary, Joe just had to touch him. His fingertips brushed his shoulder. Joe jerked back as if he'd gotten an electric shock and he had, but it wasn't painful. It was a rush of sudden unexpected warmth.

He stared after the boy, but he was already far in the distance, headed toward the highway, and then Joe Bear Claws blinked again. The boy was gone, just as magically as he had come. Joe sat there, never having moved off the four-wheeler, the sun continuing to rise behind him, flooding the desert sand with its golden light.

He turned, looking toward the notch the boy had walked through. It was gone, too.

CHAPTER 2

The man sat on the dirt floor of his thatched hut, cooking— the butchered remains of the bonobo monkey he had caught in his snare just outside of the village. There had been tribal murders, the Fang forcing the Bantus, his tribe, off their land from the northeast of Equatorial Guinea, and hunting too far from the village was increasingly dangerous. The man took a bite of the greasy meat and chewed it as he hoped the warfare would soon settle down. He swallowed with a loud gulp, working to get the meat down.

He hated monkey meat. Unclean. Carrier of disease, but better to eat than starve. Raiding a different tribe's farmland seems to come every spring and then be over, but now it continued deep into the summer. It never seemed to end. He felt his stomach tighten and threaten to reject the meat. Fighting gagging and feeling suddenly violently ill, he rose to his feet, and managed to stagger outside. He found himself in the middle of several huts and looked around, about to call out to his fellow villagers, but he coughed hard before he could get the words out.

Blood sprayed out of his mouth. It hit his lifted hand, frightening him. He was seriously ill, maybe even dying. The thought dawned on him before he could call out again and panicked, he staggered toward the nearest hut. Someone had to help him and quickly, but he realized there was no chance of that. There was no help in the village, not the kind that came from the doctors with their white coats. Their village didn't even have a witch doctor who had traditional herbal remedies.

He coughed again. More blood sprayed. People stopped to look at him. Others were appearing from their huts, talking and gesturing at him, but no one approached. They were afraid of him. They knew he was sick and dying. It could spread from one to the other. That happened with the sleeping sickness and the creeping sickness and all the others, what they called Ebola, then SARS, then some kind of new typhoid, but the diseases had been coming faster and faster. The village was losing people. They all knew it and now they saw one of their own sick and dying again.

The man dropped in the dust, coughing his last spray of blood into the air and didn't move anymore. The villagers watched him, keeping back, murmuring among themselves, held in place by fear. They would burn the body and the clothes; make sure the sickness, whatever it was, didn't spread. But first let the blood dry.

One of the villagers suddenly coughed, his rib cage convulsing again and again, spraying blood with every heave. The others moved quickly away, fear and terror spreading. Then another and another and another, male and female, young and old, coughed, gouts of blood flying.

Everybody standing about whirled and fled screaming down the narrow dirty paths between the huts, the people left behind hacking and falling.

CHAPTER
3

Terry Lathrop was pulling the bearings on the rear wheel of an ATV he and Joe rented out. He was under a corrugated metal roof next to the office, the quads, four-wheeler dune buggies, and dirt bikes parked in a line, leading to the back and the desert out there. He and Joe had been lucky to get the store, but it had been on reservation land, so they had an in. 'Course, it had been abandoned three years or more and the one mechanic who'd worked it until he keeled over of a heart attack hadn't put any money into it since he'd bought it, which was probably in the seventies.

In other words, the place had been a wreck when they'd taken over, but it was together now. Not spic and span, but functioning in a way that gave them a good business when the fall came and the fierce dry heat retreated.

Only one of the two gas pumps out front worked and the paint was near blasted off the wood sides of what he and Joe Bear Claws called the office and the store, but the place had found renewed life for the rental and repair of sand buggies. This section of the park had some of the best trails. No dunes to speak off, but the scenery was spectacular and that brought a constant stream of tourists, except in the deep summer, like now, when the heat was inescapable.

Terry was satisfied. He'd just crossed into his forties, and had cleaned up from the drugs and booze and now he had his own business. He and Joe "Bear Claws" Arachro. Amazing what you could achieve sober and with an Indian friend.

His walkie-talkie squawked on the barrel where it lay. "Joe-1, out by Elephant Ears. Come back."

Terry knew the area. A whole bunch of bushes that fanned out and popped up at the ends, just like the ears of a pachyderm. They had wireless at the shop, but it wasn't good out in the desert. Terry wasn't sure anything was but short wave.

He picked up the talkie. "Terry here, Joe. When you coming in?"

"You're not gonna believe what just happened," came the voice from the tinny speaker. It always made Joe sound like he was at the bottom of a well. "I was just staring at a mesa, maybe a hundred yards across at the top and a second one, long and narrow at an angle, maybe a hundred fifty feet high, right next to it. Now it's not there."

Terry frowned. "I'm not surprised. There's nothing out there like that." He knew the Tonto desert as well as Joe. He grew up in a double-wide, not very far from where the dune buggy shop was now.

"I know there isn't, but I blinked and it's come back. I'm looking at it right now. It's come back." Joe paused, as if he was thinking about how much to tell. "This kid appeared between them."

"What?" Terry frowned as he listened. What the hell was a kid doing in the desert this early in the morning? Not to mention a mesa that came and went. A glance at the clock on the wall told him it was eight straight up.

"Yeah, he came out of the sun," Joe said, like he didn't quite believe it himself. "He looked funny, too. Real pale, like he'd never been outside, but there he was in this notch between these two mesas, walking toward me. It was like something religious or spiritual or something."

As Terry listened, the hair on the back of his neck started to rise. Someone was watching him. He could feel it. He whirled, staring out the open front of the corrugated shed. The kid was standing there, bathed in the hot morning sun. A pale skinny kid with golden lava like sunlight running off him.

Book 1: THE FIRST DAY

Terry gulped. "He's here, right now. Standing near the pumps, looking at me."

"That's crazy," Joe said. "He was just here, five, ten minutes ago. I'm two hours out and the kid was on foot. He couldn't possibly be there that quick."

"Well, he's here and he's still on foot," Terry said, watching as the kid turned, looking past the pumps and down the road. He walked away, disappearing from sight.

"Wait a minute, he's gone," Terry said and stepped out from under the shed where they kept the bikes and buggies. He looked past the pumps, down the highway in the direction the kid had disappeared, but there was no one there to see. Terry looked the other way. The highway was empty in both directions. He lifted the talkie back to his ear.

"There's nobody on the road," he said slowly, a note of awe in his voice. "He couldn't just have disappeared like that. It's not possible."

"He did the same to me," came Joe's tinny voice. "There's something different about him, Terry. He just came out of the rising sun, one second he wasn't there and the next he was. Then I touched him and he was gone."

Terry licked his lips and looked around. The kid was gone here, too, down the highway. "Something's gonna happen," Joe continued over the walkie. "This was just the beginning. I can feel it." Terry didn't know why, but he believed him. Absolutely totally believed him. A shiver ran up his spine in the hot morning sunlight.

CHAPTER
4

They were in the Chevy van. It was six years old, a dirty white with a ding on the right rear bumper that had been there forever. Whitney hated it. She was seventeen, too old to be riding around with her family in a van. Especially one that was old and beat up and embarrassing. However here she was, she thought with a sigh, captured, a prisoner of her, oh, so boring parents.

Her father, Big Don, was behind the wheel, her mother, Helena (Gawd, could you believe how old-fashioned her mother's name was?), in the bucket seat next to him. They were watching the desert roll by, the radio (the radio - ugh) playing classic rock (Classic rock; what was that? Almost as old as their parents). No satellite, no play lists, no ear buds, no streaming, just listening to the stupid AM radio that nobody but her parents listened to anymore. Her brother, Donny, (really Don, Jr. but he hated it so much that nobody used it, except their father when he was really pissed) was on the bench seat next to her. He was into his device, some game. That's all he did. Play games. On any screen available. At least he hardly spoke. He was sixteen, younger than her by almost two years. It didn't seem much, but as far as she was concerned, the gulf between them might as well have been a hundred years.

They had nothing in common. Absolutely nothing. She was convinced. She hardly even bothered talking to him anymore. At least his buds were in, so she didn't have to listen to his stupid POV shooter.

Tom Holland   The NOTCH

She was doing her cuticles with a tweezer. It was something to do. The desert seemed endless, boring white sand sweeping by with every now and then a butte or tabletop. She might have thought it was cool if she were a tourist, but she lived here. Worse, with her family. They were on the way back from Grandma's. Every time they went there, their father, Big Don, said it was their last time, because Grandma would surely be dead any day. But she never died, she was as permanent as the peaked mountains in the distance or the flowing sand, but their parents kept saying it so she and Donny would be nice to her.

As if they would be anything else to the old lady. Whitney loved her Grammy; so did Donny, but the two of them were too old to spend a weekend at Grandma's anymore. They were anxious to get out of there after a few hours, even if they felt guilty about it.

The van hit a bump and lurched to the side. The sudden movement shifted Donny into her arm, forcing the tweezer to jerk, digging into her tender skin. "Ouch," Whitney cried. "You hurt me."

"Sorry," her brother said absently, never looking up from his game.

Whitney glanced down. A sliver of blood was slicking the bottom of her nail. A cuticle was torn. "You cut me," she said, sucking at it.

"I said I was sorry," Donny said. "What do you want? I didn't cause the bump in the road."

"Who's that?" their mother suddenly said, looking out the front window. They and their father followed her gaze. After all, they didn't have much else to do.

There, in the distance, was a lonely figure. A narrow boy, not much more than five feet tall, walking along the side of the highway. His loose clothing flapped around him with the kind of freedom that let you know they were newly washed and threadbare.

20

Book 1: THE FIRST DAY

"Who is it?" Donny said, peering over his mother's shoulder to see.

"It's a boy," their mother said turning off the radio and finally getting rid of the screaming guitars.

"Out here in this blazing sun, with no cover?" Whitney said. She leaned across the back seat for a better look. Sure enough, it was a kid ahead, younger than her or Donny given his size. "He must live around her somewhere."

"Around here there's nothing but desert," Donny said with a nod out the window. They were slowing, the sand becoming less of a brown/white blur. Helena put her window down as they stopped by the boy. He didn't seem to notice them, just tromping ahead, not stopping for them. His pace wasn't fast, but it wasn't slow either.

Determined, as though he had someplace to be. "What the hell's wrong with him?" their father said, letting up on the brake, and pacing the boy.

Helena called out her open window. "Whoo-hoo, where you going? You need a ride?"

The boy came to a stop. So did Big Don, so they were all looking out their open windows at him. Donny dropped his window, too, as far as it would go, so he and Whitney could stare out at the boy. His face was alert, but expressionless. Passive, flat, almost deliberate, like he wanted to make sure you didn't know what he was thinking, if anything. He had extraordinary eyes. They were pale with a hint of blue. His hair looked bleached by the sun, almost white, but with a trace of gold running through it.

"You think he's all right?" Big Don said, leaning across his wife for a better look. He made no effort to lower his voice. "Looks odd to me."

"Don, don't say that in front of him," their mother protested.

"He doesn't seem to mind," their father shrugged, nodding at the boy. He hadn't so much as blinked, standing there, staring at them.

"He looks fine to me, just like maybe he doesn't want to talk. Not that I blame him," Donny said and flopped back in his seat, threatening to return to his game.

Whitney didn't move, still examining the boy through the open window. "His hair is bleached, he's been out here so long," she said. "Whoever heard of walking in the desert without a cap or something?"

"Might have some albino in him," her mother said, peering more closely at the boy.

Whitney knew that was stupid, but didn't say anything. "Mom, don't say that so he can hear," Donny said, looking up from his game. He was embarrassed for his mother. The boy standing out there didn't seem to care very much one way or the other, though.

"Well, so, you want a ride or what?" Helena said to the boy, ignoring her own son.

"What are we gonna do with him, he don't talk?" Big Don asked, being sensible. "What if he doesn't tell us where to take him?"

"Then we'll drop him at Willy's Truck Stop," Helena said, equally sensible, referring to the next and only gas station on their way home to Cordes Lakes.

Whitney continued to study the boy. His eyes were shockingly clear. Not inhuman or anything, but there was no real color to the pupils. Maybe just the wisp of a blue, as if the overhead sky might be reflected there.

"What do you say?" Helena said to the boy. "You coming or not?" She reached back and opened the back door.

"Mom," Donny said, complainingly, but he slid out, giving the kid room to get in. "I'm not sitting in the middle," he said to the boy, as if he understood every word that was being said. Still silent, the

Book 1: THE FIRST DAY

boy climbed into the car, next to Whitney. Donny got back in and closed the door behind him. He was instantly back to his game, his head down, his attention there.

"Okay," Helena nodded at Big Don, and looked back at the boy as he pulled out onto the road. The boy sat perfectly still and quiet between her two children. "You want any water?" Nothing from the boy. She shrugged. "Okay, just let me know."

She turned back to looking out the front window. Whitney sucked at her torn cuticle. The sting was going away, but too slowly for her. She cast a look at the boy. "You talk?" she asked. He said nothing.

"Leave him alone," Donny muttered without looking up from his game.

Whitney pulled her injured forefinger out of her mouth, investigating the damage. "Still hurts," she said to no one in particular.

The boy turned his head and looked at her. Rather, at the tip of her finger. She felt his eyes and glanced up. "What?"

The boy didn't answer. His pale eyes didn't meet hers either, but he reached out and enclosed her forefinger in his hand. She found it soft and warm, comforting almost. He held her finger for a moment. She frowned. There was something clean and serious about the boy's face. As if he was concentrating. The pain seemed to lessen; the stinging that was more a distraction than a hurt going away. The boy opened his hand, freeing her finger, and sat back, as though his job was done.

She glanced at him, curious in spite of herself, and raised her finger, looking at the torn cuticle. Only it wasn't torn anymore. The skin was healed, completely, totally, the finger looking like it had never been hurt. Her jaw became slightly unhinged. My God, he had made it all better, she thought. Without kissing it. But nobody could do that. Could they? She lifted her gaze to the boy's face, but he was staring over the back seat, out the front window, paying no attention to her.

23

It was as though his touching her had never happened. But it had. She knew it. Her brother never looked up from his game. He missed everything, she said to herself with a shake of her head. His choice, but he had just missed something incredible. Out here, with their old fogy parents, in the middle of nowhere.

A miracle.

CHAPTER
5

Whitney looked up as they pulled into Willy's Truck Stop. It was huge, banks of pumps, diesel and gas, a section for idled trucks, a store with an eatery and hot bunks and showers for drivers to crash a few hours and clean up before getting back on the road. It was the last stop before a long stretch of desert and every traveler seemed to know it. The radio speakers were playing, now with a news break as they pulled to a halt facing the convenience store. Whitney couldn't help hearing, if only with half an ear, something about a spreading plague in Africa.

"Restroom time," her mother gaily called as Big Don turned off the car, killing the news. Whitney's mother stepped out. Her father was right behind, taking the keys with him. Her brother didn't move. He was still into his stupid game.

"You wanna come?" she said to the pale boy next to her. He didn't move or say anything. His gaze was still focused straight ahead, as if they were still on the highway. Only he was staring at the dirty white wall of the convenience store. She looked across him at her brother. "He doesn't want to pee."

"I do," Donny said with a shrug and finally slipped his device into a pocket and slid out his door, leaving her alone with the boy.

She focused on him. "You haven't had anything to drink. Is that why you don't have to go to the bathroom?" Maybe he sweated it away, walking along that road. Still nothing. She lived in the desert and knew what it was like to be out there. Bareheaded, he was lucky he didn't have sunstroke.

She held up her hand, showing him her healed forefinger. "How did you do this?" More nothing. "You're headed someplace, aren't you, and you're just using us to get there?" It was a guess on her part, but it made sense.

Still nothing. "Okay, sit there," she said with a shrug of her own and slipped out of the car, heading for the woman's room. She hoped it was clean. It usually was at Willy's. They always stopped here on the way home from Grandma's. Had a counter and good food inside, coffee fifty cents a cup. It was a real trucker's place. Whitney liked it. For some reason, the busier the gas station, the cleaner the bathrooms.

She was about to open the door to the woman's room and step inside when she suddenly stopped. Her eyes were flashing a burning white, interrupting her vision. She shook her head, and it stopped. She blinked and looked up to see her father lying dead on the ground. There was a spray of blood around his mouth. "Dad?" she managed to squeak, not able to believe her eyes.

She looked around. Cars and trucks were stopped. She could see the wall clock through the window into the convenience store. 8 PM at night it read. That's when she realized it was dark (but it had just been day; how could that be?). Nothing was moving. Dead bodies lay everywhere. She took a step forward. Many of them had blood around their mouths, others had been shot, their weapons dropped nearby. There was a big SUV near a stand of pumps, destroyed by an explosion and resultant fire. It was still smoldering, sending up a plume of black smoke into the night sky, but it wasn't the death and destruction that seemed so frightening. It was the absolute, total, otherworldly silence.

A bathroom door banged open behind her and she whirled to see her mother stagger out. She was coughing blood, her lips smeared

Book 1: THE FIRST DAY

with it. She managed a few steps and fell at her daughter's feet. She coughed once more, spewing blood, and died.

Donny, her brother, where was he? Whitney whirled, looking about. She saw him lying by the bathroom door to the men's room. He was dead, but it wasn't from any blood around the mouth. He'd been shot, several bullets tearing through his sixteen-year-old body. Her entire family was all dead. Except for her and maybe the boy. She hadn't seen him. Where was he? Could he still be alive?

She looked around the desolate truck stop, littered with dead bodies, nothing moving except the smoke from the ruined SUV rising, and then she saw him, near the highway. The boy. He was looking at her, the huge moon behind him, silhouetting him in its pale light. As she watched, he turned and walked down the highway, headed deeper into the desert, toward Phoenix, she realized with a start.

She blinked again, trying to get rid of the horrifying image. Her brother banged out the bathroom door, startling her. She jumped and realized she was back in the present, daylight making her blink. Donny seemed surprised to find his sister standing there. She must have looked pale and about to collapse because he frowned. "Hey, sis, you okay?" he said, truly worried. "You look sick."

She didn't answer, looking around, even more wildly now. Willy's Truck Stop was alive with cars again, vehicles, small and big, trucks, diesels, and people, glorious people, all moving about, doing their business in the blessed sun. Not threatening night, but the daylight of the living. But the boy. Where was he?

Her gaze swerved to their van. It looked empty. She ran over to it, throwing open the side door. There was no one inside. Whirling, she looked down the four-lane road. In the distance she saw a flatbed truck roaring away, heading toward Phoenix. The back was piled high with crates, strapped in place, and between them, leaning back against the cab, seemingly relaxed and enjoying himself, his face lifted to the sun, was the boy.

She took a step after him, but she knew it was too late. He was already gone, the truck rumbling toward the city. She couldn't stop him. She knew that. He wanted to go to Phoenix, but where did that leave her and Donny and her parents?

She was only seventeen. She didn't deserve this. What in God's name was going on?

CHAPTER 6

Mickey Meyers sat behind the wheel of the truck, taking crates of lettuce, tomatoes, and potatoes into Phoenix for a vegan health food store. Of course, crates of vegetables, even if they were totally natural and overpriced, couldn't make him any real money, so at the bottom of each were six pounds of killer sativa marijuana. That could make him a lot of money, especially since it was Purple Haze, a strain of cannabis he'd developed himself. He and his much-loved wife (common law actually; not his fault), Lilli, the real horticulturist.

He grew the vegetables and the weed together in a hydroponic farm behind his house at Mary's Landing. The sides of the truck he was driving were stenciled with his name and logo: "Mickey's Organic Vegetables—Eat Healthy." It showed an array of anthropomorphic vegetables, seemingly exploding with good health, dancing happily about. He and Lilli, who had Photoshopped it for him, knew it was stupid, but everybody needed a logo today. Branding; it was all about branding.

He was pushing fifty, if you called forty-nine pushing it. The Landing was a smallish town far away from the city, between desert and more desert, which suited him and Lilli just fine. They wanted to be out where a lot of neighbors wouldn't be asking him what he was growing in his greenhouses, a place where people were friendly, but didn't stick their noses in your business. Also, where there wasn't a lot of law enforcement. They had medical marijuana laws in Arizona, but God help you if you got caught growing and selling. Mary's Landing was the perfect place for what he and Lilli did. Everybody knew, but nobody said a word, 'cause everybody needed cash flow as bad as he did. Or worse.

He lifted a hand to scratch his nose only to grimace in pain. He'd been trying to get Lilli dinner last night—she had ALS, Lou Gehrig's Disease, and her right side was damn near useless—and he'd grabbed the handle of the old iron frying pan without realizing it was still blazing hot from the steaks he'd been frying. He'd screamed and dropped it, but too late. His palm was badly burnt. He'd coated it with unguents and wrapped it in gauze, but it didn't stop it from hurting like hell.

He'd dropped a Valium—he wouldn't touch opioids—and smoked his best bud before he'd left the Landing—he hated to leave Lilli in her condition dependent on a walker, but they needed the cash. Lilli had lost mobility. She could hardly shuffle and only one hand was any good. He'd taken over the cooking, house cleaning, and even clerking at the small organic grocery they had set up in the back of their house, which was on the main street. The plastic greenhouses were also there, down a tight alley off the main drag.

Even supplying dope dealers in the city like he did wasn't generating enough income to pay for the rising doctor bills. Rehab was costing a fortune. They were too young for Medicare, too old for an HMO, he'd like to say as he ground his teeth and tried to figure out how to keep everything going. With the bills for Lilli he needed to sell weed, the more the better. Get her body working again, hold the disease back for as long as they could. It was all he cared about, keeping her comfortable and alive, even though he knew it was a losing cause.

ALS was a crippler and a killer; it shook you apart like Parkinson's, only worse, 'cause it paralyzed the muscles at the same time, until

Book 1: THE FIRST DAY

you were stiff and suffocating in your own body. The only question was how long it took, which drove Mickey crazy with frustration. He loved Lilli. He couldn't lose her, but he couldn't save her either.

So to make the coin for what she needed and having no choice, he made dangerous runs into Phoenix to deliver the contraband. There was a lot of demand from people who didn't have the doctor's card to get medicinal. It was real dangerous, 'cause if he got busted he'd go away for a long time, and he didn't know who was going to take care of Lilli then. She was five years younger than him, but neither of them had any family, so it was up to him, no matter how he had to do it.

Dropping his burned hand with the gauze bandage, he raised his eyes, glancing reflexively in his rearview mirror. He did it out of habit, and because he didn't want to think about his still hurting hand or his disabled wife. He was shocked to see a boy standing in the truck bed between the crates, his hands out as if he were flying, his hair blowing in the wind.

Mickey almost jammed on the brakes, which would have sent the kid flying, maybe done some real damage, but he had the presence of mind to feather them, bringing the truck to a rolling stop on the soft shoulder.

He leapt out, looking up at the boy, still standing there. He wasn't even bothering to hold on to the crates, strapped down tight in the bed. "What are you doing up there?" Mickey said, running his good hand through his still long hair which he had tied in a ponytail that reached his shoulders. It was gray but still impressive for a man his age. He was more upset than he wanted to be. He looked up and down the highway. A few cars passed, but traffic wasn't heavy. He didn't need this, not when he was ferrying weed and had a burned hand. Where the hell had the kid come from?

He looked at the boy with a frown. "You hop on at the truck stop? That what you do?"

The boy didn't say anything, but he finally deigned to look down at him. Mickey blinked at the pale eyes staring at him. He'd never seen a human being with colorless eyes before. His hair was washed out, too, but the kid didn't have that pink look of an albino. He was something else, something Mickey had never seen before.

"C'mon, outta there," he said, holding up his hands. The boy stepped forward and leaned down, letting Mickey take him under the arms and lift him off the truck. Mickey was careful to make sure his damaged palm didn't take any pressure, but it still flared with pain. He sat the boy down in the dust beside the highway, staring at him and trying to ignore the throbbing.

"Why'd you get on my truck?" he asked. "You running from someone, unhappy at home, abused, something stupid like that?" The kid still didn't say anything. "What? You deaf and dumb?"

Mickey shifted his weight, looking back toward the truck stop. It'd take him time to get back there, and he had to be at the vegan shop in Phoenix at two. Hector, the owner, had a buyer who wanted what he had in back, under the lettuce and tomatoes. Wanted it bad enough to pay extra, Hector had told him.

"Shit," Mickey said, not knowing what to do. He looked at the kid who seemed to be looking back. No, that wasn't right. He was looking through him, as though he was staring at something far in the distance. "Something wrong with you?"

Mickey was calming down. The kid did seem strange. He certainly wasn't talkative. Maybe there was something wrong with him, but Mickey didn't have time to worry about it now. He threw open the passenger side door with his good hand.

"Okay, go on, get in," he nodded. The boy turned toward the

Book 1: THE FIRST DAY

open door, but didn't move, not fast enough for Mickey. "All right, I'll help."

He grabbed the boy with his good hand and lifted him into the truck, slamming the door behind him. He crossed around to the driver's side, fuming as he went. He shoulda known this day wasn't going to be good. Burned his hand last night, his wife was dying at the same time, and now a mute boy had turned up in the middle of the desert.

He climbed behind the wheel, shooting a look at the kid next to him. "Tell you what, I'm gonna take you into the city with me. I'll have you back to the truck stop like in four, five hours. That okay with you?" The boy didn't say anything, just looked straight ahead, as if he already wanted to be on his way.

"Yeah, I guess it is okay," Mickey said with a nod and fired the engine. As he gave it a little gas, warming it up, the boy turned his head and looked at his bandaged hand, as if he was interested in him for the first time. The boy reached for his bad hand. Mickey jerked it away, "Hey, easy, it hurts like hell," he said.

The boy delicately reached out and with a forefinger touched the bandage on his burned hand. Mickey wanted to flinch, but didn't. The boy spread his fingers, until he was touching the bandage on the entire area. Something in the boy's motion, his absolute confidence, the calm in his face made Mickey know it was gonna be all right.

The boy took his hand away, and as he did he also took away all the throbbing and pain. Mickey could feel it lessening and disappearing. He lifted the burned hand, wonder filling his face. There was no pain at all. He carefully probed the gauze with his good hand, kneading it with his fingers. Still no pain. Not able to understand what had happened, or how it had happened, he carefully pulled the bandage off his hand and looked at his palm.

It was like he'd never burned it the night before. The raw flesh, the charred burned skin peeling away, it was all gone. He was staring at a perfectly normal hand and it was his. He looked at the kid next to him. He had settled back into his seat, staring straight ahead toward Phoenix.

"Yeah, sure, kid. Wherever you want to go," Mickey said in a croak, awe in his voice, and pulled the truck out onto the road.

CHAPTER
7

Mickey Meyers was deep into Phoenix, the boy still beside him on the front seat of the truck. Mickey had his cell plugged in, listening to C/W. He still hadn't gotten his head around his hand healing, but he couldn't deny it had happened. Damn, he could look at it and see it wasn't burned. What the hell was he dealing with in the kid?

Part of him said to keep calm, that if he told anybody what had happened they'd think he was stoned on his own shit. Or take it as some new age kind of healing thing. Crystals anyone? He didn't know. He just didn't think it was something he'd share. Maybe to Lilli, his companion and the love of his life, although she was too spiritual as it was with the ALS. Shit, she'd even started going to church.

He cut the kid another glance. He seemed the same. "This where you wanted to come?" He nodded out the window at the city streets sliding by. There were a lot of people about, walking, talking, and checking their devices. Traffic made him go slow. It was a shopping area that would bring him to the vegan store where he sold his contraband.

"Busy enough, isn't it…" he said, glancing at the kid as if he couldn't see him enough. The words died on his lips. The boy was gone. Which was impossible. He had just been there beside him. But the seat was empty now. Mickey checked out the bed behind him in the rearview. The crates of vegetables were still there, but no kid. Only Mickey in the truck. That was it.

The kid had no-shit disappeared. Mickey swallowed. What the hell was he? Who could disappear and cure pain? No, "what?" What could do those things? Holy shit. Wait until he told Lilli about this.

CHAPTER
8

A young girl came to a stop with the crowd at a crosswalk deep in the busy city. She was fourteen or fifteen and had a small furry white dog on a leash. The girl started across the street with the animal, just as the light began to change, flashing yellow. She did not notice her dog straining at the leash to get to the other side, as though it sensed danger. The light went green and an anxious driver, one who hadn't been paying any more attention than the girl, leapt forward, turning the corner before the girl and the dog had made it to the other side.

The driver, spotting the girl at the last moment, swerved to the side, thankfully missing her, but smacking her dog. With a cry of terror and pain the animal was sent flying, the leash ripped from the girl's hand. The driver slammed on the brakes, screeching to a halt, and leapt out. She was a middle-aged woman, full of apologies. Cars stopped around them, but the girl wasn't paying attention to any of them. Her gaze was fixed to her dog, which lay in the gutter, a ball of now dirty white fluff, its long hair blowing softly in the breeze, but no movement from the body.

The girl rushed to her unmoving dog, staring down in horror.

People had gathered. Traffic had halted in the immediate area, although other drivers were already swinging out around them in their hurry to be on their way. A dead dog laying in the gutter wasn't going to stop them on their intended route. The drivers and passengers in the stopped cars watched as the young girl knelt beside her animal. Several pedestrians gathered, watching, either moved by pity or more likely, having nothing better to do.

"We should call 911," a man ventured.

Another shrugged. "That's for people, not dogs."

The girl was oblivious, reaching out and touching her animal. The dog did not move. Tears sprang into her eyes and she began to weep.

Across the street, the boy, who had appeared as if from nowhere, watched, his face not giving any feeling away. He stepped off the curb and walked to the girl and her dead dog. She sensed him and looked up, her face tear-stained. "I was just taking her for a walk," she said with a sob. "She's a rescue. I loved her."

The boy squatted beside her, looking intently at the animal. The few people standing about quieted. "What's he doing?" a woman who'd been waiting for a bus asked.

A teen and his girlfriend standing nearby didn't answer, just watched. Same with a couple of clerks that had come out of a corner dress store. The boy put out a hand, laying it lightly on the dog's side, letting its furry coat slip through his splayed fingers. He pressed harder, his pale bluish eyes focusing on the dog. He pressed his lips together. His eyelids slid half-closed.

The girl was watching him closely. She knelt next to him and could feel his total concentration, as if he expected something to happen. She put her hand on her dog. She could feel the heat of her beloved pet leaking away with death.

She didn't know what the silent boy was trying to do, but nothing was happening. The dog was still unmoving, people starting to walk away, traffic flowing by once more. Then the girl felt it, a surge of heat rushing into the animal's body. She looked up. Her eyes widened. She could swear she saw a ball of bluish light leaving the boy's hand and disappearing into her dog.

Book 1: THE FIRST DAY

The animal suddenly shuddered, its chest heaving. The girl's heart almost stopped. Her eyes bugged out. The dog raised its head, looked about and whined. Its pink tongue lapped out and licked the boy's hand. Maybe he smiled, maybe it was just a hint, the girl wasn't sure, but he removed his hand, as if his work was done.

The fluffy white dog whined again and the girl gently took her in her arms. The animal lifted its head and licked her cheek. The girl was overjoyed. "Oh, thank you, thank you," she said to the boy. She didn't know how, but she knew he was responsible.

People had stopped and turned back, watching. The woman who had hit the dog returned from her stopped car, watching open-mouthed as the seemingly just dead animal squirmed in its owner's arms. The boy stood and while everybody was concentrated on the dog, babbling, their cell phones out, recording everything, he slipped between the people gathered about and disappeared from sight.

"What happened?" the woman who'd hit the dog said to a nearby couple who'd been watching, rooted to the spot.

The teen with his girlfriend swallowed hard and said: "He brought the dog back to life. The boy did." His girlfriend nodded agreement, as serious and shocked as he. It was as though they'd witnessed something special, something they'd never seen before or believed possible; certainly, something none of them had words for.

"Shit," one of the men watching said. He was old and disheveled and looked a step from living on the streets. "Where'd he go?"

He looked around. So did the others, but the boy was gone. The girl clasped the dog closer. It greeted her with a big wet sloppy kiss.

CHAPTER 9

The Data Storage Center was a row of four-story concrete buildings in Bluffdale, Utah. They were built in a line, one after the other, marching across the horizon. The sheer size was daunting, over a million square feet of above ground reinforced concrete with multiple sub-basements. There was a regiment size guard force with its own barracks for its 24/7 protection. It was surrounded with concrete blocks, electric fencing and motion detectors that never stopped humming. Guard stations provided the only egress or ingress. Surveillance cameras were everywhere, with high intensity searchlights, and armed K9 patrols with standing shoot-to-kill orders.

With good reason. The heart and brain of a nation plus its accumulated knowledge was there. Everything that had happened or was happening in America first, and then the rest of the world, was gathered, compared, filtered, sliced and diced, and turned into mega data there. Storage sections were buried so deep they were beyond the reach of the most powerful nuclear bombs. Hopefully. Inside were server farms and storage units, kept at near freezing temperatures, powered with a constant flow of electricity, backup provided by banks of generators in case the hard wires failed. Data Halls, they called them. There were acres of them, all run under the unimpeachable auspices of the National Security Agency.

People in lab coats and wearing ID badges, each with their own code, moved quietly about, as though they were supplicants and priests tasked with caring for the most valuable—and deadly—of monsters, ones made of chips and leads and micro-scopic processors, zipping content through the air in webs of Wi-Fi. It was storing all kinds of communication, written, tex-ted, videoed, coded, and spoken, gathered from everywhere in the world. And it never slept.

There was another Data Hall, as long as a football field, where all the mega data was strained and sorted, algorithms not even the programmers could explain, building on themselves in coils of arti-ficial intelligence, growing ever more sophisticated, working in milliseconds, to keep up with the data pouring in.

What made it out of there went to other places, to the screens of those who ran the facility and were responsible to those way above, in Washington, D.C., and other hardened redundant facilities where the might of the country lay in wait for whatever might occur.

Everything hummed with tranquil professionalism. One could tell by the overwhelming mood of calm that prevailed.

Dr. Catherine Hurungzy sat in a large office, her walls a bank of screens. They were eating the cloud, pulling out and modeling data from all over the world. It was instant and the streams unending. Catherine was a mature thin woman with blue eyes like chips of ice. She was project manager of all and any Black Swan events at the NSA and FBI, and much more than that. She carried the responsibility with a thin sheen of perpetual anxiety.

A screen pinged and a face popped up. Morgan, NSA regional director. He was in his forties, short with a roundish face. He spoke with a controlled calm that had its own edge. "There's a contagion outbreak in western Africa. Are you aware of it?"

She checked her screen that gave the still limited geo parameters of the disease. "It's still small, but growing."

"We've lost a WHO inspection team. We don't know why yet. We're working on it."

Book 1: THE FIRST DAY

That stopped her. The World Health Organization didn't lose contagion teams. They were too careful. The only explanation was that they had faced something new, something they didn't expect and couldn't protect themselves from. "Let me know when you find out," she said and clicked off.

There had been multiple outbreaks of viral hemorrhagic diseases since Ebola, but nothing as bad as that. Marburg, Dengue, Rift Valley, Lassa, they'd all burned themselves out and it wasn't uncommon for the doctors to never find out the reason, but none of them had ever lost the entire team. Was this different?

She didn't know, but her attention was snagged by another feed, way down on her "oddities" filter. An unknown boy had saved a dog that had been mortally injured by a car. If only all of life was that simple. Have a boy touch you and all your troubles, even death, disappeared. With that dismissal she went back to study the emerging configuration of this new disease.

CHAPTER 10

Adan Cuarto and Magda Rodriguez sat in the follow car. They could see Samosa and Frodo sitting in the old car farther down the street. They were parked like them, tight against the curb, but they'd take off the second they saw the truck turn the corner behind them. They'd lead the truck and mid-block they'd jam on the brakes, forcing the truck to stop. Adan and Magda would crowd his rear so the driver couldn't back up. Unless he wanted to crash into them. Which maybe a few had thought of but a flash of a pistol dissuaded them. Both cars were boosted less than an hour ago and would never be traced back to them.

"Damn," Magda whispered, looking at her cell. She had thick dark hair that fell to her shoulders and green eyes. She was in her late twenties, though she would never say how late. Youth had been kind to her, that and her looks, her curves, and high firm breasts made her devastatingly attractive to men, most men anyway, but she hated relying on her looks, knowing they were fading with every breath she took. She'd been an orphan, homeless, abused, pimped out, kept as a mistress, and what she had learned from growing up hard was never to be reliant on anyone. Especially a man, so she had decided to learn a profession, not whoring, but something important, something she could always depend on. Like becoming a very accomplished thief.

Adan could glimpse live news on the screen of Magda's phone. He was thirty-two, tall and narrow with dark hair and watchful brown eyes. Women loved him, but he never had time for them, except for a quick coupling and hardly ever more than once with the same chica bella, not until he met Magda. He loved her almost as much as he loved money, but his attention was elsewhere at the moment.

"Madre de Dios," she murmured once more in shock.

"What?" he said. He was sitting there, unable to stop himself from looking over his shoulder, expecting to see the truck they were jacking turning the corner at any moment. It was already ten minutes late.

"People saying this kid brought a dog back to life," she said, nodding at the cell phone.

"What kind of kid?" he asked, his interest momentarily snagged.

"Nobody said yet." She nodded at her phone. "They're interviewing people who saw it."

He glanced at the rearview mirror to see the truck turning into view and rumbling down the street toward them. Finally. "It's here," he said, forgetting all about the boy.

Magda twisted in the seat, looking back. It was a semi, more than big enough to carry a shitload of cigarette cartons. That was what they wanted. Smokes with a state stamp that made them super easy to fence. The semi was accelerating toward them. Adan already had his phone on speaker. "Truck's coming," he barked to Frodo and Samosa in the lead car ahead and fired his own engine.

Ahead of them, Magda could see a thin line of smoke coming from Samosa's exhaust. The big guy and Frodo were ready. Before she could blink, the truck sped past and Adan hit the gas, falling in behind, but giving it room, waiting for the sharp stop.

In front, Samosa roared away from the curb, got directly in front of the truck and slammed on the brakes, stopping at an angle so the truck couldn't swing around him. The driver hit the brakes with both feet, bringing the big semi to a squealing stop.

46

Book 1: THE FIRST DAY

"Here," Samosa said in his beater car, pulling a sawed off shotgun from the floor and grabbing the throw off Frodo's lap. He used it to hide his useless legs. His chrome wheelchair was collapsed in the back. Samosa used the throw to cover the shotgun. He was big, mostly Samoan, but he wasn't sure what else. He was six feet two and over two hundred and sixty pounds, all of it muscle. Just his size was enough to make others back down, but in case the driver didn't, Samosa had the shotgun. He jumped out, motioning toward the driver high up in the cab, still in shock at almost having hit them.

"Outta the truck, now," Samosa yelled as he advanced, doing his best scary thug imitation.

In the old car, Frodo dragged himself across the seat, until he was poking his head half out the side window. He fumbled out his small-bore pistol, waving it so the driver could see. Adan skidded to a halt behind the truck, blocking it from behind, and he and Magda hopped out. They came up to the side of the cab, Magda hanging back. She had the lower half of her face hidden now with a scarf, but the small pistol in her hand was clear to see. The goddamn truckers had all sorts of little cameras stuck about their vehicles these days and she didn't want to be ID'd, facial recognition was getting more and more sophisticated. The gun being spotted she didn't mind.

"Out," Adan said, motioning with his pistol. The driver slid out, his face flushed. He wanted to put up a fight, but there were the guns waving around, plus what did he care about his cargo? They weren't paying him enough for this.

"The keys and your phone," Samosa said. The trucker passed both to him. Samosa held them up. "Put these back in your cab after we're through." The trucker nodded and took off down the street, hotfooting it back to the depot.

"Let's check the cargo," Adan said with a grin. He and Magda tucked their pistols away and headed for the back of the truck, Samosa following.

Once they'd seen what they'd gotten, they'd deliver it to Gordo's Used Car lot and go over to the bar for their money. The Fat Man, for that's what El Gordo was, had it all figured out. A one-stop shop for thieves. He'd set up the hit, for a price, of course, fence the stolen goods, take his percentage, and give the rest to you. Problem was his piece of the action was sixty percent, which meant his workers always had to keep stealing, just to stay even. The Fat Man loved it that way.

Adan was the first to reach the back of the semi, using the keys to open the double padlocks, and pulling the chains from the bolts. He shoved the sliders up and threw the doors open. He and the others froze in shock. They were looking into an empty truck, all fifty feet of it. There wasn't as much as one carton of smokes inside. It was clean, newly swept, not even any dirt to be seen.

"They musta off-loaded back at the depot," Samosa said when he finally found his voice. Magda and Adan said nothing. They were just as shocked.

"What's in the back? How many boxes?" Frodo asked as he rolled up in his shiny chrome wheelchair. He couldn't stand being in the car by himself anymore, and had made it on his own into the chair and over to them. He slowed to a stop as he saw the vast empty cargo space. His face fell damn near to his ruined knees. "Oh, shit," he muttered.

CHAPTER 11

Mickey Meyers was in back of the vegan stall in the Phoenix Mart, watching the guys unload the last of his truck. Hector Esterban, the owner, looked on. He was impatient, wanting to get past the stupid lettuce and beans to the crates with the Purple Haze.

"The stuff's good?" Hector asked him.

Mickey nodded. "Like always."

"Wife? How's she?"

Mickey shrugged. Hector was a good guy. He had been buying his produce for a decade now. Mickey knew he was mercenary, but he still had a heart. Hector knew Lilli. They'd had dinner a couple of times, when he came to check out the grow houses. "Same, getting a little worse every day."

"I fucking hate ALS, ever since I seen that Lou Gehrig movie," Hector said and looked like he wanted to spit on the floor. "Made me cry."

Mickey looked down at his hand thoughtfully. "Burned my hand last night." He turned the palm this way and that.

Hector looked at it. He frowned at the pink skin. "Looks fine to me."

"Yeah, doesn't it?" Mickey said, not daring to tell him about the boy who had touched him. It was just too crazy. But his palm had been painfully burned. God knows, it had hurt enough.

The guys in the back of his truck found the marijuana, one of them grinning at Hector. "It's all here, boss," he said. As Hector walked to the crates to check it out, a nearby TV screen suddenly started flashing breaking news.

Mickey couldn't believe his eyes. He approached the screen, staring at it. Some newscaster was rattling away about what had just happened, the street and crowd behind her, including the object of interest: a young girl holding a puffy looking and very alive white dog.

"Esther's dog here, Aerial, was hit by an errant driver," the newscaster was saying. "The animal was killed. But now it's alive again. Many observers got it on video. Watch it now. This boy came out of nowhere and laid his hand on the dead animal."

Video flashed as she spoke, cell phones showing a boy from the back, his face hidden, bent over the animal. It gave a sudden sign of life, as though struggling to awake, and finally lifted its head. It licked its owner's hand, and the boy rose and walked away. He disappeared into the crowd, the camera never catching a glimpse of his face.

But Mickey knew instantly who it was. It was the boy that had suddenly appeared in the back of his truck. He could tell from the pale, straw colored hair. No one else had hair like that. It was the same boy who had touched his hand and made his burn heal and disappear. No doubt about it. Mickey raised his hand, looking at it again. It was as good as new. Hell, it might be better than new. Now the kid was doing it big time, bringing an animal back to life. Move over Lazarus. It was splattered across the news, which meant it had hit social media. He didn't have to check his device to know that.

But what the hell was he supposed to do about it? If he called the news and told them he'd had a similar experience, not as bad to be sure, he wasn't dead, but the kid had touched him, too. What then? The news would be all over him. He'd be famous for a minute, and then gone. Or maybe not. But then it might mean something

Book 1: THE FIRST DAY

to Lilli. The idea shot out of nowhere and stabbed him in the brain. It was crazy, but if the boy could heal his burned hand and brought a dog back to life, why couldn't he help Lilli with the ALS that had her in its deadly grip?

Hope surged up inside him, threatening to drown him. Also the warning voice deep inside his skull that said the whole idea was stupid. That rose up, too. He was clutching at straws. Of course he was, he knew that, but what the hell else did he have to clutch at? Suddenly he just wanted to get out of there, get out of the city, and figure this out.

He turned to Hector Esterban, about to say his good-byes, only to jerk to a stop. Hector was lying dead on the floor. Several other workers were sprawled about. All had blood on their lips, splashes painting the floor near their mouths.

There was one man left standing. Another nameless worker. He was weak on his feet and sagging against a doorway. A hand was held up to his mouth. It was dotted with red. The man coughed. More blood sprayed and he collapsed to the floor, just as dead as the rest.

Mickey stared at the scene in horror. He lowered his head, fighting not to throw up. "Hey, you want your money or to watch TV?" Hector said. Mickey looked up. Hector stood there, shockingly alive, waving a wad of cash in the air. The rest of the workers were unloading the crates. Everything was back to the way it had been a few moments ago.

Hector pressed the money into Mickey's stunned hand, and said in a low voice: "I put an extra five hundred in there. Help with Lilli."

Mickey blinked and swallowed, not knowing what to say, caught somewhere between gratefulness and being stunned at his vision. All he knew was he sure as hell wanted to get out of there. He grabbed the cash, jumped in his truck, and sped away without saying a word to Hector, not even a thanks.

CHAPTER 12

"So whatta we gonna tell El Gordo?" Frodo asked from the back of the Beemer. He was a small man with a wispy beard and twisted legs. He sat there as Samosa drove quickly through the back streets, busier now, small businesses like auto body shops and food wagons dotting the way. They had ditched the booster cars, wiped them clean, and hopped into their car, an old Beemer. People were around. Fuck 'em, Frodo thought. Wage slaves, peasants, all of them sending cash back home to Mexico or wherever the hell they were from. Frodo sat with Magda in the back, his chair collapsed and shoved on the floorboards.

"We tell him somebody musta ripped them off before we got there," Samosa growled from behind the wheel.

"He ain't gonna believe that," Adan replied next to him. He rode shotgun. "He ain't gonna wanna hear anything, except that we got his money for him."

"Yeah," the big guy said, nodding his broad face. "He'll have heard we lost out before we get to the bar. He's gonna want his dinero."

"I'll argue with him," Adan said, but without much conviction. "It's not our fault. It's Gordo's territory. His info sucked."

"El Gordo ain't gonna care," Frodo replied from the back. "You know he won't."

"Everything sucks," Magda said, looking up from her phone in the back.

She hadn't wanted to think how bad things were for them and had lost herself in her news feeds. Half of them were about the healer kid, and the other half about this coughing sickness in a place called Guinea. Lot of looks into grass huts where people heaved up blood as they died. "They say that sickness in Africa is spreading."

"What sickness?" Frodo asked, in a lousy mood and ready to hear more bad news.

"Coughing sickness, and at the same time we got this kid who's a healer," Magda said.

"What kid?" Samosa asked, looking at her in his rearview mirror.

"The one who brought the dog back to life," Adan said, butting in. He made a face, checking out his own cell for the Twitter feed. "Social media is having a shit fit."

"Well, at least there's some good news. Things ain't all crap if a kid is saving dogs," Magda shot back as she dialed up video about the boy. It wasn't hard to find. He was dominating everything on her mobile.

"Here, look," she said, about to hold her phone out, only to have Samosa suddenly slam on the brakes. Tires screeched as they were all thrown forward, Magda getting her hands up just in time to stop herself from banging off the back of the front seat.

"What the hell are you doing?" she said as she straightened and got her hair out of her face. Even Adan in the front, Mister Cool, looked shaken. Thank God the traffic was light. A car behind them would've plowed into them for sure.

"I almost killed a kid," Samosa said, nodding out the front window. He was gulping like a fish with his own shock, making his thick neck bulge.

They all looked out. A kid, narrow and straight, not much more than 9 or 10, stood there, staring through the glass at them. They couldn't have been more than a foot or two from hitting him. "What

Book 1: THE FIRST DAY

the fuck," said Adan, pissed off and recovering from his surprise. He banged out the front door with Samosa and Magda following. Frodo lowered his window, and stuck his head out, watching as the others gathered around the kid.

Adan stopped in front of the Beemer, staring at the boy who had not moved. Samosa and Magda flanked him, all looking at the boy. "What the hell were you doing, kid?" Adan barked. "We almost ran you down."

The boy didn't react. He was staring at the car, but his gaze had a thousand-yard look, like maybe he didn't know what he was staring at. "Something's funny about him," Samosa said, cocking his head. "Like maybe he's not right in the cabeza."

"Mierda," Adan said, crouching in front of the boy. He looked at the pale eyes, bluish maybe, but he wasn't quite sure. They were looking right through him. "His eyes are crazy," he said to the big guy and Magda behind him.

"Colorless," Magda said, studying the boy, but making no move to get closer. "Look at his hair. Like that kid all over the web."

"The healer?" Samosa asked. He was looking at the kid. If that's who he was, he didn't get it. The kid was skinny, had a brain-damaged, vacant look, and his clothes were ragged. He was sockless, wearing a pair of canvas shoes that were torn, the laces frayed. The only good thing the big guy could see was that the kid was clean. Unusually so, his clothes, too, like both he and they had just been popped out of the wash.

"Yeah, the healer," Magda said, still studying the boy. He was just a kid; another ragged homeless boy. Probably abused, already using whatever drugs came his way, sleeping rough, but at the same time she knew none of those things were true. There was something special about him, his almost supernatural calmness. His coloring, too. His skin looked normal, but the rest of him looked drained.

"Forget it," Adan said; rising to his feet. "He's mental or something. Whatta they call it? Autistic. Musta wandered off." He looked around, but didn't see anything out of the ordinary. They were in a street of fast food joints to either side, and nobody seemed interested in them or the kid. "Shit, nobody's looking for him."

"Hey," Frodo called out of the back window of the Beemer as a car went around them with a blare of the horn. "We're blocking traffic, you know."

"Leave him," Adan said with a shrug and turned back for their Beemer.

Magda didn't move. "We're not leaving him here. You can't leave a kid that isn't right out in the middle of the street."

"I'll leave him on the sidewalk then," Adan said, reversing direction, grabbing the kid by the arm, and starting him toward the curb. The kid didn't come easy and Adan had to drag him.

Magda instantly leaped forward, breaking his grip on the boy. She grabbed the kid, pulling him to her. "Leave him alone. We drop him anywhere, it's a church."

"Okay, it's a fucking church," Adan snarled, starting to get edgy. Fuck. The day was already shit. The truck was empty, no cigs, they owed money to El Gordo, what the hell else could go wrong?

He stalked back to the car, Samosa following.

Magda looked down at the kid. "You all right?" He didn't move. He didn't look up at her. He didn't react, like she wasn't even there. She shrugged. Well at least he wasn't going to talk her head off. "C'mon," she said, and pulled him toward the car. Unlike when Adan had him, he came easily, as though that was where he wanted to be.

CHAPTER 13

They'd been home a few hours, Whitney and her family. It was a smallish one story white house off the dusty road in Cordes Lakes, three bedrooms, all small, two baths, one of them a half. Lakes was a road stop that had turned into a small town for a lot of people that worked at the nearby salt flats. Like her dad, Big Don.

She had spent the entire time since they got home on her laptop, her tablet opened up next to it, her TV on, but muted. They were all filled with video of the boy. Different angles on what had happened in Phoenix, when the boy brought the dog back to life, ran on the bigger screen. None of them showed his face, a glimpse maybe, a sideways angle, a back of the head, but no good look at him. The tablet had a screen grab of the kid from behind, just a sliver of his face visible. He was frozen in place, but she knew in her heart it was him.

She found her brother frustrating beyond words, but if she wanted to talk to someone she figured she didn't have any choice. She didn't want to speak to her parents about this. They wouldn't believe her, so it was him or no one but herself to talk to. She texted him, asking him to come in. If he could tear himself away from his stupid war games long enough.

A moment later he appeared, walking through her door. His buds were in. He couldn't hear a word she said. He stopped next to her desk, looking over her shoulder. "Yeah?" he said.

She nodded at her screens. "You see this?" she said, figuring he'd get her meaning.

"Yeah, I've seen it," he said, pulling his buds and dropped them in his shirt pocket, a big concession for him. "You think it's the kid we gave a ride?"

"Yeah," she answered, impressed that he'd put it together with their unusual passenger. It was a rhythm they had. Like she was gonna "yeah" him to death.

"Only you don't see his face. Ever," Donny said with a shrug. "You sure it's him?"

"They were his clothes," Whitney said. "Look at the hair. You don't see that hair everywhere." She turned and tapped her screen, blowing up the image of the boy from behind, trying to get a closer look at his almost white hair, only to have the pixels dance and the image turn fuzzy.

She frowned. Noise. She hated noise on her screens.

Donny shrugged. "What do you care? He hitched a ride with us and then he disappeared. If that's him," he nodded at the screen, "he's doing okay."

"Sit down, would you." She nodded at a nearby chair.

Donny sat, like he wanted to be anywhere else as long as it wasn't with her, but then he caught her expression. Seriously upset. He lost his attitude. They hadn't been close in years, but he knew when his sister was worried, and she was very worried.

"After we realized he was gone..." she started and trailed off.

"Yeah? What happened?" he said, trying to urge her along.

He wanted to get back to his screen but maybe not about this. She'd thought he was gaming all the time, but he was also working on a book report. He wasn't a total idiot. He didn't want to end up working in the salt flats like his dad, but at the same time he didn't want to spend forever with his sister. She had gotten so full of herself, he could barely get through dinner with her. But then again, the boy they'd picked up was odd, different, and strange. Then there was that dog.

Book 1: THE FIRST DAY

"C'mon," he said, starting to fidget on the chair. "What happened?"

"Remember when I cut my cuticle?" she asked.

He nodded with a shrug. "So."

"So he healed it with a touch. Just like he brought that dog back to life." She lifted her finger, so he could see the cuticle in question didn't have a scratch on it.

"Okay," he shrugged, "I'll take your word for it. Is that all?"

"When we realized he was gone at the truck stop," she said, "something flashed in front of my eyes, and when I looked up it was night. Eight PM to be exact, I saw the clock inside the store, and everybody was dead."

"What?" For first time there was no casual "yeah." Donny straightened in his chair. His sister was as serious as a heart attack (his father's expression, applicable in this case). "Me and mom and dad, too?"

Whit nodded gravely. (Donny called her The Whit Monster when he really wanted to piss her off). For once he could understand why she seemed so serious. Didn't mean she saw anything real though. He was into sci-fi and Stephen King, but he hadn't lost his mind. Yet. "What killed us?" he asked.

"This," she said and hit a key on her laptop.

Video of the coughing disease in Africa popped up, people dead where they fell throughout a shanty town of huts and lean-tos in some major city, a vast slum of corrugated aluminum and every other castoff material, old wood, tarps for roofs, and animal skins. Some guy was on screen, blathering about how the coughing sickness started in the bush, but was now spreading to major cities. The African was yelling in broken English that no one knew how to stop it. They needed help. Help, please!

He had a drone, he was saying—Whitney couldn't believe it—and he was using it to record video and send it out over the web, real time, because nobody was telling what was happening and he was convinced he would be dead any second from the sickness and he wanted to warn the world. Using his phone as a control, he sent the drone up and away, looking down on him and the shantytown as he ranted. Just as the drone started to gain altitude, he coughed, spraying blood, and dropped.

Whitney and Donny watched, transfixed with horror.

CHAPTER 14

Adan, Samosa, and Frodo looked out from the car at the curb as Magda tried the church doors. It was tall and steep with a cross at the top, its sides brown stucco. The boy sat in the back, next to Frodo, staring out the front window, never turning his head. He could have been a statue. Outside, Magda couldn't get the church door open and stomped back to the car, beyond frustrated.

She climbed into the back, slamming the door behind her. "Who the hell ever heard of a church with the door locked?" she complained. She wasn't happy. "Doesn't anybody believe in taking a kid in anymore?"

Samosa pulled the car back into the street. Frodo looked across the boy at her. The kid was wedged in between them and Frodo's knees were bumping against his collapsed wheelchair that was stuck in the well. "Used to be open all the time where I was a kid."

"How would you know?" Samosa grunted from the front seat.

"Fui monaguilla durante un tiempo," Frodo answered. He gave it in English in case the dumb Samoan missed it. "My grandmother took me." He was white, but had grown up in the barrio and knew all the slang, especially the taunts.

"You were an altar boy?" Adan twisted, looking at him over the seat. Frodo nodded. Adan turned back to the front. "Shit."

Magda fell into her phone, playing with it as the guys talked. "What are we gonna do with the kid?" Samosa asked from behind the wheel. They were getting closer to El Gordo's bar where they had to settle up. That could be a real mess. He wanted to get rid of the boy before that.

"Hey," Magda said, looking up from her screen. "It's total news about the kid and dog or this coughing sickness. It's killing people all over Africa."

"Yeah, sure," Adan said, blowing it off. His eyes checked out the passing street, looking for another church. He didn't see one. "Social Services maybe," he said, "drop him off there?"

"I'm not putting him with some case worker. You want him put into that system?" Magda snapped at him. "Didn't you have enough of it when you were a kid? I did." Shit, what was wrong with him? Wouldn't leave Phoenix, wouldn't stop stealing, didn't want kids, never showed any interest in the one she had. He was cut off, a wall around him that no one, certainly not her, would ever scale. Now he wanted to dump some poor brain-dead brat who probably couldn't make it across the street by himself. She buried herself back in her phone.

"We can't take him into the bar with us, not when we gotta deliver bad news to El Gordo," Adan said, cutting a sour glance at the kid in the back. He was sitting there like a dummy, that thousand-yard stare in his pale eyes.

"Why not?" Magda said, looking up from her phone. "Didn't you hear? The news of the kid keeps spreading. He's blowing up. Look. Remind you of anyone?" She shoved her phone in front of Adan. It was an image of a boy, being snapped just as he turned away. You couldn't see the face, but it sure looked like the kid in the back of the car, the one they just picked up.

"Okay," Adan said, passing the phone back. "So maybe he looks like our kid. Sure isn't saving anybody right now, is he?" He jerked his head at the kid who was sitting there, like he didn't understand a word they were saying. "He's brain-dead or something. He can't do shit, much less get a dog breathing again."

Book 1: THE FIRST DAY

"Maybe he's deaf. Deaf and dumb. Anybody think of that?" Samosa said with a glance in the rearview mirror at the kid.

"Maybe he isn't right," Magda said, peering more closely at the boy. He seemed oblivious. "Maybe he's autistic, something like that. He doesn't relate to people at all."

"I think Magda's right," Frodo chimed in, his brows pinched. "The kid's there, he's just not interested. He'll be fine at El Gordo's."

"Why would we take him in there?" Adan asked, twisting in his seat to look at him. Frodo was pushed in the corner, looking frailer than usual.

Frodo didn't answer, looked at Magda. There was a wiliness in his eye. "You thinking the same thing I am?"

"Maybe, let's see," Magda said, shifting her attention to Adan. "El Gordo's got cancer, doesn't he?"

"That's what he saying, tumor in his gut, but he's taking his sweet time dying," Adan said and added for good measure: "It ain't gonna do us any good when we walk in and tell him we came up dry. So what?"

"So we tell Gordo the kid's the one everybody's talking about. The Healer," Samosa said. Even him, the big guy with the ape brow was getting it. "Sell the kid for what we owe the Fat Man."

"That's sick," Adan responded. "Fuck, he's only a kid." He nodded at the silent boy who still hadn't batted a bluish eye. "'Sides he's not going to do anything we tell him. Look at him. There's no one home." He turned to Samosa. "Stop at the curb, we're getting rid of him."

"You get rid of him, you get rid of me," Magda snapped. He didn't have to look at her. He knew her jaw was set, her lower lip pressed tight against the upper, cutting a red slash across her face.

"Come on," Adan said, turning back, trying to calm her. "Kid could get hurt, you know."

"Since when did you give a damn about a kid?" Magda shot back at him. "Or even a baby?"

Adan clamped his mouth shut. Bitch had one child down in Mexico and acted like it was his fault. He wasn't the father and didn't want to be. He didn't want a bunch of brats running around. That's what was really going on. She wanted another kid and he didn't and she had settled on the idiot in the back seat until she got her way.

"It's never gonna work," he said stubbornly.

"You don't have gut cancer," she shot back. "You have that you'll take any chance you got, even if you know it's bullshit."

"She's right," Frodo said softly from the back. "It's worth a try."

Adan said nothing, but his silence spoke louder than any words. Magda was right. When you were desperate, you'd take any chance you could get.

CHAPTER 15

Catherine Hurungzy sat behind her desk. Her cold blue eyes had turned frigid. Her machine beeped. She stared at the spreadsheet covering one of her screens. The figures were changing, the percentages being recomputed every second, an unending flow of information and odds. Behind her was a window that showed one of the ten guard towers that ringed the impregnable facility.

She was in the OTD, the FBI Operational Technology Section, and the gathering point for all domestic and national information that might affect national security. Not only did they have their own sources of information, they were also plugged into the Utah Cyber Security Data Facility, the biggest raw collector of everything that moved on the net, via wire or wireless.

Nothing worldwide escaped its maw, but only the FBI Tech Division could filter and collate it, and put it into actionable information for Homeland Security. Percentages, projections, risk tolerance, probabilities, the Division had it all.

And she had the Division.

The door opened and Morgan, her, oh-so-in-control assistant, slipped inside. They'd already gone 24 hours without sleep, but it didn't seem to matter to either of them.

"It's exploding," he said as he took a seat beside her, facing the screens. Chunks of West Africa were turning solid red now as the coughing disease spread. Smaller dots worked their way farther out, into adjacent countries. "We've lost every medical team we've sent in."

She nodded. "We're closing down all international flights in and out of the affected area. Capitals in other countries are considering stopping all population flows."

"Quarantine?"

"Let's hope it doesn't come to that," she said as she checked security on a digital flow. "The loss of GDP may crash the world."

"Eyes and ears only on this one," he said as he leaned over, showing her his device. She studied the new screen. "48% possible connection between the sickness and the boy, even though it can't be defined yet." He pointed at a trend line on the screen. "It's growing."

"We've had higher and they've been false flags."

"Tell me that after you see this," he said with a shrug. "Fingerprints. Several of them anyway. Here, the dog he touched in Phoenix. Contrast CAT scans."

He passed his cell to her. She studied the screen. It showed a scan of the dog on its side, the handprint of the boy clearly visible, as though burned into the flesh. "The boy?" she said in a hoarse whisper.

"The boy." His face was alert and hard. "One might even say it's not human. Humanoid perhaps, but not human. Here." He punched a key on his screen. A fingerprint came up.

She studied it. "Completely normal."

"Completely," he said with a nod. "Too normal as a matter of fact. The perfection to the mean is a statistical anomaly."

Her eyes flicked to her screen. "The sickness has spread into Central Africa. China has shut down its borders. Same with India. They must have unreported cases."

"It won't stop it," he said. "It's airborne."

"Let's hope you're wrong. They're going to shut down all international travel soon. No choice. If that doesn't work, God help us." She

Book 1: THE FIRST DAY

leaned back in her chair, tapping a front tooth with a red fingernail. Tap, tap, tap.

"The cost is going to be in the trillions," Morgan said. "Markets will crash, trade will stop. The ramifications are horrifying."

"Not as scary as the coughing sickness," she said, her mind finally made up. "Get us a jet to Phoenix where the boy was last seen. Focus our domestic assets there, medical as well as paramilitary."

"Done, plus Homeland Security-FBI liaison when we land," he said, unable to keep the tension out of his voice. "Plane's waiting. Change of clothes and toiletries are already onboard."

She looked up. Their eyes met. He had known what was coming and moved on it. It was what she liked best about him; he acted, unilaterally if need be. He was a bureaucrat that didn't act like one. They had been dreading something like this forever. The coughing sickness, a Black Swan event, a true worldwide threat had finally arrived. It was the reason why the agency had been created, why they had been trained and employed. She'd never doubted it would come, they'd spend years preparing for it, but she had prayed it wouldn't be in her lifetime. So much for prayers. Here it was in all its horribleness. Especially when all their preparations looked useless, and they had no idea how to stop it.

But what did the boy have to do with it? Probably nothing, but she couldn't get closer to the coughing disease, not with that kill rate. But she could to the boy. He wasn't killing anyone. Quite the opposite, although she was sure there was no truth to it. Collective hysteria perhaps.

There was also the computer modeling that said there was a connection, even if it was inexplicable. If so, she had to find it, in the hope that it offered a defense, any defense, against the seemingly unstoppable disease.

CHAPTER 16

dan and the others stepped inside the Fat Man's bar. It was dark and steamy with cigarette smoke. It stank. The windows were shaded and the neon beer signs threw swatches of hot color into the dimness. A few people were scattered at the bar and tables. None of them looked prosperous or happy, pimps, whores, thieves, borrachos, drug addicts, and hangers-on, the worst of the worst. There were big screens hanging from the ceiling in various places, all of them showing the same thing: news about the boy, with every now and then a passing mention of the coughing sickness.

Magda stopped to watch. The boy was everywhere, and she had his spitting image with her. She was holding his hand right now. She looked down at him. The kid was vacant-eyed and passive, which was fine. Why the hell shouldn't they try to sell him to Gordo? Especially when their butts were on the line.

"Hey, you coming?" Frodo said to her, looking back from his wheelchair. He and the others were at the bar.

Magda tore her eyes away and joined them. She tried to stop herself, but she couldn't help but go back to watching the closest screen. It played the same grainy video of the boy, some cell phone watching him disappear into the crowd. The boy's face was blotted out by the sun. That was good. If their kid had the wrong face, Gordo wouldn't know it. The coloring was right. Way he held himself, too. That was the thing.

"Well, we're here," Adan said with a sour face.

He was staring across the smoke-filled room at El Gordo's table. The Fat Man was the only one seated, two hundred sixty, seventy pounds plus, none of it muscle. His face was broad and fleshy with a smashed-in nose and greasy strands of black hair laid across his balding scalp. He was chowing down on a strip steak and fries, shoveling the food into his mouth with a grim determination.

Behind him, standing to one side, was Tomas, as pretty and slick looking as a paid killer could be. He favored dark silk shirts and gabardine slacks. He was El Gordo's mano derecho, right-hand man, and the really dangerous one. He had a talent with knives and preferred them to guns, so Adan always kept an eye on him. The other thug against the wall nearby was One-Eye, a tall man with an eye patch, a shaved head, and a spade beard. If that wasn't enough, there was a skinny hood, Perez, at the front door.

"Hey, Adan," El Gordo shouted, spotting him and his little group. "You got my money?"

"The truck was empty," Adan answered. "Figured you already heard."

"Asshole called, told me about it. Said they unloaded at the depot, deadheaded it back," El Gordo said, giving him a sour look. "That don't let you off the money you owe me for giving you the truck. Not my business they changed the route, someone still gotta pay."

"That ain't fair," Magda said, raising her voice to be heard across the bar. "Contact feeds you info about a jack, they gotta be accurate, otherwise you don't owe them anything."

"Yeah, I see your point," Gordo said, waving his steak knife at her, "but the guy still wants to be paid. No payment from me, no more info." He swallowed a piece of meat and gestured at the boy next to Magda with his knife. "You bring the kid like maybe he's protection, cause he ain't." The Fat Man grinned, amused at his own humor.

Book 1: THE FIRST DAY

"Course, you could always leave Magda behind. Don't figure she's worth ten grand, but a few of my hombres might enjoy finding out."

"We ain't got your money," she said, "but maybe we got something better." She took the kid by the arm and dragged him out in front where everybody could see him. Adan and Samosa froze. Frodo stopped in his wheelchair. They hadn't expected this, not this fast.

Magda gestured at the boy. "This is the kid who just saved the dog. The one that's all over the TV. You forget what you owe us and I'll have him touch you."

"What the fuck you talking about?" Gordo snarled.

"The cancer in your gut," Magda answered. "Everybody knows you got it. Look. That's him." She thrust a finger at a screen. Everybody in the bar looked. They caught a glimpse of the boy just turning away, a flash of faint golden hair, the spindly build, but not the face.

"You can't see it's him," the Fat Man noted, making a face.

"We almost ran him down in our car," Adan said, finally realizing Magda was selling him and backing her. "One second he wasn't there, and then he was. Tell him." He nudged the big guy next to him.

"Yeah," Samosa said. "It was like, I don't know, magical."

"Yeah, if he's so good," El Gordo barked, thinking it was all bullshit, but then again cancer was silently eating away at him. "Have him touch Frodo and if he walks over here to me it's a deal."

Frodo just shook his head. He was already miserable, but Adan was making it worse. "I can't walk," he said to him and the others. "Why do you think I've been in this horrible chair for the last two years?"

"You have to do it," Magda said quietly. "For all our sakes." She lifted her head, looking over at El Gordo's table. Tomas was still eyeing her tits. Bastard. The only thing she wanted him to kiss was the barrel of the little .32 in her purse.

71

CHAPTER 17

"G'mon, kid," Magda said taking a deep breath. She grabbed his hand and led him to Frodo, sitting close to a barstool. Adan and El Gordo watched, along with much of the bar. They had stopped talking now, everybody waiting to see what happened.

Nothing. The boy just stood there, staring at Frodo in his wheelchair. They were almost at eye level. The kid could not have cared less. He was totally unresponsive, staring at and seemingly through Frodo with that blank stare.

"Okay, touch me," Frodo said with growing nervousness, and pushed his hand out. The kid didn't move, like he didn't want to be disturbed. Everybody in the bar was fixed on the boy and him, their interest now definitely snagged.

El Gordo sat at his table, his eyes fixed to Frodo and the kid. He let out a loud guffaw when the kid didn't move. "It ain't working, Adan," he said in a booming, mocking voice. "You trying to make some money to pay me back, you'd better try something else, 'cause I want my cash."

The boy's sky blue eyes seemed to focus, as if he had been listening, just hiding it, and knew what to do. He held his hand out on his own over Frodo's skinny ruined legs, partially hidden by the throw. The boy's fingers splayed wide. The bar was dead silent now, but the boy did nothing more. His hand just hovered in the air, over Frodo's ruined legs.

"Come on," Adan murmured, sensing the kid was taking too long, that the crowd was getting restless. "Touch him, dammit."

Nothing happened, the seconds ticking past. That was it for Adan. He grabbed the boy's wrist, shoving his hand down on Frodo's thigh and holding it there, but still nothing happened. Magda leaned forward, putting her hand on top of the boy's. She whispered to him. "Just make it look like you're doing something, would you? Like you're thinking hard or something. "

The boy looked up. His face was the same, but she saw something in his eyes. They were smiling at her; not his face, but his eyes. She could feel them, and then a power moved down his arm. An electric current or something, she didn't know. Adan didn't know either, but he felt it, too, passing beneath the skin. It was hot and slow moving, rolling wavelike into Frodo's legs. He pulled his hand back in surprise, letting go of the boy. Same with Magda. She let go of the boy's hand.

"Damn," he murmured in surprise.

"I felt it, too." Magda looked at him in shock. "What was it?"

"Electric shock," Adan said, keeping his voice low. He didn't want anything to distract from the boy touching Frodo. "Look." He nodded at the kid's hand, now firmly clamped to Frodo's pipe stem leg.

Frodo swallowed. His face was pale and expectant, but the irrational hope slowly drained out of him. He finally shook his head. "I don't feel any..." he started to say and then stiffened in his chair. A soft blue blur seemed to pass through the boy's fingers and into his legs.

"I feel something, I really do," he suddenly cried. "My legs, they're tingling."

He arched up and a shiver passed through his body. It only lasted for a moment, and then he sagged back into his seat with an exhausted thud. It broke the boy's grip on his thigh and the light disappeared. Frodo lowered his head, panting for breath, as if he had just run a sprint.

Book 1: THE FIRST DAY

He finally looked up, seemingly as surprised as everyone else in the bar. "Jeez," he murmured, "I really felt something."

Adan, Magda, and Samosa had been watching, as rooted to the spot as anyone else in the room. "What did you feel?" the Samoan asked with a wrinkled brow. "What was it?"

"I, I don't know..." Frodo fumbled. He looked down at his legs, leaning forward to feel them under the throw. His eyes widened. "Gosh," he added like a small child, "my legs. They feel better."

The boy suddenly stumbled back, as if exhausted by the effort, and threatened to crumple to the floor. Magda grabbed him, holding him erect. "You all right?" she asked with a worried frown. "What is it? What happened to you?"

She peered closely at his face. It was drained. He was paler than he'd been before, shrunken, whiter, his hair limp and colorless. The vague sheen of golden color had been drained out of him. The crowd was equally stunned, holding their breath, listening and watching. She looked up at Adan with a worried frown. "Something's wrong with him."

"Come on, crip," One-Eye yelled at Frodo, breaking the moment, "stop with the bullshit. Nothin' happened and you know it."

It pulled Magda's attention away from the boy, who no longer seemed in danger of collapsing, even if his color was gone.

"Yeah," Tomas joined in, as if trying to shake off the magic the moment had cast over the bar. "You trying to tell us the kid is really a healer? Demierde, man, that's what you're selling, shit."

"How do you know what Frodo's feeling?" Magda snapped, whirling on him and the rest of El Gordo's table. Her dark eyes were flashing in the neon glow of the beer signs. "How do you or One-Eye know anything except beating people up and breaking their legs?" She was still pissed off about that night they ran Frodo over, Adan and all of them were.

El Gordo regarded them, stuffing some lukewarm French fries into his broad fleshy face. "Walk," he said to Frodo, exposing the half-eaten food in his gob. "Walk over here, you want us to believe it, walk, crip."

Everybody turned to Frodo, waiting to see if he'd accept the challenge. The skinny man licked his lips, pulled the shawl away, and looked down at his flimsy legs. They were covered in loose flowing pants, the right one twisted at a bad angle and several inches shorter than the other, the results of a knitting that had gone terribly wrong. Both limbs were weak and thin as pipe stems.

Frodo stood up anyway, holding on to the arms of the chair for support. "This enough for you, Gordo?"

The Fat Man stopped eating, watching Frodo. "Over here, crip," he snarled. "A grand for you if you do it." He flipped a wad out of his pocket, counted off ten C notes, and threw them on the table in front of his gobbled meal. "Otherwise nothing, except maybe I shoot you and your crew."

Frodo stared at the Fat Man. He knew he meant it. He'd destroyed his legs. He'd take his life and that of his friends. No choice. So much of his life had been "no choice." He was sick of it, but he never had a choice. Life had fucked him, but what was he going to do. He let go of the wheelchair and took a halting step toward El Gordo. He figured he could do one or two more before falling, making a fool of himself, but he had no choice. Not if he wanted to save himself and his friends, especially Samosa, the only ones he cared about.

Steeling himself, he took another step and then another and another, his eyes widening in disbelief as he finally made it to El Gordo's table. He grabbed the back of a chair there, saving himself from collapsing. "Fuck you," he said to El Gordo, breathing hard, not able to believe he'd made it. He scooped up the green just before his legs finally gave out, Samosa appeared with the wheelchair

Book 1: THE FIRST DAY

behind him. He collapsed into it, the Samoan wheeling him back to the bar and his crew where he spun about, crowing at the Fat Man at the table, staring at him with his beady eyes. Steak grease ran from the corner of his mouth, but El Gordo seemed unaware. His eyes were fixed to the skinny man with the twisted leg that hadn't been able to walk since he ordered them broken—until now.

"That enough for you?" Frodo challenged in the rush of victory. "I couldn't move before and you know it. You saw to it."

Gordo stared at him, his small eyes narrowed with fury, but instead of going after Frodo or Adan he suddenly gestured at the entire bar. "Get out of here, all of you," he snarled, everybody watching him and the boy, the barrachos, the whores, their pimps, and the thieves. "Go!"

They all jumped. Fear was thick in the bar. They knew El Gordo and where he came from you never messed with the Fat Man. One-Eye straightened against the wall and moved forward, pulling his gun. Tomas did the same, both of them gesturing with their weapons at the door which Perez guarded.

"You heard," One-Eye snarled. "Everybody out."

The bar quickly emptied through the front door, held open by a grinning Perez, who was happily flashing his pistol.

CHAPTER 18

Perez was about to close the door behind the last of them when he stopped, staring out into the street. There must have been 15, 20 people standing about, looking toward the bar. More were coming down the sidewalk to join them. They were all poor, straight out of the barrio. "Shit," he said, swinging toward El Gordo. "We're drawing a crowd outside. Word's getting out about the kid."

"Well, close the fucking door and lock it," El Gordo growled, falling back into his chair. It creaked under his weight. El Gordo's gaze slid to the boy, Magda with her arm around him. The fat man hawked, rolled the spit around in his mouth, swallowed it, and lifted his gaze to Adan.

"All right," he grudgingly said, "The ten K you owe me is forgiven—if the kid fucking works. Now have him touch me."

"Debt is completely paid," Adan quickly replied, "even if he doesn't do you any good?"

"It's all a scam, isn't it?" The Fat Man's eyes sharpened and his mouth pulled down. "You set me up for it."

"It's not a con," Frodo said from his chair. He nodded. "Look at my legs. Did they look like this before the boy touched me?"

He leaned down and pulled up his pants, revealing his skinny white legs. They were hard to see in the murk, but the bad one still looked twisted.

"They look just as bad as before," El Gordo said, leaning back in his chair, studying him. He finally shrugged. "What the hell?

Tom Holland The **NOTCH**

The debt is paid, no matter what happens. Now have the kid touch me."

"Maybe we should wait," Magda said, looking at the boy. He still looked even paler than before to her. "Give the kid a chance to recover from what he did to Frodo."

"He does it now or he don't do it at all," Gordo snarled. "I don't have time for this shit."

"You got it, El Gordo," Adan said, hurriedly breaking in with a big grin. They were gonna get out of there clean without owing any cash. That was better than he ever dared to hope. If Magda didn't blow it. "You're the man, you want the boy, you got him."

He grabbed the kid, trying to pull him away from Magda, but she unexpectedly wouldn't let him go. "Didn't you hear what I said?" she said, staring at him hard. "He's not himself yet from what he did to Frodo. He needs time to rest."

Adan looked at the kid, wetting his lips. The boy was pale, sure enough, but they had to move. Now. He could feel El Gordo's patience running out. "Is it true?" he asked, bending down to the boy, looking intently into his face, "you feel okay?" Nothing from the kid, but Adan hadn't expected anything. "What about touching El Gordo? You know, giving him some of what you gave Frodo? Is that all right with you?"

"He don't talk," Magda said. She knew he was playing her. He was always playing her. "You know that."

Frodo and Samosa watched, not saying anything.

"He didn't say no, did he?" Adan said, straightening to face her. "That should make you feel okay."

She met his eyes. His mind was made up. She understood that. There was no choice, not with El Gordo sitting there with his men sharking them with their hungry looks. But she hated Adan for taking the easy way out and putting the kid's health, maybe even his

Book 1: THE FIRST DAY

life, in danger. Like always, she thought, he didn't give a damn who he hurt, not when he wanted something.

But Adan was right. They could all end up being cut. Bad. Tomas loved the knife.

She loosened her grip on the kid's hand, letting it slip away. "Don't you let Gordo hurt him," she said to her lover. "I mean it."

Adan saw her eyes flash and gave a short nod. He dragged the kid toward the Fat Man at the table.

CHAPTER 19

Adan pulled the boy to a stop before El Gordo. The kid was like a dummy, happy to go in whatever direction he was led, if you didn't move too fast. Adan thought he looked weak on his feet, but he didn't put out a hand to steady himself. They lay at his sides, loose and relaxed. Either that or he didn't have the strength to lift them.

"You ready?" Adan said to El Gordo. Better to get on with it, he thought. Maybe Magda was right. Maybe the kid was weakening. Maybe working his magic took something out of him. Maybe he didn't have any magic, and Frodo had just gotten into it. He sure hoped the kid had some of whatever he'd given Frodo left. He was about to pull off his greatest scam. One where he could get himself killed, not to mention Magda and his amigos, but they could also be famous in the barrio forever. He knew that. Word would spread about this con. It'd be famous. If they got out with their lives.

"Where you sick?" he asked the Fat Man in the chair.

"Here." El Gordo pulled up his florid silk shirt. It wasn't hard to do. He wore it outside his pants to cover his big gut and it came up easily, exposing an ugly white hairy belly. The fat shook at the effort. Adan was disgusted, but he kept his poker face. Expose nothing about how you really felt, never fucking apologize, never hesitate, that was his mantra.

Not that El Gordo was looking at him. His eyes were clamped on the kid with his dangling arms and blank face. "You can't do anything, can you, nino?" El Gordo said, staring at him. His lips twisted, like he had a sour taste in the back of his throat. "You're just a dummy, ain't you?"

Adan looked down at the boy. Nothing out of him. He wasn't hearing the Fat Man. He nudged the boy forward with a push on the shoulder.

"Go on, touch him," he said, nodding at El Gordo's jelly belly.

But the kid didn't move, and whatever hope El Gordo had was disappearing fast. "Nobody's home," he snarled. "How's a kid without a brain ever gonna help anyone?" He pulled a pistol from his pocket, a neat little .38 snub nose. Not very accurate, but who cared when your victim was only few feet away.

"Damn it," Adan snapped, starting to panic. He grabbed the boy's hand and pressed it hard against the Fat Man's stomach. He whispered urgently in the boy's ear. "Now, do it, kid, do it, before he shoots all of us."

El Gordo sat there, watching the boy, his hand pressed into his belly. The Fat Man was hardly breathing, like he was waiting for something to happen, but he didn't know what. "Nothing is going on, the kid ain't doing nothing," El Gordo finally growled, slowly releasing his breath. His hand tightened around the grip of his pistol.

"Give it a chance." Adan flashed the Fat Man a glance. "Hijo de puta," that's what El Gordo was, a whore's spawn. Adan pressed the boy's hand harder into the man's belly. It gave, compliant to the touch, but wet and clammy, like the flesh of a dead bloated fish.

"Nothing is happening, damn it!" El Gordo exploded at Adan, leaning forward, almost trapping the boy's bony thin hand in his rolls of fat as he lifted his pistol. "He's a fake, it's a lie, all of it."

Adan looked at the boy with a swallow. He was really desperate now. He could feel the sweat popping out on his forehead. "C'mon, kid," he hissed. "Do it, please." He was almost ready to grab his own gun and go down firing.

Book 1: THE FIRST DAY

Then something happened. Adan could feel it, like a spurt of heat running the length of the boy's arm. He looked down. Maybe it was a trick of the throbbing neon light, but something seemed to run from the boy's hand into the rolls of fat of El Gordo's stomach. A bluish glow? That and some of it went into Adan.

He felt, he felt…he didn't know what he felt; a flash of heat, a momentary elation, and then it was gone. A little like what he'd felt when Magda had forced the boy to touch Frodo's ruined legs, only it was stronger this time.

It was only for an instant, that gathering of light or energy or whatever it was, Adan wasn't sure, but he damn well felt it. Most of the heat had gone into El Gordo and then it was over, like it had never happened. Adan still held the boy's hand, but it was normal and cool to the touch again.

"Goddammit." El Gordo leaned into Adan, until their faces were just inches apart. "I don't feel nothing." He stopped. A frown wrinkled his thick brow.

"What?" Adan stepped back, letting go of the boy's hand. The kid dropped it to his side, like nothing had happened. "I felt it. This heat. What did you feel?" Adan asked again, wetting his lips. He desperately wanted the Fat Man to at least feel what he had. Maybe he could talk him into it. "Did you feel it?"

El Gordo looked at him, still leaning forward, breathing hard, but silent as he probed his guts with his stubby fingers. He was checking himself inside. "I still don't feel nothin'," he finally growled, but his voice was softer and questioning, as if he wasn't so sure. He poked his belly harder.

He must have found something he didn't like, because his face bunched up, like maybe he was going to cry. "I can still feel the fucking tumor," he whimpered. He looked at Adan, his eyes turning mean and small. "I still got it."

Tom Holland   The NOTCH

"Look, El Gordo, I didn't guarantee anything..." Adan began.

"You sonavabitch," El Gordo roared, coming out of his chair, his loose shirt flapping around him. He waved the snub-nose pistol, staring at Adan and the boy. "Give me hope, false hope, make me look stupid," he said, his fat jowls trembling with rage, "I should kill you both, you and your fake kid."

He began to bring the pistol up to shoot. Magda launched herself across the room, leaving Frodo and Samosa behind. She grabbed the boy from Adan, yanking him back. She thrust him behind her, facing El Gordo. "It's not his fault. He's only a kid, he's not even right in the head."

The Fat Man hesitated, turning his beady little eyes on her for a moment as he considered whether or not to kill her and the kid. They finally shifted to Adan and he hefted the small pistol. "It's you, you're behind all this..."

"I got the kid to try, he touched you." Adan threw up his arms and stepped back. "We had a deal. All I had to do was make him try and he did. I can't help it if didn't work."

"You think I care?" El Gordo said, white spit bubbles rising on his thick lips. "It didn't fucking work."

Near the front window, Perez stiffened, looking back at them. "Cops outside, driving by," he yelled. "Don't shoot, for amor de Dios."

Gordo swallowed, got a grip on himself, his broad face flushed, his gun hand trembling. He finally nodded at Adan and his gang. "Go on, get outta here," the Fat Man said with a wet rattle. His words were choking him. "But I still want my money for spotting the truck, I don't give a shit nothin' was in it, and it ain't ten grand anymore. It's twenty and you'd better fucking have it tomorrow. If I see that albino freak kid again, I'm gonna kill him and the rest of you for sure. Now get the fuck out of here."

Book 1: THE FIRST DAY

With that he waved his pistol toward the front door. It was all the encouragement Adan needed. He turned, grabbing Magda and the boy, and pushed them toward the door. Samosa followed, wheeling Frodo in his chair, El Gordo staring after them, his red rage slowly dissipating. Tomas and One-Eye holstered their pistols, both of them looking sorely disappointed.

Even Perez at the door looked forlorn as he slammed it behind Adan and the others.

CHAPTER
20

Catherine sat in the jet with Morgan at 35K feet. There were COMLITE specs present, feeding them constant information. It was all bad. The sickness was spreading. Even collecting specimens was a problem. Hazmat suits had not stopped the microbes. The WHO medical teams sent to investigate the sickness were dying before they could learn anything.

The bodies themselves were still infected, even though they were no longer breathing. There was now a worldwide quarantine. All the international terminals had shut down, but that hadn't stopped it from spreading across Africa and there were several outbreaks in the Middle East, but the contagion had been stopped or at least slowed down by strict limitations on all travel. There'd even been news about a spreading contagion in Germany, at the Hamburg Airport, and the soldiers, under strict orders, had not allowed anybody to leave. They had shot everybody who tried to flee.

The sickness was stopped from spreading in Europe, but the world was quickly grinding to a halt.

At the same time information about the boy continued to be downloaded. Thugs and lowlifes were already after him. He'd been kidnapped by several of them apparently, but it was all hearsay and rumor. Homeland Security and the FBI were on it now, rushing assets into Phoenix, trying to locate the boy.

"I want all communication between any of the people involved with the boy, the faster the better. Anyone they touch is under surveillance."

"Done," Morgan replied, tapping on his device.

She turned to her screen. The red dots indicated the spread of the disease was slowing. But why? It had been full speed ahead since it had started.

"Something's happening with the sickness," she said. "It hasn't flared up here."

"I think it's burning out," Morgan said excitedly. "People exposed to it have suddenly stopped dying, even when they're in the same town or city."

"Are you sure?" she asked with a surprised frown.

"For the moment. We'll need time to confirm, at least an hour, maybe more."

"Find out why," she said. "If it stops we'll be able to get closer, at least get some samples. If we can ID it we can work on an antidote." She looked up, her frown deepening. "There's got to be a reason. Why would it suddenly slow down? Everywhere at the same time?"

He shrugged, his face relaxing. "Just be grateful. I thought we were in real trouble. Worldwide apocalypse trouble."

CHAPTER 21

Mickey drove down Mary's Landing's one and only Main Street, pulling into the back of his produce store. It was actually his and Lilli's house, but they had converted the first floor to a grocery with living quarters in the back. They sold what they grew behind the house. He stopped before the greenhouses, three of them, all glass and thick plastic strips to let the sun in. The farthest back was the grow house, and it stunk to high heaven. He had fans that dispersed the odor, but never quickly enough. There was an office adjacent to the nearest greenhouse. That's where he and Lilli hung out. He stepped out of the truck and headed for the door. He had a lot to tell his sick wife.

Inside, he shucked his coat and called out: "Hey, where's my favorite bookkeeper?"

There was a flush behind the bathroom door and it opened, Lily pushing herself through. She was using a walker. The doc had been wrong. The disease had been quicker than he said, eating her nerves and leaving her right side useless. She listed that way, the right hand digging into her side like a claw, the fingers stiff and useless, unable to bend. The right side of her face had begun to sag and her speech was slightly slurred, but he knew it would only grow worse quickly from this point on. It was her mind that worried him most. She had begun to forget what she had started to do or why, and she was now making lists to remind herself. With her one good hand, the left one, while the bad one held down the paper.

"Hi," Mickey smiled. "Miss me?"

"Of course," she said, returning his smile, using the walker to approach. Drag, drop, drag, drop, it went with that scrape he hated and she gave him a kiss. "Got some money for me?"

He passed her the cash. She was the bookkeeper and ran the supplies and billing. It wasn't much, all electronic, but he couldn't have stayed in business without her. They had never married and had been a happy couple, enjoying the outdoors so close at hand with the desert all around them, and the familiarity of a small town. Then the ALS had appeared, out of nowhere, like a huge black tidal wave roaring toward them, something so overwhelming it couldn't be escaped. He had pushed her to marry him—her last name was Dollans, his Meyers, think how much nicer it would sound if she could be Lilli Meyers—but she wouldn't do it. She didn't want to be a burden on him, and he stopped asking, hoping that she'd realize they were living together anyway, had been for years, so why not? But that day hadn't arrived. Not yet anyway.

"You see the news about the kid?" he asked, nodding at the screen, wanting to bring up what little good news he could.

"The one that healed the dog?" Lilli said with a shrug. "Hard to escape." Sure enough, the screen showed video of the kid with the fluffy white dog coming back to life. It was on a constant loop.

"Yeah, that's it." He looked back at Lilli and kept his voice flat. "I think I gave him a ride into Phoenix."

"What?" Lilli looked up with a jerk.

"I picked this kid up at Willy's," Mickey said, keeping his gaze on Lilli. "I'm not sure it was him, but he wasn't there when I stopped for gas and then he suddenly was when I drove away."

"What happened?" Lilli asked. She could see how important this was to Mickey, but she wasn't quite sure why.

Book 1: THE FIRST DAY

"I saw him in back of the truck and pulled him into the cab. Didn't say a word, just sat there all the way into Phoenix."

"Then what?" she asked. She was as curious as anybody who'd seen him raise the dog from the dead. Anything about the kid fascinated her. She was sure anybody with a device or a TV felt the same way. Miracles were in short supply, especially with news of the spreading coughing sickness, which was horrible beyond words.

"I got into downtown Phoenix, stopped for a light, and when I looked up he wasn't there anymore. Didn't make sense, but then I saw him on the news, bringing the dog back to life."

"Too bad he didn't do that to your burned hand," Lilli said with a regretful smile.

"He did," Mickey said, his face intent. He held up his hand, palm open. The skin was pink and healthy. She stared at it, her mouth falling open. He'd been cooking for them last night when he'd grabbed the red-hot frying pan. He'd screamed bloody murder and scared her to death.

"It was the other hand you burned," she said quickly, trying to figure out an explanation. He was fooling her. He had to be. He held up both hands. Neither was burned. She looked like she might faint and gripped her walker so tightly her knuckles turned white.

"He touched me," Mickey said as he reached out and steadied her. He looked at her hard in the eyes, his face softening with love. "If he could touch me, maybe he could touch you. If we can find him again."

CHAPTER 22

Samosa drove through the city, Adan beside him, Magda, the silent boy, and Frodo in the back, "Mierda," he said with a whistle, kneading his legs. "I was sure Gordo was gonna shoot you. You could see how desperate the fat fuck was. He's gonna hate us forever."

"Hey, we made it," Adan said a grin. "That's the important thing. Concentrate on that. That's not too hard for you, is it?"

"I didn't think it was easy," Magda said with a scowl. "I thought we were all gonna get shot."

Beside her Frodo probed his legs harder, digging his fingers into his skin and bone. "My legs, they feel better," he said with a quizzical frown, looking at Magda. Adan didn't say anything. Neither did Samosa. Frodo leaned over from the back. "Did you hear what I said?" he asked.

"I don't care what you said," Adan replied, holding his open hand out. "Pass over the thousand the fat fuck gave you."

Frodo did so without objection, but he wasn't done yet. "My legs don't hurt as much, that's what I said."

"So what?" Adan said as he counted the cash. "You walked 'cause you wanted to, 'cause you had to, to save yourself and us. Thanks, but it had nothing to do with the deaf mute kid."

"The kid did something in there with his touch," Frodo insisted, looking at Adan. "You felt it. I saw your face."

"I didn't feel anything," Adan said, counting the green once more, just to make sure El Gordo hadn't shorted Frodo.

But he *had* felt something, which made him ask himself just what had he experienced? He didn't know, heat, then elation, and then? He fucking didn't know, but, shit, the situation with El Gordo was so loaded with danger, he could have pissed himself and probably not have noticed.

He peeled two hundred from Frodo's money and passed it to Samosa who pocketed the bills as he drove. He passed another two to Magda, pocketed another two for himself and passed the remaining four back to Frodo who was still leaning forward. He said, "Don't put it all up your nose, would you. We're gonna have to eat at some point."

One for all, all for one, especially when you were broke. Especially when the fat fuck was saying they now owed him twenty grand by daylight tomorrow.

In the back Frodo stuffed the spending money into a pants pocket. His eyes were on Adan. "Look, you can't avoid it," he said. "Saying nothing happened when the kid touched me doesn't make it true. You felt something. I saw your face."

Magda looked up at Adan, the boy stuffed in between her and Frodo. "Did you feel something when the kid touched him?" she said.

"Yeah, well maybe I did," Adan said grudgingly. "What difference does it make? We're alive and we have enough to keep going for a while. At least until tomorrow, when El Gordo will come hunting for his money." Shit, he hated being broke, no matter how much they had it was never enough. Money, finding it, making it, spending it, staying alive another day, it was all any of them thought about.

"You okay?" Samosa said, cutting him a look from behind the wheel.

"Yeah," Adan grunted, "I'm breathing anyway."

He grimaced. Samosa didn't care whether or not he was tapped out, exhausted, sick of him and the others. Samosa probably didn't care if he died, as long as Adan had good ideas and kept them in business. Samosa was a follower, an ape that was strong as hell. He

Book 1: THE FIRST DAY

was his best friend, too, next to Frodo. The big guy and he had been together from times ditching high school, when they had both been from broken homes with no one to take care of them. No father, he had a mother, Samosa didn't. It was his grandmother that had raised him and the big guy. Sort of. Then Samosa bonded with Frodo when he was in juvie, bringing him into the small crew when Adan got out.

Welfare, yeah, Social Services that had kept some money flowing, but not enough to do more than pay the shithole rent and buy crap food. His mom had a beat-up clunker that never seemed to run. She took the bus to work, which was cleaning up a bunch of fast food joints late at night. All of them were filthy as hell 'cause they were all in shitty areas, but she did it with a maintenance crew.

Finished at five, his mom was usually home by six in the morning. She tried to make him and his brother and sisters breakfast before they went to school, but she fell asleep more often than not at the kitchen table.

He and his brother had started taking care of themselves and their mother, his sisters doing the cooking and cleaning in the hovel they called home, the brothers doing their best to keep the plumbing working, to fix the leaks in the roof, to board up the broken windows and keep the cold out in winter and cool when the summer heat hit and sent the temperatures soaring.

Somehow Adan was the smartest. Shit, he'd known that from the time he was nine or ten. He had been the one to bring in extra money that gave them a few nice things. At first it had been spare jobs when he could snag them, doing deliveries for the local bodega, helping at the auto shop on the corner, but then he started to see the dudes making the green were dope dealers, and he'd become a runner for the local pandilla, the 12th Street Barrio. That was cool, he was going to join, or at least that's how he'd thought around twelve years old, but then he and four other runners, all holding, had been braced by another gang, the West Valley Crazies, and Fuerte Hector had mouthed off. Guns flashed and exploded. Guys dropped, bullets whizzed. He'd gotten out with his life, but not Hector and Sanchez, they'd died on the spot, and everybody else had scattered.

Not him though. He'd stayed and watched Hector dying, begging Adan to call his madre, tell her he loved her, and get some cash for her and his sisters. Hector had been laying there on the street, his lung making a horrible sucking sound from a bullet hole. It was a sound that Adan would never forget. All Hector had thought about was his mother and sisters, even as he was dying. That had hit Adan harder than a bullet. Family was everything. Then the terrible sound had stopped. Hector had died.

At that moment Adan, the aspiring gang banger, had died along with Hector and Sanchez and Adan, the independent contractor, the thief, burglar, pickpocket, the fixer, the one who could see the edge, the leader of the crew, had been born. He got the little cash he had to Hector's mom, and decided that was the last good thing he would do. From then on it was going to be about him. So it had been ever since.

Keep the group small, steal smart, always find somebody to ally with who was stronger, who could teach you, who could sharpen you, until you were strong enough to go out of your own, with or without the support of the guy who'd brought you along. And if he got in the way, well, look at Scarface, asshole. "Say hello to my little friend," bang, bang, bang. The kind of style Adan loved.

So it had always been and always would be.

It had seemed to work, too, right up till this morning when everything was getting confused. It was the goddamn kid, the kid he'd thought he was using, the kid who was the smart move, the only move, the kid who was now screwing everything up.

Book 1: THE FIRST DAY

"We should make a run for it," Magda said, giving up on Adan, who sat in the front, staring numbly out the window. Something had hit him when the kid had touched Frodo. She didn't know what, but she'd felt it, too, when she had him touch Frodo. If Adan didn't want to talk about it there was nothing she could do, but she could at least be honest with herself.

Like with their relationship, her thoughts tumbling over each other in her head said. It wasn't just the kid and what happened in the Fat Man's bar. It was other things that were turning them bad with each other. His insisting on keeping on with the gangster life, his shutting her down whenever she talked about kids. Not marriage, just the mention of a baby turned him off.

They were left with nothing but guilty looks and a refusal to discuss anything, which was what they were left when they were alone. That and humping. The junk, the crap left over at the end of the evening, the bad taste in your mouth when you finished making love and had faked coming, the kid, the bar and El Gordo, it was all going bad.

She did love Adan. At least she thought she did. Or had. She also thought it didn't make a lot of difference. Life took over; it swamped feelings. What had to be done, you did, the real down dirty and gritty, no matter what, because your very life was at stake, and you quickly learned how you felt didn't have much to do with what you had to do.

Survival trumped everything else. Certainly love.

CHAPTER 23

The shadows were lengthening as Whitney sat in her bedroom, in front of her laptop. She had been busy ever since they'd been home at Cordes Lakes, researching. Donny entered with his screen in hand. "Hey," he said, "you see this stuff about the kid? They're making it up now. All kinds of people saying they've seen or been touched by him."

"I don't believe any of it," she said. "So far it's just us and the dog and maybe the guy whose truck I saw him in."

"That's how he got to Phoenix?" Donny said.

"Yeah, him and us. At least I think so. You saw him, but he didn't touch you. He healed my torn cuticle."

"That's no big deal," Donny said, back on his device. "Bringing a dead dog back to life is though. We could tell people we gave him a lift, you know."

She looked up, startled. She hadn't thought of that, but now that she did she hated it. "We do that, we'll never have any peace. It'll make us special like for the rest of our lives."

"Hey," he grinned, "wouldn't it be cool in school, all the kids asking us about the boy?"

"Yeah, until like maybe the one millionth time." She made a face. She really didn't like the idea. "Mom and Dad still haven't figured out the kid in the news is the one we picked up in the car?"

"Nope, haven't mentioned it anyway," Donny said with a shrug. "Don't you wanna put out a video that we saw him? Just the two of us?" he ventured again.

"No, but if the kid keeps doing miracles, you can expect a mess of people claiming they're best buds. Maybe in the millions. All the nuts and attention seekers are gonna be saying the boy saved them." She nodded at her screen. "Take a look at this."

He glanced at her device and frowned. There were screen grabs of some foreign city littered with the dead and dying. "What are you doing?" he asked with a frown.

"The coughing sickness," she said. "I've been tracking it. It seems to have slowed."

"What?" he said, sitting on a corner of her bed. "They haven't stopped it yet?" It was a surprise to him. He was into his games, not watching a bunch of people puking their guts out.

"Not yet," she said with a shake of her head, "but it isn't spreading as fast. They're hoping it burns itself out, but they don't know."

He looked at her screen. Red dots all over Africa, spreading out from a chunk that was solid red. He peered closer at the dots. They were still throbbing, but they weren't growing. "You're right," he said with a low whistle. He checked his cell. "No definite word yet. It's a good thing, isn't it, if it slows? Better if it stops?"

"Yeah," she said, "but I saw that vision. I'm worried it's coming back. I'm worried it's coming here to America."

"Why? Because of that vision you had at the truck stop?" He didn't look up from his device.

"Would you pay attention to me?" She reached out and took the cell phone from him. "Yes. If you'd seen what I saw, you'd be scared to death, too."

Donny looked at her. "Doesn't mean it's gonna happen," he said, trying to shrug it off.

"No, it doesn't," she said with frown. "But think of this. He gave me a vision of the coughing sickness before we even knew there was such a thing."

Book 1: THE FIRST DAY

Donny looked at her, his eyebrows going up. "What are you saying? He knew about it before anybody ever heard of it? That they're somehow connected, the boy and the sickness?"

"You have a better idea?" she asked, leaning forward. He looked at her, not knowing how to answer, but all of a sudden getting as paranoid as her. She relaxed a little, seeing she at last had gotten through to him, at least a little. "Listen," she continued, "I don't know what any of this means, but for now maybe we don't tell Mom or Dad. They wouldn't know what to do and it would only upset them. Okay?"

He slowly nodded, but she still didn't trust him. He always had a big mouth, but she needed someone to talk to and he was it. If he would just keep his trap shut until she figured out what to do. Maybe he could even help her. She was scared, and scared wasn't something she usually felt. She didn't like it, not at all.

CHAPTER 24

El Gordo walked out of the bar, hitching up his pants. He was flanked by Tomas and One-Eye. They stopped at the curb, waiting for Perez to drive up with the car. El Gordo looked around, a few pedestrians scurrying past, avoiding eye contact.

They knew who he was. He enjoyed their fear and twirled the mahogany cane he used to help him walk. The tumor was putting pressure on his left kidney, and his leg had begun to go numb, but it seemed fine right now. Without thinking he began to whistle tunelessly.

Surprised, Tomas turned to him. "You feeling better?" the slick looking killer asked.

"What if I do?" El Gordo growled back. Yeah, maybe he was, but what business was it of his?

"You're not using your cane to stand up," One-Eye said, using his good orb to check him out.

"That's so I have it handy if I see that besugo, Adan," El Gordo growled, using the Spanish term for idiot or worse. Much worse.

A black SUV with tinted windows pulled up, Perez behind the wheel. Tomas whipped open the back door and El Gordo climbed in, followed by his right-hand man. One-Eye slipped in the front and Perez took off, keeping the speed low. The boss didn't like fast. Too many estupidos on the street and behind the wheel. Drunks, borrachos, and addicts. Gordo hated addicts, you never knew what they were going to do. He wouldn't have any of them working for him. He settled his bulk into the back seat, enjoying the comfort of the leather package he had ordered for the vehicle.

Perez eyed his boss in the rearview mirror as he drove. "Home, Gordo?" he asked.

El Gordo grunted. The tension of the crap in the bar was finally leaking away. The rush of hope the kid had inspired in him pissed him off. He'd almost believed it. Him. A mark, him? He hated the fucking thought of it.

He pulled out a cigar, a real stogie from Cuba, a hundred apiece, and cut the tip with his pen knife. He was about to fire it up when he paused. He frowned, for the first time really mentally checking his body.

He was fat, he knew it. What the hell did you expect when a man had a cancer growing in his gut? What other pleasure was there besides eating? After all, a tumor was like having an alien wrapped around your bowels. It even made taking a crap an ordeal, but...he did feel better. He had to admit it. God damn, he was breathing better, his head was clear, the soft ache in his belly, like a threat of terrible things to come, was muted, or maybe even gone.

Gone? The word echoed through his brain and he put the stogie and pen knife down on the seat. He probed his ample belly with his thick stubby fingers, trying to feel the tumor. It was big and hard and he checked it a dozen times a day, trying to figure out how fast the deadly mass was growing, and how much closer he was to dying.

The fucking oncologist had told him he couldn't do anything. None of the docs could help. He wanted to kill all of them before he died. He dreamed of it. The final revenge. Take the useless pendejos with him, just a few days before he expired, like some old time pharaoh who had his slaves buried with him.

Book 1: THE FIRST DAY

He dug deeper into his gut. He couldn't feel the tumor. Anywhere, no matter how hard he pressed. "Shit," he muttered, his eyes widening with surprise.

One-Eye looked back at him from the front seat. "What?" He was used to El Gordo's panic attacks about his cancer, but this was different. He could hear the shift in the Fat Man's voice.

El Gordo shoved his fingers deeper into his belly, holding them there. "It's gone," he whispered, true awe in his voice. "My tumor. It's gone."

"You're shitting us," Tomas said, looking at him, trying to figure out if it was some sort of sick put-on his boss was doing.

El Gordo didn't answer, his eyes snapping to Perez behind the wheel. "That scanning place," he snapped at the driver, "the one where I got that MRI of my cancer. Take me there."

"It's after four," One-Eye said, checking his watch. It was a Patek Philippe, and he'd paid the fence a fortune for it.

"I don't give a fuck," El Gordo snarled, his jaw setting. "They'll stay open for me." His gaze shifted back to Perez behind the wheel. "Do it."

Perez changed direction, taking the first corner they came to tight, making the wheels squeal.

CHAPTER 25

Magda looked out the car window, her mouth turned down. Phoenix sped by outside, one bland, sunbaked neighborhood after the other, none of them connected, like the people who dwelt there. Shit, they didn't even talk the same tongue a lot of the time.

"We gotta get the hell out of this city," she said, for maybe the millionth time. "No way we're coming up with El Gordo's dinero tomorrow."

"Yeah, fine," Adan said, finally coming to life. He stared out at the road ahead, slowly feeling better. His nerves were settling down. Or was it that flash of warmth that he'd felt passing from the kid to El Gordo? What the fuck was that about? But he had felt it, hadn't he? It just came out of nowhere, and it was so damn real it was screwing with his head.

"Where do we go if we leave here?" he said, trying to concentrate on the conversation and not the echoes inside his brain. "Who do we know, what connections do we have? Anybody here ever been anyplace else?"

"I been to Guanajuato," Frodo volunteered from the back. "They got an old school down there. All those mummies stacked up in this hall, this old opera house, too, and enough drugs pass through we should be able to skim something."

"I ain't going to Mexico," Samosa said, gripping the wheel tighter. "Easier to get killed down there than here." His friends thought he was stupid, but at least he knew going someplace else didn't change who you were inside.

"You don't have to deal dope or steal everything, you know," Magda said, glancing at the driver and Frodo. "There are other ways of making a living."

"Not as lucrative or as quick," Adan said. "'Sides, I ain't leaving Phoenix. It's my city. I like it."

"So what are we gonna do then? Tomorrow's coming fast, and you know that fat asshole El Gordo gonna want his twenty Gs," Frodo said.

He felt his leg, the really bad one that hadn't knit right. Damn, it was feeling better. Besides, he'd heard this argument before and it always ended the same. With them figuring out the next move to make some money and never leaving the city, much less even taking a day trip somewhere.

Fuck, they couldn't even make it to Sedona to drop some shrooms and X, and that was with Samosa claiming he had some Indian blood, even though they all knew his mom was from Polynesia, wherever that was. They talked about getting out whenever they were tanked, but nobody ever got in a car. They were like hamsters stuck in a wheel, going round and round, except at least the rodents got to rest sometimes.

Frodo glanced at the kid squished in between him and Magda. He was sitting there up straight, staring ahead, but the eyes were blank, the face like a piece of stone. "What do we do with the boy?" the handicapped man asked. His broken legs were feeling better, weren't they? he asked himself, massaging them. There was a sense of lessening pain, but he couldn't believe it was real. It was like a persistent whisper he couldn't quite hear.

"Drop him off somewhere," Adan said with a shrug from the front. The last thing he wanted was the kid hanging around. Not now, with all this crap going on. "He'll find his way home."

Book 1: THE FIRST DAY

"No, he won't," Magda reacted, looking up, her dark eyes flashing. "He hasn't got a home. You know he hasn't. He doesn't even have a name."

"There's a church a few blocks from here." Frodo nodded toward the front window. A spire could be seen poking up behind a building. "We can drop him there."

"We already tried that, remember." Magda put an arm around the boy and pulled him closer. He leaned against her, as though he liked it, and it softened her. She could feel the warmth from his skinny body and it felt good. Maybe Adan wasn't going to give her a kid, but she suddenly had this one, and he needed her. "We gotta find his folks."

"His parents?" Adan twisted in his seat, looking back at her. "What parents? He's a runaway, or maybe they just dumped him. Who wants a dummy around anyway?"

Magda gave him a look, her eyes glinting. "Don't call him a dummy," she said, holding even tighter to the boy.

"I'll call him whatever I want," Adan snapped back.

"Screw you," she said, the fight escalating. "We find whoever he belongs to. Until then he stays with us. He's not a dummy either. He's probably autistic. Lots of kids are autistic these days."

"Aw, shit," Adan muttered, but didn't look at her. He was stuck with the kid for sure, until he could think of some way to get rid of him that wouldn't drive her loco.

"Hey," Frodo said from the back, studying his device, "the coughing sickness is slowing down, maybe stopping. The UN guy is making the announcement."

"Well, one good thing happening anyway," Magda said with a sigh. Nobody said anything, all of them talked out, and certainly not the quiet boy sitting between her and Frodo.

CHAPTER 26

Hummmmm, clickety, click, click went the Magnetic Resonance Imager as it carried El Gordo into its cigar-like guts. The fat man lay flat on his back, on a carriage inside the long thin cylinder, looking up at the smooth metal ceiling as the machine moved him deeper inside. His fat gut stuck out so far it almost scraped the top. The carriage finally reached its end point. There was another series of clicks and the machine reversed direction, carrying him back toward the little circle of light at the far end.

It was like being entombed in a coffin with creamy tight sides, vaguely alive with its muted rattling. It was only fitting he held an unlit cigar between two fingers. It matched the interior shape of the machine. It brought out his fear of being trapped in small spaces, made his breathing harder. He had his shirt off. The stupid assistants had insisted. They hadn't been strong enough to make him give up the cigar, but they had insisted any outer covering of his belly would interfere with the imaging. He couldn't think of anything worse than being trapped inside this thing again 'cause he messed up the first scanning, and finally complied.

So there he was, without a shirt, his pants unzipped, exposing his dead fish white belly, being penetrated by magnetic rays he couldn't see, taking pictures of the inside of his gut.

He hated every moment of it, but he *had* to know. Had his tumor shrunk? He appeared out of the far end, sitting up in the room of the imaging center. A white coated technician stood to the side, terrified by the closeness of Tomas and One-Eye. The man knew they carried weapons and would use them at the patient's order. It made him excessively compliant, which is how El Gordo liked people.

He put his feet on the floor, and started to button his shirt, staring up at another technician in a small room, separated by a glass window. No use talking to him from here. He'd never hear. El Gordo got up and stomped to the small room, still carrying his unlit cigar. He threw open the door and looked inside.

"What do you see?" he barked at the tech, who stood with Perez behind him, just as scared as the tech in the imaging room.

The man started, looking up from his screen with damp eyes. "I don't see anything," he said, his voice trembling.

"What do you mean you don't see anything?" El Gordo stepped inside, looking over the terrified tech at his greenish screen. It showed skeletal views of his stomach. He peered closer at it. "Where's my tumor?" he asked.

"I, I don't know, it's just not reading," the tech said, desperately studying the screen. He licked his lips, his hands fumbling with the keyboard. "Here's the one from six weeks ago." An image came up on the screen.

The tech frowned at it, losing his color. "That's, that's impossible," he mumbled.

"What's impossible?" El Gordo demanded.

The tech pointed at a mass, clear on the screen to see. "You have a tumor here," he said and then quickly shifted to the first scan. "But the MRI you just did says you're clean. Your, your tumor has disappeared."

El Gordo looked at the scan, his jaw sagging. "What?" he squeaked. His voice had gone suddenly weak. The idiot tech was right. There was no tumor there, and yet in the other scan just taken six weeks ago it was clearly visible. It was gone. His cancer was gone. He was cured. By the touch of a white trash boy whose name he didn't even know.

Holy shit.

CHAPTER 27

Samosa pulled up in front of the taco stand and he and the others got out. The big guy came around to help Frodo, but the handicapped man was already up and standing on the blacktop, an arm hooked over the open back door to support himself. Samosa opened the wheelchair while Adan, Magda, and the boy sat at one of the picnic tables outside the fast food joint.

Frodo looked down at the wheelchair as Samosa held it out to him, but didn't move. "Well, come on," Samosa said, rolling the chair closer. He was hungry. Frodo eyed the picnic table. "I think maybe I don't need it."

Samosa frowned. "What are you talking about?" he asked, but Frodo didn't answer. Instead he grabbed a cane from the back and used it to balance himself as he lurched into a stagger across the pavement to the table. He sat with an oomph as Samosa came up behind him with the chair. Magda and Adan were looking at him in surprise. The only one who didn't seem to notice was the boy. He sat next to Magda, quietly staring straight ahead.

Frodo pounded his legs. "I'm stronger. My legs are better." He looked at Adan. "You hear me now? I'm not walking far, but I'm walking."

"What are you saying?" Samosa asked, looking at him, both eyebrows raised. His forehead was so low they almost touched his hairline.

"You deaf?" Magda said, shooting the big guy a look. "He's saying the kid touched him and it worked."

115

"That's crazy," Adan said with a frown. "It didn't work on El Gordo and he left his hand on him a lot longer than he did Frodo."

"It took a while with Frodo," Magda snapped back. "Besides, maybe he didn't like that fat pig."

"So what are you telling me? The kid is some kind of, of, of whatta you call it?" Samosa said.

"He's a healer," Frodo said. There was a sureness of the converted in his voice. "That's the word you're looking for. Maybe that and more."

"This is fucking stupid. What are you doing? Starting a cult?" Adan said. "I can't even believe we're talking about stuff like this."

"Try talking about this," Magda said, and reached out, handing him her device. It showed a bunch of dead people in some dusty village deep in the African bush. "It's all over the news, along with the boy. I've been talking about it all morning, but you haven't been listening."

"Why? Is it getting worse?" Samosa asked, raising his head, only vaguely interested.

"It's slowing down, maybe even stopped. Good thing, too. Here, take a look." Frodo offered his cell phone.

Samosa took it, watching the stream from some African country. He didn't know which. It showed a dusty street in some tenth-world country, littered with dead bodies. "Fuck," he said softly. "What are we gonna do?"

"It's got nothing to do with us. Focus, keep it on the boy. We can sell him, or his services anyway," Adan said, licking his lips as he thought out loud.

"It didn't work for El Gordo," Samosa said.

"Doesn't matter. Sick people will be like the Fat Man," Adan said with a grin. "They'll grab at anything just for a chance to be cured. He's a money machine."

Book 1: THE FIRST DAY

Magda shot him a dark look. "You gonna rent out a brain-damaged kid to dying people? That's sick," she said.

"We don't know he's brain damaged," Frodo said. "He could just be quiet. Or maybe he's from another world. Who knows, point is he's with us right now."

"There you go," Adan nodded. "Focus."

Samosa eyed him. He respected Adan's brains, his ambition. He wanted money, as much as he could get, like the rest of them, only Adan came up with ways to get it, whereas the others just sat around and bitched. "What are you saying? We sell his services? Like some kind of healer?"

"Exactly," Frodo said with a cock of an eyebrow. "Pay us to have the kid heal you. I can show off how I'm walking a little now, give the boy credit. People will eat it up." He glanced at Magda. She sat with the boy, her face non-committal. "What do you think?"

"I think I saw him get sick or weak or something after he touched you. He staggered, remember? He didn't look so great after he touched El Gordo either," she said with a frown.

"So he looks okay now," Adan said with a nod.

She glanced at the boy. He sat at the table with that thousand-yard stare. Samosa brought over a pile of food and drinks. She took a Fanta Orange and a burrito and put it in front of the boy. His nose didn't as much as wrinkle. She wasn't sure he had moved since they'd sat down.

"Here," she said, and shoved her Fanta closer to him. He didn't blink. She looked at the others. "He doesn't eat or drink."

"He doesn't pee either," Frodo said, watching the kid. "Think he dumps? He has to dump." His legs were feeling better all the time. It had to be the kid. "My legs are more solid," he said, stamping them up and down where he sat.

"Didn't help Gordo's gut much, did it?" Samosa said, lifting an eyebrow.

Adan's phone vibrated. He checked it, making a face. "Guess who?"

The others straightened, looking at him. They knew exactly who it was: El Gordo.

CHAPTER 28

Adan lifted the cell to his ear as the others watched around the table. "Gordo, I'm trying to get your money, what do you want?"

Across town, Gordo sat in the back of his black SUV with Tomas, One-Eye in the front, Perez driving. The Fat Man was on his phone. He tried to sound casual, but he knew he was in a high stakes game. "Maybe I got a way for you to earn it back."

On the other end he could feel Adan tensing. Magda and the other two had fallen silent and were watching him closely. "Yeah, what's happened? Why are you suddenly being nice to me?" Adan said, the truth slowly dawning on him. "You did get better, didn't you? Is that what this is about?"

"Don't be stupid," Gordo said in the back of the large vehicle, "but I figured out hope sells. It did on me. So it doesn't make any difference if the kid really has the touch. It's the possibility that matters. You wanna talk about it? Be partners on the kid?"

Adan's face narrowed. The others around the table were listening, everyone zeroed in on him except the boy. "Yeah, sure," he replied with a swallow. "See you at the bar in an hour." He clicked off, everyone looking at him.

"Well, come on," Magda said, giving him a shove. "What'd he have to say?"

Adan's mind was spinning. He wasn't even sure what was going on. "It was Gordo. Something's happened. He wants the boy. He realizes how valuable he is."

119

"You don't think he got better, do you?" Frodo asked, his twisted pipe stem legs forgotten.

"He said no. He could be lying, but that makes no fucking sense. The kid's ours. He's a fake. We invented him. He couldn't make anybody better."

"My legs are stronger," said Frodo, pounding his thigh with a hand.

"Maybe it's the power of suggestion," Magda said, "but somewhere out there is the real kid that brought the dog back to life." She nodded at the boy. "Who's to say it isn't him?"

"Exactly," Adan said with a nod. "The Fat Man thinks the kid is still worth a lot. Even if he isn't really the kid. Even if he can't do anything. He said hope sells and he can fix us up with buyers."

"He's playing you," Frodo said from across the table.

"Everybody is jerking everybody," Adan said with a shrug.

"Why do we have to cut El Gordo in?" Magda said, leaning across the table. "We don't owe him anything, even if the scumbag thinks we do."

"That's for sure," Frodo said with a scowl. One hand rubbed the leg that had the crook in it. El Gordo and his thugs had done that, broke both of them under the wheels of a moving car.

"I like the idea, we take the kid for ourselves," Samosa said with a big grin. He was sick of the fat fuck.

Adan grinned back. "We grab the money stored at our place, and just go, leave everything behind. It ain't much, but it'll help. We'll buy all new stuff on the road. If Gordo can find buyers for a touch from the kid, so can we." He glanced at Magda. "Looks like you're getting your wish. We're leaving Phoenix at last."

"Damn," Frodo grinned. "Kid's changing everything, even my bad legs." He looked up with a grin, but he wasn't in front of the taco stand with the others. He was standing in the desert, staring up at something he'd never seen before: the notch. The sun was blazing

120

Book 1: THE FIRST DAY

high above, the day well started, but there was a startling beauty about it, as though the mesa and the jagged angled spike had been made by the hands of giants, just for him.

He blinked, shaking his head and he was back at the picnic table with the others. "I just had a vision," he said, his voice filled with awe and fear.

"What? What did you see?" Samosa asked, looking at him with a frown. They were friends, roomed together, and he'd never known him to hallucinate, no matter how stoned and drunk he was.

"This place in the desert, with this mesa and spike coming out of the ground. It formed this kind of V, like a notch. The sun was rising over it, bathing it in this golden glow. It was a special place. I've never seen anything like it."

"You pop some X or some Windowpane?" Adan said, looking at him with a suspicious frown.

"Fuck, no," Frodo said quickly. "I'm as straight as you. I had a fucking vision."

"Why?" Magda asked, looking at him closely. Frodo was the smartest of them, different than her and Adan, shrewder than them. "Why would you have a vision or whatever it was?"

Frodo's eyes moved to the boy, who staring straight ahead, looking at something none of them could see. "You think it's because of him?" Adan asked, trying to understand.

"I think it is him," the disabled man answered. "He gave me something when he touched me. I felt it, this energy, this warmth, it flowed into me, like some kind of strength. It was clean, too. I mean it wasn't all fucked up with stealing and boosting people with guns."

"You're outta your mind," Adan growled, looking at him like he needed some kind of head doctor.

"Who else has the boy touched?" Magda said slowly.

"El Gordo," Adan quickly answered. "He won't tell anybody about his dreams, if he has any. Probably think it would make him look weak. Who else?"

They all looked at each other. "Nobody but me and Gordo," Frodo said.

"Not quite," Magda said. "When I held the boy's hand to your legs, I felt something, too. This flash of warmth. It made me feel good."

"C'mon," Adan groaned, "you're both talking crazy stuff."

"You felt it, didn't you?" she said. "I saw you when you had him touch El Gordo. You jerked your hand back like you'd had a shock."

"All right," Adan said, giving up. He lifted his hand. "I felt this heat going into my hand, just like Frodo said he felt."

"But no visions?" Magda asked, looking at him closely.

"Not yet," he answered. "You?" She shook her head. He rose from the table. "C'mon, let's get moving, before El Gordo figures out we're not showing up with the kid." They all rose and started toward the old Beemer that Samosa loved, but Adan's mind kept working, trying to understand what Frodo had just seen.

A notch in the desert? What the hell was a notch? Why should Frodo see that and did it have a connection to the kid? Adan figured he'd just have to wait and see if he and Magda starting having them, and if they did, what they saw.

Once that happened, he'd try to figure out what they meant. Until then, he had to get outta Phoenix with his crew and the kid, who was suddenly looking like a possible money maker.

CHAPTER
29

El Gordo slipped his phone into his pocket. The talk with Adan was okay, *if* he showed up at the bar in an hour. But maybe he wouldn't, not if he had a clue how valuable the kid was. He glanced at Tomas. "Find Adan and the kid," he growled. "Keep an eye on them. Especially the kid."

Tomas pulled his phone, turning his head so he wouldn't bother Gordo. The Fat Man relaxed. Tomas would make sure Adan didn't take off with the kid, not without him knowing anyway. "Trust no one," that was his motto, that and "plan for all contingencies."

Gordo had to start making a list of the people who might have need of a moment with the boy, just a touch of his hand. He was going to enjoy himself for a change. He had his health back, and was going to get a lot richer and more powerful. A real chance to get to the top of Phoenix that was for sure, but maybe even bigger than that. Much bigger.

What more could a man want?

The SUV drove past a car that had run up on the sidewalk. A woman was staggering out, coughing blood everywhere. Gordo twisted in his seat, looking back in shock. The woman crumpled to the ground.

"What the fuck?" The Fat Man said.

"What's wrong?" Tomas said, looking up with a jerk as he heard the alarm in his boss's voice.

"That car back there," Gordo said with a gesture. They passed another stopped car, the driver slumped over his wheel, the passenger hanging out the open window. Neither was moving. "Stop the car, goddammit," Gordo yelled.

Perez jammed on the brakes and the large dark vehicle skidded to a halt. Gordo hopped out, Tomas right behind him, his hand on the gun tucked under his right armpit. One-Eye joined them, his pistol out. Gordo looked up and down the street. Cars were stopped, people dead or dying around them. Same on the sidewalk. It was littered with the dead. A few errant people were still standing, but they were doubled over, coughing up blood and dropping.

"What the fuck is going on?" El Gordo asked in a panicked yell.

"What do you mean, boss?" Tomas asked.

El Gordo turned on him, about to start screaming when he choked back the words. The man was sitting across from him. Gordo himself was back inside the car, driving down the street. He suddenly realized he'd never gotten out. There were no dead people on the street. There were no dead people anywhere. It had all been in his head.

"You all right?" One-Eye asked from the front, glancing back at him with his single good orb as Perez drove through the city.

El Gordo looked out at the passing traffic, people walking as if nothing was happening. What the hell had he just gone through? Whatever it was had passed now, and he hated to show any weakness. He didn't want his guys thinking he was going loco.

"Yeah, I'm fine," he growled, making it clear he didn't want to be asked again. In fact, he didn't want to think about it again. It scared the living crap out of him.

CHAPTER 30

Adan and his crew were walking from the taco stand to their car. Magda led the boy. Frodo followed. "Hey, look, I'm walking," he said, holding the cane under his arm and waving his hands for all to see.

They stopped, watching him. Indeed, he was tottering after them on his own two feet, the wheelchair left at the table. "Damn," Samosa said, looking at Adan. "You see what I'm seeing?"

"It was the kid's touch," Frodo said, coming up. "Maybe it's a miracle. I mean a real fucking miracle. Any of you gangsters think of that?" He nodded at the boy. "Maybe he is the kid that brought the dog back to life."

"Shuttup, before I throw up," Adan said. He pulled his cell, putting it to his ear.

"Who you calling?" Magda asked as she put the boy into the back of that car.

"Crazy Daisy," he said.

"You sure?" she said with a frown. "He isn't called 'Crazy' for nothing."

"He's got hard cash, which we need if we're gonna get out of here," Adan said as he slipped into the front seat. She followed the boy into the back, Frodo already there. Samosa was behind the wheel. He headed for the street, leaving the wheelchair behind as Adan listened to the cell buzz on the other end.

Crazy Daisy sat in the safe house. He was running a dozen different blocks on the west side, all selling drugs. His guys kept the streets safe and did the distribution. He personally kept as far away as possible. Except for making sure things ran smoothly and the money kept flowing back to him. He had enforcers for that, major motherfuckers who'd just as soon shoot someone and their closest friends and families as look at them.

It was brutal out there and Crazy loved it. You wanted sufficient peace for commerce; it wasn't just enough to protect the buyers, you had to put the fear of death into the thieves and robbers, the boosters and desperate crack heads. Nothing else worked. He was black as coal (who in his crew wasn't?), and didn't take "high yellers." Didn't trust bloods that had more than a drop of white in them. He knew it was racist and was proud of it. True niggas were all he trusted.

Crazy was quite pleased with himself. He could be a major exec in a legit business, except he wore a peaked do, one side shaved, and baggy blue jeans that hung down below the crack in his ass, an oversize orange T, covered by a puffy black jacket with a Phoenix Suns' logo. To dress it up, he wore some major bling, gold neck chains that clinked whenever he moved. He packed heat in a shoulder holster beneath the puffy jacket. He was long and skinny and could only be described as ugly, with a patchy beard and a razor scar down one cheek. But who cared when he had so much green stuffed in every pocket. He had to fight the coke whores off.

His best guy, Neon Blue, kept things running smoothly, issuing orders on a burner phone in a corner, only bothering Crazy when something big came up, something big meaning anything that interfered with smooth cash flow.

Nobody was stupid. Everything was encrypted. The drugs themselves came in and went out from a ratty warehouse downtown, far away from his offices, which is what he considered the safe house he was in now. Nobody bothered him; if they did, he paid them off or killed them. He also went through the ghetto once a quarter and

Book 1: THE FIRST DAY

gave away a cool 100K to his faves and the desperately poor. He even passed out leftover drugs on occasion to keep the addicts quiet. Who wanted to bust their major supplier? Not those riding the needle.

But he was still paranoid and constantly anxious. No matter how good things were, he knew disaster was just a misstep away. It was why he was the most powerful street guy in the city. He kept backing everything up. "Redundancy" they called it in business school. He'd read the stupid fucking books. Whites thought he couldn't understand them; hell, his own people thought that, but if it made him money and kept the money safe, he sure as fuck was willing to work at it. Even stayed straight during the hours he spent learning, reading and reading with a calculator beside him, trying to figure out how MBA crap could apply to the streets. No one else was doing that. Too stupid or too lazy, but Crazy Daisy was the opposite. But he wasn't thinking about that right now. He was noodling about the kid, the one he was watching in a news feed on the closest screen. He'd been watching ever since the story about the dog had broken.

Neon Blue nudged him. "Adan Cuarto," he mouthed as he passed the device.

Crazy lifted an eyebrow. He'd been hearing whispers the last few hours that connected Adan and his crew to the magical kid. It made him curious. "Talk to me, my man," Crazy said into the phone in a raspy whisper.

"My brothers and sister and I have to do a fast fade, and we need money to do it on," Adan said. "Six figures."

"Nothing's free," Crazy said, wanting to ask about the kid, but not wanting to tighten the young guy up. Crazy was over forty, but Adan was maybe thirty at most. The young guys always wanted to take down the older ones, like him. "Vig's 40% and the kid's your security, if you got him with you."

"What are you talking about?" Adan asked putting Crazy on speaker phone so the others in the Beemer could hear.

"You don't know what you have, do you?" Crazy said with grin. "Word on the street is that the kid cured Gordo's cancer."

"Shit," Adan said in choked whisper.

"Shit indeed," the dope dealer replied. Adan could hear the grin in the dealer's voice. "Bring him by the house no one comes to, you know what I mean, and we'll talk. I wanna see him. I wanna have him touch me."

"A hundred Gs then," Adan said quickly, "no vig and the kid goes with us. He doesn't stay as security for anything."

"Done," Crazy said without hesitation. If he wanted the kid bad enough, he could have his people take Adan and his bunch out real easy. "Be here within the hour. Later than that and me and my money are gone." He clicked off.

Across the city, Adan pocketed the phone and looked at the others. "We grab the money and guns out of our apartment and we're on to Crazy's."

"Then out of town," Magda said from the back, as if to remind Adan of his promise to get the hell out of Phoenix. Her arm was around the boy. He leaned into her as they rode along. She kept waiting for him to close his eyes and rest, but he never did.

CHAPTER
31

Mickey Meyers had the big screen, their only luxury, in the back office that he and Lilli shared turned on, the greenhouses lined up in the yard behind them. He was still waiting for Lilli to say something about his story of the boy. She sat in a corner of the couch, not committing to anything, watching the big screen. The coughing sickness was gone, no longer a threat. Government officials were crowing, like they had something to do with it. Back and forth it went on the TV, between the sickness and the boy, but the kid was becoming more prominent as the networks went to the story that was drawing the eyeballs.

"Hope sold," the grower thought. He's certainly bought in.

The screen scrolled through Tweets and messages as a news reader talked. "They're coming in wild and thick. Rumors of the boy's healings. He healed a guy shot in the barrio, another had him appearing in a homeless shelter, and saving a guy who was overdosing. We're checking every one of them now just for you."

"So whatta you think?" Mickey finally said to his wife. "You believe me now?"

"Maybe," she said slowly, not daring to hope.

"There's something else good, too." He nodded at the screen. "They say the coughing sickness has stopped."

She smiled. Her prayers had been answered. More than anything else, she wanted God to stop the spread of the sickness. Her own problems were dwarfed by her love for others. "Love Thy

Neighbor." It was all in the Bible, and healthy or sick, she believed it. She hadn't before the ALS, but when her body had betrayed her, she started to pray to God. It could all be in her head, but when it was bad, especially when her thoughts got confused and her hands refused to work and her legs trembled when she tried to use the walker, the praying made it better. It gathered the strands in her mind and focused her. It allowed her to carry on.

All she wanted to do now was make Mickey happy. She knew she was going away, but she wanted him to have good memories of her. She wanted him to know how much she loved him, how thankful she was for his help and support.

She hadn't believed before, but she did now. With every prayer she fought off the disease, and slowed the advance. Who could refute the proof of their own body? Of her own mind. It was because of her belief in the Lord and his Risen Son.

God bless him and Mickey.

CHAPTER
32

Samosa drove, Adan beside him, the others in back. "So what do we do about El Gordo? He's gonna come after us, especially if the boy cured him," Magda said. She was on her phone, scrolling through it absent-mindedly. The boy sat beside her with his ever-present vacant stare and beside him was Frodo, also lost in his device.

"I don't know," Adan said, looking out the window. Darkness was falling, streetlights were going on. "He thinks we're coming to the bar, but he'll get nervous if we don't show. Maybe we have an hour before he sends the guys after us, maybe not that long."

"He means to sell the boy," Magda said, her mouth tightening.

"For sure," Adan said with a nod. "The question is how much does he offer us?"

"What about the kid?" Magda said, looking up from her mobile. The edge shot into her voice again. "Or don't you care?"

"I'm with Adan," Samosa said, throwing her a grin over his shoulder as he drove. "The hell with the kid, I want the dinero."

"You get the dinero, you become slaves to El Gordo forever," Magda said, her edge growing sharper. "Which is what we are now. When he gets tired of you, he gets rid of you. In the meantime, he does whatever he wants with the boy."

She cut the kid a look. He hadn't budged, like he didn't care what happened to him. Or didn't understand what they were talking about. Gawd, she wished he would say something, react, frown, pee himself, whatever, just so she knew someone was in there.

"Whoa," Frodo said softly.

"What?" Magda looked across the boy at him. The man with the formerly useless legs was staring at his phone.

"That coughing disease, it's on every feed." He held up his screen. "It's stopped cold. Worldwide."

"Screw the sickness," Adan said sharply. "We got problems here. We gotta figure out where we're gonna run."

"Run?" Magda said. She looked down at her device. "The kid is starting to pop up more. Going viral. There's gonna be no place we can run."

"Not as long as we have him with us," Frodo said.

"You wanna get rid of him?" Magda shot back. "He gave you back your legs. That how you repay someone doing you a major favor?"

Frodo turned his head to the window, not answering. She knew no way he was feeling guilty. He didn't have a conscience. How could you feel guilt when you didn't have a soul? But then maybe she didn't have one either, but she felt the pull of the boy. It was like he was part of her, and she'd known him for just a couple of hours.

"We talk to Crazy, he'll know where to run to out of town," Adan said. "Fool believes in voodoo, he wants the boy to touch him."

"Fuck, word's out we have him," Samosa said, his eyes on the road. "This keeps up, the kid's not gonna be able to go outside any-where. Frodo's right. We're marked as long as we have him with us."

"So whatta you want to do? Get rid of him, too?" Magda said, really starting to lose her temper. They were all assholes. Ungrateful assholes. And the number one scumbag was the guy whose bed she shared: Adan.

Fuck him, fuck all of them. Only thing that bothered her was she suspected she was no better, but at least she knew it.

CHAPTER 33

Mickey couldn't take it anymore and strode out into the back, by the grow houses. To the side was a wide drive that led to the street. Cars buzzed by out there. They might go past him and his store, but they all saw his sign: "Mickey's Natural Produce," with an arrow down the alley to the back of the house. He'd had the sign made in bright green and it lit up at night. Lilli had designed it with dancing vegetables. People couldn't miss it.

He had more than one customer who came in looking for organic weed, always with a medicinal card. Most of the time anyway. The smoke got them in, but the produce sold itself. Gleaming vegetables and fruits, piled up in the stand to the side of the parking area. All the vegetables, including the sativa, under the table for those in the know, all grown here in the parched desert. It didn't make him and Lilli rich, but as they say, it was a living.

But the boy had shoved all that out of his mind. He had to be one of the first people to see the kid. Somebody must have gotten him to Willy's Truck Stop, but the boy could have hitched a ride with anyone. Instead, he'd chosen him to get to Phoenix. Mickey knew that deep in his gut. He knew that meant something, but not what.

Maybe he could use it to help Lilli. That was the crazy thought, almost as crazy as the boy himself. He looked back at her through the open door into the office. She was still staring at the screen, fixated by news of the boy. He knew she was caught by the surge of hope. He figured that was a gift. There was so damn little of it in the world, even if she didn't realize it, but she would when she settled down.

Even if the boy didn't heal her, even if it was all a mistake or fake or Mickey himself was a deluded schizophrenic, for even thinking his wife might have a chance, the boy had brought hope to a lot of sick people everywhere. Like him for Lilli and Lilli maybe in the boy. He figured everybody should be thankful for that.

White flashed in front of Mickey's eyes. He blinked, momentarily blinded. As the light cleared, he found it was night and he was staring at the parking area in back of his house, only it wasn't like it was a second before. It had been clean then except for his old truck and a van he kept for him and Lilli to take little trips before she'd been struck by the ALS. Now there was a wrecked car to one side, a black SUV. Its windows were shot out, the side pockmarked, as though a burst of gunfire had stitched it. There was a man lying dead, face down by the open front door.

It looked like the car and its occupants had made an assault on the grow houses. Mickey stepped forward, looking inside. A man lay dead, splayed back in the front seat. Another man, one of the guys from the car no doubt, was sprawled in the dust closer to the office. He wasn't moving either.

Mickey's dread began to grow. He didn't see Lilli. Where was Lilli? He rushed toward the back of the house. Was she in there? He could see through the open door. It was empty. He looked around, becoming more frantic. Had she gotten away? Was her body here somewhere? Then he saw a leg sticking out from behind some vegetable crates.

He stepped forward. It was a man, not a woman, but what man? He jerked to a halt as he saw who it was. It was him! He was looking at his own dead body. Oh, God, he was riddled with bullets, his blood sinking into the sandy loam.

Book 1: THE FIRST DAY

He gasped and snapped back into the present, staring into the house. It was still daylight and Lilli was sitting in her chair, watching the boy on the big screen, transfixed. Mickey looked around the parking area. Just like it was before he'd had the vision. Everything was back to normal. But it wasn't, not really.

Mickey knew that. How could it ever again be after what he'd seen?

CHAPTER
34

Samosa pulled to a stop at the curb, in front of Adan's apartment building. Day was fading into twilight now, lights on in the windows and street.

"What are these people doing, standing about?" Frodo said, breaking in. He was twisting in his seat to look up and down the block at clots of people dotted about.

"The boy," Magda said, realizing what must be going on. "Word is spreading about what he did in the bar."

"Shit," Samosa muttered, impressed. "It's gotta be true, he cured El Gordo. You think we picked up the kid who saved the dog?"

"Fucking-A, joke's on us," Frodo said, looking out the back window. "We got company."

Magda twisted in her seat and saw the car parked behind them. "Who is it? No, don't tell me. Gordo's guys?"

"Es verdad," Frodo said, catching a glimpse of familiar faces behind them. El Gordo's guys, keeping the evil eye on them.

"Whatta we do?" Samosa said to Adan as he opened the door to get out.

Adan stopped, looking at him and Frodo. "Go around to the alley. We'll grab the money and guns and be right back out." He opened the door and stepped out, Magda joining him with the boy.

Outside on the street, Adan eyed El Gordo's guys as Magda looked down at the blank-faced boy. "You're causing a lot of trouble, you know that?"

Frodo slid out the back and took Adan's place in the front, next to Samosa. He did it all by himself, moving with an ease he hadn't had in years. Maybe the bad leg wasn't straightening, but it was definitely stronger. Magda and Adan stopped for a moment on the sidewalk, staring about. There were a lot of people on the street, standing with family members. Many of them were in wheelchairs and with crutches and braces. Others had limbs and heads wrapped in bandages and slings, all sorts of injuries and sicknesses.

"Damn," Adan whispered in awe.

"Yeah, right," Magda said, "We got the real deal and didn't know it. Whatta we gonna do? This thing is getting out of hand."

Adan and Magda with the boy moved toward the shabby entrance to their building. They'd gotten only a few steps when a farmer rushed up to them with his wife and a baby in her arms. Their clothing was ragged, their faces sunburned, his with lines etched in his forehead and dirt under his broken nails that would never come out. He babbled something at them. Adan frowned. A peon, a peasant, more mestizo than anything else. He didn't understand the Mexican dialect, and he was fucking Mexican.

"He says his baby has a heart defect, that he's dying," Magda said, translating for him. "He wants the boy to touch him."

"Shit," Adan swore, nodding at the street. You could see the people pushing in for a better look of what was happened. A hundred or more, starting to crowd them. Just what they needed with Gordo's men watching them from their car at the curb. "He saves the baby, we'll be mobbed."

"So you believe he can do it?" Magda asked, giving him a good look."

"I believe they believe," he said, glancing at the people gathered around. "Now let's get into our place." He went to grab her and the kid, but the boy suddenly pulled away with more energy than he'd

Book 1: THE FIRST DAY

shown since the Fat Man's bar and took a step toward the peasant wife and the baby in her arms. She lowered the child, as if offering it to him, and he reached up and lightly touched its forehead. The baby, which had been bawling and fussing, suddenly quieted.

The boy turned and joined Magda once more, gently taking her hand. She rushed him toward the building. Adan backed after her, looking at the crowd, many of whom were now joining the farmer and his family. The man raised the baby in its bundling above the crowd and cried out: "Mi bebe se cure! Él salvó a mi bebé!"

A cry went up from the crowd, a long moan of collective praying and Adan turned and raced into his building. He was scared to death.

CHAPTER 35

Zio Benito lay in his lounger, watching a big screen next to the huge river rock fireplace. The great room of the mansion was huge, with rafters overhead marching their way to the French doors that gave onto sweeping green lawns. Business was quietly being done around him, several of his best men keeping the money flowing, but he didn't care. His attention was fixed on the news feeds whipping by.

The boy had just saved a baby. There were crowds in front of a shabby apartment building somewhere in the barrio, dying grass, weeds, and old trucks dotting the front lawns, but all they were talking about was how the kid had touched this baby, and healed his heart, just like he touched the dog. For the first time since he'd started watching news about the boy, he was clearly visible. A skinny kid who looked like an albino, but wasn't. No pink eyes, no pink skin, but damn near.

Was it personally important to him? Fucking-A. He was sucking oxygen through plastic clips in his nose, which went to a big shiny chrome machine that acted like bellows, forcing air into his almost useless lungs. Zio was pushing eighty, a small wizened man with yellowish skin and beady black eyes. Everything was failing him except his brain and his will to live.

Aslanian came up to him, bent down so Zio could hear him above the soft thump of the oxygen machine. He was one of his top men, quiet, contained, and deadly, the way Zio liked them.

"Word on the street is that this big slab of fat got his cancer cured by the kid."

"Name," Zio said, stiffening at the news.

"El Gordo. He and his crew are after the kid right now."

"Get him on the phone. Let him know who he's talking to."

Aslanian nodded and moved away. "If" the kid was the real thing, Zio thought, "if, if, if," his mind shouted at him. Maybe someone could help him, even save him. "No, you old fool," he told himself sharply. Couldn't be. A miracle worker? A blessed kid? That was fucking crazy. He was raised Catholic, but that was many, many murders ago. But he still wanted to know more.

No, he didn't. He knew enough to know what he wanted right away. Now. In his mansion, in front of him. The kid. He wanted the stupid kid to touch him, even more than he wanted another gasping breath.

CHAPTER 36

Adan and Magda banged open the door into their dingy apartment. He went behind the kitchen counter, and started taking out drawers, trying to get to the satchel of money and guns kept hidden back there. It wasn't much, a few thousand, but they were gonna need everything they had. Magda stopped with the boy, and turned his shirt collar back, looking for a tag. There was none and she started going through his pockets. Adan gave her a look as he felt for the satchel.

"What are you doing? Grab your stuff and let's get out of here," he yelled as he dragged the bag out.

"He's got no ID on him anywhere," she said. "I'll get a backpack." She headed for the bedroom, only to stagger. He leaped to his feet, dropped the satchel, and grabbed her.

"Magda," he said and gave her a gentle shake, but she was gone on her feet, her eyes wide and as empty as the boy's.

Inside her head, she was standing in the desert at dawn, looking at the sun rising through a notch at the end of a table top mesa. It filled the slice of horizon and blasted through, blinding her as it rose. She raised an arm to shield her eyes and when she lowered it she found herself back in their apartment, Adan staring at her.

"You all right?" he asked.

She nodded shakily. "I…I had this vision, this notch in a mesa in the desert. Dawn was rising and sun came streaming through." She stopped, looking at Adan. Her eyes were shining. "It was

143

glorious. It was like being in church after confession, when you feel so clean."

"Stop it, would you," he said, looking at her with a worried frown. "We have to get out of here now. Grab a change of clothes and let's go." She nodded and dashed into the bedroom. He turned to the boy. "What are you doing? You're the one giving her the visions, aren't you?" He reached out to touch the boy's immobile face, wondering if he'd feel the warmth of human flesh.

Just as his fingers touched the boy he was staring down a street at a grocery store. "Mickey's Natural Produce" it said, with a gleaming neon green arrow and stupid dancing carrots and turnips that pointed down an alley to the back. "The best vegan in Mary's Landing" it said. He blinked, trying to figure out what he was seeing, and found himself back in the apartment, just as Magda appeared from the bedroom, a pack over her shoulder. "Come on, let's go," she said, but he didn't move. "What's wrong?" She peered at him.

"I had a vision, too, but not of some sunrise. It was a street in some small desert town. Place called Mary's Landing. I was staring at a grocery."

"A grocery?"

"Yeah, I know. Sounds stupid. Come on, let's get out of here." He took the backpack from her and shoved the satchel inside and threw it over his shoulder. She grabbed the boy and they slipped out the door.

CHAPTER
37

The man sat in a wheelchair, watching a big screen on the wall. He was beyond old; he was ancient, much older than Zio Benito, whom he didn't know, and also much more powerful. His billions had bought him the best that medical science offered, and it had pushed him into his ninth decade. But to what end? He was small but thick, crumpled into low chunks as his body shrunk with the decades. He still had white crinkly hair, but that was almost all that was left of what he used to be. The screen was showing the barrio where a man was holding up a baby and yelling he'd been cured. Tears streamed down his weathered face and that of a woman who could only have been his wife.

The old billionaire could not have cared less.

The penthouse duplex looked out over Central Park. His wife was in a chair across the room. She lolled forward in a sightless stare. She was in the final stages of dementia, pneumonia thankfully not far away. Up to this moment he had expected to join her at any moment. She was in her late eighties and he had hopes of making 93, but the pain and discomfort were becoming overwhelming. It left him yearning for release.

His mind was still good though. That was his curse, to be trapped in a crumbling edifice of a body with the sense to know it. Then he had seen the first video of the boy and like others he was sure, he had reacted wildly, flooding with hope, and now he was seeing another video of the boy saving a baby, not even moments ago. It was cell phone video, crap, but you couldn't miss how extraordinary the kid was. Drained of color, otherworldly almost, but not quite. Some kind of mutant maybe, but who cared?

It left the ancient billionaire no choice, especially given his physical deterioration, but to reach out. He had many people—and governments—where he had a presence. In fact, control, although he made sure to remain as invisible as possible. At one point he had been considered one of the most powerful men on earth. A man who controlled policy for a large portion of the world's population, even if they did not know it, which they never did. The puppeteer always had to remain behind the curtain.

He lifted a finger. One of the nurses who had been waiting in the shadows stepped forward. He whispered to her. An assistant, a young man of conservative dress, slipped into the room. He leaned down, his ear to the old man's lips.

"We have assets there?" He nodded at the screen that was now reporting the boy had saved the baby with a bad heart. He was outside a rundown apartment building, crowds of immigrants lolling about and chattering excitedly in Spanish. "Put someone in that we can depend on. We need eyes on this situation."

The assistant nodded and silently glided away. The old man went back to his screen. The sickness had stopped spreading it seemed. It was dying out in Africa and the Middle East. If he were a religious man he would have been impressed, but he was not superstitious or given to vain hope. However, he was sure every scientist and biologist in the world couldn't wait to get their hands on the boy and take him apart, trying to figure out what he was.

No way, he thought. Me first.

CHAPTER 38

Adan and Magda hurried the boy into the back alley just as Samosa pulled up in the Beemer. He jumped out and threw the pack in the trunk as Adan got Magda and the boy in the back with Frodo. He slipped back inside, looking over the seat. "Magda and I both had visions."

"Shit," the formerly handicapped man said. "It's catching. What about?"

Samosa climbed behind the wheel. "What's going on?" He put the car in gear, starting down the alley.

"We had these visions," Magda said. "I saw this mesa somewhere in the desert, just like Frodo did, and Adan saw a grocery."

"A grocery?" Samosa said with a stupid grin on his broad face. "I'm hungry."

"It's not about eating, Dumbo. It's where we're supposed to go," Adan said with a sudden certainly.

"What?" Samosa said, giving him a look as he drove, careful to avoid the garbage cans piled to either side. "How do you know that?"

"I don't know," Adan said, trying to figure it out. He glanced at Magda in the back with boy and Frodo. "He touched all of us. That's why we're having them."

"He didn't touch me," Samosa said with a grin. "I'm feeling left out."

Another vehicle came roaring down the alley behind them. It was Gordo's guys from out front. One of them was leaning out the window, shooting as they came. Bullets punched holes in the back of the window. Magda screamed, grabbing the boy and ducking down in the seat. Frodo pulled his gun and stuck it out the side window. He fired back without bothering to aim.

Adan did the same, firing out the shattered back window as Samosa stomped on the gas. They roared down the alley, the car behind trying to keep up, only to clip the back of a garage and skid along a stone wall, sending sparks flying before coming to a grinding halt in a pile of garbage.

CHAPTER 39

Dr. Kindi Obiang relaxed back into his seat in first class as the pilot announced their approach to Heathrow. London and England, at last. He breathed a sigh of relief. He was with the World Health Organization and had been sent from Pretoria to Equatorial Guinea just the day before. There had been an outbreak of some Ebola like coughing disease that seemed to kill people almost instantly. He and other WHO doctors were being assembled on site to begin interdiction and investigation of the disease.

He had taken a bush plane to get to the outer edge of the disease, which seemed to be burning itself out, at least according to satellite messages. He'd finally landed almost three hundred miles from the origination point of the disease, in a dirt village of tin huts with thatched roofs. It was desperately poor, probably much like the one where the disease had begun. Obiang was born a Hutu and his parents had avoided the slaughter in the Congo and fled to South Africa. That's where he'd become a doctor, and highly valued by the UN for his experience with disease outbreaks in-bush.

But he hadn't seen anything like this before. The village was deserted except for the band of WHO workers and government troops sent to guard them. They eyed the doctor as he came up to the portable contagion lab. They were nervous, as if they were ready to break and run at any moment.

They were terrified of the disease and he couldn't blame them, not from the little he had been told. As he stopped before the makeshift lab his self-doubts increased. It was made of loose sheets of heavy plastic hung over flimsy wooden beams. The bottom ends were staked into the dirt. A WHO comm unit was working out of a van to the side.

He met Dr. Rumarsky inside the changing room. The other man was just tightening the straps on his contagion suit. He looked up as Obiang put his briefcase down and took off his jacket. They knew each other well. Rumarsky worked for WHO, but also was the liaison to the U.S. CDC (Centers for Disease Control) which would get the word out instantly on any new outbreak of disease.

"Need some help?" Rumarsky said, stepping over to seal the strap on Obiang's back without waiting for a reply. "My third time. I'm getting expert at this."

"How bad?" Obiang asked as he started to step into the lower part of the suit.

"Very," Rumarsky said. "Air-borne, as near as we can tell, instant death, maybe in less than a minute. There are certainly no survivors to tell us different."

Obiang nodded toward the sealed off section of the room. Inside, through the plastic, he could see blurred figures moving about an autopsy table. He knew the section to their left, heavily sealed, contained corpses and body parts of the victims. He was starting to wish he'd brought an aerator.

"You isolated it yet?" he asked.

"The disease? No." Rumarsky frowned. He didn't look well, Obiang thought. "We've lost three mobile labs."

"What?" Obiang said, stepping back. Suddenly the heavy plastic lab suit didn't feel protective anymore. It felt heavy, like something that was trapping him, making it impossible for him to get out of there quickly. "Three?" Obiang repeated in shock.

He'd never heard of WHO losing any portable labs, not even one. Then he noticed strange movement inside the autopsy room.

Book 1: THE FIRST DAY

His eyes widened. Rumarsky turned, following his gaze. The white suited figures within were staggering about, three of them, as though struggling. One of them could be seen ripping his face mask off, then another. They were bent over, as though coughing, and then they began to fall.

A fourth doctor suddenly hit the plastic wall in front of them, pressing it out with his face. He coughed, splattering the plastic with blood and slowly began to slide down. He left a red smear behind.

Obiang backed away, throwing aside the plastic bottom of the suit, and tearing at the upper half, desperate to shed it. Dr. Rumarsky advanced on him, his plastic suit on, but still no headpiece. "You don't have to worry about me," he said, trying to sound reassuring. "I've been in there several times and I'm fine…"

He suddenly coughed, spraying a cloud of red mist. He raised his hand to cover his mouth as he coughed again, spraying more blood. He looked down at his hand, as if amazed that it was covered with red.

With a scream of panic and terror, Obiang whirled and raced out of the contagion lab. He yelled at the bush pilot standing near the small plane that they had to get out of there. The man was about to ask why when Dr. Rumarsky staggered out the front of the lab, and coughed one more spray of blood before he dropped to the dirt.

The soldiers screamed, dropped their rifles, and ran as one. The WHO comm truck took off without waiting for anyone, leaving a trail of dust behind. Obiang and the pilot got into the plane and out of there in what seemed like record time. They'd made it to Nairobi and the nearest international airport. Obiang had pulled rank and hurried on to the first international flight, but not before he texted his report to his superiors. He alerted WHO and the CDC, the health office of the African Nations, for what they were worth.

Tom Holland   The NOTCH

He knew they were facing a catastrophe that the international agencies certainly could not contend with. It was a possible apocalyptic event. The world was in danger, not just some country or even continent. The world. The thought scared the shit out of him. He told that to every official he could get hold of as he got on the jet and took off for London. He might be a coward, but he had a job to do.

He kept telling them he had no idea how to fight the disease—the coughing sickness—but to flee like he was doing. That was all any of them could do in the face of this cataclysmic epidemic.

"Quarantine," he yelled on his cell as he'd gotten airborne and lost connection. They'd put him in the cockpit, where he could talk to leaders worldwide. He'd done that almost the entire flight to England.

"Quarantine," he'd screamed again and again, until he was exhausted and had fallen into a dark dream where he was in a maze with no exit. The plane had landed at Heathrow and now they were exiting to customs. He wanted to yell in joy. He hadn't survived, not really, but he had run ahead of the disease. He was safe for the moment. No sickness, no urge to cough. "Thank God," he murmured to himself. He was suddenly beginning to believe in Him again. No, not believe, just desperate for someone, anyone, to appeal to for help. Even some phantasmagorical entity born of superstition.

"Mercy" some part of his brain kept whispering, even though he knew it was stupid. "Mercy, please, Dear Lord, mercy."

His cell buzzed. He saw an official hurrying toward him. The local airport authorities, UN and WHO, undoubtedly the Disease Unit of the UK, were just behind him. The leaders of the agencies, anxious to confab with him, for all the good it would do any of them.

Flee and quarantine a defensible area. An island perhaps. It was the only answer. Kill anybody who tried to enter. Let the disease burn itself out. Hopefully. If it ever did.

Book 1: THE FIRST DAY

He stopped as the group surrounded him, peppering him with questions, but before he could answer any of them his lungs heaved and he coughed. He didn't have to look down at the hand he'd raised to his mouth. He knew it was covered in blood.

The people who surrounded, men and women, backed away. A second person coughed and those who were still healthy (but not for long) screamed and ran in the opposite direction.

For all the good it would do them, Obiang thought, and then crumpled to the floor, dead before he hit.

Book 2:
THE FIRST NIGHT

CHAPTER
40

It was dark when Samosa pulled up in front of the safe house. It was on the outskirts of the city, where the workers lived. The house was a shabby two-story clapboard with flaking white paint. Crazy's Bazaar, the chunk of the hood where he sold drugs, was miles away. The last thing he wanted was any attention on his bolt hole.

Crazy mainly used kids to deal, the younger the better, twelve up if they were really smart, who would go to juvie, not to trial and jail, but here around the safe house were older more serious guards. Killers, in fact, every one of them. Only the best to protect the boss. There were four in front, spread out, lurking in the shadows.

One guy was sitting on the rickety porch. He was huge. Big Sammy, thought Magda as she and the others peered out from their beat up Beemer. You couldn't miss his bulk. Inside would be Crazy and Neon Blue, Crazy's shadow and second, them and a shitload of money, maybe some dope, but not much in case of a bust. Crazy's black Range Rover sat in the drive.

"You think maybe Crazy would switch vehicles?" Magda said, eyeing the Rover in the drive.

"Maybe," Adan said. "We can't keep driving around in this one."

Samosa scowled. "Shit, I love BMWs." He patted the well-worn dashboard.

Frodo knew how the big guy drooled over the Kraut machinery. "We'll grab another one after we get the money," Frodo said, trying to make him feel better.

Tom Holland   The **NOTCH**

Adan got out, the others following him, and started toward the house. Samosa was in the lead, him, Magda, and the boy in the middle. Frodo was behind them, bringing up the rear. He no longer needed the wheelchair and was adjusting quickly to his newfound mobility. He was feeling almost human, a snug .38 in his pocket.

As they mounted the porch, Big Sammy opened the front door for them. Adan stopped, shaking his head. "We meet, it's out here," he said.

Big Sammy studied him for a moment, as though he hadn't heard right, but didn't say anything. He disappeared inside. "You sure he'll give us the money?" Magda said to Adan.

He shrugged. "We'll find out real quick."

Crazy stepped out, tall, lanky, and darker than the night. Sure enough, Neon Blue was with him. Skinny supple body and always dressed in a gleaming blue sharkskin suit. Crazy nodded at Adan, but his eyes went to the boy next to Magda. "Hi, there. This the kid?"

"You see another one?" Magda asked. She could feel the four guards closing in around them in the shadows, ready, just in case something went wrong. She didn't like it.

"Looks like any kid," Crazy said, his eyes on the boy. "Paler maybe."

"His coloring's odd," Frodo said. "Just on the edge of being an albino."

Crazy lifted his gaze to the skinny man with the patchy beard. "He really make you walk again?"

"I'm not in a wheelchair, am I?" Frodo said, indicating his legs. "You know me. I couldn't walk after what El Gordo did to me."

Crazy looked at Samosa. "What about you? The kid ever touch you?"

"No," the big guy growled. "Only one he hasn't. I'm starting to feel left out."

"The kid's the real deal," Adan said, shifting his feet. "Especially now we know he saved El Gordo. Unfortunately. What about the money? We gotta get out of Phoenix."

Book 2: THE FIRST NIGHT

Magda watched, ready for anything. She could feel the four guards around the long porch. They were closer now. Not to mention Big Sammy who stood on the porch, glowering at them. Samosa was having the same reaction as her, his hand creeping toward the pistol stuffed in his belt.

"He touches me, you got a deal for 100K," Crazy said with a nod at the boy. The kid was strange, staring straight ahead, like none of this was going on. Crazy frowned. "What's wrong with him?"

"What's wrong with any of us?" Adan shot back. "What do you want him to touch you for? There's nothing wrong with you."

"Call it insurance," Crazy said with a lopsided grin that displayed a gold grill across a couple of his lower teeth. They didn't make him any prettier. "Besides, I'm curious." He pulled out a wad of bills, waving them in the air. "Real green." He shoved the money inside a paper sack with a lot more. He held it up. "100K, all old bills, untraceable. For a touch."

"What about a car switch? You can have the Beemer." Adan nodded toward their car, parked at the curb.

"Here, my Rover." Crazy said, pulling a pair of car keys and dangling them in front of Adan. "After the kid touches me." Before Adan could answer a car screeched to a halt in the street in front of them.

"It's Gordo's men," Adan yelled as one guy jumped out and the other leaned out the front seat, opening up on them. Boom, boom, boom went an auto shotgun, the AR going rat-a-tat-tat, buckshot flying and bullets stitching their way across the parched lawn toward the front of the old house.

159

CHAPTER
41

"Save the kid," Magda screamed and grabbed the boy. She dragged him through the half-open door into the house as Adan and the others dug for their guns and tried to take cover as slugs whipped around them. The two guards in the front were cut down before they could even move. Boom, boom, went the shotgun blasts from the guy bracing himself on the hood of the car. Crazy's last two guys dressed in black to either side went flying.

Prone on the porch floor, Adan and Frodo opened up, Magda crouched in the entry behind the door, holding the boy close. Crazy and his two guys, Big Sammy and Neon, had their guns out, and were shooting back, but hadn't had the time to take cover.

Big Sammy got stitched across the chest in another burst from the AK and went stumbling back against the siding and collapsed. Neon Blue wasn't any luckier. A slug went through his forehead and he dropped without a sound. Another burst of fire stitched the wall behind where he had just stood.

Inside the house, hugging the wall by the door, Magda held the boy close. Slugs tore through the front door, whistling past their faces and pockmarking the walls. The boy was oblivious, nestling easily in her arms. Magda stared at him as bullets ripped holes inches above their heads. He never blinked.

Outside Crazy turned into his name and stepped off the porch toward the car. He was screaming, spraying saliva and bullets as he came, a pistol bucking in either hand. "You fuckers, you think you can just kill my niggas, fuck you!"

A shot got him in the side, spinning him about, but he stayed upright and fired back. The hit man with the AR jerked back before he could fire again and dropped out of sight inside the car. The other was drilled and slid off the front hood to the street. Silence settled over the house. Clumps of gunsmoke were rising into the night air, heavy with the heat.

Crazy looked up from where he stood in the middle of the yard. He dropped one of his guns, holding his side. It was stained with blood. "Motherfucker shot me," he said, his eyes wide with shock and disbelief.

Adan sprang to his feet, meeting Magda just as she stepped out the front door with the kid. "You okay?"

She nodded shakily, checking the boy. "What about you?" He didn't reply, even though an instant before slugs had been whipping by, somehow missing them. Another miracle, she thought. "We gotta get out of here."

"My Range Rover," Crazy said, holding his bloody side. He nodded at the vehicle in the drive and tossed the keys to Adan. "Boy can patch me up in the car. Get my touch at last. Wahoo, whatta you think of that?"

Samosa got behind the wheel, Frodo next to him. Adan helped Crazy into the back seat, Magda and the boy climbing in behind him. The doors slammed shut, the engine revved, and the car backed out of the drive, and roared down the street.

CHAPTER 42

The bodies were still warm as El Gordo screeched up in his black Range Rover. He jumped out of the back, Tomas sliding out behind him. One-Eye stepped out from the wheel and joined them. Gordo hardly glanced at his man lying in the street, his shotgun nearby. He stopped on the grass, looking at the other, half spilled out the front window, leaking blood down the side of the car.

"Estúpido hijo de puta," he snarled and turned to the house. Adan and the kid were gone. Tomas and One-Eye were already searching the safe house. People were appearing, standing on the curb across the street, looking at them.

"What do you want? A show?" he yelled, flashing a pistol. People disappeared. They'd never talk to the cops. This was the hood. His men appeared from the house.

"Empty," said Tomas.

"Fuck," Gordo said. The kid had gotten away. "What were they driving?"

"Not that," One-Eye said nodding at the old Beemer in front. Its back windows were shot out.

"Mierde," the Fat Man spit out, looking at the other two. "Find out what the Moreno is driving."

They set to work as his phone buzzed. The one that he kept as his personal, encrypted and juiced up, just for him. He checked the screen. No number. He clicked and lifted it to his ear.

"You friends with Zio Benito?" a quiet voice asked.

"I know who he is," the Fat Man said, growing more guarded. Zio was old school Mafioso out of Kansas City. The most powerful Dago west of Chicago. He had tentacles everywhere in Phoenix, even if it was all run by others now. No liquor or wine moved in the city without the old man's okay.

Shit, Gordo thought. The guy had to be ancient by now. More of a myth than a reality.

"Hold on," Aslanian said.

A papery old voice came on the line. "I hear you lost the boy. What do you need to get him back quickly?" Zio Benito asked.

Gordo looked around, suddenly realizing the old man had his eyes on him. But how? It could be anybody watching, one of his own men, one of the drug dealer's, who knew. Regardless, he could use the old Mafioso's connections. "They just took off with the kid in a drug dealer's rig. Crazy Daisy. I need the location. The faster we can get that, the quicker we get the boy back. How much do I get for doing this?"

"You stay alive," came the papery voice. "I'll be in touch." Zio Benito broke the connection.

Gordo stood there, hoping he hadn't made a deal with the devil, but knowing he had. The only choice he had was to get to the kid before the old man. Until then, maybe he could use Zio Benito. Guy must be in his eighties by now. Gordo was sure he was dying, given how weak his voice was, but he didn't know of what. He didn't care either.

But the money he represented. And the power. Oh, my, si, yes, he could use that.

CHAPTER
43

Catherine and Morgan flew through the air, on their way to Phoenix. She lay back in her seat, a sleep mask on to protect her eyes from the glow of the myriad screens. She needed rest. Morgan didn't, at least not now. He was a tech geek, but he was also a climatologist and biologist. One of the reasons she had hired him. For him it was the challenge of putting together a real-time info flow that could be applied to cataclysmic events, whatever they might be.

He monitored two things, the boy and the sickness, and one of them was going bad again. The sickness. There had just been an outbreak at Heathrow airport.

He nudged Catherine, not bothering to be polite. "Wake up. We have an alert."

She replied without moving the sleep mask. "What is it?"

"There's been an outbreak at Heathrow. Big time, lots of dead."

"Oh, no," she said, sitting up and taking the mask off. "Has it hit the news yet?"

"Any second. They've sealed off the airport and told the people inside they can't leave until the sickness burns itself out."

She paled. It made her icy blue eyes stand out. "It's a death sentence."

He nodded. "They're shooting everybody who tries to leave. Just outside London, killing their own citizens. The government has given notice that the country is under martial lockdown. Any outbreaks will be quarantined permanently. Anyone within a mile has to shelter in place."

"Oh, God," she said, realizing with a terrible certainty the world was going crazy. Either that or being eminently sane. Whatever it was, it would never be the same again.

CHAPTER 44

In the back of the Range Rover, Crazy clasped his side, his fingers sticky with his own blood. Samosa drove steadily, getting the fuck out of Phoenix.

The dope king looked at Magda. She was holding the boy tight, as if not able to believe he was still alive. "C'mon," he said, "have him touch me. I'm in trouble here."

Adan was against the door, holding the slumped Crazy in his arms. He looked across the dope dealer at Magda with the boy. "Can he do it?" he asked.

"I don't know," she said, studying the boy. His face was alert, but he looked at no one.

"I'm dying here, man," Crazy said. His voice was weakening, his eyes starting to lose focus. "I feel myself draining away." He wasn't looking good. His face was strained, his lips colorless.

"Come on," Adan said to the boy. "You gotta do it. He saved us all out there." He nodded at Magda. She lifted the boy's arm and held it out to Crazy's side. The kid stiffened, forcing her to stop. "He doesn't want to do it," she said to the others, as confused as them.

"Fuck that," the dope dealer said and pulled his pistol out of his waist band. He aimed it at the back of Samosa's head. "Have the kid touch me or I'm gonna put the big guy down."

Adan swallowed. He knew Crazy meant it and he didn't think there would be much recovery for Samosa if his brains were blown out.

"You kill him while he's driving, we'll all crash," Frodo said from the front seat.

"You think I care? I'm dying already." Crazy said and cocked the automatic, keeping it leveled at the back of Samosa's head.

"Please," Magda whispered to the boy and placed his hand, no longer fighting her, on Crazy's bloody wound. The gangster stiffened, waiting for something to happen.

The seconds ticked past. Crazy let out a breath and slumped against Adan, still grabbing his wounded side. "Nothing," he said, his face drained. "Why?" He nodded at Frodo in front, next to Samosa. "Why the hell would he save you and not me?"

"Maybe cause he's not an asshole," Samosa ventured from behind the wheel.

"Fuck you," Crazy whispered back, his voice weakening. He swung the pistol on the kid, pointing it between his bluish eyes. "Do it or I'll blow your fucking head off, you freak."

The kid lifted his face to him. Everything about him seemed set in stone, but his eyes. They were clear and intent, focused on Crazy. "Shit," Frodo whispered from the front, watching intently. "Someone's home."

The boy didn't shy from the barrel of the pistol, but his eyes were locked with Crazy's. He reached forward and pressed his palm into the dope dealer's bloody side. Crazy stiffened in his seat with a groan. The others looked at him, Samosa behind the wheel checked him out in the rearview mirror. He could see the skin where the bullet had torn into his ribs begin to heal.

Holy shit. His eyes widened. The blood on the dealer's side was beginning to dry and chip away.

Adan checked the boy's face as it was happening. His cheeks were sucking in, his face and hair losing what little color they had, his forearms shrinking. "Something's wrong with the kid," Adan said, alarmed.

Book 2: THE FIRST NIGHT

Crazy looked up at the boy. Even as he got better the boy got worse, the face pulling in, the body becoming rickety, like the life was being sucked out of him. "Easy man," Crazy said. "Don't go spending yourself all on me."

The boy, almost comatose now, sagged back, breaking contact. Magda caught him, lowering him into the back seat. She looked at his face, the sunken cheeks, the bruised eyes, and deathly pale face. "It almost killed him."

Crazy looked down at his side. His eyes widened. "My wound," he said, "where the slug tore into me, it's completely healed. There's no wound, no blood, no nothing."

They all looked. His shirt was torn where it had been ripped by the bullet. It was covered with blood, now dried, but his wound was gone. His side looked as skinny as ever, but his black skin was smooth, no damage anywhere.

"What do we got here with this kid?" Frodo said, eyeing the boy with awe. "He fixed my legs, he can stop your bleeding, bring dogs back from the dead, save babies with bad hearts, gives us all visions. What else can he do? Who is he? Where did he come from? Why's he here?" He was shouting now. "I mean who the hell does these things?"

"Shut up, Frodo," Adan said, looking at Magda, with the boy. He was leaning his head against her breast, his eyes open and staring, but hardly breathing. "He's really in bad shape, whatever he did for Crazy really took it out of him."

"Why didn't it happen with me?" Frodo asked. "He got faint, but he didn't fall like this."

"Maybe he's like a battery," Samosa said from behind the wheel. "He's been running down and we haven't given him a chance to recharge."

"He'll make it," Adan said, "but he needs rest." He looked at Samosa in the front seat. "We ditch this car first, then go to ground at the first motel you see."

Samosa nodded, tight-lipped. Yeah, they had to get rid of the Rover. The cops would know it was Crazy's and they needed a crash pad. Bad. The day had been hell. He couldn't compute what he'd seen, Frodo walking, the baby and Crazy healed. He couldn't figure it out, accept it, his head kept wanting to reject it, because he knew—it couldn't be true.

But it was. Frodo and Crazy in the car with him proved it. "You know what happened, don't you?" the big guy said to the others. "We picked up the kid and used him, thinking he was a fake. Only he isn't. Joke's on us."

"Shit," Frodo muttered, realizing the big guy was right. The joke was on them.

"Here, this is where we go," the healed Crazy said from behind him and passed him his device. A map was on it, a motel not that far away pinned with a red flag.

"You sure it's safe?" Magda asked.

"Better be," the drug dealer said. "I own it."

CHAPTER 45

"Catherine," Morgan said. She was laying back in the chair, the sleeping mask on as the jet flew them through the night. She said it made her concentrating easier; he thought it was the only shelter she had from the cascade of terrible news.

She answered without lifting it. "What?"

"It flared up in clots all over the airport, then flared out. They figure half of the people were killed before it stopped."

"Stopped?" She lifted the mask and sat up. "It just stopped with people in direct contact still alive?"

He nodded. "Like someone gave an order. They're processing the survivors now in hangars. Several thousand of them. It could take days and then they'll isolate them, trying to figure out why they're still alive. That and counting the dead. They're at six thousand and rising."

"What is it? Like a faucet someone is turning on and off?" she asked. A sudden thought jumped into her head. "Where's the boy? He still on the grid?"

Morgan tapped a screen. A crime scene came up of the shootout at the safe house. "Just happened," he reported to Catherine. "There was a drug shootout. Eight dead. They're reporting several of the survivors fled with the boy."

"Damn," Catherine whispered. "The sickness stopped in London. Do we have any way of knowing just what happened at this gunfight? Did someone do something that would have pleased the boy?"

"What are you thinking?" Morgan said, looking at her out of the corner of his eye.

"What's the chance of a connection now between the boy and the sickness?"

He tapped some keys, looked at a screen. "It's up. Fifty-two percent." He couldn't believe the number, but there it was. They exchanged glances, but neither said anything. His satellite com pinged and text came up. He read with a frown. "The CIA is placing a special agent with us. One with contacts to Homeland Security. He'll be meeting us when we land in Phoenix."

He looked up at her. His round face was worried. "Somebody's interested in what we're doing."

"Yes," she answered, "someone with a lot of power in the government."

CHAPTER 46

In the office in back of the grocery, Mickey and Lilli sat on a threadbare couch, watching the TV.

A reporter was on, the slaughter in front of the safe house her backdrop, eight dead they were saying. She was talking to a home-owner, across the street from the shootout. The fat woman was blabbering, in her bathrobe, her skinny husband next to her, nodding at everything she said. A snotnose kid, woken from his sleep, clung to her dirty terry cloth hem.

"I saw him get shot down, this big guy, up on the porch. Crazy got hit, too," she said with a nod that set a triple chin wobbling. "He was bleeding bad when they got him into the car." The woman looked back at the house across the street. It was lit up with special floods, the front yard crawling with cops.

She paused and leaned in, dropping her voice, in awe in spite of herself. "They had the boy with him. The one from the news, I swear, the Healer. He shouldn't have survived, not with all those bullets whizzing by. But he did. I saw them put him into the car with Crazy Daisy and take off. Crazy was wounded. Bet he's all healed up by now."

Her eyes turned, looking directly into the camera lens. "Everybody, all of you out there. Get ready, go to church, go to temple, go to your mosques, go wherever you want. Make peace. The boy's a sign. Get ready is all I can say."

She turned and walked off, the little kid still holding a side of her frayed robe. The skinny husband hurriedly followed.

In their grubby little apartment, Mickey looked at Lilli. "We gotta get the boy here," he said, "You know he can help you. He's probably healing a bunch of thugs right now."

"How are you going to call him? He's not gonna answer a phone, you know?" Lilli said, her heart suddenly thumping. Hope. She was flooded with it. She couldn't help herself.

Mickey sat there a moment, his jaw setting. "He touched me. I've been having those visions ever since he did that."

"What kind? Have there been more?"

"One more," he said and lied. "Just a flash of the store, like it was some kind of picture. Then it was gone." He didn't want to tell her about all the dead bodies, or the fact that he had been one of them.

"He's touched others," she said, her brow creasing. "They may have the same vision?"

"I know," he nodded, "but we don't know for sure. It could be the boy reaching out to me. It could be happening to that man he saved. Whoever he touches." He got up.

"Where you going?" she asked.

"Outside, to see if I can reach him with my mind or that other fellow he touched. Maybe even the dog. See if I can get the boy to come to us." He grinned, about to slip through the door.

"Here, take this with you," she said and held out her well-thumbed Bible.

He had too much respect for her to refuse. He took it and stepped outside, Bible in hand. He figured he'd done the right thing. Not telling her about what he'd seen, the results of the gun fight, and the worst part: him dead. But she was ready for the boy to touch her. She wanted it, even if she couldn't say it.

The only problem was how to bring the boy to him. Whoever had gotten away from that fight in the safe house would have him. The police hadn't identified anybody. The boy was Lilli's only chance.

Book 2: THE FIRST NIGHT

He had to reach out to him. All those he'd touched were connected through him. He was sure of it.

He sat in the swing, listening to the hydroponic sprays inside the grow houses quietly hiss. He took a hit from his vape pen and tried to picture the front of his store, looking down the street at it, hoping the boy would see it. Mary's Landing's only vegan grocery store. It was stenciled on the side of his house along with his name and the silly dancing vegetables, facing the street so everybody driving by, headed in either direction, could see it. But it wasn't clear in his memory.

He gripped the Bible harder and muttered to himself. "C'mon, help me."

The image cleared. The name of the town, Mary's Landing, was clear to see in his mind's eyes, beneath the name of his store: "Mickey's Vegan; Go Green." Anyone who saw his vision would see that. He knew they would come, and they'd have the boy with them.

He wasn't a religious man, but he sure as hell believed in the boy. And any help he could get. He raised the Bible to his lips and kissed it, saying a silent prayer.

CHAPTER
47

Crazy made a call and they drove around to the back of the motel at the edge of the strip mall. Almost out of the city, but not quite. They came to a stop in a parking space, looking at a bank of rooms. Crazy nodded with a grin. "All of 'em are ours," he said, and slipped out of the back seat. From the way he moved a casual observer would never have known he was badly wounded only a few hours ago. The rest of them followed.

"How safe is it?" Frodo asked, looking at a long line of rooms, facing a busy highway.

"As safe as my money can make it," Crazy said. "I pay everybody off to not notice it. Should be good for tonight, I hope, but I'd keep your guns close." He nodded at a room. "That one's mine." He headed toward it, one hand feeling his healed side, as if he still couldn't quite believe it.

Crazy moved through the anodyne room into the bath, stopping before the mirror. He stripped off his shirt. It was still crusty with his blood and he dropped it to the tiled floor, studying his naked side in the mirror. He ran his fingers over it. He felt wonder and awe, emotions he wasn't used to. It took him a moment to recognize it. Something miraculous had happened to him. The dumb kid had healed him with his touch. He had saved his life. Why? The kid didn't owe him anything. He wasn't even sure the kid felt anything, like what he owed and didn't, loyalty, he called it, or right and wrong his Meemaw Callie would have called it.

"Shit," he said silently to himself. He hadn't thought of her in years. She'd died in the old falling down house she'd raised him and his sisters in, much like the safe house he'd bought. Maybe that was why he was so comfortable there. It was the last time he cried, when she'd passed because of a heart attack, or so the doc had said, when he'd threatened to kill him if he didn't bring her back, the man wept, saying she was gone, and even God couldn't do that.

"Tyrell," he heard her say his name behind him and he whirled. Meemaw Callie stood there, a big black woman with shoulders wider than his. She was alive. She couldn't be alive, but then neither could he. He'd been shot, bleeding out, no way to stop it, fading, the world turning black and then the boy had touched him and now his Meemaw stood there, staring at him with her broad face and terrible wig with the straightened hair askew on her head.

"You haven't been doing like I raised you," she said, her mouth turning down in disappointment. "I taught you better than this, I took you to church, you heard the preacher, and what have you done? You made money, yeah, you and the others, but how many died? How many have you killed with that shit you sell? You know it kills, kills the users, but kills the dealers, too, inside. You're dead inside, you know you are." She stepped forward, raising an aged hand to his face, touching his cheek with her fingers. "I love you, Tyrell. I raised you better than this, to take care of your sisters, to be a father to your children. When was the last time you saw one of your babies? What did I do wrong? What happened to you?"

Tyrell stepped back, shaking his head, unable to find the words. He spun about, looking at himself in the bathroom mirror. There he was, half-naked, tears streaming down his face. There was no Meemaw Callie behind him in the reflection. He whirled back, but she was gone. He was in the tacky stupid motel bathroom again and he was alone.

He had lost his Meemaw again and the tears were still rolling down his cheeks.

CHAPTER 48

Frodo looked at his buddy, Samosa, as they stepped into their room. "Come on," he said. "Let's wash up and see if we can find a beer."

"I wanna check the news," Samosa said, flicking on the TV, him and Frodo watching. More about the coughing sickness, but this time it was different. It had reached Pretoria, almost at the end of Africa, and then—it had stopped, just like that, in a whole bunch of places. Ghana, Guinea, Saudi Arabia, Europe, England, everywhere it had stopped.

Frodo and Samosa stepped out of their room, half stripped, their devices in their hands. "Hey, you seeing this?" they called toward Crazy's open door. "That sickness has stopped cold."

Adan and Magda appeared from their room. Her hair was a mess and he didn't look any neater. "You saw the news about the sickness?" Frodo said with a half grin. "It's another miracle, just like the boy healing Crazy."

"Yeah, I'm thrilled for him," Samosa said, looking at Magda. "Get the kid to touch me, huh? I don't wanna be the only one who's not in on these visions."

"Crazy ain't had any visions," Frodo said.

"Yes, I have," Crazy said, stepping out of his room. He looked shaken and was wiping at his eyes. They all looked at him.

"Yeah," Frodo said, looking at him doubtfully. Crazy wasn't the kind to have visions, not unless he was jacked up on some of his own product. "What kind of visions?"

"None of your motherfuckin' business," the dope dealer said, anger sweeping his face, warning the others to leave him alone. They did.

Next to Adan, Magda looked through their open doorway into their room. The kid sat there, staring at the screen, now filled with news about the contagion stopping. He saw it and didn't.

"Yeah sure," Magda said absently, "none of us care about anything except cash and staying high." She looked at the boy again; still sitting there in front of the screen, some newscaster blathering on joyfully that the coughing sickness had seemingly stopped. If the kid was responsible, she thought, you sure as hell couldn't tell looking at him. It was like the last thing the boy cared about right now. Or maybe he cared about everything, including them. You just couldn't tell looking at him, but then what the fuck did any of them care about. Or anyone in the world for that matter, except themselves.

CHAPTER
49

Joe Bear Claws had spread a tarp over the four-wheeler and made himself a little tent with a campfire in front. It was in clear view of the notch. The moon was high behind it, shining down. Only the notch wasn't there, at least not right now. Terry Lathrop, his partner in the rental shop, sat with him on the ground. Supplies he'd brought up were piled to the side. Terry was looking in the direction of the non-existent notch.

"Right there?" he said, making no effort to hide his doubt.

"When it shows," Joe said with a nod.

"Joe," Terry said, "you sure about this? He touched you, so maybe you've got this special power, but there's nothing but desert out there."

"You saw him. Maybe that's enough to make you like me. Regardless, you've changed. You just don't know it yet."

"Oh, stop it," Terry said with a laugh. He'd been watching the news, checking social media. He knew the boy glimpsed in the video was the one he'd seen stepping onto the highway. He had been using the walkie-talkie to get Joe the latest info on the kid and his healings. Shit, bringing animals back from the dead, saving a baby, and some dope dealer shootout. Spooky. But still, seeing tabletop mesas that weren't there? It was too crazy.

"Just seeing somebody walk by, grazing your hand, isn't enough to do anything to you," Terry said, trying to reason with his Indian buddy. Joe Bear Claws cocked a doubtful eyebrow, but said nothing. "Okay, let's say it's true. He is this miracle worker. What's he doing appearing in the middle of nowhere? How can he be coming out of a notch that isn't…?"

He suddenly stopped, blinking, staring through the darkness into the distance. The tabletop mesa was back in the desert. A little apart, a jagged escarpment, reared out of the desert at an angle, like it was gonna tip over, and in between was the notch. There was something beckoning about it, welcoming, like a forefinger, motioning you closer. The only thing missing was the sun rising.

Tabletop mesas that came and went, millions of tons of dirt and rock, disappearing and reappearing? What the hell? Terry's mouth came unhinged as he lost his voice in total shock.

CHAPTER 50

Sgt. Noel Getty walked up to her partner, Det. Dan Wilson. They were both in their forties. Wilson had a hangdog face, like a bloodhound, which described his nature. She was better looking (who wasn't?), but she seemed pale and tired these days. She'd had a health scare four years back, breast cancer, but had beat it. He kept thinking he should ask her about her current health, but wasn't sure he wanted to know. They'd become close working together over the years, and the last thing he needed was something else to worry about. They stood in front of Crazy's safe house. It was crawling with LED lights and CSI. The dead bodies were being packed into the meat wagon.

"The boy seems to be the real deal," she said, "touching people and curing them, or at least helping." She checked her device for names. "Somehow he ended up with an Adan Cuarto and Magda Rodriguez, both known to us. At least the kid was with them when the gunfire happened."

Det. Wilson frowned. "Shit. Gonna get the kid killed. Background on the two?"

"Small time thief and a whore," Noel replied, "Both of them are working their way up. There are two guys who run with them, looking for names now. They work for El Gordo Halazar, big time fence, loan shark, and killer. Maybe past tense. Looks like they had a falling out. His guys." She nodded at the car peppered with slugs and the body slumped in the front seat.

The other on the ground was being bagged and lifted on to a portable stretcher.

"Shit," Wilson said. "You know everybody is screaming about this kid."

"That's what happens when you save a baby," she said dryly. "Raising a dog from the dead wasn't bad either."

"What about what happened here?" The detective looked at the crowd of onlookers, held back by a string of officers. Media were there, too, network, cell phones, streaming live, it made no difference to him. "Kid's the hottest thing in the country."

"The world, this keeps up," Noel said with a nod. "That and the coughing sickness. Yin and Yang."

If only the kid would touch her, she thought. They'd found breast cancer four years ago. They'd cut it out and she seemed clean, until four months ago when she found a lump in her other breast. She wanted experimental treatments that she couldn't afford. Dimly she hoped that she and Wilson were the ones to find the boy. Maybe she could ask him to touch her, though she knew for a certainty that all this excitement about the kid was a crock of shit.

A skinny kid who healed whoever he touched? Damn, people would believe anything.

CHAPTER 51

Crazy exited his motel room and sat in a cream-colored beat-up aluminum chair, next to Samosa and Frodo. They looked out at the night, past the parked cars to the busy highway, traffic zipping by. There were several of the scarred metal chairs before each of the rooms in a line. Typical cheap motel, from the outside anyway.

None of them said anything. Crazy pulled a joint from his shirt pocket. Not a fat one, a skinny one, long and discreet. He checked his device. It was all over the net and airwaves, the shootout at the safe house. Regular fucking FBI's Most Wanted list, that's what they'd made. He'd be proud of himself if it wasn't so fucking inconvenient.

For once, he regretted being a professional gangster. (He really regretted it after seeing Meemaw Callie, but he wasn't going to tell any of them about that; make him look weak.) He still couldn't figure out the kid, the boy, but then his wound was healed (and there was no denying the fucking vision). No denying any of it, but what did it mean? What did anything mean? He glanced down at the phone. Fucking coughing sickness had stopped. What? He stiffened in his rickety chair. How could a contagious disease just stop cold? WTF was going on?

The kid? Did it have something to do with the kid? (It had to; everything did.)

"How you feeling?" Samosa said to the dope dealer, noticing his strained face.

"Okay," Crazy said, swallowing hard and trying to hold it together. "Just trying to figure out all this insanity."

"He still hasn't touched me," Samosa said, feeling left out. "You wanna talk about what you saw?"

Crazy glanced down, avoiding his gaze. (Did he have a dream? Fucking-A, the mother of all dreams, the one guaranteed to rip his guts out.) "No," he said, short and curt. It was the last fucking thing he wanted to talk about. He nodded at the new car parked in front of the room. A nice-looking Lexus. "You ditch my Rover?"

"Sure did. Deep sixed the plates, too," Frodo answered. He jerked his head at the Lexus. "This is clean, at least till the guy who owns it wakes up and finds it isn't in his driveway anymore. Switched plates on it, too."

Crazy glanced at Samosa who leaned back in the metal chair. "We're lucky, all of us. We coulda been killed at my place."

Samosa looked at the two of them. They were both smarter than he and he knew it, but he didn't resent it. He was shrewder than them about people though. Something was wrong with Crazy; he felt it, the guy was almost vibrating inside, but Frodo didn't feel it. The big guy looked at him and said, "We all been saved by the kid, haven't we? I mean, it started in the bar when he made you walk."

"Yeah," Frodo said, massaging his legs reflexively. "I'm still trying to deal with it. What it might mean. It weakened him when he healed me and Gordo, but it almost killed the kid when he had to save Crazy. We all saw him turning into a skeleton."

"Yeah, scary," Crazy said with a thoughtful nod, as if it might really have affected him. "I was watching as he made me better. Face started to draw in, eyes flickered, like he was dying right in front of me."

Book 2: THE FIRST NIGHT

"I've been watching the kid since," the big guy said with a frown. "He couldn't do anything after he saved you. He was done. He got better in the car, but it was slow going."

"Meaning what?" Frodo asked, his eyes narrowing.

"The kid has too many to help at the same time, he ain't going to be able to make it," Samosa said with his deep frown. "Someone's gonna die. Like permanently. I'd say two at a time was his max. Maybe only one. Depends on how rested he is. Also, maybe if he saves you once, you don't get a second chance."

They all sat there in the night heat, watching the cars pass on the road, and thinking that one over.

CHAPTER 52

Inside Adan and Magda's motel room the TV played softly, showing video of the gunfight at Crazy's safe house. Some nosy neighbor had grabbed it on their phone, but they weren't watching. They were entwined on the bed, making love, not fast but slow and deliberate, like they knew it might be their last time and didn't want to hurry it. The boy sat in a chair, facing away from the bed. Magda had insisted. Having the boy watch them while they made love made her uncomfortable. Her mother would have called it having "a sense of decency," something that none of her other friends would ever accuse her of.

Adan cried out as he climaxed. Her moan joined his as they both clasped each other, holding tight like they didn't want to let go. He slipped off her, both of them trying to get control of their breathing, the sweat rolling off him, her hair damp and matted. "It's all over the news," Magda said, sitting up and getting her hair out of her face as she watched the TV on the bureau.

It was on mute, but all the video was of the boy or the coughing sickness. There had been an outbreak in London, at the airport, but it had stopped. "Burned itself out," they called it, but there was no explanation beyond that given. As to the boy, they kept playing video of him in front of their apartment house, pulling away from her and touching the baby. He was clear to be seen now, no doubt he was their kid, but they didn't have any good video of the gunfight at Crazy's. They had some grainy cell phone footage, but you couldn't see anything. It was mixed in with interviews of the neighbors, all claiming they'd seen more than they had, and preening in front of the TV cameras.

She could see herself and Adan at their apartment, watching as the boy slowly reached out for the baby, the crowd watching with bated breath. No hiding the boy or themselves anymore. The boy touched the baby and it stopped squalling. There was a shot of the baby, gurgling happily in its grateful mother's arms. It was magical.

Adan got up on one elbow, ignoring the screen, bending over to kiss her naked shoulder. "Did I ever tell you how beautiful…?"

"Look," she said, cutting him off as she hit "sound" on the TV. She didn't want to hear his love talk. He didn't want to marry her; he didn't want kids, so it was all about the sex and nothing more than that. She didn't need to get married, but they could be a couple, have a family. She didn't expect that, who the hell did these days, but she had this need for another child, someone for her Sophia to play with. She'd save some money, get her back into America. She'd have that family she wanted so bad, even if she couldn't explain it to herself.

He glanced at the screen. It had changed, the boy gone, buried by news of the sickness. It showed Heathrow airport, soldiers in gas masks and Hazmat suits, armed and waiting at some distance from the buildings, weapons ready. They were the only movement. The news reader was going on about how the sickness hadn't started again, but all the people inside the terminal who'd had contact with the dead would not be allowed to mix with the general populace until they had been treated in quarantine.

"How can that be?" Adan said, sitting up naked on the bed. "What happened? Why's it suddenly stopped?"

"I don't know, but it's got to do with the boy," Magda said with absolute certainty. She got out of bed and walked to where he sat in the chair in the corner, facing the wall. Adan watched appreciatively, his eyes on her beauty, the hell with the kid. She was always going

Book 2: THE FIRST NIGHT

on about another child, she wanted him to give it to her, but he said no way. He wasn't sure he'd be alive tomorrow, how the hell could he want what he knew he could never have. He'd be condemning a child to grow up like him and he couldn't stand the idea.

He watched Magda, enjoying her sensuality. She had not wanted the boy to watch them, but now she wanted to see his face. She turned him to the room, scooting his chair around. He looked better, healthier, but he didn't react. His face was as passive as ever, the eyes with that thousand-yard stare.

She knew he could be here, with them, sometimes. Now just wasn't one of them. She took a sip of water from a plastic bottle, and looked at her lover. "What now?"

"I don't know, but he does," Adan said, nodding at boy, looking out at them with his blank eyes. "We've both had visions of that notch in the desert, haven't we? That has to mean something."

"We have to head there?" she asked. "You sure?"

"Who's sure of anything anymore, but I also saw that grocery store. That desert town, Mary's Landing. We got to get there first, to that stupid vegan store with the dancing vegetables. Stupid, but that's where we gotta go."

"I thought you said you weren't sure?"

"I'm not, but he is," Adan said, nodding at the empty eyed boy. "It's what he wants, even if he can't say it."

Book 3:
THE SECOND DAY

CHAPTER 53

The early morning sun beat down on a small roadhouse. Martha's by name, one of the last mom and pops on the highway out of Phoenix. Adan and the others sat inside and ate a hurried breakfast. Their new wheels, the dirty white Lexus, sat just outside the glass window. They were all crammed in at a circular booth of cracked yellowish Naugahyde. The boy sat in between Magda and Adan, Crazy to his side, Frodo and Samosa on the outside.

"So, what are we gonna do?" the big guy asked, spooning oatmeal into his mouth. He liked it with banana and raisins.

"Whatever it is, we'd better do it fast," Frodo said, checking his phone. "It's five to eight. El Gordo has to be closing in on us."

"How?" Frodo asked.

"You tell me, but you know he is," Adan said with a worried look. "He won't stop. This is too big." He raised his cell. "They have this to track us."

"We shoulda dumped them and gotten burners," Frodo said, trying to be intelligent about this.

"Why?" said Crazy. "You think that's gonna stop El Gordo finding us. No fucking way. He'll buy the info, you know he will, and the cops have APBs out on us. We're famous, remember?" He flashed his phone, scrolling it with his thumb. It showed mug shots of them, one after the other, and, of course, the now famous boy. "We're lucky we haven't been recognized in here yet."

"The sickness hasn't started up again," Magda said, riding her device. "Maybe it's over."

"They said millions are dead already," Frodo said with a frown. "Sure as hell hope they find a vaccine in case it comes back."

"We need to know where to go," Magda said, looking at the others. "Adan and I have had a vision of this mesa and a rock outcropping. What about you?"

Frodo shook his head. "People dying of the sickness, yeah, I seen that. It was this truck stop in the middle of nowhere," he said, thinking of the vision he'd had, "but someplace we're supposed to go? No, not yet anyway."

Adan looked at Samosa. The big guy shrugged. "He hasn't touched me. Guess I have to get shot first."

"Don't say that," Crazy said with a grimace. "Hurts like hell."

Adan glanced at the boy. He had bacon and eggs before him, but hadn't had a bite. "I had a vision of this desert town and I didn't have to get shot to have it. Mary's Landing. It's on the way to the desert. I think that's where we head next."

"Not the notch?" Frodo asked.

"The Landing first," Adan said with a shake of his head. "Maybe it leads to the notch. 'Sides, we don't know where it is." He looked at the unmoving boy, sitting in front of all the food. "Has he eaten once since he's been with us?"

"You know he hasn't," Magda said. She glanced at the boy. If he was hungry he didn't show it. His nose didn't even wrinkle at the smell of the food. Same as yesterday.

"You sure he don't ever pee?" Samosa said as he spooned the last of the oatmeal into his gob. He couldn't believe the kid didn't piss or dump, but then he couldn't believe what was happening to them either.

"Not once," Adan said with a scowl. He was having a hard time putting it all together, too. His cell buzzed. He didn't need to look at it to know who it was. He keyed it, lifting it to his ear. "Hey, Fat Man, how you doing?" he said cheerfully.

"Don't fuck with me," he heard El Gordo's angry snarl.

"I'm not fucking with you. You're the one who's calling me."

"I get the boy, you get the money. A million dollars, split between you and your crew."

That stopped Adan cold. "A million…" His friends looked at him. Every one of them heard the number and were poleaxed by it. Even Crazy. The only one that wasn't interested was the boy. "I'll think about it," Adan said, fighting for time to figure it out.

"Fuck you, you little Latino…" El Gordo said, starting to rant, but Adan cut him off with a click.

He slipped the phone into his pocket, looking at the others. "I think it's time to get out of here." He rose, throwing some money on the table and headed for the dirty white Lexus outside. Time to move.

The others followed, Magda leading the passive boy by the hand. "A million dollars? He offered a million dollars?" she called after him, as if she couldn't believe the number. She couldn't.

"Yeah," Adan said. "We split it."

"That's a lot of coin," Crazy said with a low whistle. "That include me?"

"Could if I negotiate right," Adan said with a sly smile.

"Stuff it," Magda snapped, holding the boy by the hand as they stepped outside. "We don't sell the boy for anything. I'll kill anybody who tries." Her eyes drilled into Adan. "Which way to this Mary's Landing?"

Adan looked up into the morning sun. Mary's Landing was to the west on the map. The sun was rising from the east. In the vision he'd had, the sun had been behind the kid. Maybe the Landing was on the way.

"East," he said. "We head east, into the sun."

CHAPTER 54

El Gordo sat in the shiny black SUV, speeding through the streets. Everybody fucking loved black. It made no sense in the Arizona sun, but there you were. The AC was cranking hard. He was thinking about his "fuck you" talk with Adan.

Money wasn't going to get to him, especially if the million hadn't turned him, but there were other ways. He looked at the geek, sitting in the front, nervously watching his screen. Zio Benito had supplied him. A genius with the data, his guys had said. Fuck them. One-Eye was behind the wheel. "You get it?" the Fat Man asked. The geek had promised to track Adan down if Gordo only got him on the cell. Well, he'd done his part.

"Yeah," the geek nodded, a jerky grin pulling at his tight lips. "They're at Sun Desert."

"That's twenty minutes away," One-Eye said, keeping the heavy vehicle moving as he checked his Waze. Stupid fucks hadn't dumped their phones. Burner cells, that's what they should have had. Not that it made any difference now.

El Gordo looked at the geek. "Can you follow him?"

"I've tagged his phone," the nervous man replied. "As long as he's got that we got him."

The Fat Man nodded, not particularly mollified. Talking to that smarmy thief, Adan, put him in a bad mood. Magda was beautiful, but she'd chosen a loser with that one. He thumbed his phone, raising it to his ear.

"Yeah," came a breathy squeak of a voice. It was Zio Benito himself.

El Gordo chose his words carefully. "They're outside of the city, Sun Desert. We got a fix on them and are on our way." He was about to click off when he saw a flash of a street in front of his eyes, like he was standing there, staring at "Mickey's Natural Produce: Stay Healthy in the Landing, live long, shop at Mickey's."

Fuck, he thought, why did I see that? There was only one explanation. The Fat Man blinked and found himself back in the black SUV, staring at Tomas. The man noticed. "You okay?"

"Yeah," Gordo nodded, shaken. He swallowed and spoke into the cell. "A town, Mary's Landing. Find it. A grocery store named 'Mickey's.'"

"Grocery store?"

"Mickey's Natural Produce. The kid will be there," Gordo said to Zio Benito. He looked at Perez behind the wheel. "You got it?" Off the driver's nod, he spoke back into the phone. "By the way, I want 50% of the action you get from him. Forever."

"You'd fuck with me..." he heard the old man begin on the other end.

"Stuff it," Gordo said, cutting him off. He was freaked. "I'm having these visions. He's talking to me, not to you. Because I've been touched by him and you haven't. Without me, you haven't got shit. Until you're touched anyway, if it works for you like it does for me. So fuck off from now on and we both get a vote. Full partners, until death do us part. Now head for Mary's Landing if you wanna be in on this."

"Hold on," the old man yelled over the phone, just as Gordo was about to break connection.

"What?" he snarled.

"Ten million," the dying man said breathlessly. "I'm coming

Book 3: THE SECOND DAY

after you. I can carry that amount. Tell them. It's all theirs if they just let the boy touch me. You understand?"

"Yeah, I understand," growled the Fat Man. He understood if you were that desperate, he owned you. He clicked off, feeling the best he had since he'd found out his cancer was gone.

CHAPTER 55

Whitney walked into the kitchen where her mom was busy puttering about. Her dad had already eaten and left for work, but her brother was there. He was eating his cold cereal at the table, spooning it in as he watched his tablet. Helena watched the small TV on the counter, playing the news of the gunfight the night before and the boy saving the baby.

"Feeling better, honey?" Helena asked, referring to her upset stomach as she loaded several dishes into the washer.

"Yeah, Mom, fine now," Whitney said. She had pled not feeling well the night before so she could avoid her parents. She didn't want to discuss the boy, because she wasn't sure he was the one they'd given the ride, but seeing him save the baby last night had ended any such doubts. She nodded at the screen. "Donny tell you I think he's the kid we picked up?" Her brother glanced up, his face filled with guilt. Not that it surprised her. He never could keep a secret, especially if it concerned her.

"Yes, he did," Helena said with a worried frown. "I will admit it looks like our boy, when he saved that baby, but I hate the idea of getting involved. It would turn our lives upside down. Donny said you felt the same way."

"For sure," Whitney said. "We'd never be able to live normal lives again." She looked out the kitchen window at her mother's car parked in the drive. Did she dare "borrow" it? She had to get to the truck stop by eight tonight. That was imperative. Lives depended on it, that of her entire family. "I'm thinking of going over to Sandra's later, and maybe from there to the library. Can I borrow your car?"

Her brother looked up at her, his eyes narrowing. Whitney knew he suspected something was going on. Not her mother, who said: "Depends. How long you want it for?"

"I don't know. A couple of hours, maybe three. Sandra wants some new workout gear. She's become a health freak."

"Sure, I guess," her mom replied, going back to cleaning up the counter.

Whitney turned, staring at her brother, her eyes narrowed. He looked back at her. "Whatta you doing?" he mouthed.

"None of your business," she mouthed back and whirled, flouncing out of the kitchen, letting him know how irritated she was with him.

She'd only gotten halfway across the living room before her brother appeared hurriedly from the kitchen behind her. "What's with you?" he said.

"I'm gonna take the car and head for that truck stop," she said, turning on him. "There was a clock in the window of the store in the vision I saw. It was eight at night, straight up."

"You think you have to be there by then?" he said, looking at her with raised eyebrows. She nodded.

He studied her. He was younger than her, and he hated her most of the time, but he knew when she was serious. "All right. What do you think it means?"

"I'm not sure," she said, "but it's some kind of message. It's connected to the people I saw dead there."

"Me and Mom and Dad, from the coughing sickness?"

"Has to be." With that she turned and headed for the stairs. He ran after her, catching her at the bottom. "I'm coming with you," he said.

"No, you're not," she answered. "If you come, you die. Maybe if you stay here, you don't. Now leave me alone."

She hurried up the stairs, leaving him staring after her.

CHAPTER 56

Samosa drove west as the burbs turned to desert, stubborn and vast. He said, "So it's this notch we have to find? But it doesn't exist?"

Frodo looked up from the back. He was on his device. "I haven't been able to find it. No landmark like it anywhere in the state." Crazy rode next to him, looking out the window. The boy was in the center, Magda by the door. She was also on her device. "But Mary's Landing is on here, straight ahead through the desert."

"Everything is still quiet with the sickness," Magda said, checking her screen. "No outbreak since that London airport," she said.

"What difference does it make?" Frodo said, thumbing through his screen. "They've shut down all air travel, worldwide. Nothing's moving. Everything's quarantined and the UN is saying people are gonna start starving and economies are gonna crash if they don't lift it." He made a face and stuffed the device in his pocket. "Shit, you'd think they'd be happy people aren't coughing themselves to death, but, no, they just wanna go back like it never happened. Give 'em a week and they'll forget that millions just died."

"What does it mean?" Magda asked, looking down at the boy. Nothing from him. She glanced up at the others. "You know the sickness is connected to the boy, don't you? Has to be. He's been sent here by someone."

"Who?" Samosa asked, looking at her the mirror.

"God?" she replied in a small uncertain voice, feeling stupid for even suggesting it.

"Bullshit," Adan exploded in the front. "I don't wanna hear any healing religious shit. Kid's got something, sure, but we don't know what. He could be a fucking alien for all we know. Or maybe we're experiencing—what do they call it—mass hysteria. Now leave it alone."

"Mary's Landing," Frodo said. "I think maybe getting there will answer a lot of these questions."

Samosa punched it up on his dash map. "Forty miles away." He frowned, his brow wrinkling. "I'm the only one who hasn't had a vision," the big guy complained. "I'm starting to feel left out."

Magda took the boy and pulled him forward, taking his hand and placing it on Samosa's shoulder. "Here," she said, "Consider yourself touched."

Samosa grinned, glanced back at the boy. "I think I have to be shot first, like Crazy…but I'll tell you, unlike him." He stopped. The boy was staring at him in the rearview mirror, meeting his gaze. Someone was home. A surge of heat passed from the boy's hand into his shoulder and the big man stiffened. He almost drove off the road.

"Hey," Adan yelled as the heavy Lexus swerved back onto the highway and then straightened out.

"You okay?" Frodo yelled from the back. He reached forward, grabbing Samosa by the shoulders.

"Yeah," the big guy said, shaken. His heart was beating faster, his breathing quick. "He, he really just touched me. I felt this flash of heat go into my body." There was wonder in his voice. "Just like the rest of you."

"Great," Crazy growled. "Now you can have a vision, too, and go stupid insane like the rest of us."

"You saw something," Frodo said to him, unable to contain his curiosity. "C'mon, what was it?"

"Go fuck yourself," the dope dealer snapped back and looked back out the side window, watching the desert whoosh by.

CHAPTER
57

One-Eye drove, the greasy tech kid tech next to him. El Gordo and Tomas sat in the back. The Fat Man lifted his cell. "Ready?" he asked.

The tech nodded, his eyes bright. "Do it. I'm gonna hit a phone, I don't know whose, try to message them. I'll get their location that way. Maybe they won't notice."

El Gordo nodded and punched the button. He was calling Frodo again, because he knew who was at the end of the line, not that he would answer. The phone buzzed on the other end, but there was no answer.

The greasy haired guy brightened. "That's all I need, I'm in," he said happily. He tapped his laptop, looked at One-Eye. "They're six blocks away."

He lifted his device so the visually impaired man could see the map with the pulsing red dot. One-Eye took the next corner so sharply the wheels screeched, and roared down the street. El Gordo pulled his automatic, loading the breech with a ka-chunk. One-Eye and Tomas did the same.

The Fat Man looked at his men. "We hit 'em, block 'em," he said, "and we jump out and shoot everyone. *Except* the kid. You don't shoot near him, I don't care if someone is using him for cover. You die first before you put the kid in any danger."

Tomas clicked the safety off with a small snap. "You hearing me?" the Fat Man snarled at him.

"Sure," the stylish killer said with a grin, "but we're okay even if he gets wounded, right? I mean, he can heal others, he can sure as hell heal himself."

"You as much as nick him," El Gordo said, barring his teeth, "I'll kill you."

Tomas' smile slipped away.

El Gordo lifted his phone. "I'm gonna send a little message to Frodo. Fuck with his head." Now it was his turn to smile. Making a crippled loser like Frodo suffer made him happy.

CHAPTER
58

In the Lexus, Frodo felt his phone vibrate. Now what? Gordo had tried to call him and he blocked his number. He shouldn't be able to reach him. He pulled his device, glancing at it.

Crazy looked at him in the back seat. "The fat fuck again?"

"He's messaging me," Frodo said, checking his phone. The words he read made his blood run cold. "You wanna know who got your legs broke?" it said. What could the Fat Man tell him about his broken legs? He'd ordered it done, 'cause he thought Frodo shorted him on the haul from a burglary. A stupid ring that had disappeared from the loot when it had been dumped on his desk.

He turned his phone off and slid it back into his pocket. Fuck El Gordo, he'd never talk to him again. But then it started working on him, sucking him back into the past. The Fat Man had spotted a target to hit, a big mansion, he had gotten the floorplan, the security, even where the safe was. This was when Adan had first started working for him, and they were doing high-end burglaries. They'd made a haul all right, bonds, legal papers, and a lot of jewelry. Jewelry that sparkled with diamonds and stones Frodo didn't know set in shiny gold.

They'd dumped the haul on the Fat Man's desk in the used car lot he kept as a front. It was late at night. He had his office there. One particular ring had popped out; a blue sapphire, set in platinum. It had sparkled in the overhead light in the office, but people stopped oohing and awing when Gordo finished his count. He had given them their share in cash, and they'd stepped outside, heading for their car amid all the wrecks for sale. That's when Gordo and his favorite thugs, Tomas and One-Eye, had come for them, yelling that Frodo had copped the sapphire ring. He'd run, thinking he'd lost them among the cars and the dark. He'd started for the fence to join Adan and the others when a car had roared out of the darkness. He'd tried to jump aside, but smashed into one of the parked cars and fallen back, right into the path of the car. It ran over both of his legs, Tomas inside, hooting his joy at running him down.

Frodo snapped back into real time as he caught a black SUV roaring out of nowhere, directly for the side of their car. Whap, before he could react it smashed into their front wheel on Samosa's side. It knocked the Lexus to the right, Frodo with it, all thoughts of his busted legs gone. It scraped the Lexus along the side of a parked car and ground it to a halt. El Gordo and his two men were jumping out of their SUV, firing their guns as they came. Frodo saw a guy with greasy hair duck out of sight inside the SUV. Bullets went wild, shattering the Lexus's windows.

Adan screamed at Samosa, "Go, go!" as he and Crazy pulled their pistols and fired back. There wasn't time to aim and bullets whizzed by on both sides. The Lexus was punctured in multiple places, windows shattering, slugs puncturing the metallic sides and whizzing like maddened wasps. Magda screamed and pulled the boy down on the back seat, covering him with her body. Frodo had his pistol out and fired over Crazy's shoulder as Samosa stomped the gas.

The wheels grabbed for purchase, scraping along the side of the parked car they were shoved against. Screechhhh! The gunfire kept up, bullet holes pocking the doors on the driver's side. The Lexus slammed into the nose of Gordo's black SUV, forcing the shooters to duck out of the way. They continued to fire, but they hadn't had

Book 3: THE SECOND DAY

time to aim yet. The Lexus, dented and torn, broke free and leaped down the street, One-Eye firing after them.

El Gordo shouted at them. "Into the car."

One-Eye was the first one in, throwing the black SUV into gear as El Gordo and Tomas jumped in the back. They started forward only to hear a terrible ripping noise on the front side of their car. One-Eye jammed on the brakes, and jumped out, looking at the front of the SUV.

El Gordo shoved his head out the back window. "What the hell's wrong?"

"The fender is bent. It's scraping the wheel," One-Eye said. Tomas got out and crossed around the front of the car.

"Well, get it straightened out," El Gordo barked. The kid had gotten away. He climbed back into the damaged SUV and looked at the greasy haired tech guy in the front. He was just pulling himself off the floorboards. "Tell me where they went," he ordered.

"Trying," the guy said shakily. He was ghost white and looked like he'd throw up if he had the time. He didn't. He was working his laptop again.

El Gordo watched him in disgust as he tried to figure out whether or not he should tell Zio Benito what had happened. The old man was already on his way with ten million. What the fuck, he decided, and pulled his cell.

"Yeah?" Aslanian said on the other end. El Gordo was beginning to hate the killer's voice. Always smooth, almost placid, no matter how bad things were.

"Zio," the Fat Man said.

Zio came on the line a moment later. "Speak," he said in his breathy voice.

"I lost him again. Lots of gunfire, but none of us hurt."

"Too bad," Zio growled. "Where are you?"

El Gordo looked at the greasy kid. "They want to know where we are."

"Got it," the tech said, tapping keys. "Sending it on."

"You should have it any second," El Gordo said into his phone.

There was a dead space on the other side and then Zio came back on. "We're only an hour away. Go after them and we'll follow."

El Gordo swallowed. He didn't know Zio was personally coming after them. It told him how incredibly important the kid must be. But he already knew that. "Mary's Landing," he said into the phone. "They're headed for the same store as us in Mary's Landing."

"You sure?" the old man's breathy voice said.

"Who's sure of anything, but it makes sense. You want a shot at having the kid, meet us there." Gordo clicked off. He looked at the tech as his guys climbed back into the SUV. "You failed, you stupid fuck," he yelled at him. "We didn't get the kid."

With that the Fat Man shoved the barrel of his pistol against the back of the seat, and pulled the trigger. There was a muffled bang and the greasy-haired guy stiffened and sank back to the floor.

"Fucking failure," Gordo growled to Tomas next to him, and slid the pistol back into his pocket. He hated people who didn't do their job right. One-Eye leaned over, opened the door, and kicked the greasy dude out, careful to avoid the blood on the floor.

Gordo smiled. The balance he liked, him on top and in control, was coming back. One-Eye hit the gas and they roared down the street.

CHAPTER 59

It was early afternoon, time to get moving. Whitney rose from her desk in her bedroom, picking up her backpack. She had her laptop and other devices inside, including her spare cash and one credit card. It was good, she'd just used it. She'd begged it off her dad so she could pay for sports stuff for soccer. She felt guilty, but she knew what she was doing was more important. She just didn't know how to tell him or her mom.

She could stay in touch with what was happening on her cell as she drove to Willy's truck stop. If she got there early, she could watch the coughing sickness continue to spread on the laptop. It had slowed down, but it hadn't completely stopped a second time. All air travel was shut down, and borders were closed tight. The Army had been called out in every country that had one. Wherever the sickness hit, the country ground to a halt. Great Britain was frozen by the outbreak at Heathrow. It had stopped there, but it had appeared in Iran and Afghanistan. Small outbreaks, but harbingers of things to come. Nobody knew how it got there. Martial law had been declared in the most vulnerable countries. Border crossers and refugees were being shot on sight.

All the news did for Whitney was raise her already incipient panic. The importance of being at that truck stop at the appointed hour was growing in her mind. She didn't know how they were connected, the boy and the sickness, but she knew in her heart they were. She also knew she had something to do with it; she even had an appointed hour.

213

Eight tonight. Now if she could just take the car without arising her mother's suspicions. She headed downstairs.

She entered the kitchen and stopped. Her mother wasn't there. Her brother looked up from the table where he sat, playing on his screen as he bit into a shiny red Macintosh apple. "She got a call from Molly," he said, referring to Molly Hascomb, who was Helena's best friend. "Her dog ate a sock and was throwing up. She needed someone to drive them to the vet."

Whitley whirled, looking out the kitchen window. Their car was gone. "Oh, shit," she said and hurried out the back door, her pack thrown over her shoulder. She stood in the drive, looking toward the street. Empty, no car or anything.

Her only chance of a ride was gone. She looked at her brother who had followed her, stricken. "What am I gonna do? I have to be at Willy's by eight tonight."

"You got plenty of time," Donny said, only to be distracted by his device. He frowned. "The sickness is popping up again. You think maybe your being there can stop it?"

"I don't know, but I do know it's bad if I don't make it in time. Maybe very bad." She paused, wet her lips. "You been following what's been happening with the boy?"

"Yeah," he said with a nod. "They've left Phoenix. They're headed in this direction. Leaving a bunch of dead bodies behind them. Not exactly kid stuff, and we're kids." She didn't say anything, just stared at him, her pack thrown over a shoulder. "Jimmy Newsome's family went up to Denver to see relatives," he added with a shrug. "The house is empty."

"Great," Whitney said with a frown. "What's that have to do with us?"

"Mister Newsome asked me to start his car a couple of time while he was gone. Just to make sure the battery stayed good." He

214

held up a pair of car keys, dangling them in front of her. She smiled. "I'm coming," he said, smiling back.

"No, you're not," she said, her smile gone, and took a step forward, grabbing for the keys...only to find herself grabbing at nothing. Donny was gone. She looked around. How could he disappear like that? What the hell was happening? She called out. "Donny, where are you?" She heard the front door bang open. She whirled and dived back inside, racing through the house to the entry before she skidded to a halt. She saw her mother dead on the floor, the front door open. In stunned silence, Whitney moved past her, stepping outside.

It was worse out there. Her father and brother were dead on the sidewalk, cars crashed, neighbors who had been taking a walk felled, their pets, too. A few people were still coughing, in the last seizure of the sickness before they dropped.

Unable to take any more of it, Whitney spun about and dived back into the house.

"Where are you?" came her brother's voice and she looked up to find herself back in the driveway, outside the back door, with him dangling the car keys in front of her. "You want to go or not?"

She numbly nodded. Why not? He was dead if she left him here and he was dead if he came with her to the truck stop. What did it mean? Could she save her brother? Her parents? What was the boy doing to her and why, why her?

Oh, God, please, someone, tell her.

CHAPTER 60

"They know the car," Samosa said as they sped down the street in their trashed Lexus. He wanted out of the burbs and into the desert, but he didn't want to do it in a hot car with the side windows shot out and one side with half the paint scrapped off.

"Fucking phones," Frodo said, "he knows all our numbers." He felt like throwing his cell out the shattered window. He never wanted to hear from El Gordo again, not with his poisonous messages. He knew he was being mind-fucked, but he also knew he couldn't do without his line to the flow of information. He had to have his screen. Too much was going on, and it was speeding up.

Frodo looked over at Crazy. He was slumped against the door, on the other side of Magda, and hadn't moved. "The fat fuck call you yet?" he asked. "He knows your numbers, don't he?"

The black gangster glanced at him. There was soft dreamy smile on his face. He raised his cell phone, but didn't seem to have the strength to say anything. For the first time, Frodo noticed Crazy was holding his side, red dampening around his fingers. Magda saw it, too.

"Oh, shit," she said. "You're hit." She leaned forward, pulling his hand aside to see the bullet hole there. It was pumping blood with every breath he took. "You're wounded again. In the same place." There was horror in her voice.

Adan looked back from the front. "Damn it," he said, "there were so many bullets flying it's lucky we're not all dead." He shifted his gaze to the boy. "Do it, kid, one more time."

The boy didn't move, sitting in between Magda and the wounded man. As always, he was staring ahead with that same blank stare. "Come on," Magda said. "Touch him like you did before." The boy didn't move.

Adan frowned. "He's strong enough to do it, isn't he? He looks okay."

Crazy blinked, trying to focus on the boy with the last of his flagging energy. "What do you say, kid? One more for old times' sake?" The kid didn't react. Crazy poked him with a bloodstained finger. "Hey, you hear me? Can you do it?" He looked up at Magda. "It really ate into him the last time. Maybe he's run out."

"He can do it," Magda said as she took the boy's hand and placed it on Crazy's bloody side. "Come on," she said, "it's in the same place." Nothing happened, no bluish light passing from him to the black dope dealer.

Then it began.

The boy slowly turned his head, looking at Crazy. His gaze lowered to the wound, his hand laying on it. The boy slowly pressed down. Crazy stiffened, watching him. They all did. You could see the power growing in him, as though he was gathering it inside. At the same time his face began to change. It thinned, it lengthened, as if he was being drained of weight; as though gravity was dragging it down.

"Oh, God," said Frodo in horror. "Look at his body."

They all stared, shocked and terrified. The boy was turning into a living skeleton in front of them, a starving child, so skinny he looked as if he would collapse at any moment and fall into a heap of bones and a few gibbets of flesh.

Crazy stared at him, watching the boy dying trying to help him, only to have a flash of sunlight momentarily blind him. When it cleared, he was staring at the notch. He instantly knew what it was from the descriptions he'd heard from the others. He saw the sun

218

Book 3: THE SECOND DAY

rising, pouring through the break in between the mesa and the jagged spire of stone, blinding him.

He blinked, clearing his vision to find himself back in the car, the boy's hand pressed against his bleeding side. But even as he did so, the boy's head sagged farther forward on his frail chest, his eye flickering. Right behind him, Meemaw Callie leaned in, looking over the boy's shoulder at her grandson. "I raised you better than this," she said to Crazy. "I raised you to do right. You ain't done much of that. Now's the time to do it."

Crazy looked up her, his eyes widening in shock. "Meemaw," he whispered through dry cracked lips. "You came to help me, just like always."

"Who?" Magda said, her eyes sweeping the others. "Who's he talking about?"

"Grandma," Frodo said, "I think he's talking to his grandmother."

"There's nobody there," Adan said, looking into the back at Magda and Frodo, the boy leaning into Crazy who was pressed against the bullet-pocked door with the shattered windows.

"There was nobody there with any of you either," Samosa, his eyes widening behind the wheel. He knew something was happening. Shit, something special had been happening ever since they'd almost run down the kid.

Crazy looked up at Meemaw Callie. "Do what's right," she whispered. "Make me proud of you." Her image flickered and faded, but she left something behind; a flood of conviction, suffusing his body, touching his heart. He felt like he had to do something good, maybe for the first time in his life.

"No, no more," he gasped, knowing he had to do it. He hoped Meemaw Callie knew it, too, even if she was gone. "He's not killing himself for me," he said and with his last rush of strength, he pushed the kid away, breaking physical contact with him.

Magda gathered the boy, holding him close, horrified as she felt his starved body. "He's nothing but skin and bone."

"Shit, man," Frodo said, looking at Crazy. The blood that had slowed now slicked his side again. "You're dying."

"Yeah? So?" The dope dealer nodded at the kid. "He's gotta get someplace." He looked at Adan and the others. "You gotta get him home, back to that notch."

Adan looked back at him. "You saw it? You had a vision of it, too?"

Crazy laughed a little. "Yeah, promise me, all of you," he asked as the last of his life flowed out of him. "Get him back to the notch, for all our sakes…please, and I never said that before in my fucking life." His body went limp and his eyes froze and went empty.

CHAPTER
61

Adan and the others looked at the dead man, slumped in a corner of the back seat, Magda, holding the boy, and Frodo staring at him. Adan couldn't fucking believe it. The kid had tried to save him and almost killed himself doing it. Crazy hadn't wanted that. Cold stone, kill everybody in his way, Crazy Daisy had sacrificed himself and at the same time begged them to get the boy to the notch, no matter what.

Just the thought of it stunned Adan. What the hell had the kid done to him? Samosa slowed down, as though the car no longer had to speed into the desert. More like a slow funeral cortege.

Frodo slumped back in his seat, the dead body next to him. "We're fucked. The kid couldn't save him."

"He tried, he just didn't have enough of whatever it is left," Magda said, lowering her head, trying to recover. The boy slumped against her. He hadn't stirred. "He's passed out."

Frodo looked at the kid closely. "He's already looking better."

"Fuckin' Energizer Bunny, which is good," Adan said. "At least we can still sell him if he looks okay."

Magda's head snapped up, her eyes flashing. "What are you talking about? We're not selling him, not now, not ever. You heard what Crazy said. You gonna go back on a dying man's last wish?"

"The kid's touch didn't work this time. You think it will again?" Adan said, trying to dig his way out of what he'd said. "Crazy didn't have a choice. He knew he was dead anyway. He knew the

kid couldn't save him. He wasn't sacrificing himself. He was facing reality, accepting what he couldn't change. He was also seeing
something, his meemaw, what, his grandmother? He was delusional.
Who pays attention to people raving as they die? Nobody."

"The boy will come back once he's rested, but does he come back
as good?" Frodo said, starting to worry. "Will he be able to heal more
people or whatever it is that he does? Word gets out he failed, he'll
be worthless."

"Maybe it's better that way," Samosa said from behind the wheel.
"That happens, maybe El Gordo will leave us alone."

"No way," Adan said, suddenly getting a conscience; more of
one than he wanted anyway. "Kid's too famous. They'll be after him
till they get him, and if he doesn't work, if he doesn't heal people
anymore, they'll take him apart like a piñata, trying to figure out
why not." Adan turned forward. He knew he was right. The kid was
condemned no matter what happened now. But it didn't mean they
had to be.

"See, you can't sell him," Magda said from the back, giving his
shoulder a shove.

He didn't say anything. They had a dead body in the car and a
million dollar offer on the table. Those things were more pressing
than the health of the kid. At least for the moment.

CHAPTER 62

Lilli looked up from her desk in the office as she heard Mickey working outside in the arboretum. The pain wasn't bad today, just the stiffness in her arms. They were dead to her; she knew they were there, but they wouldn't do anything she asked them to. She couldn't lift them to shoulder height. With the lack of use, they were atrophying. Her entire body was wasting away, but she still had some strength left on her left side.

With some effort and the help of her cane, she hefted herself into her walker and stepped outside. Her right arm was tucked into her body like a claw and she listed to that side. The weakness continued in the leg she was dragging. Her entire body was freezing up as the ALS destroyed her nerves. Soon major organs like her lungs would begin to fail and she'd suffocate to death, unable to protest even her own death.

Mickey was out there in the sun, in the big parking space next to the grow houses. He was sticking small things in the ground. "What are you doing?" she asked.

"All the spy cameras I got covering our crop, I'm putting them around here," he said. "I'm going to put out whatever happens live."

"What are you talking about?" she said with a frown. She didn't like the idea of anybody seeing her ask the boy for help. If he showed up at all.

"People have a right to see. The boy either makes your body straight again or he doesn't," Mickey said, "but one way or the other, the world has the right to see what happens."

"You believe he's really coming?" He nodded. "Sent by God?" she asked, hardly able to believe her ears. Mickey believed in a lot of things, but a Higher Spirit wasn't one of them.

"More your department than mine, but maybe," he said, straightening up. "Maybe the devil sent him or he's from outer space, but this is bigger than us. Maybe bigger than the world."

She took a breath, gazing at him. A skinny middle-age man with a long, gray ponytail and a short spade beard. Silly looking, but she was proud of him. "What makes you so sure he's coming?"

"He wants to," Mickey said. "He's the one sending me these visions. He wants to be brought here. He's also told me something bad is coming."

"What's that?" she said stiffening. She could see how grave he suddenly was.

"I saw it out here, after he touched you," he said, nodding at the parking area, big enough for the truck and several cars. All part of the business of having a nursery. "There'd been a fight, it looked like. Several bodies and a wrecked SUV." He looked at her and brightened. "But you were all right. You were standing straight and healthy. I could see it in your face. You were healed."

"Well, well, that isn't so bad," she said smiling, having expected worse.

"Yeah," he nodded, his eyes growing softer, "but I was one of the bodies."

"Oh, God, no," she said, reaching out and grabbing his arm. She squeezed hard. He looked back, tears wetting his eyes. He couldn't imagine leaving her. He leaned in and gave her a long kiss.

CHAPTER 63

Samosa walked through the parking lot of the strip mall, a key fob in his hand, pressing it repeatedly, waiting to get a beep or flash of light. He had a whole bunch, stolen, and when he needed to jack a car he just tried one after the other. They needed a new car to replace the one that had turned into Crazy's hearse. Frodo moved with Samosa, slower and hobbling a bit, but under his own power.

"You remember the night Tomas ran over my legs?" the hobbling man said.

"Yeah," the big guy nodded. "What makes you bring it up now?"

"Gordo blamed me for stealing the ring, but I didn't do it."

"I know, you been saying that forever," Samosa said with a nod, still working the key fob. Where the hell was a car that matched? "What difference does it make now?"

"'Cause somebody else had it. Somebody else copped the ring and let me take the fall. Was it you?"

"What?" Samosa jerked to a halt, turning to stare at him. "How long we been together? Since we were kids, right? I ever steal from you? I ever dime you, snitch you, rat you out, fuck no."

"Okay, okay," Frodo said, holding up at his hand, as if to stop the onslaught. "But somebody ended up with that ring. If not you, then who?"

"How the hell should I know?" Samosa said, looking at him like he was outraged at just the suggestion.

225

"It isn't you," Frodo said with a frown. "I believe you. Which means it's either Adan or Magda."

"Why not one of Gordo's guys? Tomas or One-Eye hate us enough to try to lay it off on one of us."

Frodo shook his head. "No way they'd fuck with the Fat Man. Too scared of him."

"Why the hell you bringing this up now?" Samosa asked, shaking his head at his friend's craziness. "We need to be together, not fighting each other."

"I got reasons," Frodo said, taking one of the fobs from him and clicking it. A late model Caddy parked a few cars away started making sounds. Frodo smiled at the big guy. "Hey, looks like we got a new ride."

He headed for the car, Samosa about to follow when his phone beeped. He looked at it. It was a message from El Gordo. So he had the number of his phone, too. The text read: "A million for the boy, in cash—or I'll tell Frodo you took the ring."

Samosa stared at it, terrified. He knew he was huge and strong, everybody thought he was a human bulldozer, but Frodo was his best friend. He didn't want him to know he was responsible for his legs being crushed that night. He didn't want him to know he'd been lying to him for years.

Samosa felt the panic surging up in him, putting a sour taste in his mouth. What was he going to do? How could he stop El Gordo from ratting him out?

"Hey," Frodo yelled to him, startling him. "You coming?" He was sitting in the Caddy, the driver's side door open, looking back at him.

"Yeah, sure," Samosa said with a sick grin. He stuffed the phone back in his pocket and headed for his usual place behind the wheel. Fuck, he hated lying. He was terrible at it, but maybe the boy would give him a vision, tell him how to get out of it, but so far nothing.

Shit, no visions, just a shitload of guilt piling up.

CHAPTER
64

A government C-37 Gulfstream jet landed at the Luke Air Force Base outside Phoenix. It was small, for groups of ten or less, but quick. The door opened and Catherine Hurungzy and Morgan stepped out. They wore practical clothes, relaxed but ready for work. They slipped on dark glasses and descended the short stairs into the hot sun.

A white van awaited them. Mark Goodman stood there, a tall man in his forties with a solid build. He wore a light suit. All three of them looked indistinguishable, like they worked for the same employer, which they did: the Federal Government.

Catherine and Morgan stopped before Agent Goodman. "Not that you need this," she said and flashed her ID. Morgan did the same.

"I understand completely," Goodman said and showed his federal badge. "Mark Goodman, Homeland Security. The Executive Division thought we should have eyes on the ground here, and that's me. The boy seems to have drawn a lot of attention."

"Meaning what?" Morgan asked, cocking an eyebrow.

"Meaning a foreign government may have interest in him. I'm here to stop that if it proves true," Goodman said, his face hardening. "If the boy turns out to be the real deal, I'd think you'll find more agents here. A lot more."

Catherine and Morgan looked at him, neither liking what they were hearing. "The boy's changing everything isn't he?" she said, making a face. Morgan said nothing.

Goodman shrugged. "I'll stay in the background and report anything I find to you as well as back to Washington. In other words, total transparency about whatever I observe." He smiled tightly and opened the sliding door of the van.

"Do the locals know we're coming?" Morgan asked before getting inside.

"I've already established contact. They're at another crime scene that involved the boy right now. They're expecting us."

"You can tell us about it on the way," Catherine said and got into the van. Morgan followed. Inside, Catherine checked her device. She frowned.

"The sickness?" Morgan asked, sitting next to her.

"Still quiescent," she said. "Doctors in Hazmat suits have gone into Heathrow, autopsying right now, but no evidence of disease. The survivors are still confined, but healthy."

"That's impossible," Morgan said. "It kills everybody it touches and then stops? Like at the push of a button?"

"It's only been four hours since the tests began. I'm sure by tonight they will have ID'ed the microbe," Catherine said, trying to be positive. Too much pressure now. Keep everybody cool, especially herself.

"From your lips to God's ear," Morgan said.

"Media is gonna be all over this if the sickness doesn't start up again. Who, why, what was at fault?" Morgan said with a frown as Goodman climbed behind the wheel, closing the door behind him.

"The boy?" she said to Homeland Security agent. "I assume you've been accumulating info. Would you care to share?"

Goodman began talking as he fired the car and headed for the street. They both listened intently.

CHAPTER 65

Magda stood before a shopping mall, holding the boy by the hand. His looks had improved but he was still parece enfermo, as her mother would have said. She was in front of the parked Lexus, looking through the window into the back. She could see Crazy slumped there, his head to one side, his eyes closed. Adan had arranged his jacket under his head, as though he were asleep.

Adan and Samosa had agreed maybe he wouldn't be discovered for a while, maybe until night when the stores closed. Magda wasn't too sure. She turned as Adan emerged from a convenience store, a plastic bag swinging in his hand. He held it up as he came up to her.

"Something to drink and eat," he said.

"Great," she said and plucked out some turkey from a pouch and began eating. She looked around the parking lot. "Where's Samosa? He was supposed to boost a car by now."

"Probably can't find anything fast enough for him," Adan answered, looking for him.

Magda nodded at Crazy, in the back of the Lexus, cloaked in shadows. "We should say some words over him," she said.

"Why?" he said, looking at her quizzically. "He's dead."

"That's horrible, that you'd say that." She looked at him with a deep frown. "Did you see how he died? He understood the boy couldn't save him. He didn't want him to kill himself trying."

"So, what are you saying?"

229

"You ever know Crazy to think of anything but himself? He was all about money, power, and shooting people. Mierda, he wanted the kid for himself when this began. Remember how he tried to grab him at his place?"

"Yeah, so?" Adan looked away. He hated it when she got like this. She was Catholic, baptized in a church. He was surprised she wasn't rubbing her rosary beads by now. Only he didn't think she had any.

"He changed him," Magda said, her voice confused and yet a little awed. "The boy changed Crazy."

Before Adan could answer, Samosa pulled up in the Caddy, Frodo in the back. He leaned over, flipping open the passenger side door. "Get in," he said.

Adan opened the back. Magda pushed the boy inside with Frodo, following him. Adan climbed in the front, looking around as Samosa drove for the street. He thought about what she'd said about Crazy. Some of the same things he'd thought. Crazy had saved the boy. He could've kept fighting for his own life, but he decided the boy was more important. Why the fuck would he do that?

Maybe cause he wanted to go out as the good guy? But Adan didn't believe it. He was talking to his meemaw, whoever that was when he was slipping away. Could that have something to do with it? Shit, he was hallucinating. He didn't know who he was talking to. He was raving. Adan shook his head. He didn't know what he believed anymore.

CHAPTER 66

Whitney backed the new Acura into the street, reversed direction, and took off. She drove with the studied intensity of the new driver, her hands grasping the wheel a bit too tightly, sitting up too straight in the seat.

Donny tried to settle down next to her as she drove through town, heading for the highway. "You have any idea what we're gonna do when we get to the truck stop?" he asked.

"No, but the boy is going to be there, I'm sure of that. I don't know who's going to be with him."

"Why you and not me? How do you know all this and I don't?"

"'Cause he touched me. He didn't touch you. Maybe you're not included. You were dead back in the house, you and Mom and Dad."

"I know," he said unhappily, "You already told me."

She nodded. "I think maybe the vision was telling me you were going to die anyway if I left you home, so it was better if I took you. It was like if we don't stop the sickness, it's gonna take out our home town, as well as a lot of the world. Maybe all of it. Certainly Mom and Dad and maybe you."

"It's getting dangerous being around the kid," Donny said with a frown. "I thought he was like autistic or had ADD, but that's not what the news is saying. People are ending up dead cause of him. Those dope dealers. They may have him right now."

He looked out the window as they left the town behind and headed into the desert. "I got a question for you. Why you, why us?

Tom Holland   The **NOTCH**

How did we get involved in this? What was he doing walking in the middle of nowhere as we came past?"

"Maybe it could've been anybody, but it was us," she said as they turned on to the highway. Now it was a straight shot of long miles of desert to the truck stop. There were no turn-offs, or at least none they'd be taking. "More than that," she continued. "I think we're like signposts or places along the way. We're meant to get him to where we found him, but that isn't where he came from. We're supposed to get him closer to home, I'm sure of that."

He looked at her, his eyes getting a little wide. "What are you talking about? He's like E.T.? Is that what you're saying? Going home?"

"I don't know, but somehow that's our job. That's what we're meant to do. Me anyway. I also don't think we're very important in all of this. Whether or not we die doesn't make much difference."

She blinked and was no longer driving the car. She was standing in the desert. She was staring at the long tabletop mesa with the end crumbling, leaving a long sliver of rock rising into the air. It created a notch between the two, like a huge V. The sun was blazing through as it rose. It was awesome.

"Look out," Donny yelled in her ear as the car veered off the road, jerking her back into the present. He grabbed the wheel, straightening the car out.

She took hold of the wheel, steadying it. "I'm sorry." She was shaken.

"What happened to you?" her brother asked, looking at her like she was going to drive them off the road again at any second.

"I...I had another vision," she said.

"Of what?"

"Where we're supposed to get him, I think," she said with a smile. "I've seen it before. A notch in the desert, with sunlight flooding through it." A warmth was gathering in her. She knew what to do now. It made her feel so much better. If her brother didn't get killed doing it, that is.

CHAPTER
67

Det. Wilson peered through the open back door of the Lexus, looking at Crazy in the back. The corpse looked asleep, but his side was crusted with dried blood. A tech with plastic gloves and white apron was doing a scan of his wound with an instrument that looked like a huge camera. The shirt had been pulled back, revealing the bullet hole.

State of the art tech. It shot out a purple light and took images of whatever was revealed, mainly blood splats.

The detective stepped back. CSI were climbing over the car, taking snaps and video, brushing powder into cellophane envelopes. Several of them were new, people he hadn't seen before with different looking equipment; more sophisticated, more digital, more expensive and connected, feeding back into a laptop.

"Who are they?" Noel Getty said, stepping up to him.

Wilson shook his head. "Feds, that's for sure." He nodded at several men wearing dark suits and short haircuts. They all looked the same and worked with a smooth efficiency.

Sgt. Getty nodded, and started to play with her phone as a white-colored van pulled up behind them. Agent Goodman got out. Wilson could tell from the way he carried himself that he was a practiced fighter. He had a sleek blond woman, early fifties, and a man with him, forties, smallish and closely shaven.

Goodman set off a small tripwire in Det. Wilson's brain: Homeland Security. The kid was attracting all kinds of attention. Important attention. He nodded as they came up.

"Agent Goodman, Homeland," the man said, flashing his ID that hung around his neck. "You know we were coming?"

"Mayor's office called," Det. Wilson replied. "We're to give you whatever you need."

"Good," the agent said with a tight smile.

Det. Wilson pressed his lips together, looking up as Catherine and Morgan stopped before him. The blond woman met the cop's openly curious gaze. He saw cold eyes, calculating and ruthless, but also highly intelligent. He'd seen them before, but only when he was dealing with the guys who ran the Mexican cartels or some big politician. The man, Morgan, looked like he belonged lecturing in some college.

"You're Detective Wilson, our Phoenix PD liaison?" she said.

"Chief Investigator actually," Det. Wilson said. "Until you showed up." He indicated the tired looking woman standing next to him. "Sgt. Noel Getty works with me."

"We'll be along with you from here on in," Catherine said, flashing him her ID. He didn't have much chance to inspect it, but it was NSA. She outranked him by a lot. He figured maybe the governor of the state took orders from her. It was in her bearing. "This is a federal emergency," she continued, "we're just not declaring it. Not yet anyway."

"May I ask why?" Det. Wilson replied, his voice dry. Getty was listening hard.

"I'm sure you've already figured it out," Morgan said, looking at the dead Crazy in the back of the car. He pulled a device out of his pocket, swiped at it with a thumb which connected it to the on-site computer. He looked at images and data. "Look at this." He passed the device to Catherine.

She stared at it, licking her lips. She looked up at Wilson and his partner. "You want to know why we're here? This is why." She passed the device to the cop.

Book 3: THE SECOND DAY

Wilson looked down at the image on the screen. Sgt. Getty leaned in to study it. It showed Crazy's corpse, limned in green, with a purplish color over the wounds. It was shaped in a clear handprint, not just one, but two of them, one slightly offset against the other.

"Is that what I think it is?" Getty asked. Her eyebrows went up. She couldn't believe what she was seeing.

"His wound," Catherine said and nodded at Crazy, slumped in the back of the Lexus. "That's where the boy touched him. He tried to save him, twice from the look of it. It just didn't work."

"What the hell is going on?" Det. Wilson said. He and his department hated the FBI not to mention Homeland Security buzzing around them, but this was different. The woman had a graveness to her. He realized it was underlined by desperation.

She stepped in to him and Sgt. Getty and lowered her voice. "I normally wouldn't tell any of you anything." She glanced at Goodman, her Homeland Security spy. "Not even you, but there's something going on here and there's no time."

"The coughing sickness?" Det. Wilson guessed, the thought popping into his head. He didn't know why. "I thought it was stopped?"

She shook her head. "Momentarily, but we don't know why it stopped. It's unnatural. It just didn't burn out. That's fake news, to dampen panic in the public. It literally stopped in the London airport with almost a third of the people there dead. There were people in the near vicinity of those coughing and dying when it stopped. They weren't infected."

"That's impossible if it's airborne," Det. Wilson said. "Isn't it?"

"As far as we know," Catherine said with a nod. "It was as though someone gave a command, or drew a line, but infectious airborne diseases don't demarcate who they're going to kill and who they're going to let live, not when it's been wiping out everyone indiscriminately. There is no scientific explanation."

"We don't understand," Sgt. Getty said with a frown.

"Neither do we," Morgan chimed in, grim-faced.

"The kid is part of this?" Det. Wilson said, his eyebrows going up. "How does a kid doing healings tie in with the coughing sickness?"

Sgt. Noel Getty stood there, listening harder than ever. She wanted to know, too. Her hand went instinctively to what was left of her breast where the cancer had so recently come back.

"We don't know if there is a connection," Morgan said, speaking through his white teeth. "But when he starts leaving his handprint on people, well, yeah, we're dealing with something pretty special. The intersection of unexplained phenomena, so to speak. The coughing sickness and the boy."

"We need all surveillance video you have," Catherine said, looking at the stores lining the strip mall. She figured all of them had cameras. Everybody did today. It was the only way to protect yourself. "All eyewitness reports. Keep interviewing. Any details you can squeeze out would help. We'll start reviewing all of it right now."

They all turned as the coroner's assistants carefully bagged the body and lifted it out of the vehicle and onto a gurney. "Get that dog he touched, the baby, too," Catherine said to Morgan. "Take over a ward of the best equipped hospital in Phoenix, the contagion ward if they have one. I want to know if there's been any change in the animal. I mean any."

"If you don't mind," Goodman said, stepping forward. "I think it would be better if I stayed here with the two officers. The agency would very much like to be involved in finding the boy."

Catherine met his gaze and nodded without hesitation. "Yes, of course." She looked at the two cops. "Special Agent Goodman is going to stay with you. You three will be our eyes on the ground. Report everything to me and Mr. Morgan. We're going to set up a command center at…" She glanced at info on her device and then back at them. "The St. Luke's Medical Center. If you need

Book 3: THE SECOND DAY

anything, and I mean anything to track the boy down—and keep him safe—just let us know. You have the full support of the Federal Government and all its resources."

Det. Wilson and Sgt. Getty stared after them as they moved away. Wilson looked at Goodman. "Seems like you're our new partner. Mind telling me what's going on?"

"I think Dr. Hurungzy just did a pretty good job. Nobody knows if the boy is real or not, or if he has any connection to the sickness—but nobody wants it screwed up. Especially not the Federal Government. Not with millions of people already dead." He gave the tight smile again, the two cops trying to figure it out.

CHAPTER
68

"**S**o, what happened to that ring I was supposed to have stolen?" Frodo said as Samosa drove them down the highway, headed for Mary's Landing.

Adan looked up from the back, the boy between him and Magda. "Who the hell cares? That happened years ago."

"Only three," Frodo said. "September 18th, 1:20 AM. See, it's branded in my brain. That happens when your legs are crushed and you're put in a wheelchair for those three years. Just struggling to get up to take a leak burns it in your brain."

"You can walk now," Magda said, looking up at him. "You should let the past go. Everybody says so."

"Yeah?" Frodo answered. "Well, they don't have a past like me. I didn't steal that fucking ring."

"Meaning what?" Adan asked. His eyes were squeezing shut. He didn't like the past being dug up, especially a past that could split them apart, not with all the shit going on with the kid.

"Well, if I didn't do it, then one of you must have," Frodo said. "Somebody dimed me, don't you think?" He turned in his seat so he could see each one of them.

"Well, don't look at me," Magda said. "I didn't take the stupid ring."

"Me either," Adan said. "Which leaves Samosa, but he's too dumb. 'Sides, he's the closest thing you got for an amigo, so that leaves one of Gordo's guys. Maybe even the Fat Man himself, so he'd have a chance to fuck us up."

"It wasn't one of you that got their legs mangled, it was me," Frodo said, turning back to the front. "It wasn't Gordo setting me up either, stealing his own ring. It was one of you. I hope whoever it is has the guts to tell me. You owe it to me. I was the one who lived in constant pain and couldn't walk for three years."

Samosa drove on in silence. No one else said anything, but the big guy was thinking furiously. Frodo was going to keep after it, trying to find out who had copped the ring. Eventually it would get back to him. He wasn't smart enough to lie smoothly, not if Frodo started pushing, asking questions rapid fire, like why he had done it.

They had stood there around the desk in the office that night, the Fat Man divvying up the loot. He had spotted the mansion for them, even gave them the location of the safe. Adan had drilled it quickly and easily. His hands were good, sensitive, always had been. They found some legal papers inside, a manila envelope with some money, thirty grand to be exact, and the real score: jewelry for the old lady, whoever she was. Among the jewels had been one particular ring that really caught Samosa's eye.

It was blue set in gold, maybe a sapphire, he didn't know, but it was pretty enough to melt any girl's heart.

He was seeing a pole dancer at the time and knew she would be hot for him forever if he gave it to her, so he had palmed it off the Fat Man's desk, never thinking that he'd notice it gone. There was a shitload of sparkly diamonds; the ring wasn't even that valuable.

But El Gordo had noticed it had disappeared and sent his guys after them as they were leaving. He was sure Frodo was the thief, because in his clumsiness he had knocked the jewels off the desk and when they were gathered up, the ring was missing.

Samosa had it. But El Gordo blamed Frodo, thought that his clumsiness had been a feint to grab the ring. But it wasn't. It was

Book 3: THE SECOND DAY

him, Samosa, the big dummy with the hard dick who had taken his chance and slipped it into a pant leg cuff. All so he could get laid. Because of that his best friend Frodo's legs had been crushed, broken, and twisted and he would never forgive himself, 'cause he knew deep inside he was the guilty one.

He loved Frodo, loved him to death, loved him in a way he couldn't explain and would never admit, not even to himself. He was hot to bang the pole dancer with the big floppy fake breasts but his true love was for Frodo, who had saved him from himself when nobody else gave a shit. He'd been heavy into coke, mixing it with meth, just so he'd have something to do, just so he could escape his shitty hopeless life and then Frodo had crashed with him, and it had stuck, the two of them as roommates. It was Frodo who told him what the shit he was smoking and snorting was doing to him, how his skin was turning bad, his teeth loose, and his hair falling out. It was Frodo, the funny little guy with the wispy beard, who made him clean up. It was that someone, even another guy, cared enough to try to save him from himself. He owed Frodo, and yet he had been the one who had gotten his legs broken and turned him into someone who couldn't move without a wheelchair.

He'd never forgive himself, but he could never cop to it. He was afraid of losing his best friend.

CHAPTER
69

Zio Benito sat in the back, being chauffeured out of the unending suburbs that seemed to surround Phoenix. When he'd first come here as a kid there had been a small downtown, a few hotels whose main business was providing rooms for western movies from Hollywood. Old stars like Errol Flynn, Roy Rogers, and Gabby Hayes, even John Wayne had made movies near here. There was an old western street, a standing set that was used for two decades if not more. Now they were all gone, like him almost.

Aslanian sat next to him, on his device as usual. Krekorian drove. At least he kept his eyes on the road. There was a rack of shiny oxygen canisters behind, in case he ran short, and ten million in the back well in canvas satchels. There was also a Porsche behind them with the Black Widow, the most dangerous and expensive assassin he knew of, and he knew a shitload of killers. She wore skintight black tights and a skeleton mask that covered her face from the nose down, but her skin tone and the shape of her eyes said she was Asian. She had her favorite helper with her, a Ninja she claimed. He looked the part, wearing loose fitting black clothes. Zio didn't know his name and didn't care. Not a lot of people in his crew, but all highly trained and easily able to handle the Fat Man and his bumbling thugs.

Aslanian turned to him, holding up his phone. "Just got a message from our people in City Hall. Say they've found an abandoned car with a body in Carefree."

"Good," Zio nodded. "Keep 'em busy as we go after the boy."

"Maybe not all so good," the hired gun said. "Says the Feds are already here, with more on the way. Major heat. From Washington, D.C."

Zio adjusted his nose clips. He had turned on one of his portable oxygen tanks and it was helping pump his frail lungs in and out. "Now, that's interesting," he said in between pants. "They've caught on to the boy, telling us he's really special. Even they can't figure him out." He paused, throwing a thin-lipped grin at Aslanian. "We got another buyer for the boy when we get our hands on him. Maybe with the deepest pockets in the world: Uncle fucking Sam himself."

CHAPTER 70

Samosa drove down the highway, speeding their way toward Mickey's Natural Produce and his dancing vegetables, going deeper and deeper into the desert.

In the back Frodo stirred as he felt his phone buzz. He pulled it from a shirt pocket and looked. It was El Gordo, the fat fuck who was trying to drive him nuts.

"Figure out who stole the ring yet?" the message read. "Santa mierda," Frodo muttered.

"What?" Samosa said from behind the wheel. They were gobbling up the miles, long gone from Phoenix now, deep into the desert which flowed by them on both sides.

"El Gordo, wanting to know how much we want for the boy," Frodo lied, but he couldn't help glancing again at the message again.

There was a grinning emoji, its tongue stuck out, like it was mocking him. Frodo hated it, but his mind was working overtime. One of his best friends had done him in that night at the used car lot. But which one? Why was it so important to him? He looked down at his pipe stem legs. Because it had destroyed him, made him helpless and kept him that way, until the boy came along. It ate at him.

He slipped the phone back into his pocket, looking at Magda. No time to be nice, not with El Gordo after them and closing. He was going to find out who sacrificed him that night so they could save their own skins. "So was it you or Adan?" he said to her.

"Was it me or Adan what?" she said with a frown. The boy sat in between, expressionless as always.

"Who took the ring?" Frodo snapped, his eyes flashing angrily. "El Gordo knows. He messaged me on the phone."

"What the fuck are you talking about?" Adan said, looking back from the front seat.

"He's saying it was one of you that nicked it that night when I knocked the stuff to the floor. Since it isn't Samosa, who is it, cause if you don't tell me I'm gonna make a deal with Gordo."

"Whoa," Samosa said from behind the wheel, giving Frodo a glance in the rear-view mirror. "Back off, man."

"There's no time to back off," Frodo shot back. "Don't any of you realize what's going on? Gordo's right behind us. We're leaving a string of dead bodies in our wake. You checked the news in the last few minutes? I have."

He held up his phone. Video was playing. "They found Crazy's body. They're talking about it now, so the cops are on our ass, too. How long can we run, especially with the kid?" He nodded at the boy who hadn't even blinked. "He's hotter than the coughing sickness."

"How's that doing?" Magda said, checking her cell. "Is it over?"

"How the fuck should I know. Now which one of you took the ring?"

"It wasn't me," Magda said, her face buried in her phone as she flicked through it.

"Me either," Adan said from the front.

Frodo's eyes glowed with anger. "Fuck you, fuck both of you. When I find out, I'm gonna make you pay. I swear I will."

"How?" Adan barked back. "You gonna turn the kid and us over to El Gordo? He'll kill us all. You know he will."

"I'll figure it out," Frodo said, his face dark, his mouth set.

Book 3: THE SECOND DAY

"Holy shit," Adan exploded. "We got enough people trying to kill us without fighting among ourselves. That's what El Gordo is doing to you. Trying to fuck up our heads. It's all about the boy. It ain't got shit to do with you or us."

A tense silence settled over the group. Magda broke it. "How far to this Mary's Landing?" she asked.

Samosa checked the map on his phone. "15, 20 minutes," he said, still trying to figure out what to do about the cursed ring he copped and his best friend, Frodo.

CHAPTER
71

Magda felt her phone vibrate. She copped a look at it. "I know where your little girl is," it read. "What is she now? Diez anos? Sí, yo creo que es diez." Her heat sunk deep into her stomach and she clicked the phone off, trying not to think about what she had just read.

But how could she not. Ten? Her baby was ten? Anger flashed through her. How had El Gordo known she had a ten-year old? Of course, he'd know, she answered herself. If anybody was plugged into the barrio it was El Gordo. She'd only been fifteen. Matias had been two years older. She hadn't wanted an abortion.

She was too good a Catholic for that, she worshiped the Virgin, and she'd told him. He answered that he loved her, and things were going well with the gang he ran with, the Maras, who were big into dope and he'd get rich and they'd get married. But she knew the Maras had big trouble with the Zetas. Different cartels. It worried Magda, but she kept her mouth shut.

But she still had to tell her mother about the baby growing inside her. Her older sister, Alba, already had a child and was living at home. It was Magda, her sister and baby, her kid brother, Santiago, and her mother in a small apartment with one bathroom. They lived on Social Services and the sometime money the fathers of the children gave them. One of them, her real father her mother insisted, worked as garage mechanic and was around off and on. He kicked in with some cash when he hadn't drunk it up on Friday night, when the eagle flew.

Tom Holland   The NOTCH

Of course, that wasn't the one her mother was crazy about. No, that would have been too simple. Mom had several boyfriends, and now her middle daughter Magda was with child. She'd complain, but she'd let her live there. But first Magda had to tell her. She'd never gotten to that point. When she was four months pregnant, a Crip had gunned Matias down. Put a bullet in his head from behind, and left him sprawled in a puddle of blood on the sidewalk.

All thoughts of having a happy little family, even if money was scarce, died with her love. There had been a stupid, thinly attended memorial at the place where he'd fallen. A few bouquets of limp flowers, ragged Teddy Bears, and some guttering cheap candles. There was nothing of him left, only a fading blood stain. She didn't know why, but his death lit a fire inside her.

She wanted vengeance with a thirst she had never expected in her 15 year-old self. She had made a deal with a member of Tre 5th, her pussy for the life of the Crip that had gunned down her lover. It had worked, the hombre was blasted in a drive-by shooting and the Tre 5th had partied with her body late into the night, as she wept tears and said silent prayers to Matias, asking his forgiveness even as she reveled in her vengeance. After that, she had gone to her grandmother's village in Mexico with her swollen belly and had the baby. She had left the child there with her. She sent money, but she hadn't seen her in almost three years now.

What the fuck was the Fat Man doing with her daughter? Sophia, she had called her, her Sophia. A stab of fear went through Magda. The Fat Man was threatening her daughter. He was telling her he knew where she was. That he would hurt her or worse, unless she gave up the boy.

She looked down at him, sitting in between her and Frodo, staring off into the distance, as if he didn't have a care in the world. He

Book 3: THE SECOND DAY

didn't either. Or at least it seemed like he didn't. Brain dead, like Adan said. But then how did she explain the visions?

It was all spinning bad, and she had the horrible feeling she couldn't control it anymore. Adan. He'd have to help her. She looked up at him in the front, his back to her. But how could he help her? Shit, he didn't want any kids, he'd let her know that, so they weren't going anywhere. Same with the rest of them. Frodo, Samosa, they were all on a ride to hell because of the boy who was there and wasn't.

Only one thing for sure. He wouldn't help her. He wasn't even aware she was there.

CHAPTER 72

Adan looked out the window as they sped through the desert. All his thoughts were on Mary's Landing and what they'd find there. It had something to do with a stupid grocery, Mickey's, like anybody still had a dumb name like that. He'd seen the place in a vision, but who could trust a stupid vision? Like being on drugs and he hated drugs. Made you stupid and got you killed. But looking out the window now, into the fading day, he knew he was heading somewhere important, really important, maybe for the first time in his life.

Because of the kid. Always the kid. His cell beeped. He checked the screen. "It's El Gordo," Magda said from the back.

"He's messing with all of us," Frodo said. He shifted his gaze to the big man driving. "What about you, Samosa, he reached out to you yet?"

"Sent some sort of message. I haven't checked it," Samosa lied. "Probably offering me a fortune if I stab all of you in the back."

"So that only leaves you," Frodo said to Adan. He nodded. "What's he want?"

Adan lifted his phone and checked the screen. "He called me," the dark-haired young man said.

"So call him back," Magda said with a shrug. "We're only a few miles from that grocery. He can't catch us before we get there."

Adan hit the button, lifting the phone to his ear. "Ah. So you called back," came the mocking, hard-edged voice. "Wanna know about your mom? It's her birthday, in case you forgot."

253

"I don't forget anything," Adan snarled. He hadn't talked to his mother in years. Not since he stabbed her drunk boyfriend, who was beating the shit out of her. She snitched him out to the cops, cursing him for sticking her pig of a boyfriend.

He had never talked to her again.

That was years ago. Adan wasn't big on forgiveness, so he wasn't moved. "I don't give a damn about her, in case you didn't know. So fuck off."

"Yeah, I figured," drawled the Fat Man, like he didn't care anymore than Adan did. "But it is her birthday. What do you say I give her a present? What do you say I shoot her in the belly and as she's screaming with pain, I tell her it was from you?"

Adan hesitated. He didn't care. The bitch could live or die for all he cared, but he didn't want her to be hurt because of him. Certainly not shot. Or worse. "Leave her alone," he said. "This is between you and me."

"Don't give a shit about your own mamma, do you?" the Fat Man said. "Ten million for the boy. Cash. For a touch."

Adan stiffened. "Where do you get that kind of money?"

"Zio Benito," the Fat Man said. "He's got it with him."

Adan licked his lips. Yeah, the old Mafioso would have that kind of money. He killed the connection without replying and blocked another call. He punched the keys too hard in a fit of anger and fear. Fear for whom? His mother, himself, those he cared about, Magda?

"What's wrong?" she asked, leaning forward from the back.

"Nothing," Adan growled and shoved the phone in his pocket.

"Sure doesn't look like nothing," Samosa said, cutting him a sideways glance as he drove.

"He's going after every one of us where we're weakest," Frodo said from his corner in the back. "He's gonna turn us against one another. He wants the kid, no matter what."

254

Book 3: THE SECOND DAY

"You have no idea," Adan said reluctantly, but knew he had to tell them. "He just upped the offer. Ten million for the boy to touch Zio Benito."

"The old Mafioso?" Frodo said with a lift of his eyebrows.

"One and the same," Adan said, glancing at the blank-faced boy in the back. "You hear that? We're all in deep shit because of you."

"We could all be filthy rich because of him, too," Magda said. The ten million number was still rattling around inside her head. It was a number she couldn't even imagine.

"What's the Fat Man got on you?" Adan said, peering more closely at his lover. Maybe she had sides he didn't know about.

"None of your business," she said, turning away.

"Same as Crazy," Adan thought. Whatever the Fat Man threatened her with, it must have gone deep. His gaze went to Frodo. "He got to you about your legs. What about you?" he looked at Samosa, waiting for an answer.

The big guy shrugged. "Just offering me crazy money like you, but not anything like ten million. More like a hundred grand, cheap bastard."

"Shit," Frodo said, leaning back. "It's all bullshit, him just fucking with us, making us weaker and weaker, so he can grab the kid. That's what the ten million is about, too. Lies, all lies."

"Let's not worry about it right now," Magda said, taking the boy's unresisting hand and holding it in her own. "We're almost to Mary's Landing. We'll learn more there."

Everybody shut up. What more was there to say? They sped through the silent desert, the shadows crawling across the barren landscape as the sun slowly sank.

CHAPTER 73

"More news about the boy," Donny said to his sister as they drove. He was staring at his device.

"I know. More dead people, right?" she said, keeping her eyes on the road. The sand flowing past was hypnotic. Made it easy to drift, so she kept her eyes fixed on the highway.

"This is different," he said. "It's another dead body turning up, this time in an abandoned car in Carefree. Police figure it was the black guy who was wounded in the shootout back in Phoenix."

"So he'd been shot in the escape. Maybe he just died."

"Maybe," Donny said, "but what I want to know is why the kid didn't save him. He was one of those guys trying to protect him, wasn't he?"

"We don't know," she said. "There's hardly anything we do know." She paused a moment. "I had another vision. This afternoon. I didn't tell you about it."

He looked at her with a frown. "Why not?"

"I didn't want you to think I was completely insane. I saw this notch in a mesa, like it was broken apart by some huge force. The rising sun was coming through it. It was beautiful."

"I never saw anything like that out here." Donny glanced out the window, into the distance to the side of the car. Dusk was creeping up. They'd been driving this way to visit their grandmother their entire lives. Tabletops and some crumbling mesas were all he ever saw in the flatness, but nothing like she described.

"I know," she said, referring to the notch. "I searched all over the web. It doesn't exist. Not in our state anyway."

"So what are you saying?" he asked.

"Like maybe it's where we're supposed to take the kid, only it doesn't really exist. What do we do then? You know, if getting the boy there is what we're supposed to do?"

He stared at her. He didn't have an answer either. In fact, he didn't know till just now that was their job. He pulled out his pen, a vaporizer, and took a hit. He told her it was scented nicotine to get her off his back, but it was hash oil, scented strawberry to hide the smell. Everybody in high school was doing it, except her. It was cool, which she definitely was not. As he expelled the smoke, his sister shot him a dirty look.

"Do you have to do that now?"

"Grab me," he said.

"What?" she said, darting him a look.

"Grab me. You have visions. I want to have them."

"There's nothing I can do about it. He touched me, not you. It's not my fault." She blinked, rubbing an eye. When she looked up she wasn't in the car anymore. She was at the truck stop. It was night and there was a burning SUV and people lying about, all of them dead, seemingly from gunshots. One of them was herself, laying on the blacktop, bleeding from multiple wounds.

"Oh, no, please, no," she thought, looking around at the death and destruction, only for her eyes to come to a stop. There, through the fire of a burning gas pump, stood the boy, staring at her. He wasn't just staring. His eyes were drilling into her.

"Oh, God," she whispered shocked at the horror of it.

"Oh, God, what?" Donny yelled in her ear and she blinked to find herself back in the car, behind the wheel. Her brother yanked it

Book 3: THE SECOND DAY

to one side. They narrowly missed an oncoming car in the blare of a passing horn before they straightened out.

She took the wheel back. "It's okay, I got it," she said shaken.

He looked at her, trying to stop his beating heart. "What the hell happened to you?"

"I had another vision," she said with a gulp, "and in this one everybody was dead, including me."

"You saw yourself dead?"

"Yeah," she nodded. "We're both gonna die, we go to that truck stop."

"So why are we going?"

"I don't know," she said, more horrified than ever. "But we have to go. We just have to."

CHAPTER 74

"**S**o what did El Gordo have on you? What did he think would make you give the boy up?" Magda asked Adan, leaning forward, resting her chin on the back of the seat separating them. Samosa and Frodo were there, but they were occupied with their own thoughts. They weren't paying any attention to them.

"Nothing," he scowled, not looking at her.

"I'll tell you if you tell me," she said.

"He says he's gonna kill my mother," Adan said, giving up.

Magda shrugged. Adan had told her all about his mom. She destroyed him, and probably didn't even realize it. Or care. She and he had been together over a year. A lot gets shared in that time, good and bad. "You hate her anyway," she said.

"I told him, but I don't know if he believed me. Then again he just might do it for the hell of it." He cleared his throat. "What about you?"

"He says he knows where my daughter is. Mi abuela. Down in Guanajuato."

Adan set up, his lips pressing together. "If he so much as looks at her, I'll kill him."

"I'm afraid he might do it," Magda said. "Everybody knows I got a daughter down there. I send money all the time. Fat cabron can reach down there if he wants."

"You don't touch kids," Adan said and meant it. He knew money was first, but when you were a kid you were out of it, you didn't know what was going on. He hated people who fucked with kids.

"He's pushing us, you know," she said, nodding at the boy next to her. His face, as always, was passive. Ready perhaps, but not engaged. "He's directing us with his visions. Sometimes it's a little hard to figure out, but he wants us to go to Mary's Landing and from there to wherever that notch is."

"What about the ten million?"

"He doesn't want to make it easy for us," she said, sitting back and brushing the boy's hair off his forehead with her hand. He lay against her, his eyes wide and staring. "He wants us to be tempted."

Adan watched her. His eyes went to the boy and the number ten million popped into his head. Yeah, he was tempted all right. Big time.

CHAPTER 75

Adan sat in the front, staring out the window, alone with himself. Samosa drove, the others quiet. He was running the odds in his head. Crazy was dead. El Gordo was offering ten million green. He knew he had it. Zio Benito was behind him. For just a touch, one lousy touch from the kid.

Him and his crew, they'd been dragged into this because they decided to run a scam with an autistic kid. Only the dummy had turned out to be the kid in the news, the one who brought the dog back to life. Who knew? Certainly not them. It had been helped by the hysteria associated with the coughing sickness. The news was calming down now, at last, saying it had stopped spreading. As though something had happened to stop it. But what and who fucking believed the government?

He and the guys and Magda had just been using the kid, at first anyway, thinking he was brain damaged. But then he'd made Frodo walk and he'd gotten some of the energy when he'd been pressing down on the kid's hand when he passed whatever it was to Frodo. He got more when he shoved the kid's hand into El Gordo's jelly belly. They'd all started having the visions, whoever the kid touched. Why? Because they had gotten some of his power or whatever it was he carried? A charge, like electricity? Blue electricity.

But he didn't ask the kid to heal Frodo's leg, Adan told himself. He'd been running a scam. He wasn't for real, he'd been faking it. It meant he didn't owe the kid anything. The kid failed. That's why Gordo

263

had kicked them out of the bar. He'd almost shot him when the kid didn't manage to cure him right away. It was all the kid's fault, where they were right now. Only it wasn't. Adan knew that. He might not like what had happened, all the people shot up, the Fat Man chasing them, but it wasn't really the kid's fault. It was theirs, for trying to use him.

Adan didn't like anybody telling him what to do, not even a magical kid. He wasn't reliable either. You never knew what was going to happen with him. Which was an argument to get rid of him. Only how the hell could he do that now? Sell him for the ten million and get the hell out of there, leave him with Zio Benito. The old man wasn't going to let anything happen to him, especially if his touch cured him of whatever was making him so desperate to get his grimy hands on the magical boy.

"You okay, baby?" Magda whispered in his ear. She had leaned forward, her head next to his.

"Yeah, fine," he lied. She brushed his ear with her lips, gave it a wet lick, and settled back into her seat next to the boy.

He went back to his own thoughts. Sell the boy and walk away, or sell just one touch, and maybe keep the boy. How to do that if he met with El Gordo and Zio Benito and still stay alive? After whatever happened in Mary's Landing, maybe he'd have a better sense of how to play all this. And survive. Especially survive. With all that wonderful ten million in cash.

CHAPTER 76

All the cameras were in place in the parking area outside. Everything was covered and now Lilli and Mickey sat in a swing he had back there, right next to the grow houses. They relaxed, waiting for the boy to show up. Mickey had a tablet set in between them on a table, so they could keep up with what the boy was doing.

It was showing coverage of the cops crawling all over the Lexus and the body inside. Nothing was private anymore. Or secret. Nothing. Crazy's body was just being rolled away on a gurney.

"Someone said the dead man owned that house where the first gunfight was," Lilli said, lifting an eyebrow. The right side of her face was weak and sagged, underlining the damage the ALS was doing, but he didn't mention it. Hell, it had been over a year. He hardly saw it anymore.

"Lot of shooting following them, isn't there?" Lilli said with a frown.

"I've been thinking about that," Mickey said and leaned forward, holding up a shotgun he had on the ground next to him. "I also have my pistol," he said, patting the gun holstered to his belt.

"I hope you don't have to use it," Lilli said. "But you can believe the people with him will be carrying. They know how to use them, too. There were eight dead people at that dope house and now another in a car. The boy's leaving a trail of death behind him. That's not the kind of thing a holy person does."

"Maybe he's not so holy," Mickey said, "but he's not bad either, that I'm sure of, and he can heal. That I'm sure of."

"I know he healed your hand, but what about him? Was he holy in any way? Did he make you feel like you were in the presence of something special?" she asked. His face had been shadowed on and off ever since he told her.

He nodded. "Yeah, he was sure special. Holy, I'm not sure about."

She nodded, but said nothing. There was nothing she could say, but wait and see what happened. If he really showed up, she was sure she could make up her own mind.

CHAPTER 77

Samosa blew past a sign: "Mary's Landing, 12 mi. ahead." The sun was sinking, darkness rushing at them. If he was going to tell Frodo about the sapphire ring, now was the time. He couldn't say why, but he had the feeling that he wouldn't leave this town. Not alive anyway. He didn't want to die with anything unsaid between them. They'd been through too much together. It had happened when Frodo's legs had been crushed. Samosa had taken care of him. It was the closest he'd been to anybody since his mother, and she had died when he was seven.

He looked at his friend in the rearview mirror. Frodo was slumped in the back, having finally given up on thumbing through his cell phone. His eyes were closed. The boy was next to him, not moving, just sitting there. Magda was by the window, staring out, lost in her own thoughts. Adan was the same, next to Samosa, looking out silently at the passing desert.

"I was the one who copped the ring," the big guy said, seemingly out of nowhere.

"What?" Frodo said, looking up with a jerk. His eyes narrowed, drilling into the back of his friend's head. "You told me you didn't know who did it."

"I lied," Samosa said, wishing he could close his eyes and go away, but he couldn't cause he was driving. He'd known this was coming and just hated it, but he had to do it.

"Why'd you lie?" Frodo barked. He was as freaked as Samosa.

Tom Holland   The NOTCH

Adan and Magda had come out of their doze, but they were just bystanders to what was going on. As for the kid, he just sat there, like always, there and gone at the same time.

"'Cause you're my best friend. You think I wanted you to know I was why your legs got crushed?"

"Why did you cop the stupid ring?" Frodo sputtered, trying to get his thoughts straight. He had been sure it was Adan, probably taking it for Magda.

"I...I...I had this pole dancer I liked," the big guy said, unable to meet his gaze in the rearview mirror.

"Oh, shit," Adan said, rolling his eyes. The reasons why people did things just kept getting dumber. "We gotta talk about this now?"

"What happens if Frodo or I get killed at this Mary's Landing?" Samosa said, cutting him an unhappy look. Why didn't he have a vision? The stupid kid had touched him at last. He kept hoping a vision would show him a way out of the pain he was causing Frodo.

"You don't know that," Magda said from the back. "The kid heals people, he doesn't kill them."

"Yeah," Frodo said, still shocked at the big guy copping to the truth, "tell that to Crazy. Do you think Gordo cares? The boy does what he wants or he kills him." He swallowed, looking at Samosa.

What difference did the ring and who took it make now? His legs were healed. The boy had done that. He should be thankful he could walk again, rather than seeking vengeance for something that had happened a few years ago. Ancient history. Especially from the guy who'd taken care of him like a baby after the car had run over him. He'd been ready to kill himself, had the gun, a .357, about to blow the few brains he had out of his head. Samosa had talked him out of it, him bawling like a baby all the time, begging him not to leave him alone. He hadn't killed himself because of the big

268

Book 3: THE SECOND DAY

dummy. He owed him even if he had been responsible for his legs being crushed.

Now the way they'd been was changed. Their relationship. Cleaned. Secrets exposed. Fuck, why not. All because of the sphinxlike kid.

He leaned forward, touching his friend's shoulder. "It's okay, man."

"Yeah, really?" Samosa said, glancing over his shoulder back at him. His eyes were wet. "You sure?"

"Yeah," Frodo said, moved for the first time in forever. "I'm sure." He was, too. He loved Samosa. He could never tell him, shit, it had taken him forever to admit it to himself, but he fucking loved him.

CHAPTER 78

A silence had settled over the backyard of the grocery. Lilli and Mickey still sat in their swing. He was monitoring the screen on the table. She didn't care. They were quietly holding hands. It gave her peace, but not enough.

"What are we going to do," she said, "if your vision was right? What if the boy saves me, but you don't make it out of here?"

Mickey didn't say anything, but he'd been wrestling with the same thought. "I don't know," he slowly replied. "I don't think of it as sacrificing myself for you. What I'm worried about is what you're going to do if I'm gone."

Lilli smiled, trying to be reassuring. "Just because you saw it doesn't mean it's gonna come true." She squeezed his hand. "What if I stay here, but you go wait in our house?" She looked toward the door next to the alley running to the street.

"I don't think I could do that," he said. "If I'm not here, I don't think the boy will save you. I think it's all part of some great plan that I can't understand. We're all caught up in something, not just us, but others, too. Maybe the entire world."

He turned looked down the alley, toward the front street. "I'm gonna turn the cameras on and tell the world what we're trying to do," he said, and hit a button. He looked into the lens of the closest camera as a green light on top flared to life and cleared his throat.

"Hi, there," he said, keeping his voice strong and clear. "I'm Mickey Meyers and this is my life companion, Lilli Dollans.

Tom Holland   The NOTCH

Yesterday I discovered a kid in the back of my pickup. No idea how he got there. He was just there. I didn't think there was anything special about him until he leaned over and touched me. I had a bad burn from the night before on my palm." He held his hand up, palm open to the camera. "As you can see, no burn." He took a breath.

"My wife has ALS. It's crippling and slowly killing her. I'm asking the boy to touch my wife and see if he can help her. We're waiting here, in back of my place, Mickey's Vegan Produce, in Mary's Landing. I can't guarantee the boy is coming, but that's what I believe." He swallowed and tried to smile.

"I'm putting this out live because I thought all of you out there might like to see it." He paused, thinking over his words. "It's about hope, and I hope this gives you some, just like the boy has given it to me and Lilli, regardless of what happens." His eyes grew moist and a single tear rolled down his seamed cheek. "God bless you all, and most of all I hope he blesses the boy, although I suspect he already has."

CHAPTER 79

A dan stared out the window as they drove into Mary's Landing. The sign read "Pop. 1380" as they whipped past. It was one long street with brick and cinderblock buildings. There were a few streets of sunburnt houses behind them. Twilight was falling, which hid their peeling paint, but not enough. The biggest building was an old post office. There was one empty storefront after another, and one theater that looked like it closed years ago. Its marquee advertised the weekly flea market.

There were three bars, Adan counted them as they passed, all lit with neon, like they were desperately trying to snag any drivers that passed.

"Is it like you saw in your vision?" Magda said with a glance at him.

"I didn't see the town, just the sign and an alley to the back," Adan said. His cell buzzed. He checked it. "It's El Gordo. Shit, he never stops."

"We got everybody on our ass," Magda said, tight-lipped. "It isn't about us. Everybody wants the kid."

She looked at Adan. He was checking out the stores to either side as they passed. Then he saw it: the sign he'd seen from his vision, "Mickey's Natural Produce," with dancing vegetables strung out behind it, pointing down the alley to the back.

"There," he said, pointing to it.

Samosa pulled off the street, ignoring the store in front, a dispensary with the green leaf and some bullshit about health, and drove through to the back. He pulled up in front of several greenhouses. A middle-aged man with a gray ponytail and a skinny woman sat on a metal swing, as if they had been waiting for them. She looked frail and unwell.

Adan didn't know much about growing vegetables, but he could see the work in it. It took skill to get good weed. He supposed the same was true for the stuff they ate.

"Just like what I saw," he said as he, Samosa and Frodo got out. Magda stayed inside the car, keeping the boy close, but she had her pistol out. She knew it wouldn't bother the boy. Nothing bothered him.

"You gonna shoot us?" the man said, getting to his feet.

Adan noticed a metal walker next to the woman. He relaxed slightly. "No, we're not gonna shoot you. We just wanna talk."

"I got a shotgun," Mickey said, motioning at the weapon laid on the ground, next to the swing.

"I can see that," Adan said, thinking the yahoo was lucky he hadn't been shot yet. Fool leaving the shotgun on the ground, when he should have had it in his hands. He nodded at the grow houses. "I've seen this place before. Inside my head, like a vision."

"You were touched by the boy, like me. Have to be," the man said. "I've had those too. Led you to us, didn't they?" He nodded at Lilli. "This is my significant other. Her choice, not mind. I've asked her to marry me more times than I can remember, but she won't."

Lilli rose, grasping the walker. She was thin and wan, her face washed out and lined. She was twisted toward her right side, her arm pulled in tight and useless. "Hello there," she said with the flicker of a smile. She moved forward a step with the walker, holding on with her left hand, balancing with her right. "We're recording this. It's going out live, or so Mickey says."

Book 3: THE SECOND DAY

"Why did you do that?" Adan said, stiffening. He and the others looked around, spotting the cameras set up all around them.

"We're doing it for the record, history, and maybe because of what will happen here," Mickey said, pulling himself up straighter. He nodded at the boy. "We know how special he is. At least I do. I'm the one who took him into the city where he brought that dog back to life. But we don't know what he is or what he wants."

He turned his head, looking into the nearest camera. "I wanted you all out there to see this happening. It's real. I'm real, me and Lilli, these other people." He nodded at Adan and his friends. "The boy's real, too. No matter what happens here, he's real."

Finished with the camera, he looked at Adan. "You've got the boy with you?" Mickey looked into their old Caddy. He was just able to see the top of the kid's head, with the pale blondish hair. He was sitting next to the good looking dark-haired girl in the back of the car.

Lilli smiled sheepishly. "I've never seen him before. Not in the flesh."

Adan called over his shoulder. "Magda, come on out with the kid. It's safe."

"What about the cameras?" Frodo asked, not liking being recorded.

Adan shrugged. "It's not like the whole world doesn't know about him or us, not since he saved the baby. Now we're part of him and this will give us some protection."

Magda swung the back door open and stepped out, bringing the boy with her. He stood there, holding her hand, staring directly ahead, narrow and loose with that thousand-mile stare.

"So that's him," Lilli said, wetting her lips, impressed in spite of herself, although she couldn't have said why. The boy was skinny and looked like the color had been drained out of him. His pale eyes were unfocused and disconnected, but he was comfortable in his own skin at the same time. You could see it in the way he stood there, like he was waiting for something and whatever it was didn't bother him. "Has he really been doing the things they say?"

"He made Frodo walk again," Samosa said, nodding at the smallest of the guys in the group. He had a wispy beard, but held a small bore pistol. "He saved the baby, suppose you saw that, and Crazy, this guy that was with us," Samosa didn't mention that the kid had been helpless to save him the second time the dope dealer was shot.

"How do you think he does it?" Mickey asked, staring at the boy. He held up his hand. "I'd burned my palm. He touched me and it healed right away."

"We don't know," Magda said. "He's touched all of us here." Her eyes went to Adan, Frodo, and stopped on Samosa. "Except Samosa. He hadn't touched him. Big guy feels left out. He gave us all these different visions."

"I saw your store in one of them," Adan said.

"He knew you were coming," Lilli said, glancing at her companion. "He used the boy to call you for me. I have ALS and my body is going numb. It's like my limbs are dying, but still attached to my body. Mickey—and I—were hoping maybe the boy could do something for me."

Adan exchanged glances with the others. He decided to be honest, something he always avoided, like being shorted in a deal. He didn't know why, but the woman's naked need and palpable fear touched him. "We lost a guy with us. Crazy Daisy. The kid saved him once, but couldn't do it twice."

"How come?" Mickey asked. The kid was just staring off, as if he had no interest in his surroundings. He'd been like that in the truck, too, but there his eyes had been fixed on the city ahead.

Book 3: THE SECOND DAY

"We don't know," Frodo said, looking at Lilli. She was frail and her weak right side was making her list. Everybody needed something, like he needed his legs straightened. "Maybe because the boy only has so much he can give. Maybe because he can only do it once for a person. Maybe because he can't do it for some people." He licked his lips. "He straightened my legs. I couldn't walk before he touched me. Didn't happen right away though."

"Will he touch me?" Lilli asked simply. "I'd be eternally grateful."

CHAPTER 80

"Maybe, we can try," Magda said. She could feel the depth of the woman's need. It moved her. This was like the baby the boy touched. This was clean, something that wasn't corrupted and would be good to do.

"We gotta tell you something first," Mickey said. "My vision wasn't all good for us. I saw it here." He nodded at the parking area where they stood in back of the house. "It was after a gunfight. I was dead." His gaze shifted to Samosa. "You, too. You were laying here with me. I recognized you first thing you stepped out of your car." He stepped back to include the others. "There were two other people and a crashed car. Not yours, someone else's. I didn't see them clearly."

"El Gordo?" Frodo said to Adan.

Adan shrugged, his eyes were on Mickey. "What are you doing here? If you think you're gonna die? Run, get out."

"I can't," Mickey said with a helpless gesture. "You see, Lilli was gone and so were the rest of you. He wasn't here." He nodded at the boy. "So I think you and your friends and Lilli make it out, even if the big guy and I don't."

"Fuck," Samosa said, rolling his eyes and looking heavenward. It was deep twilight now, no stars in the cloudless desert sky. Did he run or did he stay? How long did he have? No fucking visions. The kid had touched him. Why was he the only one who wasn't having visons? He looked down the drive toward the street. He could see a few cars passing, but that was it. The big guy looked back at the others. "The kid gonna do some healing, he'd better do it." He shrugged. "Time's short."

Adan nodded. He could feel it, too. The seconds ticking past, hurling them toward something bad. Or good, he couldn't tell. He looked at Magda, tilting his head toward Lilli. "Go ahead, do it." Magda took the boy's hand and led him over to her. They stopped in front of the older woman, Mickey steadying her as she let go of the walker. The others watched carefully, not making a sound.

The boy was motionless, not even looking at Lilli. He stared right past her, as if she wasn't there. "I sometimes have to guide him," Magda said and lifted the boy's hand, placing it in the small of Lilli's good arm.

Lilli looked down at the boy, not knowing what to think. "I'm a believer in Christ the Lord," she said quietly. "I don't know if you're from Him or not, but I just want you to know I've confessed all my sins to God, the ones I could remember anyway. I don't know if it worked, but I've tried, I've tried so hard. So I'd appreciate you helping me, if you can. I don't have anything to offer, but I'll do as much good as I can from now on, if you give me a little longer."

The boy's gaze slowly elevated, until he was looking up at her face. "Oh, my God," Magda said softly, stunned in spite of herself. "He's looking at you. He's really looking at you."

"Somebody's come home," Frodo said softly, watching carefully.

"The kid's magical," Samosa said, stepping forward. "I don't care if I have to die or not, so long as he gets where he wants to go." He threw a ferocious look at Adan. "You hear me? You get him home. You know where his home is. Those mesas in the desert."

Adan slowly nodded. He had thought of getting rid of the kid ever since they first found him, but now he realized he was never

Book 3: THE SECOND DAY

getting away from him, not until he found out what he was. Like Samosa just said: "Get him back home."

A bluish light began to gather in the boy. It could be felt more than seen, as though it was centered high in his chest. His hand tightened on her arm. "Ah," Lilli suddenly groaned and arched her back, shoving the walker aside. She tilted her head back as though she wanted to look at the darkening heavens above.

As they watched, awestruck, their mouths gaping, they could see the bluish light, something airy and faint, running like slow-moving mercury across the boy's shoulder, down his arm, and into Lilli. She stiffened even more, her crushed right side slowly straightening. Her useless clawed hand opened in spasm-like jerks. The fingers moved, opening and closing repeatedly, like they were trying to grab something that wasn't there. Her entire body straightened, both arms slowly widening and reaching up, as if accepting a gift from a Higher Power.

"Oh, no," cried Magda, watching. It was happening to the boy again. He was being stripped of weight, whatever color he had gone, his face sucking in as his cheeks hallowed and his hair thinned. He was turning into Bone Boy in front of them once more.

He suddenly pulled back, as if giving to Lilli was more than even he could bear. He started to collapse as Magda grabbed him just in time. At the break in connection, Lilli staggered. Mickey held her close, supporting her. She slowly pushed him away and stepped forward, twirling about, standing tall and straight on her own, flexing her fingers and smiling, oh, God, was she smiling.

It was enough to light up the deepening dusk. It was more than that. It was beatific. And every moment of it was being recorded live by a ring of small cameras.

CHAPTER 81

"**F**uck me," Zio Benito murmured, "he can really do it." He and Aslanian had the video up on the screens fixed to the back of the seat in the SUV. Krekorian was behind the wheel, speeding them through the growing darkness. The kid had just been pulled back, away from the woman he had healed.

Zio's face twisted. She was twirling like some fucking nun in that Christmas movie his mother had made him watch again and again, the one with all the stupid music. Shit, he suddenly thought. He hadn't thought of his mother in years, decades maybe. He continued to suck air loudly through the tubes stuck in his nose.

His face twisted as the screen broke up and froze. "Power," he managed to gasp.

"What?" Aslanian said, looking at him. Krekorian in front strained to hear. Both of them knew this was moving beyond an old man struggling to stay alive a few more months.

"The kid is power," Zio Benito said, his voice stronger. "Every government is going to want him, every billionaire, scientist, every dictator, every fucking so-called statesman or woman. There isn't anybody who isn't going to want 'the touch'." The coughing sickness didn't occur to him. It had stopped, it was yesterday. The kid was today and he almost had him within his grasp.

He lifted his phone to his ear before it hardly buzzed. "Yeah," said El Gordo on the other end, answering the question before the little old man could ask it. "I saw it."

"How close are you?"

"Just entering the town. Some dust spot in the desert called Mary's Landing."

Zio Benito looked at Aslanian. "How close to this Landing place?"

"Thirty minutes," the killer responded, checking the map on his dashboard screen.

"We're right behind you," Zio rasped. "Nothing must happen to the kid. Got it? Nothing." With that he clicked off. "Worthless," he muttered to himself and went back to breathing through the tube, the portable oxygen tank pressed tight to his side, hissing faintly.

Sssssss....

CHAPTER 82

Catherine Hurungzy was in the Phoenix hospital, St. Luke's. They were on the 8th floor where a makeshift contagion ward had been created, using the small existing burn ward that had been converted for an outbreak of SARS in 2006. The smell of chlorine that had been sprayed to disinfect was still strong. The doors to the ward had been sealed to make them airtight, although she wasn't sure it would work.

She and Morgan were video conferencing with the team down the hall, behind the airtight doors, as they ran the dog that had been brought back to life through a Contrast CAT scan. The machine was wide enough that the animal wouldn't feel trapped, not that the dog would mind. The animal was semi-comatose from a shot of muscle relaxant.

"There," Catherine said, pointing at the screen. It showed a green limned view of the dog's side. There was a child's handprint visible over the animal's heart. It was amazing, faint yet solid, a perfect outline. Beneath it the organ pumped steadily. Catherine frowned. "What did the boy do to his heart?"

"I don't know," Morgan replied, "but it sure looks like it's beating well."

Dr. Hilda Kleinman, the woman conducting the CAT scan in ISO, looked at them through their screen. She was in her sixties and looked like she had never stepped out into the sun that beat almost constantly down on Phoenix. "Blood tests just came in," she said.

"There's an unidentified plasmid of DNA. They're breaking it down now, but it could take hours."

"It has to be connected to the healing," Catherine said with a frown.

"That would be the natural conclusion."

"Send the blood samples to the WHO Contagion Center in Washington, have them recreate the plasmid. See if they have any effect on the coughing sickness if it starts again." On the screen the scientist nodded and stepped to a keyboard, beginning to type.

"Holy shit," Morgan exclaimed, peering at his phone. Catherine turned to him, raising an eyebrow. "The world just came undone." He passed her his phone and she saw Lilli's radiant face, smiling out at her.

CHAPTER 83

Donny and Whitney were stopped on the side of the highway, watching his cell phone as Lilli stood straight and said, "The pain, it's all gone." The audio was clear. They and the world heard her joy. Slowly, wrapped in wonder, the older woman stepped back from the walker and put her arms out. It was as if she were a ballerina suddenly finding a balance she didn't know she had. She took one step, then another and another until she was twirling about, laughing ecstatically, her arms open to the growing darkness above.

She was laughing until she finally fell into the arms of the man with a gray pony tail. He held her close, weeping for joy as everyone in the world watched.

Whitney and Donny set there for a moment, speechless. She finally regained her voice. "That's amazing," she said. "She was dying and he made her walk again."

Donny nodded, still unable to speak about what they had just seen. It was magic. No, it was more than that. It was what they called a miracle. He thought that was in old books, something that happened that couldn't happen. A religious thing the minister talked about in church, but didn't seem to really believe. A miracle was something you didn't take seriously, that's what he'd been taught, but he suddenly doubted that the women in that live video they'd just seen, the one who had let her walker go and twirled about on her own, would agree.

"You saw me dead either way?" he asked in a small voice. "If I stayed at home or came with you?"

His cell rang, interrupting them. He checked it out, making a face. "Mom," he said, blocking the call so they wouldn't be bothered anymore.

Whitney tried to shrug it off, but couldn't, hating what she saw in her brother's eyes. "The last vision I had, at the truck stop, I saw myself dead. If he can make that woman stand on her own and bring a dog back to life, I'm pretty sure he can make us both dead," she said with total seriousness.

Her cell rang. "Shit," she said, knowing who it was. Mom or Dad trying her after Donny didn't answer. They'd probably seen the healing like the rest of the world and were calling to get their reaction and find out why they weren't home. She blocked any calls from both of them.

Donny looked away, shock driving tears into his eyes. She reached out, taking his hand. She had never felt closer to her brother. He was sixteen, a year younger than her. How could he even conceive of dying (how could she? She couldn't, but she worried terribly about him)? He squeezed back, brushing the tears away to meet her gaze. "I don't wanna die," he said. "I don't want you or our parents to die either. There has to be a way to stop it. Tell me there's a way."

She was looking at him, trying to think of a way to reassure him. She didn't know one. She felt wretched and worried sick for him and her parents. For herself, too. She was scared to death. "There's only one thing we can do," she finally said. "Head for Willy's Truck Stop. Our fate is waiting for us there. Let's hope we can change it."

With that she pulled back on to the road, her brother sitting beside her, neither of them feeling anything like better.

CHAPTER 84

One-Eye drove the black SUV slowly down the main street of the shit burg town. Nothing to see but a few cars driving by. No cops anywhere. El Gordo and Tomas sat in the back, watching both sides of the street. The cell phones were turned off. They'd seen enough of the healing.

It hadn't made El Gordo want the boy any less. It had just made him more determined and ruthless. He had to get rid of Zio Benito, but first things first. He never would have faced the Dago, out of respect and fear, but the old man was dying. Even if the kid touched him, it wasn't going to stop the Grim Reaper for long. But the kid was going to be alive for a long time. The Fat Man had to have him. Not the skinny dying old fuck who couldn't even breathe right.

"There," Tomas said, pointing to the store with a big sign ahead. "Mickey's Natural Produce," it shouted in bright blue lettering in the growing dusk. It was lit, stupid dancing vegetables pointing to a drive to the back. "That's where the live healing took place."

One-Eye slowed as they approached. Tomas already had his 9mm Beretta out and was checking the clip. He had a second ready to go. El Gordo had total confidence in him. He was a dead shot.

The Fat Man pulled his own pistol and looked at the man behind the wheel. "You got the heavy artillery?"

"Right here," One-Eye said, reaching out a hand and touching the AK beside him, crosswise on the seat.

Tom Holland   The NOTCH

The guard on the recoil had been filed off and jiggered with a bump stock. It wasn't an auto, but damn close; squeeze the trigger and fire off the black mag's 30 rounds in one continuous burst. El Gordo loved the sound. No matter how many in Adan's crew, they'd get chewed up by the firepower.

"Don't hit the boy, don't even fire near him, no matter what," El Gordo said one last time.

"Magda will be with him," Tomas said, excited by the thought. He wouldn't mind if she was left alive at the end of this. At least until he was through with her.

"Or wing her if you can without getting shot, and rape her. I don't care as long as she ends up dead." El Gordo nodded at One-Eye. "Do it."

The driver fed the gas and they turned off the street, moving down the narrow alley to the back. He came to a stop as they saw Adan's old Caddy. That, a van, and a dirty truck parked in front of several grow houses.

The Fat Man raised his pistol and said to the other two: "I think we finally settle with Adan and his punk ass crew."

CHAPTER 85

Mickey had gotten Lilli to a chair and she was sitting there as he watched worriedly over her. Magda and Adan did the same with the boy. His color was already returning, but he still had that skeletal look.

Samosa swung on Frodo. The big guy's face was knotted. "You sure you forgive me about the ring?" he said. There was urgency in his voice.

"What?" Frodo said, his gun in his hand, darting looks down the drive toward the front, expecting Gordo to appear any second.

"The sapphire. You forgive me for getting your legs crushed?"

Frodo jerked his head up, frowning at him. "Yeah, sure. Why you asking now?"

"I'm gonna die," Samosa said. "The guy who owns this place saw it."

"Doesn't mean it's gonna come true," Frodo said. He felt a surge of feeling and reached out and touched the big guy's arm. His voice softened. "Really, it's gonna be okay." He couldn't tell him, but he loved the big guy, wished he could share it, embrace him, even kiss him. Only he couldn't. Samosa wouldn't understand, neither would any of the others. Frodo wasn't even sure he did.

Samosa swallowed, but didn't look convinced. He didn't want to die, but maybe he didn't have a choice. He blinked and was no longer standing there. It wasn't twilight either, it was night, deep and dark and he was standing in a truck stop, watching all hell break loose. He himself wasn't there, a quick glance told him that, but the others were, them and El Gordo and his crew, and some really old guy and his gang. They were all shooting at Adan. A kid went down, really young, looked like collateral damage. Adan was dragging the kid back toward an old dirty van where Magda, a girl he didn't know, and the lady who'd just been healed stood, firing back at El Gordo and his killers, but Adan wasn't going to make it, maybe the kid wasn't either.

Then he saw what it was all about, Frodo, stepping out to the side from behind some gas pumps, and opening up on the bad guy's SUV. He was walking forward, like a real hero, an auto bucking in either hand, shooting into the open back of the SUV. He was trying to save Adan and the kid. God, for a small weak guy he was great.

What the hell was in the back of the SUV? Why was Frodo ignoring the bad guys and shooting in there? Before he could get the answer to those questions or any others, he blinked and found himself once more in the back of the vegan store with the stupid dancing vegetables signage. It was twilight again and Frodo was staring at him. "I finally had a vision," he gulped to his friend.

Frodo didn't say anything, just stared at the man he loved and couldn't tell. He knew the big guy had been moved more than he ever had before. All he had to do was look at him and knew he was no longer the same. He was, what, better? Was that the word? "What'd you see?" he asked.

"You at this big truck stop and all hell had broken loose," Samosa said when he could finally find his voice. "Everybody was firing at Adan with the kid, and you were trying to save them."

"I was?" Frodo asked. "What truck stop? There's no truck stop around here."

"I don't know, but maybe you save the kid," Samosa said. He stomped his foot as he struggled to make the right words. "Maybe that's why I die. To keep you alive so you can save the kid."

Book 3: THE SECOND DAY

"That's crazy," the smallish man with the sparse beard said. "You're not gonna die. Neither am I. We're keeping on with this kid till we get him back to this notch everybody keeps talking about."

"You promise me?" Samosa said, looking intently at Frodo. It made the smaller man uncomfortable. "Promise me. Promise me you'll keep him safe and get him to wherever he wants to go."

"Okay, I promise you," Frodo answered impatiently. Anything to stop the big guy with his talk of him dying. He hated hearing it. "Now would you shut up?"

Samosa stared at him, a broad smile lighting up his face. He finally believed him. "Thanks," the big guy beamed, as if the promise was everything to him.

"I got a question," Adan said. He stood nearby, looking at Mickey. "Where did you pick the boy up? That's where we have to go next."

"Willy's Truck Stop," the man with the long gray mane said. He nodded toward the main street. "Head east, about forty miles out. What I saw in my last vision wasn't good. People there were shooting each other and dying of the coughing sickness."

Samosa turned to Frodo with a grave nod. "See," was all he said.

CHAPTER 86

A t that moment a black SUV roared down the drive at them. Adan and the others leaped out of the way as it crashed into their empty Caddy, pushing it into one of the greenhouses. One-Eye and Tomas jumped out, facing Adan and the others, El Gordo slipping out the other side. One-Eye opened up with his auto AK, stitching a plastic grow house, the fire headed for Lilli.

"Down," Mickey yelled and shoved his wife to the ground.

He turned with his shotgun, but the bullets hit him in the chest, knocking him back. Adan had his pistol up, returning fire as Tomas shot at him. Adan's slug took the slick-looking killer between the eyes, dropping him in a heap. One-Eye stitched the ground as he swung the AR in his direction, but Samosa wasn't having it. He finally knew what he had to do and stepped in front of his smaller friend, firing at One-Eye, but he missed him. A row of slugs hit him in the chest, blowing him off his feet even as Adan and Frodo opened up on him. They hit the killer with the eye patch, knocking him back and the automatic stitched its way up the side of the wood frame house as the one-eyed killer fell into the dirt.

A heavy silence settled over the backyard, gunsmoke drifting in the twilight. The moon had come out now, revealing the bodies and carnage. The quiet was deafening after the burst of gunshots. Adan stared down at Samosa, flat on the ground, his open eyes fixed on the moon above. Stars were up there for the first time.

Frodo fell to his knees beside his friend. "He's dead," he mumbled, like he couldn't believe it, even though he suspected it was coming. "He saved me." Tears rolled down his cheeks unbidden. He couldn't help it, but for once he wasn't ashamed. Someone he loved had died, trying to save his worthless ass. If you didn't cry then, when the fuck would you?

Adan turned away from the sight of fallen Samosa and the grief-stricken Frodo. He'd known, but didn't really believe the visions were for real. It was a mistake he wouldn't make again. He looked toward the house. The guy's woman was bent over her fallen husband. He wasn't getting up again either.

Lilli looked up. She was blinking tears away. "It's just like Mickey saw in his vision," she said.

"Yeah," Adan nodded. He still couldn't accept it, Samosa being gone. She felt the same way about her man. It made him feel sorry for her (when did he feel sorry for anyone? Never, so WTF was happening?). He looked at Frodo, who was still bent over his dead amigo. "Hey, Frodo," he said, feeling a tenderness he hadn't since forever. "You okay?" It was a stupid thing to say, but he couldn't think of anything else.

The former wheelchair-bound man nodded, his face streaked with tears. Shit, everybody was crying. Magda swallowed, her head jerking up as she threw off her shock and grief. "Where's El Gordo?"

She tightened her grip on the boy. She was still holding him by the hand, even though she'd forgotten all about him as the bullets flew. By some miracle, none of the lead had come close to them (but then they never did, did they?).

"Shit, El Gordo," Adan said, realizing the Fat Man wasn't among the bodies.

He whirled, looking toward the wrecked SUV. The Fat Man suddenly darted out from the back and fired at him. His bullet

Book 3: THE SECOND DAY

missed and Adan shot back. He missed, the Fat Man moving with surprising speed, ducking behind the nearest grow house.

"I'll get him," Adan said and took a step after him, Frodo about to follow.

"No," Magda said sharply. "We gotta get the boy to that truck stop. Willy's. Perfect name. 'Sides, Gordo ain't gonna be coming after us quick."

Adan looked at their wrecked car. The SUV had driven into it, smashing in the side. Both vehicles were useless.

"Use our van," Lilli said, standing over her lover's body. Everybody assumed they were married, their love was so deep, but they weren't. She wouldn't do it, not when she was so sick, but now she regretted it. He wanted to be married and in her stupidity and misery she had denied him one of the few things that could have made him happy. The dirty white vehicle was parked next to the old truck. Somehow both were unharmed, not even a bullet hole in them. "Go on, do it, quickly," she urged as none of them moved.

Adan came alive, took Magda's arm, hustling her and the boy toward the van. Frodo took a last look at Samosa, and gently closed his eyes. He wanted to kiss him good-bye, but he didn't have the time (no that wasn't it; he didn't want the others to see. Everybody was so fucking macho, including him). He leaped to his feet, throwing the sliding side door open. They piled inside, Adan behind the wheel. Lilli stood over her dead husband, staring down at him. She had not moved.

Magda called to her from the van. "Come on. We gotta go. Bad guys are coming this way." Lilli still didn't move. "You can't stay. Mickey wanted to save you, you said so. You still have something to do, you know that."

Lilli finally turned away from the love of her life, the man who had made her believe in caring and love and charity, and hurried to the van. She was moving well for a woman who only minutes before had been bent and twisted with ALS. She paused before getting in, looking at those inside. Her jaw was set, her face determined. "I was just promising Mickey I'd get the boy to the truck stop."

"No way," Frodo said, surprised in spite of himself. "I just told Samosa that."

Magda scooted over with the boy, still and unfocused again, and Lilli got into the van. Adan started down the drive to the street, only to have El Gordo step out of hiding behind a grow house and open up on them with his pistol. Inside the van they all ducked as bullets shattered the back window, all except for Adan who hit the gas, tires screeching as he took the turn into the main street, and sped through town for the highway and the deep desert beyond.

CHAPTER 87

"What the hell happened?" Catherine yelled, standing in the hospital office. She was staring at the screen. She and Morgan had been working, adding to their growing list of tests for the boy. At the same time, the coughing sickness remained quiescent.

But all of that was forgotten by the pure power of what they had just seen on their screens. The boy doing a miraculous healing, live over the web. They and the rest of the world had seen it. The truth was undeniable from this moment on. She was sure what they had just experienced would echo throughout human history.

"They got attacked by another group," Morgan checked his device. "El Gordo, the thug who's been chasing the boy. He just made a grab for him."

"The fools. They could have killed him," Catherine said. "We have to stop them. Can we contact them?"

"We had a geo on them until just a few moments ago," Morgan said, checking his device. "Their phones are suddenly out."

"How can that be?" She looked at her screens. The survivors were piling the boy into a van and taking off. Her heart sank. The boy was escaping again. It was like they couldn't catch him, no matter how many assets they committed to it. The screens flickered and went out. "What the hell is going on?" she asked her associate.

"Nothing that algorithms are going to explain," he said, checking his keyboard. "It's as if our comm lines have been blocked." The screen suddenly snapped on, showing the now empty lot in front of the grow houses, the wrecked SUV plowed into the old Caddy, and the bodies strewn about.

"Why? Why should someone—or something—mess up our systems? Who has that kind of power?" she asked. Morgan didn't have an answer. A sudden start of fear shot through her. "The sickness? Is it still quiescent?"

"Holding," he said, checking his device.

"For how long?" She licked her dry lips. "This definitely was not good for us. Do we have a way to reach the group that has the boy?"

"Working on it," Morgan said, tapping his keys.

"This was bad, what just happened, people were killed," she said with a worried frown that edged toward panic. "The boy, whatever he is, God or alien, may not be pleased."

"That's mad," he said, his voice flat. "He healed a woman. It was wonderful. So a few people died at the end. That doesn't mean he's upset. Besides, you're also positing his morality system, if he has one, would be comparable to ours. No guarantee of that."

She looked up at him. "Meaning he has no sense of right and wrong?"

He stared at her. "Perhaps. But then perhaps not, but it sure doesn't have to be like ours."

"Get the contact numbers for the group with the boy," she said, biting her lower lip. "We have to talk to them."

CHAPTER 88

Det. Wilson rode shotgun as Sgt. Getty sped through the desert, headed for Mary's Landing. Homeland Agent Goodman sat in the back, on his cell, an earbud plugged in. The detective had his device opened on his lap, a tablet with a detachable keyboard, because he liked the bigger screen. Twitter, Snapchat, all social media was going crazy with what everybody had just seen. No CGI, no Photoshop; live, a miracle. Holy Hell.

Goodman thought maybe he was going crazy, too. Did he just see the boy make a twisted woman walk straight again? What was that line about "Your lying eyes?" Goodman was a security contractor. What made him so valuable was he also had CIA clearance, so he could work for any agency in the government. Of course, part of his charm was that he didn't ask which one—or who—was doing the employing as long as the money was right.

He'd gotten the text message and saw zeroes move into his Panamanian accounts and came down here just a few hours ago. His mission was simple: evaluate and protect the boy until he could be delivered to the employer. Oh. And kill anyone who got in the way.

That was fine with him. He was the good guy for once, not that he expected it to last. Goodman's phone beeped. It brought him out of his reverie. He didn't have to look at it to know who it was. He tapped it and it was in his ear.

"We're on the way to Mary's Landing," he said. He was always polite and totally professional, even when he got violent.

Tom Holland   The NOTCH

"Did you watch it?" Catherine Hurungzy asked.

"We all did," Goodman replied. He found it vaguely amusing that she thought he was a federal agent assigned to Homeland Security, when he was burrowed much deeper into the federal government than that. "It was amazing. I don't think any of us know how to process it."

"I'm here at the hospital, but we're leaving now," she said. He could hear the whirr of revving helicopter blades growing louder as it got ready to take off. "Every one of the people he touched, the baby, the dead dope dealer, even the dog, had his print at the point of contact. Also, all the affected organs were in perfect health. Glowing with it, the doctor said." Her voice became harder. "The boy, we must have the boy."

"I understand," the contractor said and he did, especially after seeing how the kid cured that woman who had ALS. It was a death sentence, but then the boy touched her, and she lived again. Fucking amazing.

"Good luck," she said, "I really mean it."

She clicked off. Goodman slipped the phone back into his pocket. This was no longer about simple government business. Whoever had put him here had an objective that only tangentially touched a dead dope dealer and thugs shooting each other. It was about something that affected the entire world; a boy who appeared out of nowhere, just as it was in the grip of what might be the worst pandemic in human history. A pandemic that had suddenly stopped.

Scary as hell and just as confusing. The killer smiled. It was a brilliant opportunity for someone like himself to make his own fortune.

CHAPTER 89

Eight hundred people were crammed together in airport hangar Ruffin 27B on the northwest corner of Heathrow. It was one of eight, each of them choked with people who had been trapped in Heathrow in the first outbreak and had somehow survived. The airport and all ingress and egress to London had been shut down. The international airport was ringed with troops. A State of Emergency had been declared.

Those who were trapped inside were being poked and prodded, but basically, they were quarantined, and the mood was ugly. At first, they'd been promised they could leave as they were processed, but it hadn't happened. They had just moved them from the airport proper into huge, cavernous hangers with cots, soup kitchens, and portable toilets.

Babies were crying, families were separated, people were sneaking drugs and booze. Their area of the runway was shut off, troops in jeeps with firearms waiting in case anyone tried to escape before they were properly released, which seemed never.

Outside makeshift hospitals had been set up, snaking people through a series of tents as blood and DNA samples were taken and analyzed for the fourth and fifth and sixth time.

Within the last huge hangar a fight broke out between people playing a simple card game. It was poker, but the pent-up rage and anxiety made it vicious as a man got slashed and staggered back, holding his bleeding side. He looked at his attacker in shocked surprise, as if he never expected it to happen.

"What, what have you done…" He suddenly stopped, a cough working its way up from deep within him. Everybody froze, even his attacker, waiting to see what would happen. He finally hawked the obstruction up, sending a gout of blood flying.

It smacked into his attacker's face and splattered. In horror, the man with the knife dropped it clattering to the floor, digging at his eyes, trying to clear them. Around him people started to back away, pushing others in a widening circle. People were yelling and screaming as word spread—the coughing sickness, it's started again—and they all looked toward the single man standing in the circle.

He coughed again, sprayed more blood, and crumpled. His attacker staggered, barfed up more blood as he twirled about and dropped. All eight hundred people in the hangar stampeded as one, screaming for the doors. They quickly overcame the security and poured out onto the runway.

Outside the startled military was late to act, especially Gordon 380, a special unit of the King's Guards. Captain Marshall was in charge, and although it took him a moment as hundreds of people rushed toward them like a mad zombie attack, he almost immediately yelled, "Open fire! Targets at will!"

A river of bullets poured from their automatic weapons. There was no doubt in their orders. Anyone trying to leave was to be shot down. Panicked people, women, children, all went down in the spray of lead but a thin line somehow slipped through alongside a wall. A hundred people maybe. Captain Marshall and his men and women ran after them, driven by their own fear and panic at a new outbreak of the disease.

The escapees got to a break in the fence, pushing through a narrow tear to the street outside, the troops using their automatic

Book 3: THE SECOND DAY

weapons to mercilessly cut them down. Hardly any escaped through the fence, but Marshall had to be sure. He and several others broke through to the other side, seeing several of them running down the street. The troops coolly aimed and fired and brought down, all but one. She kept screaming at them not to shoot as she scrambled to get away. Marshall was the closest and raced after her.

He found her in a front yard of a row house, cowering on the wet grass. He raised his rifle to finish her when she started to heave with that familiar cough. He suddenly felt himself in terrible danger and backed away. She coughed again, blood flying, and he lost it, whirling and dashing down the street.

He got far enough away to feel safe and whirled, finishing her with a head shot from 25 yards. Her skull burst in a spray of red. She would never cough again. He turned back to the break in the fence where his men were waiting. They must have gotten everybody who got through.

He stopped, heaving for breath as his bronchial tubes were suddenly choked with phlegm. He started coughing, trying to get it free, only to succeed, and spray the air in front of him with droplets of blood.

His eyes widened in horror—oh, my God, he had it, too—and he dropped in the gutter. His men whirled and fled down the street, their duty inside the airport completely forgotten as they desperately tried to escape that which could not be escaped.

Book 4:
THE SECOND
(AND LAST) NIGHT

CHAPTER
90

"**W**hy's everybody so quiet?" Adan asked into the silence. "We're still alive."

Nobody answered, too into their own thoughts to be disturbed. He was driving through the desert, covered in darkness. Magda and the boy sat next to him, Frodo and Lilli on the bench seat behind. They had already left Mary's Landing far behind and were speeding toward the truck stop Mickey had told them about.

"Willy's, straight ahead!" There were blinking road signs everywhere. The lettering was in red. It seemed obscene against the quiet beauty of the desert night.

Adan looked at Lilli in the rearview mirror. The older woman was looking better with every passing second, but she wasn't smiling. She was scowling as she stared at her device. "What's going on?" he asked.

Lilli looked up, motioning with her phone. "The numbers. They're playing the boy saving me all over the web. I can't keep up. Tens of millions of views and climbing," she said, hitting another key, and looking at new info. "The coughing sickness is still stopped. Not a report of one new death."

Magda looked back at her from the front. "That's good, isn't it? Besides, the public has a right to know, don't they? The boy is hope, like Mickey said. What he just did for you is going to make people realize they don't have to accept a bad world."

"Bullshit," Adan snapped. "We got her husband killed. Samosa, too. You call that good?"

Tom Holland   The NOTCH

"He wasn't my husband," Lilli said mournfully. "We lived together for over thirty years, but I didn't want to marry him when he finally asked. I thought he was doing it because I was dying." She looked out the wide window with the dark desert speeding by. "It was a terrible mistake on my part."

No one said anything. What could they say? Frodo looked up. His eyes were red rimmed. It might have been from crying. "We didn't kill either Samosa or Mickey. Both of them knew it was coming." He looked at Lilli. "Mickey accepted it, right?"

The older woman nodded. "I don't think anything could have stopped it. It was foretold."

"Mumbo-jumbo," Adan said under his breath as he put his eyes back on the road. It seemed like he'd gone to Mass a few times when he was very small, but he could hardly remember. He hadn't liked it then, all bullshit and about shaking the stupid peons like his mother down for money. He didn't like it any better now.

"I think maybe it's true," Frodo said from the back, echoing him. "I haven't been to Mass in years. I'm thinking of starting again."

"What are you talking about?" Magda asked, really surprised. If any of them were cynical, it was Frodo. "You getting religion?"

"Samosa died for a reason," Frodo said, his jaw setting. "He was trying to protect me. Said I've got my place in this truck stop coming up. Bet you all do too." His gaze raked the others.

Adan shook his head. Everybody was going fucking crazy, and Samosa was dead. Lilli's husband or lover or whatever he was he didn't know, but Samosa had been a buddy forever. Someone he depended on. Not too quick in the head, but if he needed a door busted down or someone to cover his back, Samosa was the man.

Now Frodo was freaking. He was going as nuts as the Bible thumper in the back, Lilli, with the dead lover. Everything was turning to shit. It made Adan want to bail again. The boy was the

Book 4: THE SECOND (AND LAST) NIGHT

real deal? Maybe, but so what? What did it get him? Maybe Magda would stay with him after the boy was gone, but he didn't think so. He could feel the distance between the two of them growing.

She had become the goddamn Virgin Mary. Nothing he did was right. So what? They were still alive, weren't they? So was El Gordo. The thought stopped the rant in his head. He'd seen the fat slug escape out the back of the grow houses. One-Eye and that slick fuck Tomas were finally gone. Adan knew he'd wanted to bed Magda. Well, now he'd never have her. As for the Fat Man, he'd kill him if he could. Gordo would do anything to get his pudgy fingers on the boy. Him and the others, too, Adan decided, they'd kill them without bothering to clear their throats.

He'd happily return the fucking favor.

CHAPTER 91

D r. Hilda Kleinman, in her 60s with steel gray hair, studied the cells through the powerful electron microscope in the makeshift contagion lab in Phoenix. If she could just locate the bacteria, she might have a chance to stop the coughing sickness by looking at its DNA. But she couldn't find the bacteria. One would have thought the bloodstream of the infected would be swimming with it, but by the time they'd been able to access the corpses, the disease seemed to have died with them, leaving no sign of it behind.

Extraordinary. Unheard of. She's been in constant contact with the National Institutes of Health and they'd had the same results; there was nothing there by the time they were able to draw blood from the dead. That by itself was amazing—and frightening. The NIH had the most advanced gene sequencing devices in the world, but you had to find the bacteria first.

She looked up. Her assistant, Dr. Bhatt, in his thirties and already a respected immunologist, suddenly convulsed and coughed. Everybody in the lab froze, looking in his direction. He gulped air, as if he was trying to stifle another rising cough. He looked across the bench at Dr. Kleinman, past a row of electron microscopes fine enough to see the antigens in the blood stream. His face was panicked. "Help," he mouthed and coughed again, this time spraying bloody mucous in every direction. He wasn't even able to take a step before he crumpled to the floor.

Tom Holland   The NOTCH

There were four other people in the lab. Dr. Aadhya Chorday, the closest to Dr. Kleinman, screamed: "We need breathing masks!" She dived for the masks and Hazmat suits hanging from hooks on the wall. The other three scientists rushed after her. They had hardly begun to climb into them when they were wracked with violent coughs, sending bloody droplets flying through the air.

Dr. Kleinman backed away in horror as she watched the scientists collapse to the floor, one after the other, with dull thuds. Panicked, she whirled for the pressurized door to the outside corridor. She had just reached it, about to yank it open when she froze. If she did break the seal, whatever the disease was would escape to the entire floor, and from there to the hospital, and because it was airborne, undoubtedly to the entire city. Her desperate act to save herself (how would that work? It hadn't worked for anyone else) could possibly condemn millions of people to a horrible death.

In the hall outside she could hear the alarms going off, klaxon horns blaring, warning everyone of the breach in the contagion lab. Through the double-paned window in the door she could see panicked people coming up, looking through the glass at her and the bodies, and then quickly disappearing, undoubtedly fleeing her and the building. She took her hand off the door and turned back to the lab. There was no one moving. They were all dead. She was sure she was going to die. What should she do? The moral choice would be to stay there and die. She had no one to leave behind. Her husband had predeceased her in his early fifties, a heart attack. They'd had no warning and in her shock and loss she had thrown herself even more maniacally into her work. They'd had no children, a decision they had made together. They'd felt the world was dying under the increasing burden of an exploding population, one that was ruining the environment, and rapidly making global warming worse. She was helping others, she told

Book 4: THE SECOND (AND LAST) NIGHT

herself, her duty, and her mission, even as what was left of her personal life disappeared.

She was Jewish by heritage, but considered herself secular. She hadn't been to temple since her grandparents had died, and only attended then to please them. She hadn't had a Bat Mitzvah, and had only visited Israel twice for scientific conferences. She was a proud atheist, but now she wished she had some spiritual belief to guide her in this moment.

She would probably be dead in seconds, but if she had more than that for some reason she couldn't understand, how should she use the time left to her (by who? A question she had never asked, but now seemed terribly urgent, even if she knew there was no answer). She walked back into the center of the lab, ignoring the dead bodies of her fellow scientists and friends, and stood before the most powerful electron microscope. It was so tall she had to stand on short stool to see through it. What was she going to do? Then suddenly she knew the answer. What she had been doing before the coughing sickness hit them. Discover what it was.

She picked up an empty syringe and knelt by her friend, Dr. Chorday, jabbing it deep in her arm, not bothering to be gentle about it (after all, she wasn't going to complain). Finished, she rose and went to the glass slides, preparing to do a series of smears. She was doing what she had always done throughout her life, what she knew how to do in happiness or sadness: she was going to work.

CHAPTER
92

uiet had settled over the van as they sped through the dark desert. Magda looked at the boy slumped beside her. He had been dying as he healed Lilli, but now he looked to be regaining his health. There was more color in his cheeks and the light gold was coming back into his hair. He was still skinny and pale, but he was definitely alive. It had happened the same way when he tried to heal Crazy the second time. He only had so much to give, no more, but he recovered quickly.

But those weren't the real questions. Magda realized she wasn't the most educated person in the world, but she was shrewd and street smart. There was something going on here. Like wheels and gears turning, some huge machine slowly grinding away, and they were all cogs in it. Those of them who were still alive anyway. Frodo had been talking about it. Lilli, too. Asking the hard questions. What were they doing here with the boy? Why did they find him? Or did he find them? What difference did it make? A lot had to do with the way people were dropping, if not being cut down by bullets, then coughing their bloody lungs out.

Magda leaned forward to Adan in the front.

"All of us are big time important." The others could hear her in the van. She didn't give a damn. "I don't understand it, but I figure the boy somehow chose us. We're part of something much bigger that's going on."

"It's God's plan," Lilli said with absolute conviction. "You saw what happened to me." She lifted her right hand, the one that had been totally useless before the boy touched her. She flexed her fingers, something she couldn't do before. It still amazed her. "You've seen more than anybody else. Miracles. We have to stay open and see what he asks of us."

"Who? The boy?" Frodo asked, sitting up. He was still grieving inside for Samosa, but his thoughts were turning to the truck stop and what the big guy had said was coming. "You really think he's an angel or something?"

"I don't know what he is, but he gave of himself to me," Lilli replied. "You saw how sick he got when he healed me. He was willing to selflessly give. You think he cares about anything we do, anything material?" She nodded at the still boy, sitting next to her, but unmoving. "He's beyond that. He's so far beyond our material concerns as to be incomprehensible to us."

"You're crazy, all of you," Adan snapped. "Looking for reasons where there aren't any. The only thing for certain is the world's fucked up and if we don't step right, it's gonna fucking crush us."

The radio suddenly flickered to life. A voice came over the commandeered car speakers. It was crackling with static. "Patching, EJ-480."

"What's that?" Magda asked, looking at the radio.

"I don't know," Adan said, checking his phone. He punched some keys. "My phone's on. It's frozen. I've lost control."

"Same here," Frodo said, checking his device, the two women doing the same.

"Adan Cuarto?" Morgan said through the car speakers. It also came over all their devices. They were suddenly surrounded by the conversation. "Are you all there? Can you hear me?"

Adan and the others looked at each other. "Yeah, so?" Magda said, leaning toward the radio. She figured there was a mic in there. "Who wants to know?"

Book 4: THE SECOND (AND LAST) NIGHT

"We don't have time for this," came an impatient older female voice. "Do you have the boy?"

"Maybe," Adan answered. "You haven't told us who you are yet."

"This is Catherine Hurungzy," the female answered. "I represent the Centers for Disease Control, the CDC. Do you know what that is?"

"I do," Frodo said.

"Good," she said. "You were talking to Morgan, who is NSA. That's National Intelligence Agency. This conversation is of great importance to the United States government, in fact, to the world. I hope this gives you an idea of the gravity of the situation." The voice paused. Everyone in the car was pulverized into silence.

"We direct the FBI, which is closing in on you right now," Catherine continued. "We are heading toward you in an Army helicopter. Why don't you pull to the side of the road and wait for us?"

"Why don't you go to hell, lady," Frodo growled. "We don't have nothin' to do with you. Leave us alone."

"Give us the boy," Morgan said, "and we'll do just that."

"Why's the federal government want the boy?" Adan asked, impressed in spite of himself.

Adan could feel the hesitation, as if the speakers exchanged glances before answering. "We think there's a connection between the boy and the coughing sickness," Dr. Hurungzy said.

"I knew it," Lilli whooped from the back, pounding the seat with her bony fist. "I knew it, he's been sent by the Lord to help us. It's the only answer."

"Would you shut up," Adan yelled at her, almost taking his hands off the wheel. He turned back to the radio. "What kind of connection?"

"We don't know," Morgan said as he came back on the speakers, "but the sickness has started up again in London. Thousands more are dead already."

"Anyplace else?" Magda asked from the back. Her arm was around the boy, but he didn't seem to notice.

"Not yet, but the totals continue to rise. The disease has easily killed over eight million people worldwide." Catherine replied. Her voice was grim. "Magda Rodriguez, is that you? You have a relationship with the boy. I can tell from the videos. No matter what happens, he must be protected at all costs. He is the only lead we have on how to stop the sickness."

"How?" Adan said, a shiver running up his spine. He didn't want the responsibility of some worldwide plague, especially when he didn't know what the fuck was going on. "How does he stop the sickness?"

"We don't know," Morgan said, "but if it continues to light up London, it'll move through the British Isles. Tens of millions more will die."

"So what's that got to do with the boy?" Adan asked, trying to figure it out.

"We don't know, that's why we're talking to you," Morgan replied. "You tell us."

"Maybe. It's a possibility," Magda said slowly, looking at the silent boy. "There's something about him that's special. Almost supernatural or magical."

"If we're right, if there is a connection, if the boy can stop it—or start it—but we don't know why or how he does it," Catherine said. "You figure it out. He's with you. In the meantime, pull to the side of the road and wait for us…"

Adan hit the radio, shutting her off. "Shit," he said.

"Yeah," Magda said, looking down at the boy. He sat there, staring at the back of the seat in front of him, as if it was the most interesting thing in the world. "If they get him, he'll never get to that notch."

Book 4: THE SECOND (AND LAST) NIGHT

"If they get him, they'll do to him what they did to the kid in *Firestarter*," Frodo said from the back. "We gotta get him to the notch."

Adan didn't say anything, but his mind kept going to the ten million in cash that Zio Benito was offering. He had to figure out a way to grab the loot and still get the boy to the notch. That way they'd all be happy and maybe, just maybe, he'd keep Magda.

CHAPTER
93

Bang, video of the contagion lab in Phoenix popped up on all the screens in the helicopter as it beat its way through the night, carrying Catherine and Morgan. "What?" the latter said, sitting up in surprise.

"Patching in from St. Luke's Hospital, Contagion Ward," said one of the techs.

Dr. Kleinman's worn face popped up on the screen. Behind her, among the medical equipment, several dead bodies were scattered on the floor. "Have you heard?" the old woman said.

"Heard what?" Catherine said, afraid to hear the answer.

"The disease hit here, inside the contagion ward, not the rest of the hospital." The gray-haired woman said, nodding toward one of the double-paned windows to the outside hallway. People could be seen looking through the glass, cameras in their hands, recording everything.

"We hadn't heard," Morgan said. "When did it happen?"

"I don't know, ten, twenty minutes ago," the doctor replied. "I've been busy ever since."

"It took everybody but you in the ward?" Catherine said, struggling to understand.

"Yes," Dr. Kleinman said with a weary nod. "It hasn't spread to the rest of the center, at least not yet."

"Why?" Catherine asked, not sure she wanted to know the answer.

"I don't know. Once I realized it wasn't affecting me, I immediately took blood samples of the dead. I found nothing, no bacteria, no microbes, no nothing. Their blood was totally unaffected."

"Then how did they die?" Morgan said, licking his lips, more mystified than ever.

"I don't know," the doctor said, clenching her jaw in frustration. "But there's more. I finally took my own blood, hoping there might be some answer." She swallowed hard, as if she couldn't believe it herself. "There wasn't. My blood sample was totally normal, the same as the victims." She looked around at the bodies of her stricken co-workers. Tears worked their way up in her eyes, but refused to fall.

"What's your conclusion?" Catherine asked, trying to keep calm.

"The coughing sickness isn't caused by any disease that we understand. There is some other power that is killing us, something we can't identify, and we have no defense against that which we cannot see or comprehend." Her aged face sagged with exhaustion, defeat, and confusion. "I can only believe in a higher power, something that I've never considered before. I'm sorry."

The transmission was cut, leaving Catherine and Morgan staring at a blank screen. "Oh, Christ," Morgan groaned as he slumped back in the chair, strapped in by his harness. Catherine said nothing.

CHAPTER 94

"What are we gonna do to protect you?" Whitney said to her brother as they drove through the desert. The sand was moon-swept.

"What am I gonna do to protect you?" he asked. "You've had one vision where you were dead. Was I dead, too in that one?"

"What?" she asked, momentarily confused. "I'm not sure. I didn't see you. Just myself and everybody else. I think there was a gunfight, but other people were dead because of the coughing sickness."

"Ugh," Donny said, shifting uncomfortably. "That's all we need. The sickness starting up around here."

"I wish you hadn't come."

"I couldn't stay home," Donny answered. "You said it yourself. Then everybody died for sure of the coughing sickness. At least this way we have a chance to stop it, even if one of us doesn't make it."

"You think?" Whitney said, wanting reassurance. She liked the idea this might have a happy ending. For one of them anyway.

"I'm hoping," he said. "Everything that's happening, it's gotta mean something, even if we don't understand it."

"You're my brother," she said, watching the road ahead. "If I should somehow be responsible for your death, I really never could forgive myself." She shook her head, making a face. "Jeez, I can't believe I'm saying that."

"I can't tell you how much that does not make me feel better." He glanced out the window at the darkness shimmering by. There was a full moon high in the dark sky, casting night shadows across the desert. "We should call Mom and Dad, tell them why we're not there for dinner."

"Damn," Whitney said, reacting. "I forgot all about them. Our own parents. We have to tell them the truth. I had a vision about the boy, telling me to go to the truck stop, and you went along to make sure I don't get into trouble."

"They'll go nuts, you know they will, send the police after us probably," he said as she drove.

"Maybe they'll threaten, but it's too late for them to stop us," she answered. "Maybe they'll come after us, but they won't be there by eight. Whatever's going to happen will be over right after that."

His device pinged. He checked it, his face falling. "The sickness has started up again. People are fleeing London and there are unconfirmed reports of outbreaks in the Middle East and India," he said. "People are panicking, whole countries."

"Damnit," his sister said as she drove and still managed to steal a glance at his screen. It showed a map of the world, red dots throbbing everywhere to indicate outbreaks of the disease. "It's all over the world again."

"Something's gone wrong," he said, looking at her. "We saw what happened back at that vegan place. People died. Maybe the boy's in danger, right now, it could be that, too. He's making this all happen."

"Has to be headed for Willy's Truck Stop, doesn't he?" she said, gripping the wheel tighter. "That's why we're going there, too. Eight tonight and don't be late."

"We're close," he said, checking his phone. They whipped past a sign: "Willy's Truck Stop Ahead; Take a break and have a steak!" They were close, she thought and it was only a little after seven. Plenty of time to meet the boy and beg him for her brother's life. She couldn't let Donny die. She had to talk to this strange boy.

"Oh, shit," Donny said. "We forgot to call Mom and Dad." He pulled his phone, fumbling for the speed dial.

CHAPTER 95

Night had fallen in Cordes Lakes as Big Don came through the back door into the kitchen, just in time for dinner, where he expected to see his wife cooking, maybe Whitney helping out. It was empty. That was strange. The house was silent. That was stranger. He always came home from work a little after six, and he was always hungry. Maybe it had to do with the sensational healing they'd all seen live on-line.

He'd immediately called Helena who was coming back from helping Molly Hascomb take her sick dog to the vet. They hadn't seen it, but Helena would the second she got home. Don could hardly contain himself. It was the kid they'd picked up on the high-way, the one they'd lost at Willy's Truck Stop. They hadn't been able to see his face before, but they sure as hell could now. He expected her to call him back right away, but then he had gotten swept up in a work emergency (was there any other kind?), and momentarily for-gotten, but he sure as hell expected it to be the topic of conversation over dinner, between himself, his wife and kids.

"Helena," he said, raising his voice. He waited for his wife to yell back, but there was nothing. He felt a growing sense of unease. What the hell was going on? Where was she? Where were his kids? He was getting really worried. He pulled his cell, about to call her when he heard her car pull into the drive. He'd just assumed it was in the garage. He hurried to the front door, bursting outside to see her just getting out of her car. Relief washed over him.

"What's going on, honey?" he asked, grabbing her and giving her a hug. "Where are the kids?"

"What? I just left Molly. We were watching that healing in Mary's Landing," she said, stiffening. "You mean Whitney and Donny aren't here? I've been calling them and not getting an answer."

"Maybe they left a note," he said, trying to reassure her as they moved toward the front door. "They must have seen the healing of that woman. They're probably freaking out with their friends."

"And not be home in time for dinner," Helena said. "They wouldn't do that."

"Did you call more than once?"

"Of course I did," she answered. "Five, six times. There was no answer. I figured they had their cells off." They had just reached the front door, Don opening it when they heard a loud bang behind them. They spun about to see a car under the glare of a street light. It had just driven off the street and into a big tree. The front was wrecked. A man was slumped inside, not moving.

"What the hell?" Don said and moved to help him. There were neighbors coming out of their houses to see what was wrong. One of them coughed and fell. Helena grabbed her husband.

"No," she said, her fear growing. He looked at her. She nodded down the street as another woman with two young children who'd come out to see what happened. She suddenly coughed and dropped. Her children who couldn't be more than five or six did the same thing. It was horrifying.

Don's eyes widened as the truth hit him. "Oh, my God," he said in a choked whisper. "It's the coughing sickness."

He grabbed his wife, about to shove her inside their house when she coughed in his face, dappling him with sprayed blood. He stood there in horror, looking at her. Her mouth was rouged with red, like a clown who'd lost control as she put on her funny mouth, but she wasn't laughing and neither was he. She sagged against him, the

Book 4: THE SECOND (AND LAST) NIGHT

strength going out of her body. He lowered her gently to the ground, looking at her more closely.

It was too late. She was gone. He looked around, not knowing what to do. The few people who were still alive on the street were coughing and dropping. He pulled his phone to call for help, even though he knew it was hopeless, when the first cough hit him. He sprayed blood. As he gasped for a breath, a second cough hit him, but he didn't have time to complete it.

He fell to the ground, everything going black around him, his last thoughts a jumble of panic for himself, his family, and everybody else in the world. But it was too late. He was dead before he hit the grass beside his wife. His cell fell a few inches from his limp hand.

As the seconds ticked past, his cell buzzed and when there was no answer the cell in his wife's pocket rang, but there was no one to answer either one. No one on the whole damn street.

CHAPTER 96

"They've got it in Ireland now," Magda said, looking up from her device. She was stricken. They were speeding through the night, all checking their devices.

"Germany's got it bad in the big cities," Frodo said from the corner of the back seat. "Millions are starting to flee into the country. The roads are choked. All air travel is shut down. People are stealing boats, cars, motorcycles, anything to get away." He looked up. He was stricken, wide-eyed at what was happening.

"When was the first time the sickness stopped?" Lilli said from the back. "Come on," she pushed the others, "we've got a disease to stop. When was the first time it halted?"

"Right after the shootout with Crazy at his house," Magda said, "or close to there."

"In the car when the boy closed his wound," Frodo offered. "Crazy saw he was dying trying to save him a second time, turning into a skeleton, and pushed him away. Crazy died, but the sickness stopped."

"You sure?" Magda said, trying to peg the time the sickness stopped.

"No, but I'm close."

"Maybe cause this Crazy fellow tried to do something good," Lilli said, trying to figure it out. "He realized the boy was dying, trying to save him, and didn't want him to do it. Doing something good makes the sickness stop."

"That's loco," Adan said. "So the kid is some kind of on and off switch?"

"Who knows," Frodo said, "but I bet people started coughing up blood right after El Gordo and his guys killed her husband and Samosa. That was a shitty thing to do, and the kid knew it."

Magda checked the time on her device. "That was just thirty, forty minutes ago. He didn't like us all murdering each other? I can understand. I didn't like it either, but I'm not going out killing millions of people 'cause somebody did something bad. That's stupid mean crazy."

"He's a kid," Lilli said, looking at the boy with his blank face and straight-ahead gaze. It was hard to believe he did anything, especially anything as world-shaking as the coughing disease. "Kids don't know any better."

"He's no kid," Frodo said, cutting the boy a look. "He's gotta be 9, 10, 11. Shit, by then I was running dope, guns, anything I could grab and sell."

"You weren't like this boy. None of you were," Magda said, feeling the warmth of his body so close. She looked down. He was still. The pale coloring made him seen drained, but he was maybe the most powerful thing in the world. It made her want to freak, especially since all she wanted to do was keep him close, keep him safe, like he was what he looked like, a harmless, defenseless little kid. The feeling was very strong in her. Was it him? Was it her?

Was that mothering? No. Big sister maybe. La hermana.

"We were just trying to stay alive," Adan said, breaking into her thoughts. "Fuck, it's not our fault the sickness has started up again. Anybody would do what we did. We were trying to protect the boy."

"It's not just about how we treat the boy," Frodo said with a start of realization. "It's about how we treat each other."

"Oh, great," Magda said with a groan. "Now we got some kind of responsibility for the rest of the stupid world?" She shook her head. "Forget it. No way I want that." She bent down, looking the kid in the face. "You hear that? I don't want what you're doing, if you're really doing all this craziness."

"Leave him alone," Adan said. "Maybe what's going on doesn't have anything to do with him. Maybe somebody else is doing this and just using him. Maybe he's just a tool."

"This doesn't make any difference to anybody," Lilli interrupted from the back. She was on her device. "People are dying in London, Hamburg, Milan, it's popping up everywhere in Europe. We've got to figure out a way to stop it."

They all looked at the boy. He just sat there between Magda and Frodo, looking straight ahead with that fixed stare.

"How do we reach him?" Frodo asked quietly.

"Dreams," Magda said. "That's how he reaches us. We gotta try to reach him the same way."

"Mickey did that," Lilli said. "He wanted the boy to come to the store for me. He imagined it and somehow got to him." She nodded at the boy from the seat behind. "He sent it on to all of you. He must have."

"Okay, fine," Adan said, licking his lips. "How do we make him understand we want him to stop the sickness?" They all looked at one another. No one had an answer.

CHAPTER 97

"It's down here," Krekorian said from behind the wheel of the black SUV. He pointed toward the sign of the grocery store, slowing as they approached. Zio Benito leaned forward, stretching the plastic tube that fed the air to the clips in his nose. The Porsche with the Black Widow and the Ninja was tight behind them.

"Go," said Zio, leaning back. They'd seen the gunfight start, before the cameras had flared out. El Gordo, the fool, had lost. Zio didn't even know if he was still alive. He hoped he was, he needed his visions, but the moment he had the boy, the fat fool would die.

Krekorian drove the heavily armored SUV down the drive between the building and a fence, ending up in the parking area before the grow houses. Aslanian slid out, a revolver in his hand. Slipping the portable oxygen tank over his shoulder, Zio followed. Krekorian stayed in the SUV, covering them from the open window. The Porsche pulled up behind him. The Black Widow got out, her fellow killer with her. She was wearing a black mask that hid her face. It had the outline in white of a grinning skull. Its purpose was to scare the shit out of her enemies and it did. The Ninja had an AK in his hands, watching as she joined Aslanian and the old man.

"Not much left," Aslanian said, looking around. There was a dead white guy and two of Gordo's peons. Aslanian had no respect for mestizos. Yeah, sure, they could fuck you up with a blade, but they always left a mess behind; it was in their stupid nature. Not like the Armenians. They could destroy you and not leave a blood stain, not beaten, sliced, shot, and burned bodies full of DNA evidence buried a few feet deep in the desert. Shallow graves were these stupid peasants' M.O.

He looked at his boss, Zio. "None of the bodies are the Fat Man," he said to him.

Behind him, the old man took a good breath from his portable tank and lifted his head, calling out in his thin, reedy voice. "Gordo, where the hell are you?"

The Fat Man appeared around the side of an arboretum. He was shaken, dirty with a bloodless face. His blubber shook. "They came out of nowhere," he said as he came up. "Adan's gang, they caught us by surprise." He nodded at the body sprawled in the dirt. "That's the guy who owned the place, I think."

"Whoopee. You know where they went?" Zio said with a snarl. He didn't need to listen to this drivel.

Gordo nodded. "Some truck stop. I heard them talking when I got away from them. Adan wanted to come after me, but they didn't have the time. They had to get to this place, Willy's. Stupid Yanqui name."

"Get inside." Zio nodded at their armored SUV. As the Fat Man huffed his way into the back, Zio looked at the Black Widow. "You heard?"

She nodded and turned back for her Porsche. Her helper was already behind the wheel. Zio Benito climbed into the back of the SUV, careful to keep his portable oxygen tank out of the way. Krekorian leaned over from the front to help him, but the old man waved him off.

He'd seen so much on that live cast he knew what needed to be done. Find the kid. Have him cure him. And then use him like the golden goose, with him, Zio Benito, the one and only, choosing from a very select list of elite clients, all of them rich beyond belief. The possibilities were endless, especially for a brilliant mind like his.

He got into the SUV with the Fat Man, Aslanian behind him, sobering as he realized he was going to have to listen to the slobbering inanities of Gordo. "Shut up," he said to the Fat Man, cutting him off before he could say anything. He nodded at Krekorian. The driver turned the SUV around and got them quickly out of there, following the Porsche, now in the lead, all of them heading out of Mary's Landing for the truck stop.

"Can I talk now?" El Gordo said as they sped across the desert.

"You lost your two guys, shut up." He looked at Krekorian behind the wheel. "Willy's Truck Stop. I like the sound of it. Make it happen quick." He turned his attention back to the Fat Man. "The guy with the kid, has he replied to my offer of ten million?" The Fat Man stared at him, not saying a word. It almost popped a blood vessel on the old man's forehead. He snarled, "You can talk now, blubber lips."

"No," El Gordo said, nervously. The old man could order him killed any second. "Not yet anyway."

"Well, fucking message him," Zio Benito snarled at him. "Tell him Willy's Truck Stop, one touch for ten million, yes or no?"

El Gordo nodded, fumbling his cell phone out and almost dropping it. Getting a firm grip, he began to press the keys.

CHAPTER 98

Adan drove the car through the night, his mind not on the road, but on his future. Him and Magda mainly, but Frodo, too. What happened to them when this was all over? It was gonna be over somehow. The kid was going back where he came from or the big money or the government was gonna take him. No way he was gonna be allowed to stay with them. He didn't know how Magda would take it, but he knew he was right.

Time to plan for the future. His device vibrated. He looked down, reading it quickly as he drove. El Gordo wanted confirmation of a meet at the truck stop. How the fuck did he know they were headed for Willy's? He didn't know it till the healing at Mickey's. He shoulda killed him, Adan told himself. He should have spent the time back at the grow houses and hunted him down and killed him. Fucking weak. Give somebody a break and they come back and try to bury you.

One hand on the wheel, he thumbed his device and sent the text. It was simple. "Done, but I gotta see the cash before I bring the boy out."

Magda didn't even glance his way. Her mind was elsewhere. She sat next to him, thinking about what had just happened—was happening—about miracles and death. Frodo and Lilli were quiet in the back as they ate up the miles. And the kid? Well, the kid never said anything, did he?

Beside her, Adan's phone vibrated silently. He glanced down. "The old man says deal," the text said. "Esta allí o ser cuadrado; be there or be square." Adan licked his lips. Ten million in cash, for a touch from the boy.

Now if he could only figure out how to get his hands on the green and keep everybody alive.

CHAPTER 99

Inside the helicopter, beating its way through the night, a tech barked: "Another emergency report." He hit buttons on his computer with a studied frenzy.

"The coughing sickness has hit a town near here called Cordes Lakes." Morgan said, reading a screen as it flipped to a new page of info. "We passed it approximately eight minutes ago."

"Is it spreading?" Catherine asked, stiffening in her chair once more as a local police officer, obviously panicked and confused, filled a screen. A small town street could be seen behind him, already packed with EMT and police officers. Half of them wore protective covering and breathing masks. Many of them did not, indicating how unprepared they were for what had hit them.

"This is Police Chief Bill Lansdale," the man said. His hand was shaking and he was close to babbling. "The coughing sickness has hit one street. Everybody on it is dead."

"It hasn't gone beyond that?" Morgan said, shocked.

"No, sir," the chief said. "It's like this one street was targeted, but nothing else."

"Thank you. We'll be back to you when we learn more," Morgan said, aware of how limp and helpless his reply was. He nodded at the tech who broke the connection.

"It's leapfrogging," Catherine said. "It hit just the contagion ward in Phoenix, and now it hits this place, Cordes Lakes. What the hell is in Cordes Lakes that the boy would want to kill?"

"You're sure it's the boy?" Morgan said, even though he couldn't think of anyone—or anything—else, especially not after having talked to Dr. Kleinman.

"It has to be," Catherine said. "But how and why?" She paused a moment. "Get a list of the dead in this Podunk town. See if they tie in to anybody else that's died in Phoenix, or associated with Adan Cuarto and his crew. There has to be some sort of logic to this."

Morgan nodded and started typing on his device. Catherine sunk back in the webbing of her chair, trying to ignore the rhythmic thumping of the rotors which threatened to cause her to fall asleep. That and exhaustion. And feelings of helplessness. She had prided herself on her and her team being ready for something like this.

She had been so wrong. So very wrong, and now the world might be ending and it was all her fault. Pride goeth before...and then her head slumped forward and she was blessedly asleep.

CHAPTER 100

"We got millions on the table, ten of them. Cash from Zio Benito," Adan said as he sped through the night. No reason to hide that he'd made the deal, not when they were all bearing down on the truck stop. They passed a glowing red neon billboard, like a signpost from hell. "Willy's Truck Stop, just ahead." Stupid name, but cool sign.

Magda looked at him like he was nuts. "You idiot. You can't be serious. You've been texting with that fat fuck?" Her voice started to rise. "You're gonna sell the boy to him?"

"I'm thinking about how we survive this," he argued back. "We just don't have some barrio gangster on our ass like Gordo, we got Zio Benito. He's the one fronting the green. Shit, he's got it with him, in the back of his van."

"He's a legend," said Frodo, impressed in spite of himself. "Runs the mob throughout the whole southwest. He'd have ten million in cash easy."

"Whatta we need money for?" Magda asked. "All we gotta do is get the boy back to that notch."

"What then?" Frodo said, thinking ahead for once in his stupid life. He was still mourning Samosa, but he couldn't let the others know it. He was afraid of what Adan might say. No, that wasn't it, it was worse. He might find out his secret.

"We have that truck stop to get to first," Adan said, "with Gordo and Zio almost on top of us. They have the ten million with

343

them—just to have the boy touch the old man. Once, one stupid time. After that, we walk clean with the cash and the kid."

"You stupid pindejo," Magda said, staring at him, her face flushed with anger. "They'll never let us get away, much less with the boy. Maldito diablo estúpido. You know they won't."

"Look," he said, cutting her a hard look as he drove, "like Frodo said, we get him back to this place, this notch, what happens then? He's not sticking with us. He's going somewhere. Fucking E.T. We all know that. What happens to us after he's gone?"

"No matter what happens at the truck stop, we're fucked," Frodo said. "If Gordo and Zio Benito don't get us, then the Feds will. What do you think they'll do with us? What do you think they'll do with him?" He nodded at the silent boy.

"They'll kill him," Magda said, "if the coughing sickness doesn't kill us all first." She was looking at her device. "The sickness is breaking out again everywhere. They say it hit this hospital in Phoenix where they were investigating the boy. No other word about it, but there are riots all over the world. People are fleeing Europe, France especially. Russia has shut its borders. There's no air travel; private planes are being shot down. Millions are clogging the roads, only to find out there's nowhere to go. Britain is shooting at boats trying to approach the shore. The sickness is following after them."

Lilli looked up. Her bottom lip was trembling. Her eyes were filled with alarm, bordering on horror. "We've got to figure out some way to get the boy to stop this. Before we're all dead."

Magda nodded at the boy in growing desperation. "He's giving us the visions. The one we've all seen is this notch in a mesa, with the dawn rising behind it. That means something."

She turned her neck, trying to work out a crick. When she looked back, she was no longer in the vehicle. She was standing in a truck stop. An SUV had just exploded, sending a fireball high into the air, and metal was raining down around her. Adan and Lilli were exchanging gunfire with Gordo's men. People were running away from them. Others were coughing, spewing blood, the sickness getting them. It was insane and yet, somehow, she was safe from it.

She saw a teenage girl, bent over another teen, a boy. She was pulling at him, screaming for him to get up, but Magda knew he was dead. All of it was terrible. She turned her head away, only to discover she was back in the van.

"Oh, my God," she gasped.

"What?" Adan said, looking at her. "Did you have another vision?"

A shaken Magda nodded. "It was Willy's Truck Stop. All hell had broken loose. A car had exploded, you and Lilli were firing at Gordo's people, and then over by the store I saw this girl. She was young and she was pulling at this boy, like she didn't understand he was dead. It was horrible, but it got worse. People started coughing up blood."

"The Spirit," Lilli said from the back, her eyes bright. "You shouldn't be frightened. We've all been touched by the Spirit."

"What are you talking about?" Adan growled, not wanting to hear any of this, but unable to stop himself.

"The Promise of the Spirit," Lilli answered, her face shining. "Joel 2:28. I will pour out my Spirit on all mankind. And your sons and daughters will prophesy, your old will dream dreams, your young will see visions, and I will pour out my Spirit on them all."

"I don't understand," Magda said.

"The Lord has blessed us, because we are the shepherds of the boy," Lilli said, her voice strong and full. "He is the vessel that has anointed us all. We are all servants of the Lord now, through him, here to do His bidding. Our visions are giving us alternative possibilities of what can happen, depending on what we do. They're a warning, if we can figure them out."

Tom Holland   The NOTCH

"Oh, shit," Adan muttered, turning away. The bitch had been driven over the edge by her healing and her husband or whatever the fuck he was getting shot dead. What the hell did she know anyway? She was a stupid desert rat with an old hippy lover. What the fuck did anybody know at this point, including him?

CHAPTER
101

El Gordo sat in the armored SUV, next to the wheezing old man, his two thugs in front, the Porsche leading the way as they sped through the desert night. It hadn't turned out the way he'd wanted, but he was still in the game. Zio couldn't get rid of him, not as long as he had the visions, which meant he still had a chance. The blowout at the stupid organic shop had almost gotten him killed. He hadn't expected Adan or his group to be that good.

He needed a vision now. They were headed toward the stupid truck stop, but he hadn't seen that. He'd seen The Second Healing, that's what they were calling what happened in Mary's Landing on the news. The aftermath mainly, but he hadn't seen he'd lost when they tried to grab the boy. He'd seen the notch. That's what you had to call it, with the rising sun shining through. That's where they were all headed, if he knew where it was. He'd searched and there was nothing like the notch in the Tonto desert…

He blinked and he was no longer in the armored SUV. He was at some trucker gas station, Willy's, and Zio Benito was in between him and Adan and his crew. The old man had a gun to the boy's head and was dragging him back toward the SUV.

Aslanian stood closest to the SUV, a pistol in his hand, Krekorian at the back. Gunfire was sure to break out, no way the boy wasn't getting killed, when Aslanian suddenly stumbled and coughed. Blood flew. Terrified, the Fat Man looked around. People were coughing blood and dropping all over the truck stop.

Shit, the sickness was there. Zio saw it, too, and in horror released the boy who came alive for the first time, and ran to Magda, burying his face in her stomach, as though he didn't want to see what was going on. Gunfire cracked and bullets whizzed, but didn't touch them.

Gordo's eyes snapped open. He found himself back in the SUV, Zio beside him, everybody speeding through the night, for the moment lost in their own thoughts. The kid was sending him messages. Were the others, Adan and Magda and whoever else the boy touched also getting them? Were they getting different visions?

What the fuck did it mean and how could he use it to help himself? That was the fucking question.

CHAPTER 102

Adan sat in the front, driving the van. The "touching" deal for the old Mafioso was fast approaching. In the distance, he could see the glow of what had to be the truck stop. Zio Benito had to be sick. Adan already knew he was old. He was the driving force behind all this. Or was he? Was the boy doing it? He didn't have time to think about it. "Almost at Willy's Truck Stop. Meet you there," he typed one handed, adding: "Fuck with us and you never see the kid again," for all the help it would do. He hit send.

Adan put his eyes back on the road and hoped they believed him. There was no way he was giving up the kid. He'd lose Magda for sure. "Whatta we gonna do when we get to Willy's?" he asked the others. "I get the ten million, we do the touch with the old man, and then we get out of there, with the kid, no matter what. How's that sound?"

"Sounds fucking impossible," Frodo said from the back. "Besides, what difference does it make? They'll come after us no matter what."

"Not if they've all got the coughing sickness like the visions you've all been seeing," Lilli said. "Course we'll probably die, too."

"You're gotta sneak around and get an angle on them," Adan said to Frodo. He didn't have time for this shit. They had to have a plan, no matter how stupid. "Start shooting when the boy finishes his miracle. Everybody will be looking at him." Adan caught the older woman in his rearview mirror, thinking it over. "Can you use a gun, Lilli?"

349

She smiled. It was chilling, the churchgoer gone as something else took over. "I've been living out here most of my life. What do you think?"

"In the back, behind you," Adan says. "Guns and ammo."

She reached behind her, pulling out the satchel that he'd had with him since the escape from his apartment (how long ago had that been? It was only a day ago, but it might as well be a different life). She zipped it open and rummaged through it. "Cash in here," she said and pulled a pistol. "Pistol too." She stuck the cash back, but kept the gun. A small auto, full mag. It made her feel better as she stuck it in a pocket.

"A little over a grand maybe," Adan said, "the bank that I'd kept for everyone. Ten million makes it look like the nothing it is." He licked his lips. He couldn't stop himself. Just imagining that much money, all in cash, dazzled him. It also made him ravenously hungry. Horny, too. Magda never looked so beautiful. If he could get the money and keep her and the boy…why, then he had the whole world.

"When the boy touches the old man and Frodo opens up, I grab the kid and we get out of there," he said, his eyes bright with excitement.

Everybody stared at him for a breath. Frodo shook his head. "That's brilliant, amigo. Insane but brilliant. You pick me up on the way out?"

"You'd better know it," Adan said, both of them knowing the chances of that happening were slim to none. Frodo would never survive; probably none of them would. "Lilli, you and Magda protect the boy. I'll get him back to you just fine."

"How you gonna do that?" Magda asked, her eyes narrowing.

"Use the boy for cover once he's touched the old man," he said, shocked at his own honesty. "They won't shoot him. None of them. Besides, I don't think the kid can be killed, not by flying lead. He survived Crazy's and what happened at the grow houses. I got a feeling the only thing that could kill him is if he tried to heal more than one person at a time."

Book 4: THE SECOND (AND LAST) NIGHT

"You're just hoping that," Magda said. "You don't know for sure. But maybe you can relax."

"How do you figure?" Adan asked with a frown.

"In my vision," she said, the others listening, "people were coughing up blood, with all these explosions and gunfire going on. If it happens like that, none of us are gonna escape."

Adan drove on into the night. He was shaken but he couldn't think of anything else to do. There were so many things that could go wrong with the plan but at least it was a plan.

CHAPTER 103

Det. Wilson looked at the crime scene behind Mickey's Natural Produce as he talked on the cell. Agent Goodman stood nearby, also in on the call. Sgt. Noel Getty was poking around the wreckage. The local police department, a chief and his deputy, were there, not knowing what to do as they waited for the coroner. Same with the Highway Patrol packing the place. It was a total cluster-fuck as far as the detective was concerned.

"Can you tell me what happened from looking at the victims?" Dr. Hurungzy asked over cell.

"No," Wilson replied, looking inside the crashed SUV. A dead man was sprawled across the front seat. "But it's obviously a shootout over the boy. They're gone. I assume you're tracking them."

"They're on 136 West right now, two cars behind them which we assume are the bad guys," Catherine said from the chopper.

"We're putting them into the info flow right now," Morgan said, getting in on the conversation. "What we want to know is if anything happened there that could have upset the boy? Something bad?"

"Yeah," Goodman, who was also on the call, said. He was checking out Mickey's body. "That guy whose wife the kid healed is dead. He tried to do right and lost. One of Adan's thugs, too, a real big guy. Looks like they died protecting the boy. That's good, right?" He was getting into this. "El Gordo lost three men. Why? What difference does it make?"

"We think there may be a correlation with what happens to the boy and the progress of the disease," Catherine said. Her voice was heavy with worry. "It's started up again. It's spreading across the world, Europe, the Middle East, Africa. Now it's popped up here."

"What?" Wilson jumped like someone had just tasered him. "We haven't heard."

"It's just going out now over the news," Morgan said over the wire. "It hit the contagion lab in Phoenix and a small town not that far away from you called Cordes Lakes."

Getty and Wilson exchanged glances. They'd heard of Cordes Lakes, but they'd never been there, unlike St. Luke's in Phoenix. That was too close for comfort. Maybe fifteen miles from his home, Det. Wilson thought, with his wife and three kids. "Is it spreading?" he asked, suddenly worried.

"No," Catherine answered, trying to be reassuring and failing. Agent Goodman was listening intently, but Wilson and Getty were hardly aware of him. "That's what's so frightening. The disease wiped out the contagion ward, except for one scientist left alive, and Cordes Lakes just lost one street. The rest of the small town was left alone. That means this disease is being manipulated to hit specific, and sometimes very limited areas. We're getting a list of the dead and trying to figure out the connection, but so far none is apparent."

Wilson and Getty exchanged glances, the full import of her words hitting them like a brick wall. "Lilli, the woman the boy saved, her companion is dead, but she's gone," Wilson said, checking the dead scattered about. There was a group around Mickey Meyers, the woman's common-law husband. They'd learned that much anyway. "Where are they headed now, this Adan with the boy and the guys after him?"

"Just a second," Morgan said from the chopper above, reading his map screen. "Willy's Truck Stop. They're all headed in that

Book 4: THE SECOND (AND LAST) NIGHT

direction, Adan Cuarto and his group with the boy, and Zio Benito right behind them."

Wilson looked at Getty, with Goodman watching them. Wilson spoke into his cell phone. "We know it well. Last stop before miles of desert. We're on our way." He snapped off the connection and headed for his unmarked car, his partner and the agent right behind him.

CHAPTER 104

Whitney looked out the window as they whipped through the darkness. Ahead they could see the bright lights of the truck stop, "Willy's" writ large in glowing red and white neon, stuck up high in the middle of the desert. Around it was an oasis of pumps, grocery, bar and grill. It was busy, too, rigs still coming in for the night, and cars getting the last fill-up for a late run into the deep desert.

"Like a signpost from hell," Whitney thought, "come on in and die." She cut a look at her brother. He was on his phone, calling their parents again. "You get 'em yet?" she asked.

He slipped the phone back into a pocket with a worried frown. "No, nothing. You know how regular Dad is about dinner. They should be finishing around now."

"Forget about it for a while," she said. "So what should we do? If we had any sense we'd turn around and go home. That way neither one of us would have to die."

"The boy," Donny said, "we have to talk to him, he's the only one who can change any of this."

"He never talked to us while he was in our car."

"I know, but there's gotta be way to reach him," he said hopefully. "There's just gotta be."

There was a long pause. Closer to the truck stop now. "I just wanted you to know I really care for you, like a lot," Whitney suddenly said. "Even if I can't stand you."

"Yeah," he said, not wanting to get sappy. "I know." He looked out at the dark sand speeding by. "I don't feel like a kid anymore. I feel like I grew up all at once."

"The boy," she said, "he's made both of us grow up." She pulled into the truck stop, weaved her way around the pumps, and took a parking space to the side of the convenience store. "Well, here we are," she said, taking a breath. She got out, followed by her younger brother.

She came to a stop at the corner of the store, staring past the pumps at the parked big rigs to the far side. The dark night made them see like hulking beasts, just waiting to come alive and eat you. All the bright lights popped in the clear desert air. "Is this where you saw all the dead people?" Donny asked as he came up to her side.

She nodded, a little awed in spite of herself. "Yeah, right here, and the second time everybody was dying of the coughing sickness or shooting each other."

She checked her device. "The sickness is still spreading. They say there have been breakouts in China and India. South America, too." She suddenly froze. "Oh, shit."

"What?" he asked, digging for his device, suddenly as worried as her. "What is it?"

"There's been an outbreak in Cordes Lakes," she said. "They don't say where or if it's spreading from there."

"Oh, no, don't tell me," he murmured as he brought up live video. She leaned over, watching his screen. Some colonel from the Highway Patrol was on, answering questions from frantic reporters. It was obvious he wished he wasn't there.

"No, we do not have any more information on the breakout of the coughing sickness," he said in a too-loud official voice, as if he wanted to cover up his panic. "Just that it's isolated and as of this moment has not spread beyond a single street."

Book 4: THE SECOND (AND LAST) NIGHT

The reporters yelled at him, burying him in a flurry of questions he obviously did not have the information to answer. A stricken Donny looked at his sister. "Mom and Dad," he said softly, "they're gone."

Whitney nodded, stunned. "Just like I saw in my vision." Panic swept her. "It's gonna happen here, too. You're gonna die, maybe me, too."

"The vision you had is a maybe, you don't know for sure," he said with a white-lipped nod. "What happens if tonight is worse, like maybe you didn't see everything? What happens if everyone dies of the coughing sickness, including both of us?"

"Oh, God, stop saying that stuff," she said with a sharp shake of her head. She didn't know what to say, but there was nothing to do but wait. She looked through the window of the store, seeing a big clock on the wall above the cashier. The same clock she saw in her vision.

7:25. Not long to wait.

CHAPTER 105

Everybody, including us, is converging on Willy's Truck Stop," Catherine said over the comm line to Det. Wilson. He sat next to Sgt. Getty who sped through the night in their unmarked car. Goodman was in the back, listening in on his earpiece.

"There's no doubt, is there?" Wilson asked. "We're all being manipulated."

"Sure seems that way, doesn't it," Morgan said, coming on the line. He was in love with patterns. "I don't know what's meant to happen at the truck stop, but it's more than just El Gordo and Zio going after the kid."

"What about the rest of America?" Agent Goodman asked, joining in from the back of the unmarked car. His client wanted the boy. He would undoubtedly be getting impatient. "Have there been more outbreaks outside of the hospital and Cordes Lakes?"

"No new outbreak of sickness," came Catherine Hurungzy on the wireless. "It was specific and limited. The rest of the country still seems safe. For the moment. The rest of the world, not so much."

"It's the boy," Getty said, pounding the dash in frustration with her free hand as she drove. "If he's doing this sickness thing, he's scaring the hell out of us. Is that what he wants?"

"All right, all right," Wilson said, raising a hand. He spoke into his cell, trying to keep his voice level and reasonable. He felt like screaming. "What's going on? The boy's doing this? Why?"

"We don't know," Catherine answered, "but all my instincts say it's a warning. Of what could happen if we don't handle this right."

"What's right?" Wilson asked. "How do we handle this right?"

"I don't know," came her answer, leaving Wilson and Getty totally confused. Goodman in the back seat was less so. So far his orders were to protect the boy at all costs. Nothing else mattered. At some point he would be told to take the boy and kill anyone in his way. He would do it without question. For him there was no right or wrong. They were value judgements. He didn't have the time for it.

The boy was the key to everything, including his own advancement. It made him more curious about who had hired him. He had to be very important to reach deep enough into the bowels of the government to find him. He decided to break one of his iron-clad rules and find out.

CHAPTER 106

Adan whipped by a sign for Willy's that was lit up like a blazing flare in the darkness. Lilli straightened in her seat, pointing at a large glow in the near distance. "There," she said, "the truck stop."

Frodo saw it and frowned. "How we gonna start this?"

"Quien sabe?" Adan said from behind the wheel. "It'll happen. Ride el tigre." He glanced in the rearview mirror at the boy between Magda and Frodo. As always, looking steady, even alert, but with that thousand-yard stare. "I don't know whether he's planning all this or is just a cog in a machine."

"How do you mean?" Magda asked.

Adan nodded at the boy. "Look at him. If he's got any power, you wouldn't know it. He might be a puppet in all this, just like us."

"Why? For what purpose?" Magda asked. "What do you think is really going on?"

"I don't know," Adan said, clicking his teeth together, "but something. All this just isn't happening for nothing."

"It's God's will," Lilli said, leaning over from the third seat back in the van, behind Frodo and Magda. She held out a hand, wriggling her fingers. "Look, he cured me. Just as he cured your friend's legs. He's already done so much for others." She looked down at the boy in front of her. He had not moved. "He's good and we have to protect him as he's protecting us."

"Some kind of protection," Frodo said, his voice etched with bitterness. "Samosa's dead. He was my friend. He was a friend to all of us." His mouth pulled down. "What happens if all this is just an accident, some kind of cosmic joke? What then?"

"Who cares?" Magda said, looking out the window as they pulled into the truck stop. It was big and lit up like a nighttime football game. Adan pulled to a halt near a bank of pumps, close to the store. "He's giving people hope. That's even more valuable than being healed sometimes."

"Fuck hope," Adan said, staring straight ahead. There were people filling up their vehicles, but not that many. There was a big chunk of parked trucks way over to the side, with their own diesel stations. "I want the ten million and then I want out of here." He turned and looked at Frodo in the back. "You ready?"

The man with the used-to-be bad legs nodded and held up a pair of pistols, one in either hand. He grinned, putting on a happy face, but inside he knew he was going to die. Funny thing was it seemed all right with Samosa gone. He'd promised him to protect the boy. He wasn't going to break a promise to a dead man, not one he loved, not when he might be joining him very soon.

CHAPTER 107

Zio watched the screens built into the seats of the SUV. The fat slug Gordo was beside him, staring out the window. The screens were filled with news about the second shootout, this one at the grocery store. Only this time the world had a real-time video to keep replaying forever. The "Second Healing" they were calling it. Guess the first one was the baby with the bad heart or maybe it was bringing the dead dog back to life. Who knew? It was better than any dumb scripted show. Reality did beat the shit out of fantasy.

People were going nuts, slicing and dicing what they'd seen: the boy healing the ALS afflicted woman, what it meant, the first clear shot of the albino boy—he was a fucking star—all that anybody could talk about. That and the coughing sickness that seemed to have started up again across the world and had just popped up in Phoenix and some other nowhere town. Shit, it had so far killed what, millions, tens of millions? How bad it was you didn't know. Nobody gave you figures. It was the fucking news. It gave you nothing.

But being touched by the boy, Zio thought—some fools were saying it was a blessing, the sickness and the boy at the same time, that they were somehow working in common, one feeding the other. Zio didn't understand it, but he sure as hell knew the closer you got to dying, the more you were looking for some way to save yourself.

His special phone vibrated, the one that nobody had the number to, and gave caller ID and bunch of other shit. He pulled it from his pocket and checked the screen. There was a name and WHO

365

logo behind it. The World Health Organization. He immediately knew it was about the boy. Like everything else.

Big ass government comes to big ass Mafia boss. If he was going out, this was a way to do it. He loved the attention. "Yes," he said, keeping his voice neutral.

"Dr. Catherine Hurungzy here, Deputy Director at the CDC. Is this Zio Giuseppe Benito?"

"If you're analyzing my voice, you know it's me," he answered with that familiar breathiness, the air flow from the tubes keeping his nostrils flared. He could hear the soft whirr of the helicopter blades behind the woman and looked out at the dark sky above, but he saw nothing.

"I'm putting you on speaker here," the old man said, nodding at Aslanian who punched a key. Everybody in the armored SUV could now hear the conversation, most of all El Gordo. He shifted his bulk, pricking his ears. "What do you want?" Zio asked.

"The same thing you do," she said. "It would be good if you stopped pursuing the boy."

"Not going to happen," the little old man said. "My lungs are failing. He's the only hope I have, so you see there's nothing you can offer me, or threaten me with, that's going to make me stop."

"You have to understand. There are some things greater than you," Catherine said reasonably. "Greater than any of us. We think that could be the boy."

"You're breaking my heart," Zio said, breathing in as much as he could through the plastic clips.

"There's a correlation between the boy and the sickness," Catherine said flatly. "We think that whatever happens to him slows or speeds up the spread."

Zio stopped. "Now you're playing me for a fool. What are you, some kind of Christer working for the fucking Feds?"

Book 4: THE SECOND (AND LAST) NIGHT

"We don't know what would happen if he were injured or hurt in any way. If you don't stop and pull off to the side of the road, we have a drone overhead and we will stop you by force."

"How do you know you're doing the right thing?" Gordo said, leaning his bulk over to speak into Zio's phone, though he was sure the Feds were also listening through the sound system in the vehicle itself. Everything was more and more connected all the time.

The Fat Man grinned. It forced his double chins to pile up. "We were all chosen by him, even shitheads like me." He didn't see why he shouldn't declare himself. The fuckers undoubtedly knew everything. "He touched all of us, me, too, El Gordo, the Fat Man," he continued. "I've been having visions. I've seen what's coming. You see what's coming? 'Cause I got a real serious message for you. You can't change it. None of us can."

"Morgan here," came a male voice. It was trying to be reasonable. "What visions have you had?"

"I've seen the truck stop coming up," he said. "I was there. I saw the boy touching Zio. Do you see what that means?" The Fat Man's voice became strident. "You can't kill me or stop me or Zio, because that's not his plan. Now fuck off."

"Have you seen people dying of the sickness?" came Catherine's quick response.

Gordo hesitated, thrown. He hadn't. "What are you talking about?"

"The others who've been touched," she said. "They're having visions of people getting the sickness. At the truck stop. Have you been seeing anything like that?"

"So what if I have?" Gordo said, his eyes bulging. He hadn't seen that happening where they were headed.

"Do you have idea what it means if you haven't seen it but

someone else touched by the boy has?" Morgan said from the chopper. "Is it some kind of warning?"

Gordo reached over and took the cell of out of Zio's flimsy grasp and clicked it off.

"What the hell are you doing," Zio Benito said, pissed. In the front seat, passenger side, Krekorian shifted so he had a clearer reach for his pistol. Things were getting edgy.

"They're not going to do anything," Gordo said. "They can't. Not till after the truck stop and however that turns out and maybe not even then."

"What do you see? I know you saw something happening at that truck stop. What was it?"

"Relax. I didn't see anybody coughing," he said. "'Cause what I saw was you being touched and then people pulling their guns and opening up. Big surprise there."

Zio swallowed and shifted his skinny ass. "Doesn't mean it's gonna happen," he said, getting increasingly nervous. What if the Fat Man was wrong? What if the sickness did break out?

"Doesn't mean it isn't either," the Fat Man shot back. "Maybe we don't draw our guns. Maybe everybody stays cool, and nobody starts coughing, maybe we grab the kid and Adan backs down. Who the fuck knows?"

"Yeah," Zio said, trying to figure out how to play it. He looked at his guys, the two Armenians. "No gun play—until the boy touches me. After that, go with the flow."

CHAPTER 108

Adan slid open the side door of the parked van and helped the boy and Magda to the ground, followed by Lilli and Frodo. They all had pistols, and kept them low, not hidden, but not drawing attention to them either. They stood there, looking around. Business had picked up. Vehicles filled the pumps, trucks at the diesel stations, people went in and out of the grill, patronized the convenience store where they could pick up snacks and basic groceries. The stop was the last one before a long stretch of desert and nobody wanted to be out there after dark without a full tank and munchies.

"Okay, no Gordo. We got here first," Magda said, scoping out the situation. "So what do we do?"

Adan scanned the stop, looking for something familiar from his vision, something that might tell him what was about to happen, but he wasn't seeing it. Magda spotted a young woman, a teen really. Pretty in an Arizona sort of way. Blond and natural. Magda just knew she had blue eyes. A younger boy stood next to her. It was the girl's brother. Had she seen them both before in her vision? Damn right, she had. They were the spitting image.

She nudged Adan, and pointed. "There," she said, "the girl and the boy I saw, only they're still okay." Her eyes darted about the still busy gas station. "We've arrived early. This is before it all goes to hell."

Adan and the others looked at the two teens. They were looking back as if they recognized them. "Let's find out what they know," he said and started toward them. Magda took the boy's hand and followed, Lilli and Frodo with them.

CHAPTER 109

Donny and Whitney looked at the boy as Magda and the others walked toward them. "You recognize them?" Donny asked.

"Yeah," she nodded, "from my last vision. The woman with the boy was trying to protect him when the gunfire started."

Adan and the others came up to them near the side of the convenience store.

"Where'd you get him?" Donny asked, nodding at the kid. He was totally natural and didn't seem at all surprised to see them. He must have recognized them as the ones who picked him up on the highway and brought him here, but he sure didn't seem to care.

"You know who he is?" Adan asked.

"Oh, yeah," Donny said with a nod at his sister. "We picked him up in the Tonto desert. He was just walking along and our mom insisted on giving him a lift. We stopped here and he disappeared." His face scrunched up like he was thinking about crying. "Our parents are dead. In Cordes Lakes. We think anyway." He swiped at his eyes with a knuckle and looked at his sister. "He touched her."

Magda looked at the girl. "You've had visions?"

"All the time," Whitney said, nodding at her brother. "I've seen him dead and then another time I saw myself. I also saw my parents back home, but I hoped it wouldn't happen, but I think it has."

"My husband saw himself back at our store," Lilli said, stepping forward. "He stayed anyway. You saw him heal me?"

371

Whitney nodded. "Oh, yeah, us and the world." She glanced around the truck stop. "I've also seen this whole place exploding. I saw people dying with that coughing sickness, too, those that weren't shot already. Some of you may have been among them, but the boy was gone, I'm sure of it."

"Just like Mickey," Lilli said, referring to the man she'd spent so many years with. "I wasn't there either. That's why he stayed, because he knew I made it out of there. To here, of all places." She looked around in wide-eyed wonder.

Whitney turned, looking at the clock that could be seen through the window of the convenience store. The hands showed five of 8. The witching hour. "It's supposed to happen at eight tonight. Five minutes from now."

"Holy shit," Frodo said, looking at the truck stop. It was all relatively sane; for the next few minutes anyway.

"There's gotta be a way to stop it," Whitney said with a huge start of self-awareness. She wasn't sixteen any more. Well, she was chronologically, but not emotionally. She was older now, much, much older. She had responsibilities. Like for her brother and the world, but who cared if you couldn't do anything to make it come out right?

"You have to stop it," she said to the boy. He looked blankly ahead. She knelt in front of him, trying to snag his gaze. The others watched, Frodo keeping an eye on the traffic. No one was paying them any heed, which was good for the moment. "Do you understand me?" Whitney continued, trying to get the boy's attention. "You can't let my brother be killed. Me either, if you can help it."

The boy did not react. "It's fate," Frodo said, turning back. "None of us can avoid it. Not me, not you, not any of us."

"Why didn't you both stay home?" Lilli asked Whitney and her brother.

Book 4: THE SECOND (AND LAST) NIGHT

"I tried to," Whitney answered, "I tried leaving him at home, too, but then I saw him and my whole family die of the coughing sickness if I did." Her eyes dampened. "I really wanted to save him and my family, but I think our parents are gone. You gotta help me save my brother."

"It's a test," Lilli said. "He's part of it, too." She looked at the boy who stood there, staring across the truck stop, seemingly not seeing anything; or certainly not giving a damn. "It's not him that's controlling this. It's something else."

Whitney looked at the clock. She gulped. "It's eight o'clock, straight up," she said.

CHAPTER 110

Before anybody could reply, a black SUV, followed by a powerful, low-slung Porsche left the highway and pulled to a halt next to the nearby pumps. The doors flew open and Aslanian and Krekorian stepped out, their guns pulled and ready. They were followed by a very angry looking El Gordo while Zio Benito stayed hunched inside, hidden behind a darkened window.

"Fucking idiot," Gordo shouted, spotting Adan and his crew. He waved his pistol angrily, not caring who saw it. "Look what you made us go through, asshole. You're gonna pay."

Adan didn't move. None of them did except Magda. She drew the boy a little closer. The girl in black and her Ninja slipped out of the Porsche and edged forward. Only her narrow black eyes were showing through her skeleton mask. She unslung an AK and cleared the breach. People at the pumps started noticing and were beating a hasty exit in their cars, or backing away from their vehicles, putting space between themselves and the people with the weapons.

The manager of the truck stop appeared from within the store. You could tell he was the boss because he wore a shirt and tie and some kind of nametag. He yelled at them. "Hey, you can't have guns here. This isn't open carry."

Out of the darkness of the black SUV slipped the little old man, Zio Benito, a small portable oxygen tank slung over his bony shoulder, a plastic tube running to the clips in his nose. The old man stopped, looking at the guy from the store. The Black Widow and the Ninja stepped forward, raising their weapons. The manager took one look and hurriedly disappeared back into the store, slamming the door behind him and locking it. A "Closed for business" sign went up.

"Zio Benito," Adan muttered, looking around. They were completely alone now, in the middle of a truck stop that suddenly had gone stone quiet. People who hadn't fled had pulled back, watching from behind trucks and cars. They weren't moving. They were frozen in place, watching them. It was like the entire place was holding its breath.

"No shit," Frodo murmured back, all of them watching the little old man as he stopped, facing them.

"The last of the Mafioso…," whispered Magda. Her eyes were on the little old man. He nodded at the two guys with him, and one of them threw open the back hatch of the SUV, so they could see inside. The back was full of several large duffle bags. A row of shiny aluminum oxygen canisters sat behind them, filling up the cargo area.

El Gordo stepped forward, yelling to Adan as he waved a hand at the bags. "All right, here's your money. How we going to do this?"

CHAPTER
111

Magda swiveled her head, looking at Adan. Her color was up and her eyes were squeezed with worry. "What the hell do we do?"

Adan shrugged. "We do what I said." He yelled back to the Fat Man. "Bring it over here, I'll come out with the kid. We meet Zio Benito halfway."

Zio took a step forward, staring at him. He nodded at his men. The two Armenians threw the bags over their shoulders and carried them half of the distance between the two groups, one at the pumps, the other near the store, and dumped them. They hurried back to their boss.

Zio stared at Adan and the others. "All right," he called in his thin reedy voice. "I'm coming." Waving El Gordo and the others back, he started forward. They were slow steps, but determined. The oxygen container swung from his shoulder, bumping his side. He was breathing heavily through the nose clips, as though walking unassisted was a chore for him.

Adan looked at Frodo, who stood with the two teens near the convenience store. "It's time. Work your way around them."

Frodo nodded, slipping behind their van and working his way behind stopped vehicles toward the pump. Whitney looked at the boy. Magda held his hand. "Can you stop this?" Whitney said. "Can you keep my brother from being hurt?" There was no reaction from the boy, who was facing the slowly approaching Zio Benito.

Adan turned to Magda, indicating the boy. "I'm taking him out there. You back me up."

"We're both taking him out," she said through clenched teeth and stepped forward with the boy before he could stop her.

He looked at Lilli. She and the teens were the last ones left. "Cover us when the shooting starts." Lilli nodded, pulling her small automatic, keeping it down at her side and hoping that Frodo got a good angle. The teens just stood there, not sure what to do.

"Guns," Whitney said quickly to Lilli, wanting to help. "We know how to use them."

"The back of the van," Lilli said and Whitney dived inside the vehicle. She appeared a moment later with a revolver, busily loading it, trying not to drop any bullets.

Donny shot her a look. "What about me?"

"I'm trying to keep you alive. You stay out of it."

Donny thought about insisting but got caught, watching the unfolding scene with fascinated eyes. Adan and Magda with the boy came to a halt by the bags of money, Zio stopping on the other side. They were surrounded by people hiding behind their vehicles with their devices out, sending it out live worldwide.

CHAPTER 112

"We could kill it, just let it all go black worldwide. There's no reason they have to see this," Morgan said to Catherine. They were in the chopper, watching the face-off on their feeds in real time.

"Too late," she said. "Twenty minutes to the truck stop." She swung to another screen filled with blinking red dots. "It's spreading out from London and across the world, but it looks like it's slowing."

She swung back to the screen showing the boy and the thugs at the truck stop. Zio Benito had come to a stop before the boy and Magda. The bags of money were to their side. The sound wasn't the best, but you could see his mouth move. "Have him touch me." The old man's gaze shifted to the boy. "Come on, kid, do your stuff." He held his hand out, waiting to see what the kid did.

Everyone was frozen, watching.

The boy initiated the movement and pulled away from Magda. As she and the others watched he took the old man's hand, holding it tight as he stared upward into his beady eyes. The boy's chest swelled as though some great power was gathering in him.

Catherine leaned closer to her screen, pointing to his chest. A bluish swirl seemed to be forming there. "What is that? We saw it when he saved that woman in the back of the store," she said.

Morgan leaned in. "A force," he said. He could almost see it, but not quite. "It's going down his arm and through his hand into the old Mafioso."

On the screen, the boy withdrew his hand, breaking the contact. Zio Benito slowly lifted his head, breathing slowly at first and then taking increasingly deep breaths. With a big smile, he pulled the plastic clips from his nose and threw them aside. He dropped the oxygen bottle to the tarmac. He thrust his hands wide and he slowly turned, as though inviting applause.

"I can breathe," he crowed. "I can breathe." Catherine and Morgan heard him clearly in the helicopter.

CHAPTER 113

At the truck stop, there was a smattering of applause. Enough for a suddenly boundlessly energetic Zio Benito to give a little jump in the air. He turned back to Adan and his group. He had a big grin across his shrunken leathery face. Unseen by him and unnoticed by everyone else, Frodo worked his way in behind a pump, where he had a good angle on El Gordo and Zio's killers. He was also looking into the open rear hatch of Zio Benito's SUV. With the bundles of cash gone, the shiny oxygen bottles lined up in the back were clear to see in the overhead floods.

"It is a miracle," the old Mafioso said, grinning wildly at Adan. "The boy can really do it. I can't tell you how grateful I am." He lost his smile. "But not that grateful. I'm taking the boy with me." He spun the boy about, facing Magda and the others, and snapped a skinny arm around his throat. A gleaming gun appeared in his hand, a small 9mm.

He aimed it at Adan and the others as he backed away, dragging the boy with him. The boy's eyes were wide-open, staring at them, almost as if he was begging them to help him.

Adan pulled his piece, but it was too late. Magda and Lilli stood there, frozen, the teens behind them, next to their van. The older woman had her pistol out, but she didn't dare fire. She was a good shot, living in the desert, could stop a rattler mid-strike, but she didn't dare put the boy's life in danger. Zio continued pulling the boy backward. Behind him at the SUV, the two Armenians pulled their weapons, and Gordo filled his hand, but nobody moved. The masked Black Widow and the Ninja stepped up with their AKs.

Over to the side, behind the gas pump Frodo pulled back, his gun out. Sure, he could open fire, but then all hell would break loose. The kid could get it and he didn't want that to happen. He'd promised Samosa. Besides, he wanted the kid to reach the notch as badly as any of the others.

"You're afraid," Zio crowed to Adan, enjoying his grip on the boy, stopping for a moment. "You shoot, you kill the boy. You don't want that, but you know something. I don't give a shit. What if I do it?" He pressed his pistol into the side of the boy's head. Adan stiffened. So did the two women and the teens.

"Don't hurt him," Magda cried out. Zio just laughed at her.

"He's God's Messenger," Lilli shouted at Zio, her pistol up, but not firing. "You subvert his world, you contravene his plans, and he will stop you."

"Oh, yeah," the skinny old man yelled back. "I'm alive and I can breathe again and I got the boy, so what the fuck is your God going to do to me?"

Behind him, backed up against the SUV, Aslanian tightened his grip on his pistol, only to suddenly cough. It was hard and rasping. He seemed surprised. He coughed again, harder this time, blood flecking his lips. El Gordo and the others froze, staring at him in horror.

Zio, too, the boy forgotten, as he turned to watch. The thug coughed again, spraying more blood in the direction of the Black Widow and the Ninja. They forgot their automatic weapons and backed away. Adan used the moment to leap forward, breaking into a full out dash, smashing the butt of his pistol into the old lizard's head. Zio Benito went down with a dry crunching sound and Adan grabbed the boy.

Book 4: THE SECOND (AND LAST) NIGHT

He started to pull him back toward the van, picking up a satchel of money and Magda on the way.

It snapped El Gordo out of his horror at the coughing sickness and he whirled, opening up on them with his pistol. Krekorian followed, even as he moved away from his fellow thug, Aslanian, as he crumpled to the blacktop with his blood-smeared mouth.

Behind them, those civilians who hadn't fled now turned tail and ran, all of them screaming in fear of the gunfire and the sickness.

It didn't stop Zio, bleeding profusely from the head, from crawling to his feet and making it back to the black SUV as El Gordo and their crew continued firing on Adan and the others. He and the others dived for Lilli's van, bullets ripping past. Hidden behind the pumps a flurry of thoughts whipped through Frodo's head. If he started firing at El Gordo and the others, they would kill him. If he didn't they would kill Adan and the others, maybe the boy. He loved Samosa for all he'd done for him, especially after he was crippled. He was gone, his best friend who he'd never be able to pay back, not while he was alive anyway. He'd promised him to get the boy to the notch. The hell with it, he thought. He wasn't going to end up dead, on the other side, telling Samosa that he'd failed to fulfill his dying promise to him.

He rose up and fired at the open back of the SUV. He was aiming for the canisters.

"For Samosa and the boy," he screamed and started for the vehicle, pulling his second pistol and firing as he came, both guns bucking in his hands, taking the attention of Gordo and the others. They opened fire on him.

Magda reached their van with the boy. Adan grabbed Whitney and Donny, dropping the bag of cash. He hated to do it, but their lives were more important than the cash. Lilli followed, firing her pistol. A thug went down. Near the pumps, Frodo was hit, but kept walking and firing. Zio hugged the side of the SUV, glancing into the side window and seeing the oxygen bottles lined up at the back. Slugs were hitting the canisters and ricocheting off with high-pitched metallic whangs.

"Get away!" he screamed at the others, flapping his skinny hands and backing away from the SUV which had suddenly become a potential powder keg. "Get away!"

He started to scramble back, the others not quick enough. Frodo was shot in three places now and finally fell to his knees, bleeding from multiple wounds. He used the last of his strength to raise his pistol one last time, aimed, and fired. Frodo didn't see it, he was dead, but his slug hit a canister square in the back of the SUV and punctured it. It exploded, taking the others with it, boom, boom, boom they went, tearing out the sides and top of the vehicle in a fireball that blew bags of cash high in the air, immolating millions in a fireball as it blew off the top of the pumps, and reached for the night heavens.

The Ninja was cut down, same with Krekorian. Zio hadn't made it far enough away and was crushed by a flying door that slammed him to the ground. Blood gushed out the sides, only his hands and feet visible beneath the warped door.

Adan and the others were knocked off their feet by the concussion just as they reached their van. Whitney leapt up, looking at Donny and the others on the ground. "Come on," she yelled at her brother. Magda with the boy and Adan with Lilli climbed groggily to their feet and stumbled toward the van. Not Donny. He didn't move.

Whitney ran to his side. "Donny?" she said. He still hadn't moved. She pulled frantically at a limp arm. "Donny, come on, get up." She rolled him over. There was a neat hole drilled right through his sixteen-year old heart.

Book 4: THE SECOND (AND LAST) NIGHT

Magda got the boy and Lilli inside the van and rushed back to Whitney who was still holding her dead brother's arm. "C'mon, honey," Magda said, "we gotta go." She pulled the stunned girl away and put her in the front with Adan who was behind the wheel. She climbed in back with the boy and Lilli.

Adan fired the van, but his eyes were for the cash bag he'd dropped. It was unharmed, sitting just a few feet away, plump with all that cash. He couldn't help himself. He started to climb out and go for it again. Magda grabbed him, screaming above the crackle of the fire that was sweeping the remains of the SUV and threatening to set the pumps afire. "Leave it, estupido pendejo, leave it!"

With one last mournful look, Adan slammed the door shut and took off, heading for the highway. Behind them, near the store, Gordo rolled over with a groan from where he'd been blown by the explosion. The Black Widow appeared over him, looking down. "Can you travel?" her skeleton face asked. She made no effort to help him.

El Gordo shook his head trying to clear it, and looked around. The fire continued to burn, flickering light revealing the dead bodies. "The sickness? What happened? Did it stop again?"

"Seems to," she replied with a shrug. "We're still breathing anyway."

"The boy. We have to get the boy," he grunted as he struggled to his feet.

"I know," she said, checking her device. "The bidding is over a hundred million for him, now."

"Who do you work for?" the Fat Man asked, his mouth sagging. He was charred and a mess, the fire roaring behind them as the SUV burned furiously. Ka-boom a pump went, sending the fire higher into the sky and threatening others.

"The highest bidder." She grabbed him under the arm and headed back toward her waiting Porsche, the Fat Man, dusty and torn, leaning heavily against her. It didn't seem to slow her down at all.

CHAPTER 114

"What do you see?" Adan asked as he sped through the desert night. "Do you have any idea where you picked him up?"

Whitney shook her head. She was still stunned at the death of her brother. She had tried to protect him. It didn't make any difference. She turned to the boy who sat next to her, quiet and still as always. Lilli and Magda sat on the other side. "You saw it coming, didn't you? If you could see it why didn't you stop it? We asked you. Donny didn't have to die, neither did my parents."

"We're still alive. He could have killed us back there with the coughing sickness," Lilli said. She looked at Whitney. "He was trying to protect you. It was meant to happen that way. You have more to do. We all do."

"You're crazy," Whitney said, looking at her, blinking back tears. She suddenly leaned forward, grabbing Adan's shoulder as he drove down the dark highway. "Go back. Have the boy touch Donny, bring him back," Whitney yelled at him, on the edge of hysteria. "He'll do it, if he doesn't I'll kill him myself."

Magda pushed her back. "Stop it, it's not Adan's fault. It's not the kid's either. You saw that guy coughing himself to death. The sickness has begun again. It's begun here, in Arizona. Out of nowhere."

"I know," Whitney screamed at her, "my parents are dead. They died in Cordes Lakes. Now my brother is gone. He's killed my entire family." She glared at the boy who sat in between her and Magda, seemingly oblivious. "You did it. Why, why do you have to hurt and kill everybody?"

"Cut it out, would you," Adan broke in, his voice hard. "You want to watch the fucking highway, see if you can tell us where you picked the boy up?"

Whitney wiped at her tears, calming down, as though having something else to think about took her mind off her grief. She peered out at the moon-swept road ahead. "It's too dark to tell exactly, but it was after we passed this dune buggy shop. He was coming from there."

"Four-wheelers?" Lilli said, straightening in the back. "That's Terry Lathrop's place. He rents out to sand riders, him and Joe Arachro. It's only a few miles ahead."

"I was a stupid fool," Adan said out of nowhere, his hands gripping the wheel harder. "Estupido. My greed fucked us all."

"What do you mean?" Magda asked, throwing him a look. She could hardly believe her ears.

"I wanted the money. I wanted it more than anything and I got Frodo killed because of it." He nodded back at Whitney. "I got your brother killed. Everybody is fucking dying and all I could think about was the stupid money."

"Don't feel bad," Magda said from the back. "It's all any of us could think about. Me anyway. Frodo, too. Anyway, we're doing it for the boy now. Getting him home." She looked down at the boy. She realized with a start that he was focused, staring almost expectantly down the dark road ahead.

Lilli noticed, too. She leaned over. "He's looking forward to wherever we're going," she said quietly. "He's listening also. To every word we say."

Whitney looked up. Her eyes were still red and tear stained, but the boy took her mind away from her grief and anger. "What do you mean? He's judging us?" she asked.

Book 4: THE SECOND (AND LAST) NIGHT

Adan's phone buzzed, interrupting them. "Shit," he said. He clicked it, putting it on speaker.

"That you, you fat fuck?" he asked, knowing the answer.

"Me and someone with me who can kill you and everyone with you," Gordo growled back. "The boy. I still want him."

"Can't have him."

"Where you headed?" came the greasy voice. "The notch?"

"How did you know about that?" Magda asked, sitting up in surprise. She didn't like the idea of him knowing about the notch, not at all.

"He wants me there, too. I see it. I'm gonna catch you," El Gordo said. "You know that now, don't you?"

"Yeah, that makes sense," Adan snarled. "Kill the boy. Smart move. That what you want? Fuck off and stay away, Gordo, or I'll kill you myself." He clicked off, continuing to drive down the road. They whipped past a sign that said "Terry's Dune Buggies, Quads, 4-Wheelers, whatever you want for the sand, straight ahead!"

CHAPTER 115

Terry Lathrop sat in a beat-up old chair, before the open door to the dune buggy shop. He was enjoying the night air. The quads were kept under an aluminum awning to the side, lined up real nice. They were mixed in style from motorcycle-like rail riders to full-on four seaters with awnings and shocks. They all had fat tires and could roar through the sand. The shop was mostly office and a half-ass kitchen with a cot in the corner. He was on his walkie to Joe Bear Claws. Ever since he'd seen the kid, the Indian had refused to come in. Said he was waiting for him to come back, that he was guarding the notch till then.

He'd believed Joe ever since that first walkie call, telling him the boy was on the way. Of course, seeing the boy as he walked past that morning and the news since then helped. Going up to visit him and seeing the mesa-that-wasn't-there-but-was, sealed the deal. Ever since, he'd been reporting every move the kid made to Joe and when he'd showed up in Mary's Landing he knew Joe was right. He was coming their way.

He didn't know how Mickey and Lilli had gotten involved. Maybe 'cause they grew dynamite weed, but he knew them as good and honest people. Hell, the town was so small everyone pretty much knew everyone else. He'd seen Lilli's healing, "The Second Healing" they were calling it, on his device. Then there had been the healing at Willy's, before all hell broke loose. Was there anything that wasn't streamed worldwide anymore?

Tom Holland   The NOTCH

"There was a big explosion and a fire in the distance," he said over the walkie to Joe. "It was the truck stop."

"They saying what happened yet?" Joe asked on the walkie.

"No, but they got live broadcast. This is like watching a stupid huge action movie, only it's real. The kid saved this old guy and then a gunfight broke out. They just blew up Willy's. Huge fireball. They're on their way here."

"Just like I said," Joe chuckled. "I was left here to keep an eye on the notch. Just to make sure it didn't disappear. Then he'd be stuck here."

"It still there?"

"Sure is," Joe said. "Between the table top and the crag, a couple of hundred yards above me. That's where the boy came from, out of the sun."

Terry spotted two bright headlights poking out of the darkness, the van speeding down the highway toward him. "I think they're here," he said, standing up.

"Send them up. If they're for real, the boy will show them the way." Joe clicked off. Terry stepped forward to greet the people in the van as they turned off the road. It stopped and Adan got out, followed by a hot young woman with the boy and then Mickey's wife, Lilli, and a young girl with flowing blond hair.

Terry's eyes widened. "Damn it, Lilli," he said with a grin, "you can walk again."

The older woman smiled back and hugged him. "It was Mickey's gift to me. He brought the boy to us."

Terry centered on the boy. Same kid, same wheat-colored hair and freckled pale face. The dune buggy operator nodded. "Knew he'd be back."

"You've seen him before?" Adan said, feeling a flash of hope that maybe this all did make sense. Whitney, without quite

392

Book 4: THE SECOND (AND LAST) NIGHT

knowing why, brought out her phone and started live streaming. The world had a right to know about him. It was like his entire time here was going out across the world. She figured it had to give people hope. Or at least question everything they knew up till then (and maybe stop her wanting to cry all the time, too, for her lost family).

"Yup," Terry nodded, and looked through the darkness, across the open shed of four-wheelers toward the high desert in the distance. "Came out of the sand in the early morning. Appeared over there." He glanced to the side of the shed where the desert started to end. "Just looked at me, but I knew something special had happened. He started down the road and then was gone."

"I was the next in line," Whitney said. She nodded down the highway. "We picked him up a few miles from here."

"We've got to get him home," Lilli said. "It's the notch, isn't it? We've all seen it."

"Up that way," Terry said, looking up the dirt road that legged out the back of the shed and trailed deep into the desert. "In a place Joe Bear Claws says exists, but it doesn't on any map. What you call the notch. I was there last night."

"We couldn't find it on any map either," Magda asked, letting go of the boy. He just stood there, not moving. "We've all seen it, but not all of us want him to get away. Others want to trap him and keep him for themselves. They're after us right now."

"I wasn't the first to see him. Bear Claws was, Joe Arachro is his given name," Terry said. "Knows the desert better than almost anyone." He glanced at the boy who just stared ahead, not reacting to anything. "He said the kid came out of the sun, like some Navajo god. I thought he was crazy, but then I started seeing the news."

Terry didn't tell them that Joe was stoned more often than not—shrooms; said they were more natural than the other shit.

393

Tom Holland   The **NOTCH**

Sharpened your mind, unlike liquor, weed, crack, speed, and opioids which made you stupid and insane. Both Joe and Terry knew the truth of it; they killed. Their mutual love of the desert, the unending sand that seemed to scour away all evil, the cleanliness and quiet beauty of it, had somehow saved them from their addictions.

"He's afraid if he leaves it'll disappear again," Terry continued. "He's saying the boy has to return into the sun, the same way he came. He's holding it open for him."

Adan and others exchanged glances. "Did he say why?" Lilli asked.

Terry shook his head. "Boy touched him. I saw him. That was enough." He nodded at the boy who was still staring straight ahead, at something they couldn't see. "In him. I believe in him and I don't believe in shit."

Headlights blazed out of the darkness, interrupting them. It was the Porsche roaring down the highway toward them.

"Time to run for our lives," Adan yelled. They raced for the dune buggies under the sheet metal roof next to the small building.

CHAPTER 116

Sgt. Getty whipped past the blazing truck stop, fire and smoke still rising. Agent Goodman sat in the back. The wail of sirens could be heard in the near distance, quickly approaching. Det. Wilson was beside her, on his headphones. "They're gone. Are you tracking them?" he said into his throat mic.

He looked out the side window, up at the sky, limned by a full moon. He knew the chopper was up there somewhere with Dr. Hurungzy and the guy with her. He had no doubt there were drones up there, too, and heavier aircraft on the way if needed.

"On the highway directly ahead," came her voice. "Gordo is ahead of you. We don't know who's with him, but a number of people were lost at the truck stop, including Zio Benito."

"What about the sickness?" Wilson asked. "We saw it just before the truck blew. Somebody went down with it."

"We saw it, too," Catherine replied, "but there have been no new reports. We have assets headed there right now, but you stay after the boy."

"Is there an endgame?" asked Wilson.

"The boy," she said in his headphones, "he must be protected at all costs, including your life and that of your partner. You, too, Agent Goodman. I can't put it in strong enough terms. The sickness has stopped again."

"So there is a connection?" the cop said with a swallow, stunned by the implications.

"It's getting stronger all the time. Somebody did something at the gas station the boy approved of. It's all we can think of. We're tracking you. The next time you stop we'll land." She cut the connection and looked across the helicopter at Morgan.

"You saw the video," she said. "What happened that the boy liked? He stopped the sickness there. Several people died, one of the sickness, and that was it. It hasn't popped up anywhere else in the area." She glanced at her screen. The red dots were slowing down and some were even disappearing. "At the same time it's stopping all over the world, burning itself out."

She looked out the window of the flying helicopter. She could see the fire at the truck stop below. They were circling as things developed on the ground. "The boy has to be controlling the sickness. Why?" she asked, her voice starting to rise. "Is he an alien or is he some kind of god? Was he sent by God, a messenger? Obviously, a higher intelligence. In our solar system or some other? Is he human? Humanoid? Robot? A simulacrum? You're seen the fingerprints he leaves on whatever he touches. What does that? What's he doing here and what does he want?"

"He's heading somewhere," Morgan said, looking at her steadily. "There's a constant progression. They're all people he touched. It's as though he's retracing his steps to where he started."

"Where's that?" she asked, her gaze shifting to a screen.

"We don't know," he said, his face grim and determined, "not yet, but we will."

CHAPTER
117

dan and the others reached the shed with the line of ATVs, Terry yelling at them. "Grab the packs." He nodded at backpacks piled on a work tale. "Get out of here. Follow the red light, it'll take you to Joe Bear Claws." He shoved an electronic compass into Adan's hand, another in Magda's. She grabbed it and pulled on a helmet. "Make sure the boy gets to the notch, now go."

Terry looked down the highway. The Porsche was almost upon them, its headlights spearing him. Magda jumped on a stripped-down dune buggy, Adan sitting the boy behind her. He placed his hands on Magda's side. "Hold on," he said, but the boy's grip was loose.

"Here," Terry said, throwing a tow cord around the boy and Magda, cinching him in close. She took off on the four-wheeler, roaring out the back of the shop with the boy behind her and up a dusty road into the desert night.

Adan was busy getting helmets on Whitney and Lilli when the Porsche's bright Halo headlights swept the shop as the car left the highway and went into a sideways slide that brought it to a stop before the shop, spraying sand and dust into the moonlight. El Gordo and the Black Widow hopped out. They both opened up, he with a pistol, she with her AK. The bullets ate their way across the dirt and slammed into the shed, whistling through the air around Adan and the others.

Lilli didn't hesitate. She hit the gas and roared out of the back of the shed and into the desert. Whitney followed, holding on tight to the handles as the fat tires dug into the sand and she gathered speed. Both were desert bred and handled the four-wheelers easily.

Inside the shed, Terry picked up a rifle and was firing at the Porsche. He missed, but not El Gordo. The Fat Man returned fire, the slugs hitting Terry and knocking him back against a quad where he fell to the ground. Adan leaped on a four-wheel rail, laid flat against the tank, and twisted the accelerator. As he roared away into the desert, the Widow opened up on him, stitching the air around him, but missed.

She and Gordo ran up, the Fat Man stopping above Terry. He was still alive, but blood was draining out of his chest and gut. "Where's the notch?" Gordo snarled, aiming his pistol at the dying man.

Terry smiled up at him. Blood flecked the corners of his mouth. He was hit in the lung. "You're the bad guy who has the visions, aren't you? You tell me."

The Black Widow stepped forward, nodding after Adan and the others. "Look," she said with a smile behind her skeleton mask, "we can follow their lights." Sure enough, several of them could be seen bobbing through the darkness in the distance.

El Gordo smiled and shot the wounded guy in the head, putting the asshole out of his misery. They had to get the boy. That was all he had to know. El Gordo realized how huge this was now, with the Feds involved. The Shadow Government was just behind them, giving all the orders. They'd kill all of them once they got their hands on the boy.

Gordo had to get the boy first, before anyone else. It was the only way he and the Black Widow were going to stay alive. He wanted them to be the last two left alive, them and the boy. That's when he'd kill her.

CHAPTER 118

Adan drove up to the other quads that waited for him on the rise. They looked down through the night on the ATV store and the highway. Magda turned to Adan on her ATV. "They got that guy, whatever his name was."

"Terry Lathrop," Lilli said. "Nice man." She nodded up at the dark moon-streaked sky above them. "We don't know how far this notch is. It's dark. We can't go fast."

"How's the boy?" Adan asked Magda. He was tied behind her and had laid his head on the curve of her back, as though resting.

"Fine, I think," She looked over her shoulder where the boy was strapped tight to her. He seemed almost asleep.

Adan got off his quad and checked the tie cords that held the boy. Lilli sat on her idling quad. "The whole world wants him," she said, looking at him sadly.

"I still have the same question," Whitney said, looking at the boy. His eyes were closed and he seemed to be sleeping peacefully, nestled against Magda's back. "If the kid's so good, why is he leaving a trail of bodies behind him? It isn't just my brother and parents or your Mickey or the guy who probably just died at the dune buggy store. It's tens of millions of dead people, if he's responsible for the coughing sickness. He's killing off the whole goddamn world."

"I don't know about the world," Magda said quietly, "but we're the core of it, of what's happening. It's us, the people he touched, Crazy Daisy and Samosa and now Frodo, Mickey, we're deciding what happens to the rest of the world." She glanced at Lilli. "But it's still not the boy's fault. He's not in control. We can all feel that."

"He didn't touch my parents or brother," Whitney said bitterly, "and they're dead."

"The sickness?" Adan said with a frown. "We saw it at the truck stop. Has it started up again?" He checked his device. So did Whitney and Magda. Only Lilli seemed content to look at the stars above.

"There's no news. The bars are weakening. People saw the gunfight, but not the coughing," Magda said.

"It's gonna start up again after what happened at the truck stop," Adan said, his face darkening. "I mean, look at all the shit that went on back there."

"It doesn't make any difference now, does it?" Lilli said reasonably enough. "It's just us and them." She nodded back toward the store and the highway. They could see the lights of two quads tearing up the road in the moonlight, headed in their direction.

Adan looked at the boy. "Which way do we go?" He didn't expect anything from the kid, he was already pulling out the compass Terry had given him, but the kid suddenly lifted his head.

"Look at him," Magda said, shocked. "He's coming alive." The boy slowly turned to the right, staring into the distance.

"You think that's the way?" Whitney asked, not sure if the kid did it deliberately.

"You'd better know it is," Adan said, staring at the boy. His face was still, set like stone, but the eyes were definitely focused in the distance. His compass pointed in the same direction, toward where the Indian, Joe Bear Claws, was supposed to be. He revved the quad and drove deeper into the dark desert. Magda followed with the boy, Whitney pausing a moment to look at Lilli, who was still enjoying the desert quiet.

Book 4: THE SECOND (AND LAST) NIGHT

"Is it the boy's fault? Can you think of any reason so many bad things can be happening?" Whitney asked. "Why would he kill my entire family?"

"Some of us are good, some bad, and God has a reason for everything, even if we can't understand," Lilli said with a shrug. "It's the way it's always been and always will be, but maybe somebody has gotten tired of putting up with us, the bad, anyway, and is giving us one last chance. Or maybe this is the apocalypse the Bible talks about and we're all done for. I know it doesn't make you feel any better, me either, but that's how I think about it anyway."

"What?" Whitney asked. "You think the boy is some kind of messenger from God?"

"Or judge," Lilli said quietly. "Then again, I could be wrong and he could be the devil in disguise, playing with us and corrupting us, laughing in God's face at how weak and stupid we all are."

"But you don't believe that?"

"No, I don't," the older woman answered.

Whitney put her ATV in gear and rolled after Adan and Magda. Lilli looked after the teen, wondering if she would make it or join her family on the other side. She knew she wanted her to live, just as she did herself, but it was the boy who was important. She had to get him to the notch, even if she couldn't say why.

She took one last look back through the darkness at the dust cloud moving toward them through the moonlight and turned, roaring after Whitney and the others.

CHAPTER 119

The unmarked cop car pulled to a stop in front of the dune buggy shop. Lights were on in the dark, as though people were home. Det. Wilson got out, looking around. There was dead silence. A shot-up old van sat to one side, a sleek Porsche nearby, its lights still on, as though the occupants hadn't had time to turn them off. The shop itself was pockmarked with bullet holes. Sgt. Getty and Agent Goodman slid out, joining him. They all had pistols in their hands.

"Nobody here," Wilson said.

"Nobody alive anyway," Goodman murmured. He nodded toward the sheds. He could see a body, male, thrown amid the bikes. "Looks like some of the ATVs are gone." Tense, pistols ready, they walked to the shed. Bright lights, three of them, burned under the corrugated aluminum. They saw Terry laying sprawled in the dirt.

"If the kid can save people," Wilson drawled, "he sure didn't do a good job here."

"I wish he'd touch me," Getty said.

Her partner cut her a glance, lowering his voice so the Homeland Security guy wouldn't hear them. "The breast cancer," he said. "It's back?" She gave a tight-lipped nod, but didn't answer. It was her business and she didn't like discussing it. Wilson respected her privacy; they'd been working together for several years now, and he knew how personal it was.

Goodman's cell buzzed and he stepped aside to answer it as Wilson and Getty poked around in the shed, trying to figure out what had happened. "Yes?" Goodman said into his mic.

"The two policemen with you," the cold voice said to the Homeland Security agent, "terminate them."

"What?" Goodman wasn't surprised, but he saw no reason for the decision. "Why?" he asked.

"No witnesses from this point on. Do it now and continue after the boy."

"That's all bullshit," Goodman said, his eyes on the two cops, who were still looking around. "Tell me who you are. You're not part of the government, not now anyway. If you want me to execute these people, tell me who you are."

"A man who makes and destroys governments, who reshaped continents, who decides the way of the world for generations," came the dry papery voice. It sounded very old. "I need the boy to touch me. I have so much more left to do. Now kill them."

The line went dead in his ear. Goodman respected the honesty he had heard in the answer, but he still didn't have a name. However, it was time for a winnowing, regardless. There were too many people after the boy, too many threats, and too many loose ends.

Without hesitating, he pulled his 9mm and opened fire on the closest cop, Getty. He's heard her mention her breast cancer. Well, she wouldn't have to worry about it now. The first bullet took her through the heart, throwing her back against the wall of the shed. Goodman was a dead shot.

Wilson wheeled about at the back of the shed, the side open to the desert, startled by the sudden bang of gunfire.

Wilson's eyes couldn't process what he was seeing. His partner dead, the federal agent sighting down on him. He started to raise his firearm, but Goodman shot first, nicking him in the side and

Book 4: THE SECOND (AND LAST) NIGHT

spinning him about. A second bullet cut a furrow high on his head and he was thrown to the ground.

Goodman glanced at the blood pooling around his head and wrote him off. He looked out the back of the shed, into the moonswept desert. He could see the lights of several dune buggies, a couple of miles away, making their way through the cactus, and behind them another two. He was to pursue the pursuers.

He stripped his suit coat and grabbed a padded jacket for riding, a backpack, and a helmet from the pile. Out there he'd take any protection he could get. He started a rail quad, especially fast, flipped on the brights so they picked out the sandy road, and with a roar leapt out of the shed and into the desert night.

CHAPTER 120

FBI and state police swarmed the truck stop. The CDC was there in force with Hazmat suits. A ruined vehicle, blown apart and burned, was still smoking. Same with a couple of pumps, but the fires had been put out. There were dead people on the ground, either shot or dead from the sickness. One had blood around his mouth.

Catherine and Morgan watched through a feed into the helicopter, circling high above. They couldn't land because of the sickness. They could afford to lose everybody but themselves. They were directing the entire operation. If they'd had time, they would have felt guilty about it, but they didn't. The CDC supervisor was talking to them, her face covered with a cloth respirator.

"It just stopped," the CDC super said in dumb surprise. "Only one person dead of the coughing sickness, then it just stopped."

"Does it make any sense?" Catherine asked Morgan.

"I don't know, unless the boy threw a tantrum, then calmed down," the man said, rubbing his eyes. They were tired. Stress. He hated being this helpless. "It's so hard to say."

"What the hell set it off?" she said, studying the video link of the smoking truck stop and dead bodies.

"Here, the next stop." Morgan nodded at a screen. It gave a view of the buggy shop from a drone hovering above. They could see a man escaping out the back into the desert. "It's Goodman," Morgan said. "He's killed the two cops." He swung back to the screen of the truck stop. Nobody was left standing. Nothing moved except for police, EMT, and CDC workers working the scene.

"Who's he working for?" Catherine asked, referring to Goodman.

"I don't know," Morgan replied. He licked his lips. "Someone deep inside our own government."

A face flashed on the screen. It was a tense CDC worker in a Hazmat suit, standing before a roadblock some distance from the truck stop. "We've quarantined it, sealed it off, but there's no spreading of the disease. Everybody's dead there, most from gunshots or the explosion and fire."

Morgan looked at Catherine. "He's stopped it, just like that," he said and snapped his fingers. "Hold on, playing back." His fingers flew across his keyboard. Video of the shootout started to play.

"What are you looking for?" Catherine asked, leaning forward for a better look.

"Why he might have killed that one man," Morgan said. Video came up of Zio Benito dragging the boy back toward his SUV, the gun pressed into the kid's head. It was freezing Adan and his friends, making it impossible for them to try to save their charge. "There." Morgan pointed. Aslanian, one of the Zio Benito's thugs, suddenly coughed, blood flying. Everybody froze. Zio Benito turned, taking his pistol away from the boy's temple. Adan launched himself forward to save the kid. Morgan punched a key, freezing the image. "Look." He indicated the man with the blood-flecked lips as he started to crumple. "The boy gave him and him alone the sickness to distract the others. He deliberately gave Adan a chance to save him, maybe to see what he would do."

"Sweet Jesus," Catherine said, her face pale and strained. "I hope the kid never gets pissed at us."

CHAPTER 121

Adan pulled his quad to a halt in the sandy loam as the others came up. Their lights poked holes in the night, showing the dirt road had come to an end. He stood up on his bike, looking back. He could see Gordo's lights, but they didn't seem any closer. "Something's holding the Fat Man back. He should be closer by now."

Magda didn't reply, standing up on the steel pegs of her buggy, looking in the other direction, forward, into the dark desert. "I don't see anything like the notch."

Lilli and Whitney turned, looking into the rolling sands. In the far distance, framed by the moon, they could see several mesas, but nothing like what they'd seen in their visions.

"It's not here," Whitney said, pursing her lips. They couldn't come all this way, go through all this not to find it.

"Joe Bears said you couldn't see it, according to Terry," Lilli said. "It was hidden somehow. That's why we have to trust the boy." They glanced at him. He was laying against Magda's back, but as they watched, his eyes seemed to focus. He sat up straighter, his head turning slightly, until he was clearly focused on another point in the desert.

"There," Adan said, amazed in spite of himself. He pointed. "We go in that direction."

"Maybe, but there's nothing there," Whitney said with a frown as she stared across the night strewn sand. It was climbing slightly, but flat, except for foothills of rolling sand.

"I think maybe we should get going," Lilli said, cocking an ear. They could hear the distant whine of El Gordo getting closer. "Sounds like more than one of them."

"We'll have to go slower without a road to guide us," Adan said. "Stay together. We gotta find it before dawn."

He drove into the desert, following his own headlights. Magda with the boy drove in his tracks, then Whitney and Lilli, all being careful as they went.

CHAPTER
122

Det. Wilson rolled over with a groan. He slowly sat up, wiping the blood out of his eyes. He tentatively felt his head and winced. Scalp wound, but it hurt like hell. He'd been grazed. He tried to get up, only to feel a burn in his side. That hurt like hell, too. He rose slowly, reaching inside his shirt and feeling the Kevlar vest he wore under his jacket. It had saved him from a bullet hole through his ribs, but the force of the slug hitting the vest had left a big purplish bruise. He could hardly see from the blood running into his eyes from the scalp wound. He staggered to an outdoor sink and washed it out of his eyes. He saw the first aid kit in the corner and grabbed it. He put a slab of antiseptic and fuzzy gauze on his scalp and taped it down.

His head was ringing, but he was still moving. His side ached but the bullet had plowed into the Kevlar and stopped. That's when he realized Noel Getty, his partner for over three years, was laying amid the buggies, dead. She didn't have to worry about the breast cancer now. What he didn't get was Goodman. He couldn't be Homeland Security or FBI. But the CDC gal and Morgan had thought he was. They were wrong. The killer was working for someone else and had killed his partner.

Wilson had a hangdog expression, but his jowls tightened. He silently swore to get Goodman for what he'd done. Traitor to his oath, to law enforcement everywhere, definitely to his country. They'd taken off into the desert, after the boy, all of them. That stopped the cop. Goodman must have orders to kidnap the boy. He was sure he wouldn't kill him. He was too valuable.

A sudden surge of rage flowed through Wilson. It straightened him. He wasn't as badly wounded as he first thought. He could go after him. He knew what the bastard was after.

The boy. He had to stop Goodman or whoever he was. He didn't know if it was because he hated him for killing his partner or knowing that he was a grave danger to the boy. He grabbed a jacket from the rack, threw on a backpack, making sure it had water, and grabbed another canteen, drinking of it deeply. He hooked it over his belt and checked his 9mm. He grabbed Noel's, dropped on the ground beside her body, and stuffed it into a pocket. Maybe he could kill the bastard with his dead partner's gun. True justice.

Poor lady, he'd liked her, too, but at least she'd died reaching for her gun. Wilson slipped onto an ATV, one well-padded with double seats and springs to soften the bumps on his bruised body. He turned the ignition, heard it roar to life, and twisted the hand accelerator, speeding after the others into the starry night, and trying not to let his throbbing head break his concentration.

CHAPTER 123

Goodman came to a halt on the dune buggy, staring into the night. Ahead he could see two bobbing lights, and beyond them several more. Probably the thief and whoever had survived with the boy, and behind them the hunters. He lifted his phone. He still had a bar left and hit a key, listening to it buzz as the two riders directly ahead slowed and stopped.

"Yeah, who is it?" Gordo growled. He'd chosen the strongest two-seater buggy with a wire cage to hold his bulk.

"The man behind you," Goodman answered.

On the sandy ridge a mile or so away, the Fat Man turned, staring back toward the highway below. The Black Widow was with him. They could see a single pair of stopped buggy headlights. Gordo held the phone out as he talked, so she could listen. "Who are you?"

"Goodman," the answer came, "irony intended. I was with the two cops following you. They're dead now."

"Fine, you shoot your own people," Gordo said with a twist of his fat lips. "What's it to me?"

"They weren't my people and I did you a favor," the Homeland agent said icily. "You no longer have to deal with them. How far ahead is the boy?"

El Gordo wasn't surprised at the question. They all wanted the same thing. He looked ahead, picking out Adan's lights easily in the darkness. They were closer than he thought. "Thirty-forty minutes," he said, "but why should I let you in on this?"

"Because I represent the US Government and you're gonna need a lot of help with them. There are drones overhead, circling us right now and helicopters are closing. I'm sure Dr. Hurungzy or that nerd she has with her are listening in right now." He laughed. "You listening, doc?" He laughed again. "You hear me, Fat Man. Without me, the Feds will kill you and take the kid. Your choice."

The Fat Man looked back. Riding a four-wheeler was easier than he thought, even with his bulk. He had grabbed the one with the widest seat. He could see—what was his name, Goodman?—waiting for him to answer.

"What do you think?" he said to the Black Widow.

"Let him come up. We'll wait."

In truth he was tired already and used a handkerchief to rub the dust off his face. It only put him in a worse mood. He shouted into his cell. "You hear that, Mister Homeland Security? We'll be waiting for you." Gordo broke the connection, looking at the Widow. "I say we kill him as soon as he comes up."

"If he's any good, it's not going to be easy." She looked around. "Trying to ambush him won't work. If he only sees one of us he'll back off or attack."

Gordo shrugged. "I don't wanna waste time. Make a deal with him, so he thinks we're after the boy together. We kill him first chance we get."

CHAPTER
124

T he helicopter circled some miles away from the Buggy Shop. It was the mother ship with several drones in the air. One watching the boy and his pursuers, another staying trained on the quad shop. Catherine and Morgan watched through the eyes of a drone that circled almost directly overhead. They watched Det. Wilson driving into the desert.

"Well," Morgan said. "The detective seems to have survived."

Catherine had her earphones on. "I'm listening to Goodman get his orders again." She looked up. "It's NSA or CIA. They want the boy."

"Why don't they just ask us?" Morgan said dryly. "Hypothetically, we all work on the same team."

"Hypothetically." Her mouth turned down. Her eyes caught a screen. Red dots were beginning to throb. Her face paled. "Oh, no."

"What?" he said, and checked her screen. He swallowed. "It's started up in Great Britain again."

"Same with Germany and now Egypt. China and India just starting to report. China says it's under control. As usual. Everything is always under control there." Her gaze shifted back to the drone's eye view of the buggy shop. She nodded. "I don't think we have to ask why it's starting again, do we. Gordo is chasing him and Goodman betrayed all of us. More than enough reason for the boy to condemn us."

"How did he know about it?" Morgan asked. "The boy wasn't there when the two policemen and Goodman showed up." Catherine just stared at him. "He's like us, isn't he? He knows everything." She slowly nodded. He gulped, his face grave. "You think he'd really let this sickness go? Sodom and Gomorrah, apocalypse? Wipe us out?"

"You don't?" She nodded at the video of the drone circling the buggy shop. "Time to go in. I don't think we're going to mess anything up at this point."

Morgan spoke into his throat mic and gave the order as she watched the screen that tracked the sickness around the globe. The number of throbbing red spots was growing.

CHAPTER 125

"**T**ook you long enough," El Gordo snarled as Goodman pulled up on his ATV. The Fat Man and the Black Widow had been watching his lights closing from behind. He nodded into the desert in front of them, his jowls loose. He was sweating even though it was a cool night. "They're about thirty minutes ahead."

"She knows the boy can't be hurt, no matter what?" Goodman said, nodding at the Black Widow, her face hidden behind her skeleton mask. It was like it was glued there, but her dark eyes were watchful and intent. She was the real danger, and Goodman knew it.

"Don't be stupid, we all want him alive," the Fat Man said and then without pausing: "Why don't I just kill you right here?"

A pistol appeared in the Black Widow's hand, pointed right at Goodman's heart. It didn't faze the contractor. "I'm the only chance you got once the Feds get hold of you and believe me, they will." He nodded up at the night sky above. The moonlight was cut by passing clouds. "Drones, they're up there right now. Choppers on their way. You got a cell, they got a fix on us." He shot a look at the Black Widow. "All of us." He looked back at El Gordo. "So you want to go on and get the boy—it's our only defense against the Feds—or you want to stand here and think about killing me?"

"You won't survive without the boy either," the Black Widow said and pulled off her mask, tossing it into the sand. She was smallish, compact, the body of an acrobat. She had jet black hair, light yellow skin, and narrow eyes that watched him unblinkingly. "Why should we cut him in?" she said to the Fat Man, quite practically. "If we get the boy, the Feds will deal with us. They won't have any choice, with or without him."

"So?" the Fat Man said with a smile at Goodman. "You have an answer for that?"

"Yeah," Goodman said and pulled his phone, holding the screen up. It was a camera, looking right down at them. Gordo and the Widow automatically looked up, but they saw nothing in the dark sky above. "They have missiles on it, believe me. The only reason they're not taking you out right now is that they want to know who I'm working for. I die, you die."

El Gordo took a breath and smiled. "Well, then, we have nothing to lose, the three of us, except our lives, of course. Let's get the boy."

He turned his quad, rumbling into the dark desert. Goodman looked at the Black Widow. She didn't move. He realized no way was she letting him get behind her. Bitch wouldn't be that easy when the time came, because the contractor knew he was going to have to cap both of them—and they'd be thinking the same about him.

Everybody was just waiting for their chance.

He roared into the desert after the Fat Man and the Black Widow followed, thinking exactly what Goodman thought she was thinking.

CHAPTER 126

Adan pulled the four-wheeler to a halt. He was still following where the boy's gaze took them. Unlike before, he was definitely indicating a direction, his stare fixed on some place deep in the dark sand, but there was no notch to be seen. Magda with the boy stopped by his side, Lilli and Whitney coming abreast. "We're going in the right direction," he said, staring in the same direction as the kid.

Whitney looked over her shoulder, her eyes widening in alarm. "They're catching up," she said. They all looked back. She was right. They could see several pairs of headlights in the darkness. They were moving faster than before, speeding toward them.

"There's somebody new with them," Lilli said, squinting at the trail of dust they were leaving behind in the darkness. The moonlight was picking it up. "There are three dirt bikes after us now."

"Gordo and who else?" Magda asked with a frown.

"Nobody who wants to help us, that's for sure," said Adan, suddenly stiffening as he looked back. "Wait a sec. There's another light, much farther back, behind El Gordo and the other two."

They all looked and could faintly see their new pursuer. Magda licked her lips. "After us or after the Fat Man?"

"Who knows," Adan said, "but you can damn well bet whoever it is wants the boy." He turned back to the desert in front of them. "Come on."

"Hold on," Lilli said, raising a hand, stopping him. "If anybody wants out of this, now's the time. Split off, you can get away. They'll follow the boy."

Tom Holland   The NOTCH

They all stopped, looking at her. Magda shook her head. "We can't go different ways. We've all been in on this since the beginning."

"She's not talking just about you," Whitney said, looking at the woman who'd been unable to move without a walker, now sitting tall and strong on her four-wheeler. "She talking about me, too. She's giving us a way out before we find the notch. That happens, whoever is behind us is gonna kill us to get the boy."

"She's right," Adan said, looking at Magda. He did love her, damn it, and he didn't want her to be murdered. "This is it. Maybe we find this notch and maybe we don't, but either way says we get killed."

"You don't know that," Magda said, wiping at her mouth to clear the dust. She looked back through the night, at the headlights rushing toward them, the threesome and the single behind them. "They're gonna catch up, that's for sure, unless we go."

He hit the throttle, the engine revving as Whitney yelled at him. "How much farther? If only we knew that…"

Adan was gone in a spray of sand as his thick wheels dug for purchase. Magda with the boy was close behind, leaving Whitney and Lilli looking at each other. "So why don't you take your own advice and take off?" the teen asked the older woman. "He killed your husband just like he killed my brother."

"He didn't kill him, those guys who wanted the boy did," Lilli said softly. "And he damn well saved me. I can't answer about your brother, but he saved you just like he did me. There's gotta be a reason he did it. Now why don't you take off on your own? You'll be safe."

"I don't want to die without knowing whether or not it was worth it," Whitney answered. She meant it, too. "What we've all been through. Losing my brother and my parents. I want to know why."

"Me, too," Lilli said. "It's the last gift he can give me."

Book 4: THE SECOND (AND LAST) NIGHT

Whitney stared at the older woman, realizing how much alike they were now. She didn't want to die without knowing what this was all about. She hated the boy for killing her family, and so many millions of people, but she also loved him. He had given her inchoate seventeen years of life purpose. She only prayed his use of her and Lilli was for the greater good, whatever that was.

With one last glance at the lights gaining on them, she took off into the darkness, her headlights leading the way. Lilli was close behind him, both of them picking up speed, roaring through the desert night.

CHAPTER 127

The blades of the twin-engine chopper chugged as it landed in front of the sand buggy shop. Both ends of the highway were blocked by state police. Another two helicopters were landing. Men spilled out, preparing a space for drones. Catherine Hurungzy hopped to the ground, followed by Morgan. Neither of them waited to be greeted as they made their way to the shed where the bodies lay.

FBI and CIA crawled the scene. No one else. This was all government business now, with a total clampdown on news. "Who's dead?" Catherine asked as she looked at the bodies.

"One of the Phoenix cops." Morgan was matter-of-fact as he checked out Sgt. Getty's unmoving body against ID on his device. He nodded at Terry's corpse. "That guy owned the place, I think."

"We need info, but who do we trust to get it? Anything on Goodman?" she asked.

"Nothing yet, which tells you how deeply buried he is in the Deep State. But they'll reveal themselves," he said with a shrug, still on his device. "They'll have to break cover to get the boy. They can't hide from that."

"Morgan," she said, looking up from her device. "The sickness is spreading. It's happening all over the world at the same time. If it hits here, we're only one step away from everything falling apart."

He moved to her side, looking down at her screen. It was a globe of the world and more and more dots were glowing red, throbbing faster and faster as the disease spread.

CHAPTER 128

Det. Wilson rode through the desert on the quad, using the moonlight to guide his way. He gritted his teeth against his throbbing head and bruised side. He reached into a jacket pocket and pulled out some painkillers he'd found in the first aid kit. He gobbled two. It took the edge off. Of course, he'd taken two when he'd first started out, so he had to be careful. No use getting wrecked when he was in close pursuit of the man who killed his partner and friend, Noel Getty.

He snarled low in his throat as he piloted through the dark sand, trying to avoid the bumps, the fallen pieces of sun-bleached wood, or the branches of water-starved mesquite that came as high as his head. He was taking it slow and deliberate. He knew they were ahead of him, Goodman and El Gordo and whoever was with him. He'd never met the Fat Man, but he knew the rap sheet. El Jefe, on his climb through the corruption of Phoenix, of any big city, working his way to the center, to the web of real control, which was represented by Zio Benito, or what was left of him back at the gas station.

But what about the boy and those who had him? Who were they? He'd read their rap sheets. Cheap hoods. He was surprised they'd managed to hold on to him this long. Or wanted to. Well, with any luck he'd find out. He felt his phone buzz and slipped the earpiece in as he drove.

"Det. Wilson here," he said.

Tom Holland   The **NOTCH**

"You managed to survive," came the female voice. He remembered her from when they'd first met. She was the one the killer Goodman had intro'ed him to. Catherine Hurungzy with her quiet assistant, Morgan. They'd shoved the bastard down his and Getty's throat.

"Barely," he answered, slowing the bike to a crawl so he could talk. "Your guy killed my partner and tried to kill me. I expect he's thrown in with Gordo. You wanna tell me why you put him with us?"

"We didn't know," Catherine said simply. "He came from very high up in the government. His credentials were impeccable. We're trying to find out how high right now. We're heading in your direction. The sickness has started to spread again. What happened back at the dune buggy shop? Did someone hurt the boy?"

"When we arrived, there was one body, then your guy turned into an assassin and killed my partner, and almost capped me. Why? More connections to the plague?"

"We don't know," Catherine replied. "The boy could be an alien, he could be a robot that controls plagues, he could be God if you think there is one, make up anything you want, but we aren't going to find out if he doesn't survive. Your first duty is to make sure that no harm comes to him. Do you understand that?"

"Yes, I understand," Wilson said with a frown. He'd never seen the boy, not in the flesh, if that's what he was made of, but he was following in his aftermath and it was truly remarkable; death and destruction and scum suddenly acting like heroes, or at least not the dregs they really were. But besides that were the hard facts: a traitor had killed his partner and tried to kill him, and that really pissed him off.

"You must get him to us, so we can protect him. You must not let anyone else have him, unless not to do so would put the boy's life in danger."

Book 4: THE SECOND (AND LAST) NIGHT

"I get it," the detective replied, sarcasm thick in his voice. "My life means nothing compared to that of the boy."

"If his life is the key to controlling this disease, that's right, his life is more important than yours, mine or anybody that either of us know. We are working desperately on controlling the disease. We've failed. It's spreading again. There is no antidote that we know of. So don't let the boy go. Please, and I don't use that word often. No matter what, save him."

The phone suddenly went dead in Wilson's ear. He braked the quad to a halt, looking at his device. No bars left; the wireless had failed. Too far from the highway now. Well, he wouldn't worry about it. He looked ahead. He could see two sets of lights, one ahead of the other: Adan and his gang and their pursuers. He had fallen behind.

No more time to waste. At least according to the CDC boss or whatever she was. The pain in his head was lessening, same with his side. The meds were kicking in. Good, now if his gun hand only stayed steady. He picked up his speed across the desert.

CHAPTER 129

Lilli and Whitney were roaring up the dried riverbed, following Adan and Magda with the boy. There was less brush and the sand was hard from the night dampness. They slowed as it got rockier, riding abreast, able to talk over the steady chug of their machines.

"You think we'll ever find out what this is all about?" the teen asked, speaking loudly to make herself heard.

Lilli hesitated. "I don't know, but I'm going to accept whatever happens. I know it sounds crazy, but it's preordained, what's happening to all of us. It has been since the beginning." She looked around at the dry riverbed they were chugging through, with the cactuses standing up against the night sky like warning fingers held aloft, the hard sand crunching under their fat tires. "The moment is coming for both of us, what he has planned for us."

"What moment? You mean where we die cause that's what he wants?" Whitney yelled. "That's insane, I hate it."

"I know, but I feel it coming. I know when it happens I'll be rejoined with Mickey. It'll be joyous."

Whitney kept chugging along, keeping the bike moving straight ahead, but she was filled with wonder. The woman was crazy. She'd never sacrifice herself for anyone, except her family, and that hadn't worked out at all.

"If I don't make it and you do," Lilli yelled, the going getting tougher as the riverbed sloped upward, "promise me you'll get the boy to the notch. Swear."

Whitney cut her a glance, not able to believe the older woman's faith was so strong she'd willingly die. "I swear," she shouted back, "but not for the boy. For you. If I make it."

The two women glanced at each other, sharing a grin that made them both feel a little silly. A breath later El Gordo, the Black Widow, and Goodman suddenly exploded over the embankment behind them with a deafening roar. They hit the sand hard, and righted their four-wheelers, and tore after them. The Fat Man was surprisingly agile in his four-seater.

Adan speeded up ahead, boosting himself into the air as he yelled back at the top of his lungs. "Follow me."

He took the embankment on the other side, spraying sand as he flew into the air and disappeared among saguaro cactus. Magda with the boy clinging to her back was right behind him. Lilli and Whitney angled to follow when the Black Widow opened up on them with her automatic pistol. Lilli went up and over the berm after Magda, Whitney following at an angle when she jerked forward in her seat. A bullet had clipped her shoulder.

She reached the top, catching air and losing control of her machine. She spilled as she hit and it flipped on its side, digging a deep long furrow in the soft sand. Ahead of her in the dark, Lilli jammed on the brakes and looked back. Whitney was just coming to her senses. It was her vision. She knew it was and she knew how it ended, but she didn't hesitate for a moment. Lilli whirled her vehicle and roared back, about to grab the teen only to have El Gordo fly over the side from the riverbed, almost crashing into her.

Lilli ducked as he clipped the back of her buggy, knocking it to the side. She had just started to right it when the Black Widow appeared over the embankment on her rail bike, airborne, a flashing knife in her hand. Lilli looked up, digging for her pistol, but not quick enough. The killer slashed Lilli across the throat and the older woman spun about, spraying blood. She hit the sand with a damp thud as the Widow sped on into the night.

Goodman was behind the Widow, his wheels narrowly missing the fallen Whitney. The teen dug at her eyes, momentarily blinded by the flying sand. Able to see again, she found herself staring into Lilli's dead face, the woman who had become her unlikely friend, who had been saved in the back of the produce store, only to die in the middle of nowhere, trying to help her.

Whitney gasped, feeling herself. She was still alive. Lilli was right. There had to be purpose she was still breathing and it had to do with the boy. She didn't want to break her promise to the dead woman. If she made it, she had to get the boy to the notch before dawn. Fighting shock and exhaustion, she dragged herself to her feet. She felt her shoulder. The flesh was torn and bleeding, but the slug had only winged her.

Lilli was dead, but her ATV was there, still purring. Whitney staggered to it, and swung a leg over the front seat, about to get behind the wheel when a wave of nausea swept her. She gagged trying to throw up and couldn't make it. She collapsed, sliding off the dune buggy to the sand.

CHAPTER 130

Adan tore around the side of the boulder, sand spewing, the others behind him, and prepared to accelerate across the flat desert. Gordo and whoever was with him were hot on their butts, still no notch to be seen, but they had to get away or lose the boy.

His four-wheeler suddenly died. Not only the engine, but the lights, as though the electricity was abruptly cut. It coasted a few feet and came to a halt, its front wheels turning in the sand. He looked back to warn Magda when she came around the boulder fast, only to have her engine die, her headlights flickering and dying.

She rolled to a halt and released the boy from the straps that held them together and rose, getting off the buggy as Adan joined her. He held up his device. "We've entered some kind of dead spot. No bars, no nothing."

She checked her device. "Same," she said, casting a look back. "We gotta move. They got Lilli and Whitney and they're on wheels."

He looked at the boy, still seated in the dead buggy. He pulled him off, looking down at him. "Which way to this notch? Come on, we got no time." Just at that moment they heard the roar of approaching ATVs.

Adan shoved the boy to Magda. "Go," he said and pushed them into the desert. He pulled his pistol, and started after them, looking for any cover he could. Behind them El Gordo roared around the boulder, only to have his four-wheeler abruptly die. The front wheel turned and jerked the buggy to a halt, slamming him chest first against the wheel.

The Black Widow and Goodman were right behind him. Same thing. Their ATVs died instantly but they rode them to a halt, staying in control. Adan pushed Magda and the boy deeper into the desert, quickly disappearing in the dark. Those left behind tried to start their four-wheelers again and again with no luck.

CHAPTER 131

Joe "Bear Claws" Arachro sat cross-legged on the top of the rise, his dune buggy and camping gear behind him. He had been chanting The Sunrise Song in Tonto Apache, trying to recall it. He didn't know what the words meant, "Heye, heye" something. His grandfather had tried to teach him, but he had been very young, hardly a toddler, and it was only a faint memory. There were others in the tribe who said they remembered old songs, or snatches of them, but he was never sure they weren't bullshitting. They'd always been so drunk and wasted.

It didn't make any difference, but the chanting worked for him. He wasn't going to do drugs anymore. Well, a little weed. Terry had told him about the shootout at Mickey's Produce, which produced the best organic herb. He had some and smoked it as he watched the notch and chanted under his breath. "Heye, heye, da-da-arap, heye, heye...."

It was there for him, the notch framed against the night sky, tall and dark, jagged and powerful. Close on one side, the sheer solid cliff of the tabletop mesa, on the other the jagged shaft of stone, sticking up at an angle, like it was giving the moon the finger, and in between the notch where the sun rose. Sometimes he'd take his eyes off it and then look again, only to find it gone. The first few times that happened it had scared the hell out of him, and then he realized it always came back.

But it still made Joe nervous. There was a sudden gunshot behind him, close. He heard the whiz of a bullet past his ear. He turned to find himself in the middle of a gun fight, the boy nearby, two women standing there, one a teen, the other a dark haired beauty, firing pistols. He grabbed his shotgun and sprang to his feet, shooting at one of the men coming up the hill with a fat man and a small compact woman all in black. She looked like she was out of a horror movie. He got hit in the leg with buckshot, putting him down. She raised her pistol, firing with every step she took. He was reaching for extra shells in his pocket when he felt the slug hit him high in the chest.

It punched him back flat into the sand. He tried not to, but he dropped the shotgun and fell into black.

His eyes snapped open with a start to find himself back in the present, sitting cross-legged on the sand. He had seen what was coming. His own death and it could only be moments away. He rose to his feet, taking his eyes off the notch and looking back down the rise. He couldn't see anything, which didn't make sense. The last time he'd looked, he could see two groups of lights approaching, the pursued and the pursuers. But now there was nothing but darkness, no distant rumble of dune buggy motors. What was going on? Had they disappeared or was it another vision?

He didn't know what it meant. Maybe they were stuck, their vehicles dead, but that wouldn't stop them. The riders had to be working their way toward him on foot if something had happened to their buggies. Otherwise his vision was false, but so far they had all come true, so his death was fast approaching, even if he couldn't see the killers.

He looked down at his walkie. It was dead. He tried his flashlight. Dead, too. He didn't have to look at his dune buggy. All the electronics were suddenly dead.

Joe Bear Claws knew the boy was among those headed in his direction. He had to be. Dawn wasn't that far away and they were coming with it. The Final Saving was upon them, and now he knew

436

Book 4: THE SECOND (AND LAST) NIGHT

it was one in which he died. He could run, try to avoid his fate, but he knew in his heart there was no escape. Somehow this was all tied to the tales he'd heard when he was a child, of the Turtle God who carried the world on his back, until he decided to drop the evil place, and scourge it, drive the white man and the bad Indians away, to save and cleanse those who remained.

He had forgotten the song. Now he dearly wished he'd listened more carefully to his grandfather. "Heye, heye, heye…" he sang under his breath.

CHAPTER 132

Det. Wilson came up the embankment from the dry riverbed below and stopped the quad. There was a wrecked buggy and a body beside it. He recognized the woman from the live stream of her "saving" in Mary's Landing, Lilli Dollans, common-law wife of Mickey Meyers. She had finally been able to walk and now here she was sprawled dead in the sand.

In back of her was the teen that had joined the others at the gas station. She was laying on the ground, trying to rise up on an elbow. Wilson slid off his bike and felt the ache in his ribs. He wasn't in great shape either. He helped her to her feet and leaned her against a bike.

"You all right?" he asked.

She nodded stiffly and focused on him. "Who are you?"

"Det. Dan Wilson, Phoenix PD. You're one of the kids from the truck stop, aren't you? I saw you live?"

Whitney looked at him, seeing the bandage on his head and the way he held his sore ribs. "You're a mess. You after the boy?"

"We've been following him since Phoenix. There was a guy with us, claimed to be Homeland Security," Wilson said. "He killed my partner and then tried to kill me. How'd you get involved in this?"

"Visions. He touched me. I was one of the first, maybe the first. My brother got killed back in the truck stop." She swallowed, turned, looking into the desert. "They went ahead, searching for the notch."

Tom Holland   The **NOTCH**

"The what?"

"Where he came from," she answered. "Where he wants to go. We've all had visions of it, I think because he touched us. I can show you." She tried to straighten, but grimaced at the effort.

"Can you ride on your own?" he said, holding her steady, "or do you want come with me?"

"You," she said. "Maybe I can help you."

He climbed into his buggy, helping her up next to him. She strapped herself into the seat. "They'll kill us, you know," she said. "They thought they killed me." She looked over at where Lilli was sprawled in the sand. "They murdered Lilli. She knew it was coming, but refused to leave."

"She was very brave then, but they won't kill us," Det. Wilson said. He lifted a leg and pulled a .32 hammerlock from its holster. "You shoot?"

She nodded. "I grew up out here. I also have my own gun." She flashed it, looking up at him. She was stone-faced. "If I get a chance, I'll kill them. For my family and the boy. For Lilli, too." She looked toward the dead woman lying face down in the sand.

"Why is saving the boy so important to you?" the Detective asked.

"If he'd touched you, you wouldn't ask," she answered, looking at him with shining blue eyes. For the first time he had a sense of the kid's power from someone he'd touched. He changed people. The cop wondered what he'd do to him.

CHAPTER 133

Adan stopped trudging through the sand up a slow rise, looking at the boy he held by the hand. He was still looking straight ahead. Magda came up. "West," he said.

"Where he's always looking," Magda said, glancing up at the night sky. She frowned. "It's going to be dawn in an hour or so."

"You know where you came from?" Adan asked the boy, giving him a shake. "You know where this notch is?"

The boy didn't say anything, but his eyes were focused. He slowly turned, looking slightly to the side. "Northwest," Adan said, looking out over the vast, silent, still dark desert. "I don't see anything out there."

"Neither do I," Magda said with a hopeless shake of her head. She looked back. "Gordo's on foot, but he's gonna catch up with us, you know he is, no matter how fat he is."

"Hello," came a deep gravelly voice, calling to them out of the darkness ahead.

Adan and Magda looked up, startled. "The man the guy at the buggy shop talked about? The Indian?" she said questioningly.

"Yeah, Joe Bear Claws," Adan said, stepping forward as they saw the form of a man appear at the top of the rise slightly above them. "Come on..." he said only to realize the boy had already started toward the man. He was leading the way for once. They exchanged glances and followed after him.

CHAPTER 134

Det. Wilson came around the side of the boulder, Whitney strapped into the dune buggy next to him. The power suddenly cut and it rolled to a stop. He jumped off and looked around. There were several other dune buggies stopped there. He checked them out as Whitney slipped out of their dead buggy.

"What?" she asked as he hit the ignition in buggy after buggy and got nothing.

"They're all dead," he replied, studying the sand in the moonlight. He pointed ahead at scuff marks. "They went that way."

"They're all here," the teen replied, looking at the buggies. "Adan was on that one, Magda and the boy on the other. The rest must belong to those people who were chasing us."

"The ones that killed the woman from the vegan store?"

"That's right," Whitney said with a nod. "The Fat Man and this woman all in black. She was the one who slashed Lilli. There was another man with them, but I'd never seen him before."

"Goodman," Det. Wilson said, his jaw clenching. "He was the one who killed my partner and almost did me in. Come on."

"Are you sure?" the teen said, stopping him before he could take off. "I have to go, but you don't."

"No, we both have to go on," he said grimly, "just for different reasons. Can you do it or do you need me to help you?"

She met his gaze and realized it was futile to argue. Why was she trying to save the policeman anyway; she didn't even know him, but he had rescued her and she knew he was good. She started ahead, her face set, tramping through the sand. He followed.

CHAPTER
135

Gordo huffed his way through the scrub brush. The Black Widow was in the lead, lithe and seemingly tireless. Goodman trudged behind him, moving easily and not even breathing hard. "How far ahead are they?" Gordo yelled at the female killer in the lead.

The Widow stopped, waiting for him and the contractor to come up. She wasn't pleased. "Why don't you just tell them where we are?" she hissed at the Fat Man. He was sweating heavily even in the dead of night. He wiped his forehead and looked like he wanted to snarl back, but bit down on his tongue. She continued: "Ten, fifteen minutes ahead if we keep moving. We get the boy and kill them all."

"What about after that?" Goodman said, eyeing the other two. "We're being monitored by the Feds. You know that, don't you?" He held up his dead cell phone. "You don't think the bikes and the wireless just died by chance, do you?"

"I'll distract them," the Fat Man said, looking up the soft rise. Human shapes could be dimly seen up there. "Magda, the whore with the kid ahead. I know where her daughter is in Mexico. I tell her she's dead if she doesn't give us the boy. While they're freaking out you get to the side of them."

"You think it will work?" the Black Widow asked.

"Probably not, but the whore will go bat shit crazy," El Gordo said with a nasty grin.

The threesome looked at each other. Goodman shrugged. "Worth a try."

The Black Widow checked out the rise, measuring the distance between them and the figures ahead. There was still a good deal of distance between them, too far to try a pistol shot. "Let's do it," she said, and started working her way to the side and up through the sand. Goodman followed. El Gordo wiped the sweat from his forehead, wishing the hell he'd been able to shout from right where they were, instead of having to climb higher.

He started grunting his way upward through the sand, slipping and sliding and swearing under his breath.

CHAPTER 136

I've been waiting for you," Joe Bear Claws said as Magda, the boy, and Adan reached the crest of the rise. The desert went almost flat from there on. His eyes settled on the boy. Magda stood beside him, but no longer held his hand. She realized it was no longer necessary.

"You know where this notch is?" Adan asked, catching his breath. "We were hoping when we found you, we'd find it, but there's nothing…" He swung a hand out, indicating the flat nighttime desert only to jerk to a stop. "We're here," he said in a choked whisper.

Magda looked, even the boy turned his head. The tabletop was there where it hadn't been a moment before, and the shard of rock sticking up at an angle at the end, forming a V. The notch. "I can't believe it," Magda said, her eyes wide, "just like we saw."

"What we all saw," Adan said, studying the boy. Was he magical? He still didn't fucking know, and he didn't care. His job was to take care of Magda and himself. Magda, he thought, and then it hit him. He loved her. He really loved her.

"It's why I wouldn't leave," Joe Bear Claws said with a nod at the notch. "I knew it wasn't here and then it was. I was afraid if I left it would disappear forever and he wouldn't be able to get back to wherever he came from."

"At dawn," Magda said softly.

"Has to be," Joe said with a nod. "I've been thinking about it ever since I first saw him walking out of the sun. Like molten gold it was. He had a purpose. You could see it in his walk. He came here to do something."

"Well, you can certainly say he's done that," Adan said, giving the boy a glance. He was more focused now, more alive, but he just stood there, as if waiting for something with the rest of them. "Is he an alien, brain damaged, what?"

Joe shrugged. "Maybe all of them, but it doesn't make any difference. Whatever he is, he's something bigger than any of us can imagine. Maybe that's why they have the word God." He nodded toward the sky. It was still dark with just a hint of lightening around the edges. "He can't leave till dawn."

"We have to go now," Magda said with a quick look over her shoulder. "There are people after us, after the boy really. They're killers. They'll never let the boy go if they get him."

"He still can't leave till dawn," Joe Bear Claws said with steady certainty. "He's gotta walk back into the sun, coming through the notch, just like he walked out of it. I think it's his gate."

Magda looked at Adan. "We're going to have to make a stand for it. Protect the boy." She shifted her gaze to Joe. "How long till the sun comes up?"

Joe looked up at the night sky above. The clouds were gone, giving a clear view of an almost full moon. It was paling and fading with the coming twilight. "Thirty minutes, give or take."

Adan frowned at Magda. "That's more than enough time for them to kill us. You take the kid. Head up toward the notch."

She stared at him, not moving. "You've changed," she said. "You finally care about something more than yourself."

"I care about you," he said. "No one else, not even the kid. Now get moving."

They suddenly heard El Gordo, yelling up at them from below. "Hey, Magda, I see you up there. You got the kid with you? Cause

Book 4: THE SECOND (AND LAST) NIGHT

I got eyes on your bitch daughter in Guanajuato. You got her with your abuela, your grandma, right? Well, I can kill them both, just one call and I can make that happen right now, you don't give us the boy."

"Oh, God," Magda gasped. "Sophia. She's only ten. I can't lose her."

"Chill," Adan said, checking his device. "Our phones are dead. All of them."

She pulled her device to check, only to see it suddenly snap to life. "Oh, no, we have reception again. I got full bars."

"Oh, shit," Adan said, checking his cell. "You're right." His gaze flicked to the boy who seemed totally out of it, just standing there, seemingly ignoring them. "Is this you? You doing this?"

There was nothing from the boy, but his eyes seemed to be fixed on the notch as the sky continued to lighten. "Gordo's going to kill my baby if we don't turn the boy over to him," Magda said, wrapped in sudden agony. "All he has to do is send a text. He doesn't even have to fucking call."

Adan swung on the boy. "Kill it," he said, "kill the wireless. It's the only way you're gonna save yourself. If you don't, we're gonna turn you over to the Fat Man."

No reaction from the boy who now looked almost bloodless as the moonlight fled along with nighttime.

"You can't do that," Joe said, his face almost as impassive as the boy's. "He has to go back through the notch at dawn. The world depends on it. Our very souls do."

"I'm sorry," Magda said, almost as pale as the boy, "I'm not gonna let that pig down there kill my only child."

"Magda, maybe he's right," Adan began and reached out for her. She stepped back, pulling her pistol and aiming it at him.

"Stay back," she said, "or I'll shoot. I swear to God I will. I have to save my baby. I have to."

Adan lowered his hand. Not Joe; he stepped toward her. "Lady, you can't do this…" She swung the pistol to cover him.

"Don't touch me," she said, her voice on the edge of the hysteria. Joe lowered his hand.

"So what are you going to do?" he asked calmly.

"Give them the boy," she said, grabbing the kid's hand and pulling him down the rise, in the direction of Gordo and who else she didn't know.

CHAPTER 137

The Widow and Goodman stood in the sand to the side. They could see Adan and the others, standing on a low rise above them. The fading moonlight framed them. "They're fighting among themselves," the Widow whispered to the contractor with a grin.

They heard Magda yell down to them. "Gordo, if I give you the boy, how do I know my little girl isn't in danger anymore?"

"I'll send a message to let her go, to walk away," the Fat Man yelled back. "I'll copy you from here."

"I don't believe you, you fat pig. Do it now," she yelled back. "Only when I know she's safe do you get the boy."

Goodman looked at the Widow. "This could take hours. I'll move closer and shoot them." He began to move away, the Black Widow moved after him.

"I'm gonna cover him," she said and moved into the dark, after Goodman.

Lower down, Gordo kept his attention on Magda and the other above him. "I'm calling right now," he said to keep them busy and made like he was doing something on his cell, just in case they could see him. He didn't have time to hook up with a cartel down there and off the girl and her grandmother, not now, but Magda didn't know that.

Finished faking it, looking back up the rise at Magda and the others. "It's done," he shouted, waiting breathlessly for the Black Widow and the Fed asshole to get a bead on them. It was so close to being over. He was so close to having the boy in his hands. So close to shooting his Asian partner and the turncoat Fed asshole.

He looked up at the night sky, hearing a soft whoosh overhead, and caught a glimpse in the fading moonlight of what looked like a small missile. He wasn't stupid. He knew what it was. A drone, undoubtedly relaying info back to helicopters, circling somewhere out of sight keeping an eye on them and ready to swoop in at a moment's notice. He wasn't worried. As long as he had the kid in his hands, they'd bargain with him. In fact, they'd kiss his fat ass.

He smiled at the thought of it.

CHAPTER 138

More than ten miles away, Catherine and Morgan hovered in the air in their chopper, their motors idling with bafflers on to deaden the noise. They watched their screens. They were dead. "Where the hell is our reception?" she asked, biting her words off in frustration.

"All dead," Morgan said, checking his dials. "Includes connectivity. Thank God the electricity to the choppers and drones are working or we'd be pancaking on the sand below."

"It's the boy," she said. "He wants us here, but he doesn't want us to move in yet."

The screens suddenly flared to life. The drones showed the people below in a small group at the top of the rise.

Catherine jumped. "How is this happening? How can our screens be popping on and off?"

"The boy," Morgan said, hitting the keys on his laptop. "Gotta be." He checked out the screens. The threesome at the top of the ridge were talking, but their drone's directional mics weren't good enough to catch it. Morgan hunched forward. "There." He pointed to the side of the screen. "Two of the killers moving up to their side. There's a third down there, not moving." He was indicating El Gordo, but he didn't know it.

"Oh, damn," she said, her voice suddenly sick with worry. "It's started up again." He looked at the center screen of the globe. The red dots had started throbbing once more. All the screens suddenly went black.

"Damn it," Morgan exclaimed, pounding a black screen with the palm of his hand. It did no good. None of the panels came on again.

CHAPTER
139

Down below El Gordo on the gently sloping rise, lit by the fleeting dark, Det. Wilson paused with Whitney. They'd come up behind him and the other two killers and fallen to the ground, keeping low and silent. They'd heard everything. He didn't know what to think, except that he wanted to stop the coming bloodbath, but she was terrified at the risk to the kid.

"We can't let them have the boy," she whispered urgently to Wilson. "We have to make sure he isn't hurt either."

"You stay here," he whispered back and began to move to the side, after the Black Widow and the man he really wanted, Goodman, the traitor and the killer of his partner. Whitney watched him disappear into the fading darkness and gritted her teeth. She couldn't just stay here like this and not do anything, not after what she'd promised Lilli. Gripping her pistol and keeping low to the ground, she began to creep up on the Fat Man who she didn't even know, but knew to be a deadly threat to the boy.

Above at the top of the rise, Magda kept her pistol raised, but lowered her eyes, looking at the boy whose hand she held. "I'm sorry," she said.

Adan looked at her in outraged disbelief. "How can you be doing this? You're the one who believed first, you're the one who kept telling me we had to get him here. You're the one who loved him."

She looked up at him, tears springing into her eyes. "She's the only daughter I have. Now leave me alone, I'm doing what I have to."

"You can't do this," Adan said. "The boy is the world. He's more important than any single life."

"Not to me," she snapped back. "What do you care anyway? You don't want children, remember?"

Joe saw the Black Widow appearing out of the twilight to one side, and nearby a tall man with her. Both had pistols in their hands. "Well, he is to me," the Indian said and picked up his shotgun. He stepped forward to meet the intruders. He called out: "Stay back."

Without hesitating the Black Widow fired her gun, hitting the Indian square in the chest. He shuddered at the impact and collapsed, the shotgun hitting the sand. Forgetting herself, the Widow grinned and hurried up the rise toward where Magda stood with the boy, Adan beside her.

"The boy is ours," she crowed back to Goodman and El Gordo. It was all Goodman needed. He stepped forward, took careful aim, and shot her in the back. She went spilling face down in the sand. Goodman came up behind her and shot her twice more, just to make sure.

Above, Adan pulled his gun and shoved Magda toward the shadows, whispering at her. "Take the boy, hide him, now."

CHAPTER 140

He stepped forward, firing at Goodman coming up the rise. The contractor snapped off a quick shot in reply. Magda suddenly came to her senses and stepped forward, firing down at him. One of the shots cut Goodman's leg out from under him, but the contractor fired back, his shots going wild. Magda grabbed the boy's hand, looking closely into his face. "I hate you for forcing me to make this choice."

She straightened and dragged him toward the notch, the light continuing to rise around them, but the boy resisted. He dug his feet into the sand and pulled her to a halt.

She looked up, terrified as Goodman, limping on his one good leg and Gordo, huffing loudly, appeared up the rise. "We got 'em," Goodman yelled in exaltation, "we got 'em."

"Fuck you, Goodman," came a cry from behind him, and Goodman and El Gordo began to whirl, but too late. Wilson was a little behind them, aiming at the contractor. He shot Goodman through the heart before he could fire. Goodman crumpled back into a sitting position, tried to raise his pistol, didn't make it, and keeled over, dead in the sand.

El Gordo cleared the rise, covering Adan and Magda with his pistol as he grabbed the boy. He shoved his pistol into the side of his head and whirled, yelling down at Wilson. "Shoot me and I'll kill the boy before I drop." Wilson froze a few yards below, not daring to fire. Gordo grinned, swung his gun, and shot him through the chest.

The detective was knocked flying backward, sliding down the rise, and didn't move.

The Fat Man turned his pistol back on Adan and Magda, keeping his grip tight on the boy. "Ah," he gloated. "The healer child and I have him."

Magda took a step toward the boy. El Gordo shook his head. "Feeling motherly, are you? You should know better." He raised his pistol to shoot her, only to have the boy come suddenly to life, struggling to break free.

Gordo tightened his grip. "You do understand, don't you?" He looked at Magda, the pistol in his hand centered on the woman. "Don't worry, I'll take care of the kid from now on." He began to pull the trigger.

"No," Adan cried, stepping in front of her.

"Sure, anyway you want it, gamberro," El Gordo said with a shrug and shot him in the chest, sending him sprawling.

Magda screamed and sprung at him. El Gordo shoved her away with his free hand and brought his pistol up to finish her. Just as he started to pull the trigger a single shot rang out. A bullet ripped through his skull spraying blood and ocher. He stood as though stunned it could happen to him and collapsed, revealing Whitney standing behind him, a few yards down from the rise. She held a smoking pistol in her hand.

CHAPTER
141

Whitney hurried up the rise, quickly reaching the top. She had snuck up behind the Fat Man, knowing that there was some reason the boy had placed her there. When he had shot Adan she had been shocked into paralysis, but when he raised his pistol to kill Magda, it was like Lilli had said and she had known why she was there. She had shot him without hesitation.

It looked like a slaughterhouse on the rise. Joe Bear Claws lay flat on his back, sightless eyes staring at the milky sky. The Black Widow and Goodman were sprawled nearby, the Fat Man, what was left of his face, buried in the sand. Adan lay on the ground, bleeding badly. Magda dropped by his side. "Adan, Adan, talk to me," she said, but he didn't.

Magda looked up at the boy who stood watching quietly. "Touch him, heal him, please," she said. "He's bleeding badly."

The boy didn't make a move. Wilson appeared. Magda and Whitney looked at him, shocked to see him alive. "Kevlar," he said, ripping open his shirt to expose the bulletproof vest.

The boy slowly turned and walked to Joe Bear Claws and leaned down. The others watched him, momentarily frozen. The boy put his hand squarely on the dead man's chest and pressed down. A bluish glow gathered in his skinny chest, and ran down his arm and into the Indian. As it happened, the boy's face began to suck in, his body becoming thinner and more rickety beneath his loose fitting clothing. It was as if all his spare flesh and life was being sucked out of him and into the other man.

Whitney, who had never seen the boy turn into a human skeleton, was horrified. "Oh, no," she said in a choked whisper. "He's killing himself."

"Stop, please," Magda said sharply to the boy as he became more and more rickety, not able to take it anymore. She couldn't let the boy kill himself, no more than Crazy Daisy could, not even to save the Indian who had tried to help them. She leaped forward to pull the boy free when the Indian suddenly coughed and rolled over with a groan. The boy broke contact, staggering back. Magda grabbed him before he fell. He was a living skeleton in her arms.

She couldn't help herself, looking angrily at him. His face was a skull with big bruised shadows beneath his almost colorless eyes. "You fool," she whispered. "You can't kill yourself, not after everyone has died to get you here."

She looked at where her lover was bleeding out. He lay on the ground, his breathing ragged, his eyelids fluttering. If he wasn't dead, he soon would be. She turned to Joe Bear Claws who was sitting up now. "He chose to save you and not Adan," she said, confused and furious with the boy at the same time.

"I saw this," Joe said, his voice filled with wonder. "I saw all this."

"What happens?" Whitney asked, hoping for an answer and yet not sure she wanted to know.

"I don't know," the Indian said. "All I saw was me getting shot and dying. I didn't see me waking up."

Magda turned back to Adan. He had stopped breathing. "Adan," she said, letting the boy go and falling beside her lover. She shook him gently. He didn't move. Tears rolled down Magda's cheek as she broke into sobs. The boy reached up a thin bony hand and caught one on a fingertip. He raised it to his eyes, looking at it as though it were a thing of beauty.

Book 4: THE SECOND (AND LAST) NIGHT

"What's he doing?" Wilson asked, captivated in spite of himself.

Whitney was about to say she didn't know when the boy put the finger to his mouth, and licked the tear off. He smiled as though the taste meant something to him. They were all staring at him, transfixed.

"He's, he's…" Whitney began but couldn't finish. She was overwhelmed by what she and the others were seeing. The boy was looking better with every breath, as though the tear was healing him. Color was returning to his face, his stretched skin growing stronger with muscle and sinew. The skull receded as his cheeks and hair filled out. But he didn't wait to get better, to fully regain all his strength.

He turned, looking at Adan on the ground. The boy fell to his knees by Magda, looking down at Adan. He reached out, covering his heart with his bony hand.

"He's doing it again," Wilson said. Awe was in his voice. He had forgotten being a cop, being a member of anything but humanity, moved by what he was seeing, even if he didn't understand it. Whitney and Joe Bear Claws stood watching, saying nothing either, as if they were all in the middle of some sacred ceremony they only vaguely understood.

The boy pressed his hand harder into Adan's chest, whatever health he might have gained in the last few seconds was stripped away as he turned skeletal again. Adan's chest suddenly heaved with a deep breath and his eyes popped open.

He focused to see the boy staring down at him. Adan frowned, watching his face start to draw tighter and more skeletal once more. Adan knew what he was, a worthless thief that couldn't even want a child with Magda, the woman he loved. Adan knew he was nothing compared to the boy. He was dirt, that's all he was, all he had ever been.

"What are you doing? Don't touch me," Adan croaked to him, "Don't kill yourself for me."

He pushed him away, but he was weak and the boy reached for him again. Adan knocked his hand away another time, but he was exhausted. "Stop him," he said to Magda, his voice a thin whisper.

She hesitated, caught between wanting to save the boy and the man she loved, both at the same time. It paralyzed her. "Only one of them can live," Joe Bear Claws said, watching the terrible confusion on her face. "It's your choice. You have to make it."

Magda suddenly stepped forward and grabbed the boy, pulling him away from Adan. The wounded man smiled up at her. He was bleeding heavily again. "You did the right thing," he said. His eyes moved to the boy with the last of his strength. "You take care of her." His eyes closed and he stopped breathing. Magda pulled the boy close and held tight to him.

Wilson's cell phone suddenly buzzed. He pulled it out and looked at it in surprise. "It's working again," he said and answered, noticing for the first time that dawn was finally breaking.

CHAPTER 142

Catherine Hurungzy and Morgan sat in the back of the chopper. They both constantly monitored the array of black screens, every one of them still dead. Thank God the rotors were working, keeping them aloft, but their communication had been killed as if they had flown into a blackout area. Then suddenly the screens and audio jumped on again. Catherine started in her seat.

"What happened?" she said. "Damn it, they keep going on and off." Her and Morgan's comm mics in their ears suddenly worked.

"Same here," Wilson said, looking at his phone. He was down below, on the desert rise with the others, but suddenly the CDC head was on his device. On all their devices, him, Magda, Whitney and Joe "Bear Claws" Arachro. Magda sat on the sand, the skeletal boy in her arms. He seemed to be barely alive. "Something's happened. Everything's working down here again."

"Us, too. We were flying blind, looking for you, but we were lost without eyes and ears," Catherine said, glancing at Morgan who was nodding at the largest screen. She could see the group below, the few standing, others on the ground. "Something happened to cause it. What was it?"

"Adan Cuarto just died," the detective replied. "He refused to let the kid help him because he knew it would kill the boy."

In the chopper Morgan stiffened. "What do you mean? He sacrificed himself to save the kid?"

"Definitely, several of the people here did," the cop replied. "What's happening up there?"

Catherine peered at her screen of red dots. They were frozen and fading. "The sickness seems to have stopped again. It suddenly started up just a few minutes ago and now it's stopped."

On the rise in the desert, Wilson looked at the boy. He lay back in Magda's arms, his color and strength beginning to return. "He brought a dead man back to life down here," he said into the phone, his eyes shifting to Joe Bear Claws, who was watching the notch. A few rays of light were just beginning to peak over the horizon. "I'm looking at him right now."

"Listen, you can't let the boy go," Catherine insisted. "For all we know he's an alien force, maybe God or his messenger, who knows, but for sure he's controlling the sickness. We don't know why or how."

Wilson's eyes suddenly widened as he understood. "It's a test," he said into his earpiece.

"A test?" Catherine replied, "What test?" but her voice suddenly cut off as her headphone died again.

Wilson looked at the others on the ground, the few left alive anyway, Magda with the boy, the Indian, and Whitney. "The government doesn't want us to let the boy go."

Magda looked up at the sky, rubbing the tears away. She finally turned away from her dead lover on the sand and rose to her feet. It was visibly lightening, just a hint of the sun about to shine through the notch. "Won't be long now," she said. Wilson didn't correct her.

CHAPTER 143

In the helicopter bay, Morgan turned to Catherine, lowering his mic. "It's disappeared off our settings. We're getting nothing but static."

She looked up, not understanding. "We're looking at it right now," she said, nodding at the drone's eyes view of the small group, gathered around Joe Bear Claws. It suddenly turned to snow.

"Same thing with all our systems," Morgan said. "We're blind now. He doesn't want us to land, not yet anyway."

Her private line pinged in her ear, nudging her to reply. She tapped her mic. "Yes."

"On your top security screen," a recognizable voice said.

She tapped her screen. It was working. The only other screen in the chopper that was. A very old man was seen, peering at her. "You know who I am?" She nodded numbly. How could she not? One of the most famous faces in the world, even if younger people didn't know the name. His voice alone brought a flash of news interviews through the decades into her mind, myriad decisions that started wars and ended them, that affected countries and continents that decided trade and the trillions that flowed across the globe.

He seemed satisfied. "Then you'll understand the gravity of my words. There is an international emergency, an ally who holds the balance of power over a huge swath of the world. He needs the boy to touch him. Otherwise he will fire nuclear weapons at us. America will be destroyed, wiped off the map. Do you understand?"

Catherine nodded dumbly. They always used that expression: "Do you understand?" and it was always a worldwide emergency. She recognized the words as her own to the cops, Wilson and his dead partner. The old man continued. "You must secure the boy safely. There will be an air ambulance and a full Air Force escort at the airport." He smiled. It seemed brittle. "Good luck. Your country is counting on you."

He snapped out, leaving her sitting there. "There's no end to this," she said to Morgan.

"There will be if the sickness comes back," the shortish man said. His face was as grim as his words.

Book 5:
THE THIRD DAY

CHAPTER 144

"Look," Joe Bear Claws said with a nod. They all turned toward the notch. The sun was just breaking above the horizon, the first pinkish tendrils of new light stretching out from the sky across the desert to the space between the mesa and the jutting rock finger. The shaft of light was narrowed there and concentrated, just peeking over the rock. It looked like liquid gold slowly rising in a jagged champagne glass.

The boy turned to Magda, touching her hand. She looked down and could only smile, even though she felt numb from losing Adan. She really loved him and just when she realized it, she had lost him as he had lost her. But the boy had been saved. He looked up at her and the others. His face seemed to say nothing and everything. He turned toward the notch, about to start on his way. Wilson stepped forward, grabbing him by the shoulder.

"We can't let him go," he said to the others, holding on to the boy.

"You have to," Joe Bear Claws said. A frown creased his brow as a ray of sunlight slashed across the sand in their direction. "It's why we're all here. It's why all this has happened."

"I know," the detective said, his face confused. "But we may lose our best chance to fight the sickness. This woman who's DNI or CDC or whatever she is thinks the boy is controlling it."

"How?" Whitney said, looking at him, mystified.

"She doesn't know," Wilson said, "nobody does. But if I let the boy go and the sickness comes back the whole world is wiped out. Don't you get it? We have no way to stop it."

Tom Holland   The **NOTCH**

The boy strained in his grip toward the notch and the rising sun that was shining brighter and brighter through it. "Let him go," Magda said.

"I can't," the cop replied, tightening his grip on the kid. "I've got my orders."

"You called it a test," Whitney said. "I heard you. You wanna know what's being tested? *Us.* It's us that's being tested."

"You gotta do what's in your heart," Magda said, finally understanding the boy. "That's what he's been showing us."

"Do it," Joe Bear Claws urged. The notch was blazing with slowly rising sunlight. It was cutting its way across the desert toward them. "It's time."

Nobody said anything. They were looking past Wilson and the boy at the notch. Wilson could feel the sunlight hitting his legs and climbing up his body. He didn't know why, it wasn't any conscious thought, but he finally knew the right thing to do. He let the boy go, who slowly began to walk toward the notch. Magda, Whitney, Joe Bear Claws, and Wilson watched him go.

Behind them on the sand, Adan suddenly rolled over with a cough. Magda's eyes widened and she whirled to see her lover trying to get up on one elbow. She ran to him, burying him with kisses as the boy continued across the sand, toward the notch and the rising sun.

DAWN

CHAPTER 145

Dawn was breaking in all its glory across the desert as the helicopter hit the sand behind Magda and the others. Catherine and Morgan jumped to the sand, followed by a crew, weapons out. They stayed by the chopper as the blades wound down.

"What happened? Where is he?" Catherine shouted as she and Morgan came up. Adan was being helped to his feet by Magda, but the older woman didn't notice. She was looking around for the boy. Her gaze snapped to Wilson. "You were supposed to hold on to him. Where did he go?"

"There," the detective said, pointing at the notch. She looked up. The boy was getting close to the notch, slowly being swallowed by the rising sun, but not gone yet.

"I've had orders from the top to stop him," the CDC official said.

"I couldn't do it," Wilson said. "Try if you want."

Catherine stared after the boy. The sun was starting to edge him, outlining him in the blaze. Morgan stepped up beside her. "You heard the call. The powerful will never stop trying to get him. If they do they'll destroy him."

"He could do so much good," she said, almost wistfully. "He could tell us how to stop the sickness, how to do so much more."

The sun was starting to eat him, making him look like he was on fire, a ring of it consuming his body.

"I don't want him to go," Magda said, but she made no move to follow him. Adan reached out and took her hand. A breath later the sun slicing through the notch flared, swallowing the boy up in gold fire, and he was gone. The small group stood in a desert now bathed in the early rising sun that was threatening to blot out even the notch.

"He's gone," Whitney said. She was overtaken by a peace that she had never felt before. Joe Bear Claws lowered his head, lost in his own thoughts. Whitney reached out, touching his arm. He smiled at her and took her hand. Adan pulled Magda close.

Wilson stepped up beside Catherine and Morgan, all of them staring at the notch. It disappeared in the blazing sunlight and with it the tabletop mesa.

"It's gone," Morgan said, not all surprised, though he couldn't have said why. He was a brilliant man, hardened to the realities of life, the best at what he did, and yet he stood in awe. All this time he figured there would be a rational explanation for the boy and it wasn't going to be spiritual, but it was.

He was going to have to recalculate a lot, like maybe his entire life.

Catherine's device beeped and she checked it. She read it twice to herself, just to be sure before she spoke. "The sickness has stopped spreading. It's happening worldwide."

Catherine looked up at the others and smiled. Every one of them smiled back.

CHAPTER 146

The old man sat in his wheelchair in his luxurious West Side penthouse, staring at the screen. His brain-dead wife snored lightly nearby. An assistant quietly wheeled her out. No one wanted to disturb him now. The screen was blank. They all were, except for a crawl about "Technical Difficulties" at the bottom. He knew what it meant.

The boy was gone. That stupid woman from the CDC had lost him, her and whoever else was involved. He'd had his agent, Goodman, there. He could have gotten him. Killing the others should have been easy for a man of his experience, but it hadn't happened.

At one time he had moved nations, shaped continents, and now he could not even get a boy to touch him. The screens suddenly snapped on. There was a drone eye's view of the rise in the desert, a small group of people standing on it. He leaned forward, straining to see if the boy was among them. A newsreader suddenly started intoning: "The boy is gone! First news, the boy is gone! Reports say he has disappeared back into the sun!"

The old man sat back in his chair with a creak. He was devastated. There must be something he could do. The boy had been here once, he thought with a flare of hope. He could come back. There had to be a way to reach him. To make him touch him. As if in sympathy, one withered claw of a hand reached out from the chair toward the screen, as if trying to seize something only he could see. As his mind whirled with schemes, his very old heart finally gave out, and he slumped forward in his chair.

His hand fell to the side and he didn't move.

CHAPTER 147

Catherine waved a hand at an officer from the chopper to keep their cameras away. She wanted a news blackout until she was ready to shape some kind of narrative that would reassure people. If such a thing was possible. The sun was now rising rapidly in the sky. "Well," she said to the small group. "It's over. Of course, it will never be over, not for any of us, not after this, but this part is over."

She nodded at where the notch had been, with the sun blazing through it. There was nothing there but sand and rubble now, certainly not a notch or the boy. "Anybody mind telling me what he was? Did anybody see anything as he disappeared into the sun?"

"Did you see something?" Adan asked Magda. "I didn't see anything. I had to put a hand up, the glare blinded me."

"I, I thought I saw him turn and wave goodbye," Magda said, "and then he was swallowed up by the sun."

"I saw something different," Joe Bear Claws said, stepping forward. "I heard things, too, Apache chant. I think it was welcoming the dawn and I saw a huge hand reaching down, the palm open, like it was going to lift him up."

"I didn't see that," Whitney said. "I thought I saw a golden staircase. I heard music, too, like in a church. I thought he was going home and it was a good thing."

Catherine looked at the cop. "I saw something, maybe," Wilson said, "like a door or capsule in the middle of the sunlight. Hanging there, like it was waiting for him and then the sun blinded me. What about you? You didn't answer the kid's question."

"I saw what could have been a pillar," Dr. Catherine Hurungzy said. "It was vibrating and I wanted to go after him. I wanted to touch him and then he was gone."

"What about you?" Magda asked Morgan. He was the only one who hadn't spoken. He smiled. "I saw and heard everything you all did and more. I thought it was a beam of light reaching down for him, but I'm sure he's gone back to wherever he started from. That's a good thing. For now, anyway."